Damian Nettoyer is the Empire's go-to g͏
to kill. In exchange, he and his rag-ta͏
Damian's psychokinetic partner and lover, Aris, isn't issued a one-way
ticket to an Empire-sanctioned lobotomy.

Then Damian's latest mark, a suave revolutionary named Raeyn, kicks his
ass and demands his help. The first item on the new agenda: take out
Damian's old boss—or Raeyn will take out Damian's crew.

To protect his friends and save his own skin, Damian teams up with Raeyn
to make his revolution work. As Aris slips away from Damian and his
control over his powers crumbles, the Watch catches on. Damian gets way
too close to Raeyn, torn between the need to shoot him one minute and kiss
him the next.

With the Empire, Damian had two policies: shoot first and don't ask
questions. But to save the guy he loves, he'll set the world on fire.

EMPIRE OF LIGHT

Voyance, Book One

Alex Harrow

A NineStar Press Publication

Published by NineStar Press
P.O. Box 91792,
Albuquerque, New Mexico, 87199 USA.
www.ninestarpress.com

Empire of Light

Printed in the USA
First Edition
February, 2018

Print ISBN: 978-1-950412-25-9

Also available in eBook, ISBN: 978-1-950412-09-9

Warning: This book contains graphic violence (including shootings, beatings, tasing, mild gore, depictions of a hanging, and an execution by burning), explicit sexual content (including mentions of sex work, a sexual relationship that begins in a negotiated contract for sexual services, and on- and off-page descriptions of explicit sexual situations involving bondage, control, mild pain play, and Dominant/submissive dynamics), trauma (including allusion to past physical and sexual abuse, and a depiction of a panic attack), deaths of supporting characters (including a young teen, mentions and depiction of assisted suicide, and one queer character who is a person of color), as well as substance abuse (alcohol, smoking, drugs, and a mention of an overdose).

To found families everywhere.

And to Tori, because it's dangerous to go alone.

Part One

Gambit

Shootings with a Chance of Explosions

FUNNY HOW I always had to be the guy who ended up with a gun to his head.

"I thought you said this was going to be easy," Aris said somewhere to my right. His voice was thick, the words choked out past the gun shoved underneath his jaw. The two Reds who kept us pinned were all broad shoulders and raw muscle. Huge white guys. Buzz cuts. Built like fucking tanks. In the low light of a fading sunset spilling into the empty warehouse, their leather coats gleamed like congealing blood.

The run had started out simple enough: get in, dump the cargo—a couple dozen barrels of diesel and some tech we'd snatched off a derailed train—and get the hell out. The place'd been abandoned for years, just another slouching ruin on the outskirts of Low Side. The perfect hiding spot to stash away things you didn't want the Watch to find, while waiting for the highest bidder to jump the gun. A surefire way to some quick and easy cash and still get to my real job for the night.

Standing there with my face mashed against the crumbling brick wall, a gun barrel against my skull, it looked more like a surefire way straight to a cell in the Finger of Light.

If we were lucky.

The guy above me seemed happy to put a bullet into my brainpan and chalk both Aris and me up as "casualties, resisting arrest." The Watch, safeguards of the Empire, the Consolidated Nations at their best. To protect and serve. Right.

I couldn't just tell our dear upstanding Reds to go ahead and stick their guns and handcuffs up their asses because we kind of were on the same team. I might be running the Empire's off-the-books hits for extra cash, but officially, I didn't exist. Blurting out I was on their boss's payroll wouldn't get me anything but a bullet to the head and my body dumped into the East River. Talk about employment perks.

That's what I got for double-booking myself. Fucking Murphy's Law.

And worse, I'd dragged Aris into it.

"Guess Jay was sugarcoating it a little when she said there might be slight complications."

Someone ratted us out. No way the Watch had just shown up here, far from their usual patrol routes, without any reason. The whole thing'd been a sting from the get-go, and once I found out who'd set us up—

My fingers twitched for my Colt. My Colt that lay cold and useless five feet away from me. Slim chance I'd be able to shoot both Reds before one of them got to either Aris or me, but I might get lucky and get the drop on one of them. Especially if I could piss him off enough he got stupid. At the very least I could distract them from Aris.

"You know, I kind of need to be somewhere. And I'd appreciate a little more leg room here," I said and squirmed under the Red's grip.

Honestly, by now I probably should've memorized some of the regulars' names or something. To me, they all looked the same. All fists ready to punch and guns ready to fire; neatly wrapped in black uniforms and their trademark red coats. Not like this was the first time either. By now, the Watch should issue us a punch card for frequent visits, maybe something with a rewards program.

"Shut up."

The Red jerked me around and slammed my head into the murky stained-glass window to my right. *Point taken.* A distant rushing filled my ears. Spots started to slow-dance in front of my vision. I went down hard, twisting away from the Red's reach and blindly fumbling for my Colt. I'd barely moved before his boot came down on my fingers with a dry crunch. I bit back a grunt that came out more like a breathless scream.

"Next time it'll be your head," the Red—I mentally tagged him as Captain Crunch—said, towering above me, gun aimed at my forehead. If he shot me from that angle, there wouldn't be enough of my head left for Aris to scrape out of the wall cracks behind me.

Here was hoping he had more fun beating the shit out of me than making shooting me look like it'd been his only option.

The Red didn't shoot me. Instead, his knee dug into the small of my back, his free hand going for a pair of handcuffs. "In the name of the Empire of Light, I hereby place you under arrest for—"

"Oh, I don't think so," Aris said.

He'd been standing perfectly still, his head slightly bowed, a model of the "hands above your head and don't make a move" arrestee. The unthreatening kind. The kind who came quietly and wouldn't even think to make any trouble for our dear upstanding officers of the Watch who only did their job.

When he straightened, brushing away a few errant blond curls that'd slipped out of his loose ponytail, a slow smile curved his lips. A dangerous smile, turning positively radiant until it teetered on the edge of manic as he glanced from the guy above me to the one holding him.

"In fact, I'd suggest you two start running. This is going to get messy."

His eyes flicked to me. "Damian, stay down. And get out."

And like that, all color drained out of his eyes until they were a stark, milky white.

Oh *shit*.

"Aris, no!"

Too late.

The Red pinning me tensed. He slapped his hand on his right ear to call out for reinforcements. His headset shorted out with a buzz and the burned-copper smell of fried electronics. The guy holding Aris cursed and flinched away, as if he'd been zapped by a high-voltage fence.

Aris didn't move. His expression wiped completely blank, like someone'd snuffed out the lights behind his eyes, now fixed on some point far above me.

Then he blinked.

I felt the zing of the Voyance crack through the air like a power surge. The window wall at my back blew up in a shower of broken glass and toppling bricks.

Sacred, bleeding *fuck*!

I managed to duck and roll away before half the wall collapsed on top of me. I flattened myself onto the ground and then scrambled to my feet, cursing and coughing through a cloud of red-brick dust settling on the crumbling remains scattered all over the cement floor and the cracked pavement outside.

The explosion hit the Red above me completely by surprise. I only spared him a quick glance to make sure his hunched form wasn't moving, and he wasn't faking being unconscious. Or dead. A slow trickle of blood ran down his temple where one of the flying bricks must've hit him. People died from less. I didn't push my luck.

I grabbed my Colt, its weight solid and familiar against my stiff, throbbing fingers.

"Aris?"

"Over here." His voice was a thin thread, fraying at the edges. "Told you to get out."

I ignored that last bit. Aris stood only a few feet away from me, his back pressed against the remnants of the wall. His face was gray, and he was trembling badly; he probably would've fallen over if not for the second Red who kept him pinned.

"Fucking Voyant," the Red snarled, gun shoved against Aris's temple, ready to put him down. As if Aris was nothing but a rabid animal.

Aris stood perfectly still, blood running out his nose—a steady drip down the collar of his shirt. Looking at him, knowing how easily I could lose him, hurt worse than all the bruises and broken bones any Red could ever give me.

"Damian—"

The Red's finger tightened around the trigger. I shot him in the head. His body sagged sideways and hit the ground with a meaty thud, his gun slipping uselessly from his fingers.

"Just to be clear," I said to the body at my feet. "He's *my* fucking Voyant, so back the fuck off."

Magic is not a Good Thing

"HEY." I REACHED out to Aris. "You okay?"

"Fine." Aris looked pale and shaky, eyes darting from me down to the dead Red and back. He swallowed and took a wobbly step toward me, but halfway through, his legs gave out and he slid into a crouch, his head resting against the remnants of the wall.

I dropped to my knees in front of him. "Hey, easy there. Easy. Shit, since when can you blow things up with your brain?"

"Since about five minutes ago?" Aris's breathing was shallow, his skin clammy and gray against my warm brown hand on his throat, his pulse beating a fluttering staccato.

"I'm fine," he said again, lips curved in the beginning of a smile, but his eyes weren't with it. At least they'd turned back to their usual hazel. Definitely a step up from his creepy-ass white Voyant eyes. "Liked my escape plan?"

"Escape plan. That what you call this?" I waved at the giant hole in the wall along with the mess of jagged glass and bricks around us.

Aris winced. "I guess it might need a little refining as far as accuracy is concerned."

"No shit."

"Well, it worked."

"Yeah and almost got you killed." I continued to check him over. Aris looked like shit. Worse than I'd ever seen him after he used the Voyance. 'Course, he'd never done anything even close to this. How long until he'd use too much? Till he wouldn't get up again?

It'd kill him eventually. The Voyance was like a virus that took no prisoners. It'd use him up, body and mind. And if he was very, very lucky, it'd do it in that order.

I swallowed and ran a hand through my loose curls. "Damn, Aris. What were you thinking, blasting about with the Voyance? He almost fucking *shot* you!"

Aris shrugged. He dodged my eyes. "That's what I keep you around for, remember?"

"To do the dirty work and save your ass?"

"Well, yeah. Only I saved *your* ass first. I mean, I blew up a wall. That has got to count for something in the dirty-work department." He grinned, a glimmer of mischief in his eyes. He slumped against me. "Gods, I'm glad that worked."

He reached out for my face, dabbing at something on the side of my cheek with his sleeve. It left a dark stain on the black fabric of his shirt. Blood. On the scale of gross things likely to splatter you during a casual shootout, it could've been worse.

Aris didn't pull away. His hands warm and searching against my face as if he had to make sure I was really here. That made two of us. "Damn, that was close." Aris leaned in.

"Yeah." I wouldn't let myself think about just how close.

I didn't do public touchy-feely stuff. But right then, with his face only inches from mine and his lips slightly parted, I was pretty sure I could make an exception. Just for a second.

I didn't get much further than feeling my mouth brush against his before the rustle of feet scampering across scattered rubble jerked me out of my Aris-induced stupor. I spotted the tapered coils of Jay's hair poke through the hole Aris'd blasted into the warehouse front.

"You know, I don't want to interrupt you guys sucking face—ew by the way!—but the cavalry is down the road, so I suggest you move it," Jay said and squeezed all of her five-foot-nothing frame through the opening. At seventeen, Jay might've been the runt of the gang, but she was brilliant. She'd managed to hack into the Empire's mainframe at fifteen. Iltis knew what she was doing when she'd snatched Jay up.

"Yo! One of them's still moving!" Jay jumped back from the groggily stirring Red but got in a well-aimed kick to the bastard's temple, and he sagged forward again. "Looks like someone didn't finish his job." She eyed me as I got up and drew Aris to his feet. He managed to only lean on me a little.

I glared right back at Jay. "That coming from the one who said that according to her intel, this run was going to be a piece of cake. Forgot the part about how a patrol of Reds was likely to show up in your calculations, Grasshopper?"

Jay held up her hands. "Oh, come on. There were only two of them. Used to be two Reds didn't even qualify as a warm-up for you. Getting a bit rusty in your old age?"

She turned to Aris. "Love the redecorating, by the way. Genius how you opened up the space."

"You're pushing it, kiddo."

I kicked aside some debris as Aris and I made it out of the half-collapsed building, biting off a comment about how at twenty-nine, I was a long way from "old age." 'Course, the way life went in Low Side, she might actually not be that far off. There was a reason you barely saw any old guys around there.

Also, fuck numbers, Reds could be sneaky bastards.

Something moved in the corner of my eye. I tightened my grip on Aris and turned, poised to shield him, Colt in hand and ready to fire.

Only all I was pointing it at was a heap of bricks and broken glass.

"What?" Jay said, her eyes following mine.

I lowered my Colt, but kept a hand on it, and walked over to the pile of rubble. I could've sworn I'd seen something. A shadow. A guy in a long coat with a hat...

"Nothing," I said after a moment. "It's nothing."

I peered back into the bowels of the warehouse, just to make sure. Empty except for the two Reds—one unconscious, and one very dead. Jumping at shadows. Great. I rubbed my eyes and tucked my Colt away.

Guess that's what I got for trying to run two jobs in one night: One with the crew, another one I'd finish later, a hit in the making for weeks now, with my boss breathing down my neck to make a move. Only that my "boss" in this case happened to be the commander of the Watch, the biggest and baddest Red in town, Faelle Valyr herself. You didn't keep her waiting. I may be a free agent, but Valyr took deadlines a tad literally.

I sighed. "Let's get out of this dump." And let's hope this near-miss wasn't some fucked-up omen about how the rest of the night was going to go. I couldn't afford any more.

"Best idea you've had all night." Jay skipped a step and hopped over a wide crack in the pavement.

"You got the goods stashed away in time?" I asked as we walked down the road, out of the jagged shadows of Helos's warehouse district.

Jay nodded. "Ditched the hover at the *Shadow*. I clearly can't leave Bonnie with you lot, the kind of trouble you get in."

I made a face. "You know it's weird to name things, right? It's a godsdamned hover, Jay."

"She's *my* hover and she's earned her name. Do you have any idea how hard it was to find a working transducer to make her run again?" Jay pursed her lips. "Anyway, stash's safe."

I sighed and rubbed my temples. Good thing Jay'd gotten out when she did, never mind her griping how she never got in on the action. At least we had something to show for getting our asses handed to us by the Reds.

Still, the whole idea'd been to avoid attracting attention by keeping business away from the *Shadow*. No way we'd have potential buyers of all colors of the moral gray-zone rainbow that was Low Side amble into the place where we lived. Iltis would have a fucking coronary. Right after she'd kick our asses to the other side of the moon.

We'd have to take care of that later. For now, everything sat as safe as it'd get and we needed to clear as much ground as possible before the Reds came picking up after themselves.

I probably should've saved us some trouble and put a bullet into the head of Captain Crunch, who was still conked out in La La Land, but unlike the Reds, I had standards. Which included not shooting a guy who was already down. At least I tried not to make a habit out of it.

'Sides, keeping the Reds off our backs was what good old-fashioned bribery was for.

Here in the dregs of Helos—New York before the Consolidation Wars of 2090 turned most of this world into a crater a little more than thirty years ago—money bought you everything. Life. Liberty. Protection. That kind of thing.

With the Watch, it bought you what they liked to call benign indulgence. Long as you paid up on time and didn't fuck up too big, they'd turn their backs on crookery, the occasional heist, maybe even a knifing or two. Kind of a mutual business arrangement that kept the black markets of Low Side afloat and petty crooks like us flush while lining the Reds' pockets with plenty of cash. The only catch was sometimes they'd start to ask for something other than money. That's when you knew you were in deep shit.

"I've got to go," Aris said as we turned down the Rue Lumineuse toward the Place du Marché.

"You're not serious." I caught his arm, grabbing him tight enough to bruise. "You're not going to go to Laras tonight. Not after—"

I broke off at the look Aris gave me. His stubborn we're-so-not-having-this-discussion kind of look cut right through his tiredness. He sighed, closed his free hand around mine, and something else, a desperate exhaustion he'd tried so hard to mask earlier carved into the hollows of his face. "Damian, please. I need—"

I nodded. Squeezed his hand. "You need me to leave and let Laras fuck you."

Aris bit his lip, guilt so obviously warring with relief, it tightened my throat. "Yes. Please."

I knew what Aris did, of course. That he fucked people—mostly men—for money, information, whatever he wanted in exchange. But I also knew for Aris, this was much more than making the most of his looks and people's tendency to give away way more between the sheets than they'd ever tell you at gunpoint. He loved his work, the release, taking control by giving up part of it. It was part of who Aris was. I got that, even though I didn't fully understand it.

The problem was where Dahlia Laras, Captain of the Watch, and coincidentally one of Valyr's favorite underlings, was concerned. With her, Aris showed up and did whatever she wanted, or he risked fucking over all of us. That's how it'd started. Aris assured me things had changed since then, their meetings were strictly contractual. The thing was, Laras knew Aris was a Voyant. That's where she really had him by the balls, and even the most airtight contract felt flimsy in comparison.

I sighed and forced my hand to unclench from his, waiting for my heart to do the same. "Okay. Just let me drop you off and I'll be on my way."

Aris eyed me. "Promise?"

My thumb traced circles against the inside of his palm, letting go but not quite yet. "Promise."

Aris nodded, his shoulder brushing mine. "Thanks."

I glanced at Jay, who'd hung back, looking like she very much wanted to be anywhere else. "You coming, Grasshopper?"

Jay's face split into a sudden grin. "You bet. Someone's gotta keep an eye on you and make sure you aren't going to try and shoot anyone. Again."

"I didn't—"

Jay rolled her eyes. "Uh-huh. Pretty sure those Reds back there would argue that point."

I swiveled to Aris, but he held up a hand. "Hey, I know better than to argue with her."

Jay beamed at him.

I shook my head. "Fine, Grasshopper. I promise I'll try not to shoot anyone this time."

Jay patted my back. "Don't worry. I've got you. In case you forget."

"Yeah." I couldn't help the smile. "I know."

None of us talked as we followed Aris to the Place du Marché, our breath forming silent white clouds in the cold.

Even with temperatures barely above freezing, it looked like a busy night.

The center of Low Side was packed with people, squeezing past each other in tangles of unwashed bodies. The sharp smells of sweat and alcohol mixed with food and spices, some less edible than others, wafting from the vending stands bunched along the edges of the square.

The Place du Marché didn't consist of much more than a circle of free space carved out between the huddling shacks of bars and shops cramming this part of town. Close enough to the red lights of Nightshade where crappy motels rented their moldy rooms by the half hour, it was the hub that held together Low Side. Here you got everything for the right price. You were also most likely to end up with a knife between your ribs and no one would as much as look down as they trampled across your body.

Which meant you'd want to lay low and avoid sticking out of at all costs.

With my coppery brown skin, black hair, and dark eyes, I blended in. I squeezed my way through clusters of people bartering with merchants, past hands passing credit wavers, powders, and pills in all colors of the rainbow in neatly measured plastic baggies. Hard not to stomp on the occasional foot or trip over one of the rampant children who made the place their playground while others hoped for a little extra money picking unwary pockets.

I nearly tripped over a white guy standing in the shadows of a cart that might've been a train car once, its red paint now peeling in scabby patches. He didn't seem to notice me with his hat drawn deep into his face, while he absently flicked speckles of dust off his black trench.

At the Marché, a healthy don't-fuck-with-me attitude went a long way toward making sure people stayed away or thought twice before starting something. That and I sported the scars that showed I wasn't someone who'd back down easy in a fight.

Next to me, Aris stood out like a sore thumb with his long blond curls and sharp, fine-boned features. A pretty boy ready for the taking. Never mind that he could kick the ass of anyone who tried, especially with the Voyance, but that wasn't the kind of thing you let loose in public. Not unless you were into being chased down by a mob. If the Reds didn't get you first.

Jay and I nearly crashed into Aris when he made a right into the thickest of the crowds and abruptly stopped dead in his tracks with a strangled, "Oh, no. No."

It took me a second to figure out what he was staring at. Then I saw Laras, all decked out in her red coat sporting her captain's tabs, standing at the center of a small circle people'd cleared in the middle of the square.

Without her usual flunkies for once, she still wasn't alone. She held a girl.

A tiny little thing, the girl shivered with cold or fear or both. She couldn't have been much older than Jay when we'd first picked her off the street—twelve, thirteen, maybe a year younger, all blond, blue-eyed, and terrified. Not sure how I knew she was a Voyant. I just did.

And clearly so did Laras. My stomach plummeted to my kneecaps.

Suddenly, the thick crowd packed around us made sense. They weren't here to cut deals or get the latest on Low Side gossip. They were here to watch an execution.

Of course, the Reds would never call it that. The Empire didn't kill Voyants. Not officially.

Something about it being inhumane and breaking some convention. Same kind of bullshit that went hand in hand with their claim that of course they were all duly appointed by election and keeping up democratic principles.

What the Empire did to Voyants was worse than killing them. They called it Cleansing. It got rid of the Voyance, along with everything else that made a person a person, leaving behind nothing but a drooling, empty Shell of a body without enough sense to keep from rolling in its own shit.

No one knew what happened to them after. Most Shells quietly disappeared, covered up and buried deep like anything that didn't sync with the bright and shiny image of the Empire of Light. 'Course, that image only stretched as far as Up Side, where the good part of Helos ended. Here in Low Side, rumors floated about harvesting their organs or using them for cheap slave labor, but the Gods alone knew what really happened. The few the Watch let slip usually ended up keeping the mesc junkies company, rotting away in some ditch and slowly starving because they simply forgot to eat.

I'd never actually seen a Cleansing, given how they mostly happened behind closed doors or in some dark alley with people quick to turn the other way. The thought of witnessing one now made me itch to take Aris and Jay and run.

Public Cleansings meant the Empire was making a statement. The Watch keeping the Empire's streets clean of the Voyance threat. Fucking typical pre-election posturing. Didn't matter the "threat" didn't look old enough to show more than the beginning stages of the Voyance. She'd probably shorted out some Red's headset or something. It was the main reason why the Reds kept those things in the first place. Uncontrolled Voyants fried all kinds of things, especially when they got scared.

The cold gnawed inward, turning into an icy knot of fear in my stomach when I realized Laras was watching Aris. And she was smiling. It was the kind of painted-on smile you'd get from a porcelain doll—perfect, angelic, and creepy as hells.

Jay shrank behind me, her hand slipping into mine. I squeezed it, trying to be reassuring and failing miserably.

"Aris!" Laras called. I hated the familiarity in her tone. As if she knew him at all. Worse, like she owned him. As if he was a dog who'd come to heel at her command. I gritted my teeth.

Next to me, Aris tensed like a rubber band ready to snap but still tried to keep up pretenses. "Evening, Captain." Aris tried for an easy, seductive smile. It didn't cover up the spark of panic kindling in his eyes. I wasn't the only one who noticed.

If it was even possible, Laras's smile widened, but it didn't cover the tightness around her eyes or how she lowered her voice when she said, "You're early." As if she didn't want Aris here. As if she didn't want him to see what she was going to do. Except she completely ruined that thought by adding, "Be a sweetheart and hold this for me?"

Laras shoved the girl forward, perfectly manicured hands wrapped around a thin arm. Even if Laras'd let her go, the girl didn't look like she would've run. She had that look—a deer caught in the headlights, frozen in shock, waiting for the impact.

The crowds stayed a safe distance away. The myth you could catch the Voyance if you got too close to someone who had it was alive and well in the Dregs where people didn't know better. Everyone around us had gone silent, smothering every sound to the point where I could hear Aris's throat click when he swallowed, his smile wilting as he took a step back, nearly bumping into me.

"I don't think—"

"Hold. The girl."

Aris's mouth opened and closed, but no sound came through. He let out a shuddering breath and took a step forward as if Laras was pulling him on invisible strings.

"No."

I moved before I even knew what I was doing. I couldn't let him go through with this—couldn't stop the panicked thought the Cleansing wouldn't stop with the girl but hit Aris as well. That tonight Laras finally tired of her toy and decided to kill two flies with one stone.

Even so, Aris'd never forgive himself if he just stood there.

Jay shook her head. Her grip tightened on mine.

I pulled away and put my hand on Aris's shoulder to stop him. "I'll do it."

I stepped forward, into the center of the circle.

"Damian, don't!" Aris tried to hold me back. I brushed him off. Didn't look at him. "Damian, please."

"Oh, by all means, let him," Laras said with a look somewhere between irritation and an odd, smug kind of relief. As if I'd somehow played right into whatever fucked-up scheme she was pulling. I ignored her and stepped in front of the girl. Her eyes widened. She made a small, frightened sound, backing away from me.

Now, I don't do so well with kids, even older ones. Killing people for a living tended to be an instant disqualifier in the good-with-kids department. She was short enough I had to stand hunched in an attempt to look nonthreatening and not like I towered over her.

"Hey," I said, to say anything and try to blot out the frantic voice yelling *What the fuck are you doing?* inside my head. The thought about snatching her up and making a run for it drowned it out.

I scanned the crowds for any gaps, any potential distractions that could kick up and give me least a chance at getting her out far enough she could get away. But no one made a move, some knowing all too well what'd come next, the rest anticipating it with the kind of dread masking secret relief the Watch hadn't gotten them instead. Not this time.

Whoever this girl was, she had no one. No parents or siblings coming for her, making a fuss. Another Low Side orphan crafty enough to make her own luck in the streets. I knew what that felt like too bloody well.

Clearly, her luck had run out. And didn't I know what that felt like, too.

Gods, I wished I had one of Jay's flash bangs, except she'd wasted the last of those on the Reds at the warehouse. No point. The Reds would just start shooting and take us down along with everyone else in their line of fire.

No. No turning back now. Not in all the Seven Hells was I going to let Aris do this. That left me. Me and this girl staring at me with eyes too big for her face. "What's your name?"

For a second, she just stared. Then she said, in a stumbling voice, "N-Nadia."

I nodded, trying to swallow the tight knot in my throat.

"Okay, Nadia. I'm not going to hurt you, all right? But I need you to close your eyes and hold still. You got that?"

She bobbed her head in a shaky nod and closed her eyes, her small hands curling into the stiff leather of my jacket as I held her by her narrow shoulders.

"It'll be okay," I lied and watched Laras.

"Touching," she said. "Never thought you had a weak spot for small, helpless things."

I kept my eyes on her. That way I wouldn't have to see Aris and Jay watching.

I couldn't do a damn thing to stop the Voyance from slowly chipping away at Aris until there was nothing left. But this I could do for him. I could be the monster so he didn't have to.

I clenched my teeth, kept my hands tight on the girl's shoulders. "Get it over with."

A smirk was all the warning I got before Laras reached for the girl's head and cupped her pale temples and white-blonde hair. That was all. The force of the Cleansing hit me like a bolt of lightning. The girl screamed and thrashed against me.

I didn't know how exactly the Cleansing worked. There were rumors some Reds had a low-level ability with the Voyance, enough to grab and yank.

Whatever Laras was doing, it hurt like hells—like jumping into a high-voltage current that kept my body pinned and spasming uncontrollably, unable to break free. It was over quickly and seemed to last forever all the same. The world exploded in bursts of color. Bright orange burned my retinas, like living flame, only hotter. I could make out a white glow around the girl, before it flared up right where Laras touched her and then just...disappeared. Fizzed out. Something popped between my ears. Everything faded to white. Laras took her hands off the girl and shoved them into the pockets of her coat and then pulled them back out and wiped them as if she'd touched something dirty. She let go, and the girl went limp in my arms. I sagged to my knees, almost burying her under me as I collapsed.

I came back around, blinking against dazzling afterimages of bright black and white spots dancing in front of my eyes. The world spun lazily before snapping back into focus. My body folded over, curled against something warm and breathing.

"Damian?" The voice above me sounded fuzzy and far away. "Damian, can you hear me?" It took me a second to recognize Aris was helping me pick myself up from the ground. I didn't get further than to my knees, then noticed the girl squirming and wriggling in front of me, her eyes empty. There was nothing behind them. The lights were on, but no one was home.

It was the single most creepy thing I'd ever seen.

Until she smiled and lunged at me, teeth shredding into my throat.

3

Shellshocked

EVERYTHING TURNED INTO a blur of snarls and claws and teeth, white-hot pain, and lots of screaming. I might've done some of the screaming myself. It drowned in the general chaos. I managed to wrestle the rabid girl off me, her nails and teeth leaving wet gouges down my throat and the side of my face. I barely got her an arm's length away before she came at me again, her mouth a red maw. Like a pissed-off mini zombie on fucking steroids.

Survival instinct kicked in.

Gods, I'm sorry, kid.

My Colt slid into my hand, and I pulled the trigger. One shot, point blank. That single bullet cracking through the air snapped the world back into focus.

I caught the girl—the Shell, I reminded myself, because there wasn't, couldn't be anything human left inside her—as she fell against me, her slight body unexpectedly heavy in my arms and dragging me to my knees. For a moment everything froze, a still-frame in a movie zooming in on the girl, her eyes broken and glazed over, her mouth half open and slack now, no longer biting and tearing.

If it hadn't been for the smear of blood, *my* blood, smudged across a waxy cheek, no one would've believed what just happened.

She'd been a girl, a fucking *kid*, and I'd killed her. Bang. Just like that. I couldn't stop staring at her, couldn't let go of her little body, still warm, only a hair from drawing another breath.

She'd been a threat. She'd attacked me. Would've killed me. I'd shot people for less.

So why were my hands shaking?

I should move. People bunched in everywhere, muttering like the buzzing of a hive, the occasional high-pitched voice peaking over the rest.

Somewhere above me, Aris said, very softly, "Damian? Damian are you—" Then, panic ringing in his voice, "Dahlia, *no!*"

Before I could get to my feet, Laras moved behind me and something hit me between the shoulder blades. Electric shock locked up my spine, my body flailing and jerking in pain too intense to leave room for a squeezed-out scream.

"Nobody move!"

Two Reds melted into the tiny window of my vision that hadn't blurred into jagged lines. I'd been wondering where Laras had left Pyr and Merron, her ginger twin flunkies.

Merron's fist crunched into the side of my face. And I hadn't even made a move to deserve it this time. Between the two of them, they hauled me to my feet. Everything had gone numb, but the two Reds kept me pinned with my wrists twisted behind my back. The cold pressure of handcuffs clicked into place. They left the dead girl lying by my feet, back twisted at a weird angle, thrown away like a broken toy.

Laras stalked toward to me. She managed to tower over me, never mind I had at least half a foot on her. Her doll-like smile disappeared, her painted-on mouth twisted into an unhappy line.

"Now, what did you do that for?" she asked sweetly, her head cocked at the girl on the ground, her face a mask of fake regret. "I understand this must be a new concept to you, Mr. Nettoyer, but as a matter of fact, we don't just go and kill Voyants."

"Yeah," I ground through clenched teeth. "You close the door behind you first."

Laras's thin, penciled-on brows drew together, furrowing porcelain skin before her knee slammed into my abdomen. I would've gone down if it hadn't been for her hand curled in the front of my shirt and Pyr and Merron's grip on my shoulders.

"I've got this one," Laras said.

With a curt nod from her, Pyr and Merron backed off and grabbed Aris instead, who'd been standing a few feet away, white and rigid with Jay next to him. They didn't spare Jay as much as a second glance, tiny and scared-looking as she was, with her wide dark eyes darting from me to Aris and back. I shook my head at her hoping she wouldn't do anything stupid and turned to the group locked in around Aris.

"Leave him out of this, Laras," I growled.

"Oh, don't worry. I'm merely making sure nobody does anything they might regret."

I tensed, hands clenching into helpless fists straining against the cuffs. But I didn't move. Not while Pyr and Merron were close enough to snap Aris's neck if I as much as twitched.

"Now, let's make sure this kind of thing never, *ever* happens again, shall we?" Laras said, her mouth curling in a sweet smile right before she drove her knee into my stomach again and her upper right smacked into my face. I doubled over with a grunt, arms jerking against tight cuffs at my back, trying to protect my head as I hit the chunky cobblestones. Blood trickled out of my mouth, darkening the dirt between the crevices.

I'd expected they'd arrest me. Drag me off to the Finger, lock me up, and throw away the keys. I'd fucking killed someone, right in front of the fucking Watch. Only then it clicked that of course, arrests and trials were only for things the Empire thought were *wrong*. Killing some Voyant girl? I'd probably done them a favor.

I closed my eyes against the ringing in my head.

In the end, it came down to a giant pissing contest: I'd dared to go against Laras, made her look bad in front of half of Low Side, and she'd show me. The more public, the better to earn her some don't-fuck-with-me points with the rest of Low Side.

"Dahlia, please." Aris jerked against Pyr and Merron who still held him like two robots on standby; all Laras had to do was push the right button on her Dumb Muscle remote.

"Don't," I gasped, the side of my face crunched into the ground. "Not worth it."

Laras clucked her tongue. "You sure know how to talk to a girl, Nettoyer." She kept me pinned with her boot right between my shoulders.

Coldness crept into my limbs. I'd be damned if I'd let her see me shiver.

"Just get on with it. Don't have all fucking night."

I could feel Laras's smile at my back like the point of a knife. Right before she aimed a set of well-placed kicks at my ribcage, I tried to curl in on myself, to give her as little surface area to attack as possible. No such luck. More kicks. Gods, I hated steel toes.

I must've made some sort of noise. A great deal of shuffling broke out behind me. Someone shouted my name. *Damn it, Aris. Shut up.* If I said it out loud, it drowned beneath the zap of Laras's stunner and a strangled moan when it hit my lower back.

The world went black for a second. It came back with bright afterimages swirling in front of my eyes, Aris's voice a distant rush at the back of my head.

Two hands on the collar of my shirt dragged me upright. My legs were too numb to even tingle. I licked off the coppery taste of a split lip and braced myself for the next punch.

It didn't come.

Instead, Laras stepped back and let Aris catch me before I smacked face-first into the ground.

"Hey," he said, his hands skittering all over me, trying to find a piece to hold on to that wasn't bruised or bleeding. "You're okay, I've got you. Come on."

He helped me to my feet, his shoulder warm and firm under mine. To my credit, I only teetered a little and almost kept my legs from shaking. Breathing became another issue, one that had to be tackled slowly and very, very carefully.

Laras unlocked my handcuffs and gave me an annoyed wave of her hand.

"Get lost, Nettoyer," she said and handed me back my Colt. "Next time, make sure your random acts of mercy have a contract on them."

"Right." I took a staggering step forward, suddenly glad for Jay to pop out of the crowd, wedging me in between her and Aris.

"So much for staying under the radar, huh?" she said. "You look like hells."

"Thanks, Grasshopper." I barely kept the wince out of my voice.

Jay kept glaring at me, but her hand wrapped tight around my arm. "Think you can pass up a chance of some Red beating the shit out of you for a while?"

I didn't say anything. Just gritted my teeth at the dull pain that throbbed all over my bruised body. Could've been worse. All in all, Laras probably hadn't gotten in half as many punches as she'd wanted to. Small favors.

"Now then," Laras said, "Shall we go on with our evening?" She held out her hand to Aris, who hesitated. "Unless you've changed your mind."

"No." Aris shot me an apologetic look. He let go of me, and something plummeted in my stomach.

"Aris, don't—"

His lips were a brief whisper brushing against mine. "It's okay. Go. Please."

He turned away.

There was no mistaking the tight set of his shoulders or the stiffness in his steps when he walked over and took Laras's hand. Aris knew who Laras was. What she was. But still, he went.

"Aris," I said, my voice hollow and pleading in my ears, hoping he'd turn around.

He didn't. He let Laras take him by the arm and lead him away down the street, leaving me standing there, empty-handed but for my Colt, whatever bloody good that'd do me.

I must've moved, because Jay's hand closed around my arm in a vise grip.

"Oh no, you won't," she hissed. "If you think I'll let you run off only to stupidly get yourself killed and leave me to scrape you off the pavement, you better think again. Aris is a big boy. Big boys can take care of themselves. We go. Home. Now."

I didn't budge, just stared down at my Colt, turning the polished stock in my hands, focusing on the pounding in my fingers, the broken blurs of my reflection in the blue steel.

"Sorry, but can't do, kiddo. Got to take care of something first."

"You're kidding, right? I know some guys get off on the whole 'vengeful boyfriend' thing, but—"

"I'm not going after Laras." Gods, I wanted to, but a fat lot of good it'd do me or Aris. He'd made up his mind. No, I had my own line of side jobs to take care of as Laras had kindly reminded me. Valyr's deadlines didn't give a rat's ass about bruises or personal issues. Last thing I could afford tonight was to get on Valyr's bad side when she paid me more than any of the runs with the Shadows ever would.

I tried to smother the tiredness in my voice and said, "Got to get this job done for Valyr tonight."

"A *hit*? Now? Uh, don't get me wrong, but you don't exactly look like you can take candy from a baby right now."

"Could kill a girl," I said flatly.

Jay opened her mouth, then closed it.

"I didn't mean that." She glanced at the spot where the girl's body lay— had lain. Say anything about the Reds, they got their clean-up act together. Jay bit her lip. "Double-booking yourself's a one-way ticket to a messy death, you know."

No shit. "Job hazard," I shrugged and caught on a wince. The grasshopper was right. If I had any sense, I'd call it a night with a handful of the good painkillers and half a dozen ice packs. And the image of Aris and Laras stuck in my head for however long it'd take her to finish with him. *Gods*, Aris... "Got to clear my head, Grasshopper. Shouldn't take too long. Simple point and shoot."

Jay nodded, uncertain, but she backed off. In a small voice, she said, "Be careful?"

A smile snuck up on me. The bruises made it feel lopsided. "Hey, Grasshopper?"

"Hm?"

"Thanks."

I tried not to limp as I walked out of the smog of Low Side and toward the floating holoscreens of the Core. Most of them were lit up with glowing praise of how Nymeron and his cabinet kept bringing prosperity, cleaned up the Dregs, and other bullshit to remind the rich who to vote for to get richer. Between that, anti-Voyance propaganda, and behind-the-scenes looks at who was screwing who at the palace, the Core's feeds were a 24/7 stream of what life looked like for those who'd come out on top of the Consolidation Wars.

The Core was where the Frankish names stopped. Low Side had a thing for nasals in their place names, using Frankish as they'd been the last ones to hold out against Consolidation, too stubborn to give up on what they called their national identity. Yeah, it'd been petty and made the Frankish lots of enemies pre-Consolidation. After the Wars, Frankish became a sign of defiance in the face of the Empire, something Low Siders took pride in, no matter how pointless. Which was why the Empire let them get away with it.

Apart from different names, there wasn't much of a boundary marking where Low Side ended and Up Side began. No need. Crossing over from where the trashy part of Helos spilled into Up Side and the Core was like walking through a dark hallway into a room and someone flicked on the light switch.

Where Low Side was basically one hugely sprawling junkyard, Up Side was a maze made of glinting white marble towers and glass. Even the cobblestone was polished to the color of creamy shells, almost to the point where you could see your own reflection staring back at you.

Across the part of the East River someone'd very fittingly named Hell Gate stretched the Core, the part of Helos you usually only got in per invitation. Or if the Reds knew you were on officially unofficial business for them and waved you through. There actually was a wall running along part of the riverside—transparent like someone had polished crystal rocks to the point they shone like glass—and a set of gates in each direction. In Low Side, we called them the Pearly Gates, where someone stood to judge you, found you lacking and sent you right back to whichever Low Side hole you'd crawled out of.

This was where the latest item on my list of contracts lived. Some upscale corporate fuck by the name Mael Taerien. Apparently, he'd stuck his nose a little too deep where it didn't belong and now the Empire wanted me to put a bullet into his head. Nothing new as far as the story went, and I wasn't the kind who asked questions. That kind usually ended up dumped in some ditch faster than they'd say "second thoughts."

There's something to be said for fresh air and a good icy draft going through the streets to clear your head. I stopped by one of my regular caches where I'd hidden the bag with my Ruger and other bits of bulkier gear underneath the floorboards of an abandoned factory for convenient on-the-go pickup. It took a bit longer than I wanted, but even sore and hurting like hells, I made it to Taerien's place in decent time.

'Course, two painkillers the size of horse-pills Jay'd slipped me did their share, too.

Also "place" was hells of an understatement: Taerien lived in a fucking mansion— complete with automated gates, security detail, and a moat of all things. Okay, less of a moat than a skinny arm of Hell Gate snaking along and through the wall surrounding the whole thing, but still. I climbed the rough stone by a break in the bottom of the wall, a drain of some sort to let the river run through and curve along the inside.

Thanks to a pocket-sized EMP Jay'd rigged for me, cameras and motion sensors became a non-issue; they spontaneously shorted out as I hauled myself up the wall. My bruised body didn't like that idea one bit. I made it, a panting, sweaty mess, every breath a stab of pain aimed right at my chest. I perched at the right angle to be partly covered by the wide branches of a tree and still get a good aim at Taerien's high windows. With those windows, the guy was asking to be shot.

All I needed to do was wait for Taerien to switch on the light in his study—and try not to freeze to death while I was at it. I'd scouted this place for weeks, making sure I knew when Taerien would be home, when his security changed shifts, when he went to the bathroom to take a shit. When it came down to it, assassination was horribly boring work involving way too much hiding and freezing your ass off, spying out places to make sure all you needed was one well-aimed bullet in the end.

I kept my eyes on the house, huddling in my leather jacket, bracing myself against the cold creeping into my bones. Not quite through winter yet, it was still cold enough for thin patches of ice to float on the river below. I was careful to hide the white cloud of my breath so it wouldn't give me away. Taerien's flunkies weren't the smartest bunch. Hadn't taken me longer than a night to figure out they weren't worth their shiny combat boots.

I shifted again and must've made some noise, trying to work the tingle out of my legs slowly falling asleep as I crouched in the dark. Because right then something hit me between the shoulder blades and threw me off the damn wall and into the fucking river.

4

Um, I'm here to Kill You

WHOEVER'D THROWN ME in held me under long enough for icy water to fill my mouth and nose and for flailing panic to kick in. It felt like diving into liquid ice. My body locked up in cold shock. I kicked dark water closing in, fighting its way down my throat and into my lungs. Then two hands grabbed me from behind and yanked me up and out of the water. The same hands that'd been trying to drown me a second ago.

I hit the ground choking on a fit of coughs tugging at my bruises. Eventually my hacking gave way to heaving gasps for breath.

"What the—" I hardly got the words out between chattering teeth and violent shivers. Cold burned my skin. I scrambled for my Colt, but my fingers weren't working. And there was the issue of the muzzle of a gun poking at my jugular as I lay there with the side of my face pressed against the cold dirt of the riverside. What was this, night of recurring themes or something?

"It honestly baffles me," a smooth voice said above me, "how someone with your reputation can be so completely oblivious to his surroundings. It seems your reputation is getting to your head, Mr. Nettoyer."

I twisted around, soggy clothes dragging me down and making my movements even more sluggish, but I got a good eyeful of Taerien's goon and recognized the fedora and black trench of the guy I'd nearly ran into at the Marché.

"You! How?" I forced my teeth apart, trying to keep the shakes out of my voice. "How the hells do you know who I am?"

A flash of a crooked grin. In the shadows of one of the lanterns spilling light onto Taerien's neatly trimmed lawn, the guy's hat hid most of his face.

"Mr. Taerien does go to great lengths to stay up to date on potential security threats. You will find we know more about you than you may think, Mr. Nettoyer."

"No shit," I grunted. "And cut the 'Mr. Nettoyer' crap."

A half shrug was all the answer I got. "We have been watching you for days, and we are quite aware of the details of your contract regarding Mr. Taerien. Including the sum Commander Valyr agreed to pay you upon completion. Which is rather sub-standard, by the way. One might almost be offended. But with Faelle Valyr in charge, who would expect any better? Honestly surprises me how she still finds anyone willing to do her dirty work." He paused for a second. "Unless of course, you aren't doing this for the money, but because you are desperate."

Something inside me clenched, a cold fist wrapped around my stomach, squeezing. What the hells did this guy know about the deal I had with Valyr? Worse, if he knew about that, what else did he know?

"You going to cut to the point and tell me what the hells you want or go on and monologue me to death?" Out of the corner of my eye, I caught the gleam of my Ruger, dead and useless on the ground.

"Don't even think about it." His tone was mildly amused, but the pressure of the gun against my throat increased. "I really would prefer not to shoot you, Mr. Nettoyer. It would be messy and unnecessarily dramatic, don't you think? I'm sure we can find a way to handle this in a much more civilized manner."

"Civilized, my ass," I said, but spread my hands, indicating yes, I was going to be a good boy, and no, I wasn't going to try anything stupid. For now.

Taerien's goon nodded. "So glad we are in agreement not to shoot each other's heads off. Now, Mr. Taerien has a business proposition for you. If you would follow me." He pulled back his piece but didn't lower it when he held out a pale hand to me. In the flare of bright halogen lighting, it looked white as bone with long fingers that belonged on a pianist's hands, not wrapped tightly around a gun.

I didn't take it. Just scrambled to my feet, soggy clothes clinging to me like a second skin, slowly freezing over. If he noticed me wince while I dragged myself up off the ground, he didn't let on.

Now that I got a better look at him, I saw the scars running down the left side of his face. Like a trail of bubbly, melted candle wax; they started at his temple, twisting his skin before disappearing into the high collar of his coat. Tips of silver-white hair peeked out from under his hat. There was something familiar about him. I'd seen him before. Scars like that didn't exactly make for easy blending-in.

"Who the fuck are you?"

A smirk tugged on the corner of his mouth. His eyes glinted the color of gunmetal, a gray so faint it was almost white. "I am the man holding a gun to your head. Everything else would be convoluted exposition at this point."

His crooked grin never slipped. I began to wonder if that was his normal expression, the scars pulling his mouth just a little off center. Even so, he had one of the most beautiful mouths I'd ever seen on a guy. I chased the thought away with a mental "What the fuck?" at myself.

His grin widened. "Shall we?"

Like I had a choice. Since he was the one with a gun on me, there wasn't any question of me going. I'd dropped my Ruger when I fell, and sure, I had my Colt and a knife or three tucked away, but no way in the Seven Hells would I draw them fast enough without Fedora getting wind of it. The one thing I needed to top off this clusterfuck of a night was getting myself shot.

Not that I wasn't pretty fucked already. No harm done in finding out exactly how fucked I was before my frozen-stiff corpse drifted down that damned river. Given the choice between dying somewhere inside Taerien's fancy mansion or freezing to death outside, I'd take my chances with getting warm first.

I wasn't disappointed when the heavy wooden front door swung open and warmth wrapped around me like a fluffy blanket. Aside from a good heater, Taerien's place had all the things you'd expect to be in a proper Core mansion. Heavy wooden furniture that seemed to have seen at least a century or so, colorful wallpaper, and oil paintings. Carpet. None of the scrap metal, PVC, and plastic that made up the interior of the *Shadow*. My boots left wet footprints along the polished hardwood floor of the long, narrow hallway. Every squishing step made hollow echoes thrown back by ceilings too high and way too white for my taste.

Taerien struck me as the kind of guy who did his offing in style. He'd take me out back first. Wouldn't want to ruin those expensive rugs by getting someone's brains all over them.

Fedora led me into a room three times the size of the bunk I shared with Aris. By Core standards, it probably measured up to a walk-in closet. There was a bed, the largest wooden dresser I'd ever seen, and a giant mirror that took over a whole wall.

"Given your current state, I suggest you change first." Fedora gestured at the pile of folded clothes and towels on the dresser. "You do look a bit like a half-drowned rat, if you don't mind me saying."

"And whose fucking fault is that, huh?" I glared at him casually leaning against the door.

He gave me a blank look that didn't quite cover his amusement. But he didn't make a move—just stood there, waiting.

"If you think I'm going to strip in front of you, you better buy me dinner first."

"Dear Gods, please." Fedora rolled his eyes. "Is all of Low Side this prudish or is it just you? I would turn around, but—" He waved his gun. "Feel free to continue freezing."

I swallowed a comment about what a waste of perfectly good clothes this was if I'd end up getting shot in them anyway. Instead, I turned to the massive dresser and started stripping out of my wet clothes. And tried to ignore the mirror and the way Fedora kept looking at me, his eyes brushing down my spine like a touch. Definitely not the kind of once-over you gave a guy you pointed a gun at to make sure he didn't run.

I forced myself to focus on the buttons of my shirt, one at a time. My fingers were numb and fumbling, but I managed. I shrugged off my shirt when something tore inside, and I nearly doubled over in pain. Dizziness hit. I clenched my jaw, held my breath until the twinge passed.

"What happened to you?" Fedora's voice was at my back, very close. Pale fingers reached out to poke at my ribs. I whirled around and slammed him into the dark wood of the dresser, ignoring the flare of pain the movement set off inside my chest.

"Don't. Touch me," I wheezed. He stepped back and held up one hand in a gesture that might've been soothing, if not for the gun he was still holding.

"It's okay," he said quickly. "I'm sorry, I—I'm a...a doctor, you could say. I'm trying to help." In front of the mirror, I couldn't help but notice the mess of dark bruises covering my torso. No wonder I felt like my entire upper body'd been pounded like a slab of meat.

Fedora carefully lowered his hand. "May I?"

"I'm fine. I don't need—"

"Please."

I let out a breath deep enough to make me wince and nodded.

His fingers were warm against my skin, rippling with goose bumps. Seemed he knew what he was doing. Still, I found myself clenching the top of the dresser in a white-knuckled grip, trying to keep my breathing even. It'd be okay. I clamped my lower lip between my teeth. Made myself stay perfectly still. It'd be over in a minute. Everything under control. Just breathe. Pretend it was Jay or Kovacz patching me up. No one to worry about. I squeezed my eyes shut. Slowly counted to ten before opening them again. Fuck, if there ever was a bad time for trigger issues, this was it.

I was so busy trying not to freak out at Fedora touching me, I completely missed when he let go and started going through one of the drawers in the dresser. He'd put the gun on the other side of the dresser, a few feet away.

"Don't," Fedora said, long fingers closing over the handle. "Please."

I looked away.

A smile curved his mouth. "I won't hurt you, Mr. Nettoyer. Not unless you make me."

Fuck, like I hadn't heard that one before. My jaw began to ache from clenching it so hard.

He pulled out a roll of wide elastic bandages and a tube of something with the biting menthol smell of analgesic. It chased even more goose bumps across my body but took the bite out of the pain.

"It doesn't look like anything is broken, but you should leave this on for a few days," Fedora said, wrapping bandages tight around my ribs. He'd pushed the sleeves of his coat up to his elbows. In the mirror, I could make out more scars along his arm and on the inside of his left wrist. These were faint, curling like tendrils of smoke.

He caught me watching and turned his left side away from me. Almost made it look unintentional, too, if it hadn't been for his fingers twitching short of reaching up to pull his hat deeper into his face. All about looking, but didn't want others to look at him. Interesting.

"What happened to your neck?" His eyes lowered. "Did something *bite* you?"

And we were back to loaded questions. At least he didn't push for an answer, just went for the disinfectant and another gauze pad. He paused taping me up, eyes fixed on the tattoo on my right shoulder—a raven stretched in flight, holding a broken pocket watch in its claws.

"Beautiful ink. What does it mean?"

I jerked away. "It's nothing."

Fedora raised an eyebrow but didn't comment. Good for him.

It was from a story Aris told me when I'd first gotten to the Shadow. He'd told me how the old Gods shattered the world, but when they tried to put it together again, a raven nicked a piece and flew away with it. After, the world had never been the same again. I always thought the raven had a point. If the Gods wanted the world whole, they shouldn't have broken it in the first place.

When he was done, I turned to the bed and gingerly put on the fresh clothes, not sure what creeped me out more: that they were exactly my size or that they were the near match to my soggy ones now crumpled on the floor. Then again, it did feel good to be warm.

"Think I can talk to your boss now I'm not going to drip all over his fancy carpet?"

Whatever point Taerien wanted to prove with this fucking farce, I'd rather he got to it quickly. Not like I had much of a choice in the matter, but if I played nice, I could speed things along. And maybe, just maybe, it'd give me that one second of distraction I'd need to get the jump on Fedora and the shit he was pulling.

Fedora nodded and led me back outside and to what I figured was Taerien's living room. Or they might call it a sitting room in places like this. The door was wide open, and I wondered if he'd been watching all this, getting a kick out of how much he could fuck with me before cutting to the chase. The gigantic room somehow managed to look cozy with walls painted in an accented mix of earthy red and brown, lined with tall bookshelves bent under the load of books they were stuffed with. An electric chandelier dangling from the ceiling sent broken speckles of light dancing across polished crystal glasses set out on the stained-glass coffee table and a bar in the back lined with decanters of clear and amber liquid.

Taerien stood by one of the large windows facing the exact spot I'd been using to hide. Fucking figures.

Fedora positioned himself by the door, and the guy I'd come to kill turned around and gave me a calculating once-over. No love lost between the two of us, no matter how this night was going to turn out. Even for a corporate, Mael Taerien was unremarkable. He had that standard clean-cut, close-shaven look that screamed Upright Core Citizen. It went with sandy hair, brown eyes, medium height, medium build, and the kind of skin tone they used for off-white color swatches. Someone so obviously built to be overlooked, it had to be intentional.

"So, we finally meet in person," Taerien said, his voice as bland and sleek as his looks. The kind of voice that set off my inner alarm bells. Too bad they were already ringing at max volume. At least he didn't insist on a handshake. Taerien sat down in one of the black leather chairs grouped around a round mahogany table at the center of the room.

"I suppose we can bypass drinks and small talk and get down to business."

"Actually," I said, suddenly determined to stall and put some cracks into his polished businessman facade, "I'll have some gin if you've got any. No ice."

A tight smile and casual wave at the liquor cabinet. "Help yourself."

Turned out the bottle of gin was already there, right next to an empty glass. Was there anything about me Taerien hadn't sniffed out, if we were already down to drinking preferences? Taerien didn't strike me as the kind to resort to drugging me. Not when he had me exactly where I wanted. So, I poured a double shot, knocked it back, and then poured another. Shit, bastard better not be wasting poison on some damn good top shelf gin. The stuff was surprisingly smooth and strangely flowery, not burning down my throat or likely to make me go blind like the kind of engine cleaner you got down in the dregs of Helos. Up Side perks.

"Business then," I took the bottle with my glass and sat down opposite him. The armchair was cushy enough to feel like it swallowed me. Comfortable chairs. Never a good sign.

"Talk," I said.

That got me a twitch of his thin lips that almost could've qualified as a smile if it'd touched his eyes. "How much did Valyr offer you?"

"You already know that, and I'm pretty sure you didn't just half drown me for kicks, so cut the bullshit."

"Ah yes, that introduction might have been a bit...drastic."

"He deserved it," Fedora cut in from the doorway. "And I only drowned him a little."

I didn't bother glaring at him. The guy enjoyed this fucked-up cat and mouse game way too much already.

"What do you want?" I said to Taerien.

"I want to triple your offer."

I blinked. Downed the rest of my drink. "Huh. And I s'pose I've got three guesses who you want me to off for you?"

"That won't be necessary," Taerien replied. Humorless bastard. "You already know it's Valyr's head I want. And you are the one who will get it for me."

Who will get it. Interesting word choice. "What makes you think I can be bought?"

"You are an assassin, Mr. Nettoyer. A mercenary. Being bought is part of your job description. Besides, if money fails to be incentive enough, these should serve."

He made a show of pulling open the table's single drawer and took out a slim folder before handing it over to me. One look at the stack of holosheets inside bound my stomach into a knot. I turned cold all over. This was worse than the damn river.

The folder contained detailed blueprints of the *Shadow* and the junkyard surrounding it. Holoreels looped through Jay and Kovacs climbing into the *Shadow,* their faces bright with laughter at something that didn't make the recording. Others showed Kovacs leaving La Poubelle in a counterfeit red coat, Iltis supervising the rest of us unloading cargo at a nearby container bay, and Jay kissing a girl with a buzz cut against the hood of a stripped-down groundcar, her fingers leaving streaks of grime on the other girl's cheeks, both of them clearly beyond caring.

But the one that made my heart skip before launching it into a frenzy that felt like it was going to burst through my chest was a holoclip capturing what'd happened at the warehouse only hours ago. It'd been recorded from above to our left, as if whoever'd captured it had perched outside one of the warehouse's tall windows. But even through the soot and part of the glass pane starred where a rock must've hit it, the viewer's line to Aris remained clear. It zoomed in on him as his eyes turned stark white, and a blink later, the warehouse erupted in a burst of rubble and bricks.

I swallowed and kept my breath even, unable to will the gooseflesh from rippling along my arms as the reel replayed what'd happened screen by damning screen.

Gods, Aris, we really got ourselves into a fucking pickle this time.

Taerien smiled thinly. "Think about what would stop me from slipping a tip to the Watch regarding the location of a certain ship. A ship which not only harbors a group of wanted criminals, but a stray Voyant. I'm sure they would be very grateful for that particular tip, don't you think?"

"Nice try." I lowered the holosheets, trying for nonchalance and failing. My mouth went dry and my knuckles stood out white around my empty drink. "In case it slipped past you, the Reds are dirty. Not much you can tell them they don't already know." Which was a load of shit. Bribery only got you so far. Good for covering up minor fuck-ups, but useless once they had you by the short and curlies.

Taerien didn't fall for my bluff.

"Rest assured, I am well aware. Besides, I would make it worth their time. After all, your friend Aris Maevere blasted about with the Voyance in public. Where anyone could have seen him. Think what will happen if you don't come to the rescue and shoot whoever is ready to Cleanse him next time."

I turned to Fedora. "You. It was you who called the Reds on us."

Fedora held my gaze.

Thought I'd seen a shadow whisk away right before the Reds'd busted us at the warehouse. A shadow in a trench and hat. And then it'd been him at the Place du Marché later, sneaking after me the whole time, no doubt gathering extra intel to blackmail me.

Gods, I'd fucked up big time. I'd dragged Aris and the others right down with me. So much for thinking I could take out Taerien like it was no big deal. Making rookie mistakes from the start. They'd played me all right. Game, set, and fucking match. Empire-style. Fuck.

"Fine." I paused long enough to fill my glass to the brim and knock back a double. "I'll do it. But it'll take time." Also, it'd probably end with my mutilated body dangling from the Finger of Light, right after Valyr gutted me and made me watch my entrails burn while I died. "You ready to roll over and play dead for a while till I get this sorted? Won't do you any good dead when Valyr finds out I didn't actually kill you."

"Details." Taerien waved a hand. Obviously throwing the lives of my friends into this were just details to him, too.

"We have a deal then."

I knocked back another drink. Gods. We had a fucking deal all right.

5

I've Got You

A SINGLE CLOCK strike followed me out of Taerien's place and into the darkness. The sound felt like a dark promise, a countdown that'd end with my messy, screaming death. Behind me, the moan of metal creaking open, clanging shut. Light footsteps followed.

"Fuck off, Fedora."

"Aw, you gave me a nickname. Cute." The obligatory crooked grin split his face. "Let's continue bonding while I give you a ride home."

My fist wanted to bond with his face. Probably would've, if there hadn't been three of him, blurring in front of me. Shouldn't have had that last glass of gin. Or the three before.

"'M pretty sure I've seen enough of you for one night. Now fuck off."

Gods, I didn't have time for this shit. I had to find Aris. Get him out of Nightshade and back to the *Shadow* and figure out things from there. Preferably not get myself and everyone around me killed in the process.

Fedora shook his head. "Unfortunately, it would pose a slight inconvenience to our operation if you fall into a ditch and freeze to death. Consider this asset protection."

"Asset protection, my ass."

I walked away, stumbling a bit. The road in front of me only swayed a little with its rows of houses with flower beds lining neatly trimmed lawns straight from some holocommercial of what life could be like if you were both lucky and didn't ask questions. Here, behind their white fences and doors with triple security locks, no one slept worrying about Reds crashing into their homes to arrest and brain-fry their friends just because they'd pissed off the wrong guy. Must be nice to live in the kind of place where there was money for fancy bell towers that told you the hour in chiming tones. Only had to kiss enough Empire ass and know when to turn around and look away in time or it'd be you they fucked over next.

Trying to walk off the feeling of the world wobbling beneath my feet, I did my best to lose Fedora, but he stuck to my heels like a lost puppy. Just what I needed.

I crossed over into Nightshade, where nobody gave a shit about who you were or who you fucked as long as you paid the tab. Dozens of bars and cheap motels with flickering neon signs colored the narrow streets, the scratching of dying bulbs cutting into the soft glow of red and orange lights.

Fedora smiled at two girls in short skirts and high heels crossing over to us. "You should have told me you had plans for the night," Fedora said. "I would have dressed for the occasion." At a scowl from me, they quickly turned tail, the clacking of their heels a hurried echo on the pavement.

"Not that kind of plan," I snapped and veered into one of the less-busy streets, almost tripping over a piece of broken curb in the process.

Fat chance I'd find Aris in this, even if I narrowed it down to his usual haunts, but lucky for me, Laras was predictable. The Red Garter was one of the shabbier places of Nightshade, a little off the busy main roads. Part cheap motel, part greasy all-night diner, you'd be right in for a case of food poisoning to go along with your STI. The building itself could've fit right into Low Side with black and red graffiti splattered across peeling white paint. I used to wonder why Laras took Aris to this kind of dump when she could've afforded pretty much any of the nicer places around here. Then I realized it was all part of her setting the scene.

Aris wouldn't talk of the nights he went out with Laras. He didn't have to. The bruises said enough. I couldn't bring myself to touch him for days after, he looked so sore. So breakable.

We'd almost made it to the Garter's boarded-up front door when Fedora said, "I am sorry. About Taerien dragging your friends into this."

He'd barely gotten the words out before I whirled around and slammed him against the chipped red doorframe, my Colt shoved against the crook of his jaw. I didn't give a shit about how I was still drunk out of my head and how it'd throw off my aim. He and Taerien could fuck with me all they wanted. Hells, wasn't like this was news to me. But no one threatened Aris or the others.

"Don't. Don't you *dare* act like you're sorry. We both know you're not and you're just trying to make nice with me so Taerien can use me as he fucking pleases and make me pretend I fucking like it."

"Now that's a bit harsh, don't you think? Besides, Taerien doesn't—"

"Shut. The fuck. Up," I hissed and shoved the Colt in harder. "Whatever shitty excuse you're trying to come up with, I don't want—"

"Dahlia, please. I'm fine."

Whatever else I was ready to say died in my throat, pushed away by Aris staggering out of the Garter, clinging to Laras in an unsteady wobble.

"You are *not* fine," Laras's voice snapped, then softened. "Light, Maevere, sit down before you hurt yourself worse than you already have."

I lowered my gun, suddenly painfully sober, and crossed over to them, heart tight in my chest. For once Fedora did the sensible thing and hung back, melting into an alley where dim lantern light blended into shadows.

I closed the gap between us and rounded in on Laras. "What the fuck did you do to him?"

"She didn't," Aris protested and sluggishly tried to pull away from Laras. "'S my fault. Sorry."

Apparently talking and moving at the same time seemed to take more coordination than he had. Between Laras and me we caught him as he slid down to the pavement. With his back against the crumbling wall and his legs splayed in front of him, Aris looked boneless, his shirt torn and gaping where he hadn't buttoned it right.

"I'm sure you are." Laras stepped back, her lips thin and bloodless in an icy expression I'd never seen her direct at Aris. "But not half as sorry as you will be if you ever do this to yourself again. This happens again and we are done, do you understand?"

"Dahlia—"

"Do you understand, Aris?" Laras's tone cut like a lash.

Aris's shoulders slumped and he sunk in on himself before nodding. "Yeah. Understood."

"Good." Laras turned to me. "Get him home before he catches his death out here. He's shivering."

"Yeah." I knelt by Aris. "I've got him."

Laras inclined her head. "Thanks, Nettoyer." She was gone before thinking too much about the sudden tenderness in Laras's face could give me whiplash.

"Hey," I bent closer to Aris, cursing when I took his hand. It was ice cold. "What in the Seven bloody Hells happened to you?"

"Hey." Aris's mouth curved in a lazy smile. He tried to reach for me but didn't quite make it. His hand swept through thin air, like a cat trying to bat at dust mites. He slumped forward, shivering, his head lolling against my shoulder when I caught him. His pupils were so dilated I couldn't see any color in his eyes.

Aris raised his head and stared right through me. "You're warm," he mumbled and burrowed in.

"Yeah, and you're stoned out of your fucking mind."

"Hmmm, that," Aris slurred, his grin lopsided. "Thought it'd help with the Voyance. Make things quieter. I just needed—" Something clenched deep in the pit of my stomach. Twisted at the desperation in Aris's face, the sudden dampness clinging to his lashes. "Must've taken a bit much." He shuddered, eyes sliding to half-mast before they scrunched shut. "Oh Gods, Damian, it—"

He whimpered, his body jerking in violent spasms.

"Aris? Aris!"

"Don't," Fedora said, suddenly next to me as I was trying to hold Aris down. "Turn him on his side." He began to rip Aris's shirt open.

"Get your fucking hands off him!" Seeing Fedora's hands on Aris right after his boss had fucking blackmailed me, using Aris's life as if it was nothing, short-circuited something in my brain. I tried to pull Aris to me, but he was thrashing so badly, I had my hands full trying to keep him from bashing his own head in.

Fedora let go of Aris and straightened, sudden pissed-off fury burning in his eyes. "Let me make this easy for you," he hissed. He dug around in his coat pockets and tore open a package containing a syringe filled with some sort of clear liquid. "He took mesc. Overdosed by the looks of it. He's in shock and you have two options. One, you let me help. Two, you keep at this and he dies, because his heart is going to give out if we don't do something about this."

I swallowed and jerked my head in a nod. "Do it."

"Good. Now do exactly as I say. Meaning, stay out of my way."

He unbuttoned Aris's shirt, pulled up the syringe, and rammed it straight into Aris's chest.

Whatever was in that syringe made Aris's entire body go rigid like he'd been hit with one of the Reds' stun guns. Another full-body spasm, then Aris let out something between a moan and a sigh and went completely limp in my arms.

"Holy shit. Aris?"

"And now we wait." Fedora put two fingers against Aris's throat, then nodded. "Better."

I stared at him, the syringe that'd saved Aris's life cast aside like it was nothing. Like he did this every day.

"Who the fuck *are* you?"

"Wouldn't you like to know." That signature half smirk crooked Fedora's lips, but the brief flash in his steely eyes told me I'd hit a nerve.

Fedora pulled back and fished a silver penlight out of his pocket. He was shining it into Aris's eyes when they fluttered open.

"Hi there," Aris drawled. He peered down at himself, then at Fedora. There was the faintest ring of hazel visible around his pupils. Still flying high. "Don't think I caught your name, but if it's not your thing an' you wanna get right down to business..." He fumbled with his belt and my stomach did a little flip. Aris would call me a demisexual monogamist, but sex just wasn't hard-wired into my DNA. Not like it was for Aris and not like it was for most people, I guess. It took well-established trust. Emotional connection. That kind of thing. Didn't think I'd ever get how fast Aris could switch straight to fuck-me mode. Definitely looked like he was feeling better though.

"Um, that won't be necessary." Fedora actually looked kind of awkward and drew back. Good for him, because I would've socked him otherwise.

"We should get him someplace warm," he said to me. "Shouldn't be more than a few hours for the worst to be out of his system."

"'M right here y'know," Aris muttered. At least he'd stopped trying to talk Fedora out of his pants. His hand brushed against my cheek. "Hey." Aris's brows furrowed as he tried to focus on me, but couldn't quite manage it. "You okay? What's wrong?"

Gods, sometimes I hated how well Aris could read me. I closed my eyes and leaned into his touch. Just for a second. I pulled away before I got a chance to fall apart.

"Nothing." I brushed a soft kiss against his fingers, whatever Fedora thought be damned. "Everything's fine. Let's get you home."

"Bad liar, know that?" Aris mumbled thickly, his eyes already slipping shut again. He only let out a weak noise of pain when I lifted him up and awkwardly got his body up and over my shoulder. My battered ribs didn't like it, not at all, but I shrugged off Fedora's offer to give me a hand, his face set in an odd expression as he regarded me and Aris.

"He needs to get out of the cold."

"I got him." I turned to leave.

Fedora followed me.

"Gods, there's no getting rid of you, is there?"

Fedora regarded me coolly. "He needs medical care. What exactly is your idea of proper aftercare of a mesc overdose? Patch him up and let him sleep it off? You do that and he might not wake up again."

I wanted to argue, but there was no point. Fedora and Taerien already knew anything there was to know about the *Shadow*. I didn't know the first thing about him, but Fedora'd helped Aris. That'd have to be enough.

Even with Aris's weight slowing me down and my body screaming at me, I managed to avoid the mess of potholes riddling the narrow roads into the Bande Poubelle. Didn't need to know any Frankish to figure out the Poubelle was exactly as the name said: a row of junkyards. Part of the Districte Feraille, Helos's very own ass-crack. The Reds had turned tail here long ago, making the yards the best place to hide whatever you didn't want the Empire to find.

But the *Shadow* wasn't just a pile of trash, half buried under a few disemboweled car wrecks and other scattered debris. You'd have to do some serious digging to figure out under all this crap was one of the last spaceships ever made before space travel went to shit. We'd sent people to the moon once and thought it was the beginning of owning the galaxy. Now, a hundred and fifty years later, lack of resources meant colonizing planets was on hold in favor of keeping our own up and running.

The Gods alone knew where Iltis had gotten a bloody abandoned spaceship in the first place. Far as I knew, those didn't just lie around waiting for some street scum to turn them into her personal headquarters.

Iltis wasn't particularly chatty when it came to her past, but it didn't matter. She'd had the right idea when she decided this was the ideal home for what she later called the Shadows, our gang of merry little outlaws, mostly kids no one'd ever miss anyway. She'd picked us off the street and taught us how to make a life of honest thieving and how to avoid getting caught and strung up by the Reds while making life for the Empire a little harder. The *Shadow* wasn't much, but it was better than most of us would've expected to do in this life.

Past the mesh wire fence topped with security cams that'd lost their lenses to target practice between Kovacz and me years ago, we made it to the edge of the junkyard where the *Shadow* lay like an oversized bird with its wings clipped. The light of a single lantern cast flickers like scars across its dented carcass. I nodded at Fedora to pull on one of the side hatches we used as an easy entrance whenever we didn't have any cargo with us. The door opened with a teeth-grinding screech no amount of oil seemed to fix.

"So we're clear—" I pulled my Colt out of the waistband of my jeans. It was awkward, holding Aris with my other hand, but got the point across. "—one wrong move and you're toast."

"No worries," Fedora said, crooked smirk back in place. "Just remember our deal."

Smug bastard. I gritted my teeth, a hair from reconsidering and putting a bullet in his back after all. What in the Seven Hells *was* I doing, letting the guy who'd threatened me, threatened my friends, into our home? But then I felt Aris shiver against me and I didn't know what else to do about it right now.

"Move," I snapped.

We'd barely gotten inside when Jay almost ran us over. "What took you so long? Where—" She stopped short when she saw Aris's body slung over my shoulder. Her head swiveled to Fedora. "Who the hells are *you*?"

Question of the fucking hour.

"Later, Grasshopper." I brushed her off and kept walking down the corridor to the infirmary.

The Shadow's sick bay was a retrofitted spare room in the back of the ship, past the side-shuttle Iltis had turned into her study and the loading deck, now stacked high with the barrels and crates that'd been supposed to go into the warehouse. Aris stirred a little but didn't wake up when Fedora pushed the door open and flicked the light switch. The dull-metal cubicle of a room flooded with greenish neon, only made more hideous by the walls and bed frames throwing it back in blinding reflections.

Blinking away the bright spots in front of my vision, I lay Aris on one of the beds. With a glance my way and a nod, Fedora started to pull open drawers in the white cabinets shoved against the wall like he owned the place. He'd dropped the trench over a chair, snapped on some vinyl gloves, and was starting an IV in the crook of Aris's right arm when Jay came in with Kovacz in tow.

Jay's eyes widened when she got a good look at Aris, his skin so pale, he looked almost blue in the stark neon light. "Oh shit, Aris." Jay swallowed and came closer, her voice a tad shaky. "What happened?"

"What *I* really want to know is what in the Gods' names is *he* doing here?" Kovacz cut in, adding some extra emphasis on the question with his gun out and aimed at Fedora. I would've been worried about his aim also including me and Aris, but I knew how good of a shot Kovacs was. "Seriously, Damian, not enough our resident Burner here's crossing all kinds of lines he shouldn't, now you're dragging an Up Sider into our home?"

"I have to say," Fedora turned from where he'd been adjusting the dosage on Aris's IV. "Quite a charming bunch you have here. I'm warming up to them already."

Kovacz wasn't a tall guy, but all of his short, stocky build was tense and cramped behind that gun, his blue eyes narrowed to slits making him look even more like a pissed-off imp than usual.

I sighed, my right hand rubbing at my temples. All this shit was giving me a headache.

"Put down the damn gun, Kovacz. He's okay." With the small exception that his batshit crazy boss was blackmailing me and if I didn't do as he said he'd serve our asses to the Reds on a fucking silver platter. Maybe I *should* let Kovacz put a bullet into Fedora. Tempting.

I exhaled, took Aris's hand into mine, grounded by his pulse's steady beat against my skin.

"Stop fucking around, okay? I'm not going to let you shoot him." If anyone did any shooting here, it'd be me.

"Now aren't I flattered," Fedora said. "I believe this is my signal to leave."

Best thing he'd said all fucking night.

Kovacz opened his mouth, when something rapped his hand. He gasped but kept his grip on his gun. Good thing, too, because dropped guns didn't mix well with the tight tin can of a room we were in.

"Stay," Iltis said behind Kovacz.

"Damn it, Iltis!" Kovacz rubbed his hand. Iltis might be blind as a bat, but she knew where to hit.

"Looks like someone needs a little reinforcement in basic manners, huh, Orion?" Iltis lowered her walking stick. "Which includes not waving guns around in front of guests." Her milky eyes crinkled. "Raeyn Nymeron." She smiled. "It's been a while, boy."

"Iltis." Just then Fedora's—Raeyn's—smile almost felt real. "Still handy with that cane, I see."

"Wait a fucking minute," I cut in and put Aris's hand down on the cot, if only so I could get between him and Aris. Useless as the gesture might be. Not much I could do to protect him. Not when he was who Iltis said he was. Not when I'd brought him right into our Godsforsaken ship. "You. Are Raeyn Nymeron. *The* Raeyn Nymeron. The president's son."

"Oh, I get a definitive article now? Notoriety, I like it."

His grin rolled right off him. He turned to Iltis. "Thank you for stomping all over my carefully maintained anonymity, by the way. And here I thought friends didn't blow friends' covers."

Iltis wasn't impressed. "Honestly, boy. You think that coat and hat will fool anyone? I may be a blind, old woman, but this is just offensive." She tapped the brim of his fedora. "Besides, you're indoors, in a respectable abode. Kindly lose that ridiculous hat."

For a second the *Shadow* fell entirely still, the faint hum of the generators the only sound in the silence.

"Of course. Where are my manners?" Fedora—Raeyn—took his hat off with a flourish.

I finally got a good look at his face. His eyes were a gray so faint it was almost white. The silver-white of his hair had nothing to do with age. Its tips curled around his ears. Up close, even the hat and trench coat didn't do much to hide the trademark looks of the Nymeron family. I'd only ever seen the president on holoscreens and safely far away during one of the Empire's parades, but there was no mistake. Freakishly pale eyes, white hair, and the same light skin and fine-boned build. This guy could've been a younger copy of the Big Bad himself. Fuck.

"Raeyn Nymeron's dead." The words spilled out before I could stop myself. "Kicked it years ago when the old palace burned."

"That's the official story." Raeyn stood very straight, his face tight. In the bright light, his scars stood out like knife slashes that'd destroyed a beautiful painting but would never ruin it. "Unfortunately for my father, I didn't die quite as conveniently."

"Obviously it takes more than a little explosion to do away with the truly stubborn," Iltis said, her free hand brushing strands of wispy white hair from her crinkled forehead. "Now, is anyone going to explain to me what by Helos's hairy balls is going on here?"

"Okay, wait a minute," I cut in. Maybe whatever Aris was doped up with was contagious or something, because this sure as hells'd stopped making sense to me. "You *know* each other?"

"You think he got out of that fire at the palace all by himself?" Iltis said, as if it explained everything. "Raeyn's an old friend. Speaking of, I take it you're not here for a friendly visit?" She mightn't be able to see my face, but the old crow was no fool. That and she'd sniff a lie ten miles downwind. Shit.

"He's—" I started, but Raeyn talked right over me.

"Damian and I were discussing some business matters I'm going to need his help with. The confidential kind."

"You need someone to do your dirty work." Iltis nodded, not smiling this time. Here was hoping she'd swallowed Raeyn's not-quite-lie. Smooth of him. Real fucking smooth.

"So, what happened here?" Iltis's hands hovered over Aris. She wrinkled her nose. "I can smell the mesc on him from here."

I took a deep breath and filled her in about how we'd found Aris and how Raeyn had helped. Just left out the bit how I hadn't wanted him to be there in the first place along with some choice bits of what exactly that "deal" I'd made with him involved. That'd have to wait till later.

"He should be fine." Raeyn re-checked Aris's vitals. "He's stable and needs to sleep it off."

"I'll stay with him," I said when Raeyn was done and tracked the numbers on the screen off to Aris's side as if I could will his pulse to stay strong and even if I kept my eyes on it long enough. "Grasshopper, make sure Kovacz doesn't shoot Nymeron here on the way out?" I sounded tired, even to myself.

"I don't need a fucking babysitter, Damian," Kovacz said and shoved his gun into his jeans, never taking his glare off Raeyn.

"Two words for you, hotshot," Jay said. "Drinks and cards. You owe me a rematch, remember?"

Kovacz growled something in reply but let her steer him out of the room.

"And you" —Iltis took a step toward Raeyn— "Stay. It sounds like we are desperately in need to catch up."

"Of course." Raeyn's expression stayed unreadable, but something told me he hadn't been expecting anything less. "You still prefer to do your scheming over a chessboard?"

"Only if the player's worth my time."

"Not to sound like a sore loser, but I do believe we ended our last match on a rather unfortunate draw."

"It was a checkmate, boy," Iltis said. "Clearly. You going to deny a blind old lady her victory?"

"A blind old lady who cheats," Raeyn said, but he grinned when he took Iltis's hand. "Shall we?"

Iltis's gnarled hand twitched around her cane like she wanted to whack him. "This better be good."

"I promise you won't regret it," Raeyn said and turned to me. "He should be out for a while still. Keep him hydrated when he wakes up."

I nodded, suddenly out of energy to tell him I'd dealt with plenty of hangovers before.

I was relieved when he left and the clanking of Iltis's cane echoed down the corridor. Not that I had the slightest clue what the hells was going on and how she knew Raeyn fucking Nymeron of all people or how far they went back. Not sure I wanted to know. Same as I didn't start wondering how in the Seven Hells someone blind like Iltis managed to find her way around a chess board. Gods knew even with two perfectly fine eyes I was a crapshoot at it. Had to be a tactical thing. Or she'd sold her soul to the dark side for that, her upper right hook, and her ability to sneak around places like a ghost.

Soon as everyone was gone, I got some blankets, one to carefully cover Aris and one to wrap around myself before I pulled a chair over to the bed. Only when I sat down did I notice how completely beat I was. Guess that's what I got for letting my body be used as a punching bag all night. I thought about getting some of that numbing stuff from the infirmary's med cabinet, but even the thought of getting up again sounded like way too much work.

Instead, I stayed where I was and took one of Aris's hands in mine. His wrists were circled with dark rings of bruises and scabs. She'd cuffed him. Tight. But she'd drawn the line at the drugs.

This happens again and we are done, do you understand?

Laras had meant it. I only hoped Aris had, too. I swallowed, trying to get my stomach to unclench, but didn't let go of his hand.

I leaned in, brushed a few strands of hair out of his face, and kissed his forehead. "Next time you pull this kind of shit, I *will* kill you."

I must've fallen asleep at some point, because I woke up to Aris scrambling out of the bed and staggering toward the bathroom in the back of the sick bay.

"Hey," I said, tiredness muffling my voice. "You okay?"

The sound of the toilet lid hitting the tank and Aris heaving was all the response I got.

Great. I squinted at the clock above the door. It was one of those old railway station clocks, and from this angle, it loomed menacing—as if it'd fall down any minute and crush someone in a pile of metal and glass. Four thirty in the morning. Couldn't have slept for more than an hour. Two tops.

Somewhere between the crick in my neck and my body generally deciding to go on strike, I got out of the chair and padded to the bathroom to make sure Aris hadn't passed out in a puddle of his own puke or something.

"Hey, are you—Shit!"

Aris lay in the corner of the bathroom, curled in a fetal position, shivering violently with his hands clawing at the cold tile floor, making horrible nails-on-blackboard noises. His chest rose and fell way too fast.

"Aris?" Two steps brought me next to him and close enough to feel his pulse, beating frantic and fluttered, like something was trapped under his skin trying to get out.

"Hey!" I shook him gently, trying to get him to snap out of it, whatever *it* was. "Hey, c'mon, Aris, you gotta wake up. C'mon. Aris, wake up!" No reaction.

"Raeyn! I need some help in here! Raeyn!"

Aris's body spasmed and his eyes flew open, blazing white before he threw me across the room. The back of my head smacked into the tiled wall. My vision turned black and spotty, I could taste blood at the back of my mouth.

"What the—" I didn't get any further. Aris's brows drew together in a tight line and two hands closed around my throat, dead set on crushing my windpipe. The creepy thing was he didn't even touch me, just kept staring right at me, looking as if he was concentrating real hard. The Voyance. Shit!

I gasped for breath, tried to struggle, to do anything that'd get his hands off me. Hands that weren't even fucking *there*.

"Aris. No." He didn't let go, just tightened his grip. I kicked out, frantic and pointless. Not a damn I could do to get his hands off me. My feet scrabbled against slick white tile. Aris held tight.

It went on for seconds stretching into an eternity of helpless wheezing. My lungs started to burn, heaving and trying to fill themselves with air, panic bubbling up when nothing came through. My vision tunneled, the bright neon light overhead making spots dance in front of my eyes.

Aris was going to kill me.

What are you doing? It's me. Aris, please. Let go. It's me, for fuck's sake!

I tried to get him off me, fighting against something I couldn't see, tried to get words past the hand crushing my throat, tried to stop kicking and wasting my energy on panicking, tried...

Aris, no! One last thought before everything tilted sideways and something hard crashed into me.

Suddenly I could breathe again. I doubled over coughing, sucking in massive gulps of air through my wrecked throat. Things cleared up enough to see Raeyn standing over me. Between him and the bottom of the sink I'd smacked into, I almost managed to drag myself up from the floor.

Aris's eyes'd gone back to normal and now stared at me from across the room, wide and completely fucking terrified. Recognition set in.

"Damian?" he croaked. "Oh Gods, Damian."

His eyes rolled back in his head and he keeled over. Raeyn caught him before his head hit the floor.

6

Shadows

"GOTTA HAND IT to him," Kovacz said when I filled him in about what'd happened over a couple of hands of Five Cards the next day. "Your Burner's not much for subtlety."

My jaw tightened. "Don't call him that."

"What?" Kovacz raised his chin. "He's burning through our minds before the Voyance does him in the end. Fucking appropriate, if you ask me."

"Well, I wasn't asking, so shut up and deal, Kovacz."

Even after the painkillers, Raeyn'd doped me up with, my voice had a hoarse rasp to it. Kovacz glared and went back to scrunching a deck of cards between his fingers as he shuffled.

The door separating the *Shadow*'s commons from the kitchen and the rest of the lower floor opened and Jay came through. She put a cup in front of me.

"Raeyn left this for you. He said drink it."

I eyed the cup; its contents were hot and kind of greenish. "Yeah, right. Don't think so." I pushed the cup away.

Jay pushed it right back. "Drink it. He said it'll help with the voice."

"They always say that, Grasshopper. 'Drink this. It'll help.' It's bullshit. Doctors' way of taking the piss." I lifted the cup and sniffed it, just to make sure. Wouldn't put it past Raeyn to take the piss bit literally. I wrinkled my nose. It smelled herbal in a muddy way with an underlying note of ass.

Jay shook her head, her messy corkscrew coils bouncing. "You're such a baby, you know that? You gonna drink it or do you need me to shove it down your throat?"

"Think you can take me, Grasshopper?"

"Watch me. I'll pinch your nose shut if I have to."

Across from me, Kovacz barely got his chuckles under control. "Now that I want to see. Money's on the kiddo. She fights mean."

I glared at them both and took the cup. I almost choked on the first gulp as it burned down my throat, sharp, bitter, and absolutely disgusting.

"What the hells did he put into this?" I wheezed once I was done coughing. I actually was surprised it hadn't burned whatever was left of my voice right out.

Jay shrugged. "No idea. Just said he made it 'specially for you."

"Yeah, I fucking bet."

Jay rolled her eyes. "Please. Quit whining. Wouldn't hurt you to say thank you. I mean, he patched up Aris and saved your ass while he was at it. Picking up the pieces gets kinda old, you know."

I bit my lower lip, trying very hard not to tell her what exactly was up with Raeyn's shady motives and his "everyone's best buddy" spiel. At least he'd finally left well enough alone and cleared out. Last thing I needed was Raeyn Nymeron's eyes glued to my ass with every move I made. Especially when part of me wanted to turn it around on him, preferably with him against a wall and my teeth on his skin to show him two could play his game.

Gods, Aris must've rattled my brain around something fierce the night before if my mind snagged on the thought of what Raeyn's scars would feel like against my mouth or how I'd make sure he'd shut up for once.

I washed the thoughts down with the rest of whatever plant acid was left in the cup.

Jay gave me an approving nod. "Was that so bad?"

"You have no fucking idea, Grasshopper." I shuddered and shoved the cup—and Raeyn—as far away from me as I could.

Jay snorted and flopped down on a chair next to Kovacz. Soon as she did, her gray cat, Dust, always glued to her heels, jumped into her lap and demanded to be petted.

"Anyway, business!" Jay said brightly. "I hooked Staxx up with the details about yesterday's loot. She says she wants it by tomorrow or the deal's a no-go."

"She gonna make it worth the rush?" Kovacz asked.

Jay reached for the discarded pile of cards and flicked several at Kovacz's face. "The appropriate response here is, 'Thank you, Jay, for doing all the boring legwork and making sure we'll actually get paid this time.' If you haven't noticed, it's not all that easy making a living off stealing from the rich these days." More quietly, she said, "Especially when we're one down for the count."

I put my cards down. "How's Aris?" I asked.

"He's fine." Jay turned away, but not fast enough for me to miss the unspoken *at least as fine as you are* in her face. Sometimes it was a real problem she knew me as well as she did.

Neither of us said anything for a minute.

Jay pretended to focus on scratching Dust behind the ears. "He...needs a little time."

"Funny how everyone's so concerned about what *he* needs." Kovacz picked the deck of cards back up. His shuffling got a lot more aggravated.

"Kovacz, don't." We'd had this discussion before. Kovacz was a good guy. As long as we didn't talk about Aris or the Voyance. I took a deep breath—not a good idea with my battered throat—and tried to get my hands to stop clutching the table's edge. "He didn't mean it."

"Didn't *mean* it?" Kovacz shook his head and slapped the cards back onto the table. Stacks of game chips spilled in a shower of red, white, and blue. Dust growled and jumped off Jay's lap, and Jay gave Kovacz an accusing look. "Damn it, Damian, have you looked into a mirror lately? Any of those bruises not look like he fucking meant it? Are you still going to make excuses for him once he has managed to set the Watch loose on us and they string us up one by one for sheltering a stray Burner? All because you're fucking him?"

The back of my chair hit the ground in a clatter and Kovacz's head smashed into the tabletop, sending the remaining cards and chips flying.

"Say that again," I gritted through ground teeth, holding him down.

Kovacz squinted up at me, his jaw set. "I'll say it all night long if you like. Won't change a damn thing. Times I wonder if you haven't caught it from him yet, the rate you two go at it."

My knee pressed into the small of Kovacz's back. "You know as well as I do the Voyance doesn't work that way, you fucking bigot."

Jay's hands wrapped around my arm before I could punch Kovacz again. "Stop it! Both of you. What is wrong with you two? Go find some Red to take it out on. Remember you're on the same damn side."

I could've shaken her off. Easily. Instead, I took a deep breath and stepped back.

"The Grasshopper's right, we're on the same side. So, watch your damn tone, Kovacz."

"No." Kovacz gingerly poked at the side of his face that was quickly turning into a bruise. Fury sparked in his voice. "You watch it, Damian, because it's you who can't get his priorities straight."

I almost told him just how straight my priorities were, what with the deal I'd made with Taerien, but I kept my mouth shut. We already had enough of a mess on our hands without me blabbing about batshit terrorists threatening to hand us all over to the Reds. That gig was mine to take care of. The less the others knew, the better. At least for now.

"I'm out," I said with a last glance at the mess we'd made of the table.

I walked out and onto the bridge crossing the *Shadow*'s holding bay. Rays of late afternoon sunlight spilled through narrow windows overhead. Brightness webbed the crates stacked in the space beneath me in crisscross patterns of light and shadow where they broke through the iron grid of the walkway spanning the edge of the cargo bay.

I sat down in the middle of a sun patch at the edge of the stairs leading down, my legs dangling through the steel rails above the holding bay below. Up here'd become one of my favorite spots to think, in the middle of the *Shadow*, surrounded by what mattered, and the people who'd shown me family meant more than empty names on paperwork.

Fuck if it made trying to figure out what to do next any easier.

In the end, it was simple: if I wanted to protect my crew and keep Aris safe, I'd do whatever Taerien wanted me to do. I'd get intel on Valyr, sneak up on her when she'd least expect it, and that was it. Mission accomplished. All in all, this wasn't much different from any hits I ran for the Empire. Except there'd be an army of Reds after me looking to ice my ass afterward, but what else was new. And Aris could never know. The thought of keeping this from him and the rest of the Shadows twisted knots in the pit of my stomach.

I was still figuring out details on how to keep my trail cold when Jay climbed up the stairs, carrying a plate heaped with what vaguely smelled like breakfast.

She handed it to me. "Eat," she said. "You look like you need it."

Shit, I must've looked worse than I felt if Jay felt the need to feed me.

I kept my mouth shut. "Thanks, Grasshopper."

"You can thank me after you survive my cooking." Jay plonked down next to me.

"Point," I said and barely dodged Jay's elbow jabbing at my bruised ribs. "Hey! Injured, remember?"

Jay grinned. "Still cheeky though."

Whatever genius helped Jay do her magic with machines, it definitely deserted her when it came to cooking. The eggs were runny, the toast was burned, and the bacon tasted like bacon-flavored cardboard. Which was probably what it was, given how everything we ate was basically reconstituted protein. To my empty stomach, it felt like the best thing I'd ever eaten.

For a while, we sat in silence. Me, polishing off my plate of terrible but delicious breakfast, Jay sitting next to me with her legs crossed.

"So, what's next?" Jay finally prodded after I'd finished.

I set down my clean plate. "Fuck if I know, Grasshopper." I filled her in with what I could, leaving out some choice bits about Raeyn and the Watch along with how likely it was we'd all get dead before all of this was over.

"Well, shit," Jay said and lay down on her back with her knees pulled up. "Guess I'll have to hurry up and fix this clunker so I can fly us out of this mess."

I couldn't quite fight down the smile at that. Didn't think Jay'd ever let up on her grand plans to take the *Shadow* to the skies again, never mind half the parts she needed hadn't been in existence for half a century.

"You honestly think it's any different out there?" I said, leaning back and looking up where she was staring out one of the *Shadow*'s cracked skylights where the outside hid under a layer of hundred-year-old dust.

"Are you kidding me?" Jay propped herself up on her elbows. "'Course it is. There's so much out there. Stars, planets, galaxies! I reject the thought they're all as fucked up as the Empire. Besides, we'd be *flying*." Her expression got that dreamy quality it always did when she talked about something she'd never actually experienced. It didn't shake her enthusiasm.

I'd seen those things in history books and old posters she liked to decorate her bunk with. "You read too many stories, Grasshopper."

Jay blew air out of her nose. "Whatever. If it were up to you, we'd be stuck down here until we're as rusty as the *Shadow*."

And what's so wrong with that?

The *Shadow* was home, the Empire all we knew. It was a nice dream to leave all its shit behind, but who said we'd trade it in for anything better?

Before I could say as much, the *Shadow*'s hatch creaked open and Aris came through.

Jay sighed and got up. "How 'bout you go take care of lover boy while I put my genius to work to save the day, huh?" She seemed like she was going to say something else but walked off.

I got to my feet and climbed down the stairs to the main deck. Aris hadn't noticed me. He pulled the door closed behind him before he turned around and leaned against it, sliding down to the ground with his back to the ship's rusty blast door and his head in his hands.

"Hey," I closed in and put my hand on his shoulder. "You okay?"

He startled, cringed when I touched him, and then let out a deep breath. "Yeah. I'm fine."

"Right." Didn't take a second look at his face, pale, shadows like bruises under his eyes, to figure out he was anything but. I gingerly sat down next to him, my shoulder brushing against his. "You look like hells. Since when are you up when there's light out, anyway?"

"I went to the Temple."

"The—why?"

The Temple was the fancy name for what was commonly known as the Burner Academy around here, a place that picked up stray Voyants and trained them before they accidentally killed themselves and everyone around them. No one knew how the Voyance had first started. Some claimed it was the next step of human evolution. Others thought it was some sort of alien parasite. Both theories were equally jacked. Whatever it was, it was killing its host, and no one could do anything to stop it. Least of all some group of delusional zealots armed with prayers and incense.

"Did Iltis put you up to this? Gods, I swear if she's in with Kovacz and his—"

"Iltis doesn't know." Aris hunched his shoulders. "I've had their contact info for years."

"You did." I let the implications sink in. "Why now?"

Aris' eyes lingered on the collar of bruises around my throat. There was something broken in his expression, like he could barely stand looking at me.

"You have to ask? I almost killed you. I thought I had it under control, but—" He swallowed and stared at his hands. Clenched them to control their twitching. "They told me to contact them when it got too much. They said they could help. Teach me how to stop."

"Like what, some fucking twelve-step program? You really think it's that easy? Remember the last place pretending it'd help, that it'd make things better?" I closed my eyes and pinched the bridge of my nose. Fuck me if I started even thinking about *L'Ecole*. That place was full of nothing but ghosts.

"The Temple's not like them," Aris said. His hands fidgeted in his lap. "And no, I don't think it's going to be easy. But it might be the only option I have left. Maybe it's better that way. If someone kept me...away. I mean, Gods, I completely lost it last night. And it's only going to get worse. Damn it, Damian, I can feel it, okay? It's like there's something inside of me and it wants out. And what if I can't stop it one day, what if—"

Aris's words brought back the same desperation I'd seen in his face last night and with it the gnawing helplessness that this wasn't something I'd be able to shield him from if I only had enough bullets. I knew I had to shut him up right then and there before we both fell apart, and there was only one way I knew how. I dragged him close and kissed him. It wasn't a gentle kiss, but hard and hungry, the kind that left bruises and both of us panting for air afterward.

"You're thinking too loud," I said. "Makes my head hurt."

Aris gave me a shaky laugh. "You tell me."

"You're thinking about leaving."

I could see the answer in his eyes, even before he said, "Maybe."

"Don't," I said and abruptly got to my feet, ignoring the twinge from my ribs, instinct telling me to leave or I'd hit something. Thinking better of it, I took a deep breath and held out a hand to Aris. "C'mere."

A flash of uncertainty crossed Aris's face before he took it, his hand so pale, it was almost transparent against mine. I pulled him up and sent him stumbling backward against the wall, my arms around him like a cage, both trapping him and giving him an out if he needed it.

"You're not going to get rid of me," I whispered, hot breath flittering against Aris's ear. "So, quit trying."

I closed the last inch or so between us and kissed him again, gentler this time. I leaned into him, the warmth of his body sending shivers across my skin.

"Gods, I thought that mesc overdose was going to kill you," I whispered, my forehead against his as a breath shuddered out. "Damn it, Aris, don't ever scare me like that again, okay?"

"I'm sorry." Aris grimaced and we both know it wasn't just the mesc he was thinking of when he said, "I'll try."

"Try harder."

A feeble smile was all the answer I got before his arm snaked between us, fingers tightening on my belt buckle. "Make it up to you? Maybe we both need to not think for a bit."

I let him drag me upstairs to the room we shared at the back of the ship. The door clattered shut behind us, the lighting coming on automatically, set to low. The space was tight, the full-sized bed only fit after we'd cut out the patched metal wall that'd once separated both of our bunks. Mismatched crates stacked into a cobbled-together tansu chest along one wall and that was it as far as furniture went and still have space to move.

Aris went to push me toward the bed when I stopped, suddenly very aware of Aris's hands on my shoulders. The long sleeves of his shirt slid down far enough to let me see the dark rings of bruises and half-healed scabs around his wrists.

I closed my eyes. Clenched my jaw.

Part of me couldn't bear touching Aris like this. With the reminder of how vulnerable, how fucking breakable he was written all over his skin. But a bigger part couldn't bear not to.

"Tell me what you need."

Aris thought about it. Then, his fingers trailed across my shoulders, down my arms, twitching as if torn between covering his cracks and bruises and proudly displaying them, between falling into familiar patterns and admitting the truth. "I need you to not be gentle," he said finally. "I need to feel this."

I exhaled, slowly, letting his words sink in. "You want me to hurt you."

Aris bit his lower lip and threaded his fingers through mine. "Could you?"

I stared at my hands against his, both of us lined with more scars than we knew how to talk about. My gaze traveled back up to Aris's. "If that's what you want."

"Please."

I nodded. Gathered myself. "Strip." A single word, clipped short against the thickness of my own voice.

Aris eyed me, hesitating, but then his half smile slid back into place and he pulled his shirt over his head, tousled blond curls brushing against his shoulders. He bent over slightly, shrugging out of his jeans and winced, with his hand pressed against his ribs.

"Let me see," I said softly.

"I'm fine."

"Let me *see*."

I stepped close enough for our bodies to almost be touching and slid my hands down Aris's sides. His skin rippled with goose bumps. He tried to suppress a hiss when my hand came to rest on his left side, where a series of half-healed bruises stretched across the length of his ribs in fading shades of green and yellow.

"Did it hurt?"

Aris tensed at the question. "Damian, I'm fine. Really."

There were faded bruises down his thighs, but none as bad as his ribs and wrists. I traced them with careful fingertips.

"That's not what I asked." I straightened up again, facing Aris, his back almost against the wall in the narrow room. "Close your eyes and turn around."

"Damian—"

Before I could talk myself out of it, I snatched his wrists and squeezed them hard enough to dig into his bruises. Aris gasped. His eyes widened, pupils blown with need. Desire. I swallowed. Gods.

Aris watched me, lips parted, his face flushed, and so damn eager for more.

"I said, close your eyes and turn around." Gently this time. "Now."

I let go and Aris did as he was told, facing the wall with his eyes closed. "Good."

It wasn't as bad as I'd expected. Perks of being a Voyant. I leaned in, the fabric of my clothes brushing against warm, naked skin, and kissed one of the darker bruises on his shoulder hard enough to make Aris shudder. He pressed closer, hands reaching back, fumbling with my belt. I took a step away from him, my hands catching his wrists, the only point of contact between the two of us.

"No," I said, my cheek brushing the curve of his neck, close enough to lick. "First you're answering my question. Did it hurt?"

Aris swallowed, stifling a gasp when I tightened my grip, fingers digging into bruised tendons. "Yes," he said, voice thin and breathless. "It hurt."

"Did it help?"

"What?"

His voice caught at the edge of a moan when I twisted his wrists behind his back, leaning close. No need to look at his cock to know I was right about that one. Still. I had to know. Had to be sure Aris wanted this.

"I—" Another sharp inhale when I twisted harder. "Yes! Yes, it did. It does. I—" His breath came out in pent-up pants, shoulders tense trying to keep from shaking. "Damian, please. Please."

I let go of his wrists then, one arm wrapped around his middle, drawing him close, while my free hand cupped his jaw and turned his head toward me. Aris's eyes were still closed, blond lashes fluttering arcs that sent shadows across his face. I kissed him, gentle at first, then harder, turned him, pulling him to the bed with me.

"It's okay," I said softly. "You can open your eyes now. It's okay." I pushed him down and into the mattress. Then I was on top of him, straddling his thighs, hands on his face, his torso, his hips. I only let go long enough to get rid of my belt and unzip my pants, very aware I still was as good as dressed and Aris wasn't. Somehow in this, my clothes had become armor, a flimsy shield that nevertheless kept me grounded and hyperaware of every cue Aris gave me.

I stopped him when he pushed up my shirt, bright eyes following the baring of my skin. "No. Turn over."

He did as he was told, positioned himself on his knees, spread open, his hands a tight grip on the headboard. He left me barely enough time to open the drawer in the bedside table and scavenge a bottle of lube and a condom. His hips bucked under me when the coldness of the gel hit, and I slipped a hand down his ass and between his cheeks.

"You sure you still want this?" I asked and lined up two lube-slicked fingers against him. "There's nothing I'd do to you if you don't want me to, you know that. And not only because you could kick my ass with the Voyance."

Aris shook his head, turned before he pulled me close and kissed me. His eyes were very dark and his voice weirdly steady when he said, "I want this. I want you. Just you." Aris nipped the side of my throat and snatched the condom out of my hand. He tore it open with his teeth and rolled it onto my hard cock with practiced fluidity. "Now, stop stalling and fuck me."

Aris returned to his hands and knees, rocked back his hips until I slid my fingers inside him, and he languidly, methodically, began to fuck himself against my hand.

My free hand trailed past healing bruises up Aris's spine, tangled in his unbound hair, dragged back his head, exposing the tender skin where the side of his throat met his shoulder. I leaned forward, my body covering his when my teeth found its mark and I bit him, hard enough to wrench a moan from Aris as a third finger joined the other two in his tight heat.

"Damian, now. I need—I—"

Gods, I loved hearing Aris fall apart beneath me.

With a grin, I withdrew my fingers and guided my cock to his entrance.

I must've moved too fast or Aris hadn't relaxed enough, because he locked up and let out a low whimper when I pushed into him.

"Shit, did I hurt you?"

"No." It came as a grunt, and I could tell he was biting his lip, hands curled tight into the sheets until he eased into it. "Don't. Please, don't stop. Damian don't—"

I didn't. Didn't stop. Didn't care about Laras, or the Voyance or Raeyn or how sex seemed to be the only thing that still worked out between Aris and me.

It didn't matter. Didn't matter part of me hated myself for treating him like any of his clients, like Laras, might at any given night. What mattered was this was what Aris needed. The stinging heat of a slap, the sharper, deeper pain of my teeth on already tender skin, all paired with a relentless fucking. It was what gentleness couldn't give him. It transformed Aris, transformed both of us, into something more solid. More intimate. Something no one, not even Aris's Voyance, could touch and maybe Aris was right, could be this, feeling this, was exactly what both of us needed.

So, I focused on driving all the thoughts of last night, all the guilt, clear out of our heads for as long as it lasted. Everything turned fuzzy on the edges. Nothing remained but his body underneath me, all thrusting hips and arching backs and interlaced fingers.

It wasn't perfect. It wasn't right. But it was what both of us needed— from the time I thrust into him to the point when I came, screaming into the crook of his shoulder and he followed, clenching and shuddering under me, long fingers twisting in the sheets, spilling his release.

It took a few minutes before I felt like paying attention to the world again. The first thing I saw when I did was Aris's wrist, his hand splayed out on the pillow, a smear of red seeping into the white fabric where the scabs around his wrists had torn open where I'd held them too tight.

The sight flicked some inner switch and the room around me shifted into a place I'd buried deep in my memory. Patched metal walls and shaggy rugs turned into concrete and white tile, slick with blood, forming little puddles running down the drain in the center of the floor.

The guy's name'd been Ish Vereux, and it'd started with him coming for me in the showers that night. He'd come alone this time, without

Marten to back him up and convince me to just take it. Thanks to my fists and a piece of rusty pipe, it'd ended with him bound to the complex's ancient water heater with his handcuffs. Nothing but a broken, keening pile of flesh. Too much red everywhere. He'd begged me to stop, sobbing, swearing up and down the Gods he hadn't meant it, how he wasn't ever going to touch me again. At some point, it'd all become mangled between blood and broken teeth.

I hadn't stopped. Kept hitting him even when he went down, his head cracked against the wall at a weird angle, and I heard something crunch. I forgot why it'd been Ish who'd finally made me snap. Ish'd been nothing but a sidekick. For him, it'd just been fucking. He hadn't been like Marten. He hadn't made me trust him first. He hadn't made me love him, despite everything. It didn't matter. The sounds of fists pounding meat, the sobs that'd died in Ish's throat, the smell of piss, all canceled out by the rushing in my ears and how fucking good it felt.

I only came back 'round when the pounding got deafening and I realized someone was breaking the door open, steel screaming in its hinges. In the end, I'd opened the door for them, the lock slippery in my shaking hands. There'd only been two of them, still green behind the ears. Too young to be full instructors yet. None of them lifted as much as a hand against me as I walked out, not even bothering about my clothes that lay in a crumpled heap on the floor. Behind me, I left the smears of red footprints and the sound of at least one of them losing his dinner over the body that'd been Ish Vereux, the first guy I'd ever killed. Nobody held me back as I went down the corridor and turned my back on *L'Ecole* forever.

I'd been sixteen.

Six months later, I'd run into Iltis. Between her and Aris, they'd somehow glued the pieces back together, and for years I hadn't let myself as much as think about *L'Ecole* and what'd happened with Ish.

Now it all came crashing down on me like a freight train. The inside of my left wrist tingled with the memory of me burning out the registration number that'd been tattooed there on my first day at *L'Ecole*. Sometimes I could still smell the red-hot blade scorching away black ink, leaving a patch of bubbled scar tissue. If I could've burned out my memories the same way, I'd have more scars than I could count and every single one'd be worth it.

I scrambled out of bed as fast as I could.

"Damian?" Aris's voice sounded sleepy, his eyes half closed. He reached for me, but his movements were slow and sluggish, and he didn't get a hold of me as I got up and yanked my pants back on. "Hey, what's wrong?"

"I've got to go." I couldn't even look at him, the proof of what I'd done, of how I'd used him, like any other client, like I didn't care, clear on his skin. My fists clenched hard enough to make my knuckles pop.

"Need some air." I was at the door when he suddenly appeared next to me and reached out, his hand warm against the side of my face. It was then I noticed I was shaking.

"Hey," Aris said again, his voice soft like a fuzzy blanket, his lips brushing against my throat. "It's okay. You didn't hurt me. You're never going to hurt me."

Damn him, but he was good at this, had always been, reading me like a fucking book. I couldn't look at him, my hands tense around the rough ridges of the door.

"I almost did. For a second, I lost it. I, fuck. You shouldn't have had to make that deal with Laras. Not for me."

Aris shook his head and took my hands into his. "First off, you didn't. You made me feel exactly how I needed you to make me feel. And I trusted you to stop if I had asked you to stop. Because I know you." He kissed the corner of my mouth, his eyes level with mine. "Second, I don't see Laras because I have to but because I want to. Third, and most importantly, I'd set the world on fire for you if it came to it. Come here."

His grip was gentle but firm, and he led me back to the bed and made me lie down.

"There," he said, once he'd settled in next to me, his head on my chest, lazy fingers combing through my hair. "Much better. Stay with me."

"Okay." I leaned into his touch. It melted away everything. Aris was home. Had been from the moment I first set foot into the *Shadow*. He'd held me together when I thought nothing else could. It'd been him and the rest of the Shadows who'd given me a reason to get myself sorted out. They'd given me a fucking purpose. A place to call home. Family. And I'd keep them safe if it killed me.

My arm tightened around Aris when I asked. "Are you? Staying, I mean."

Unfair question, I knew. Aris stayed silent. Then his fingers twined through mine, and I could hear his smile when he said, "You're not going to get rid of me."

7

Kiss Kiss, Bang Bang

TARANTINO'S WAS A shit hole.

'Course you had to dig through some shit, trying to tail Reds. Especially when that Red was Faelle fucking Valyr, who'd been conspicuously absent from her usual haunts for the past week now. Tarantino's might've been a last-ditch effort to dredge up any intel on her whereabouts, but after radio silence from my usual informants, I was a tad desperate. Worse, after any attempts to get Raeyn off my ass and from checking in at the *Shadow* daily, both to remind me of my obligation and because he loved to fuck with me, had failed so far.

Could turn it over as often as I wanted; bottom line: there was fuck-all I could do to get myself out of this. If I backed out, that bastard and his boss Taerien would turn Aris over to the Reds for an express Cleansing. I'd end up bleeding out facedown in a ditch before I'd let that happen. So, I'd play along. At least until I came up with a better plan.

Even through the closed door, I could catch a good whiff of alcohol, smoke, and way too many sweaty bodies stuffed into too small a space. Teetering at the edge of Low Side and the Core, Tarantino's got its extra-shitty look from the contrast to the shiny glass façades of Up Side. There was nothing bright or polished about this place. It must've spent its past life as a construction trailer before someone'd gutted and extended it with parts of junk and metal hammered into shape. Honestly wouldn't surprise me if the whole thing crashed down on us one day, looking like nothing but superglue and graffiti held it together.

Inside, the smell was worse, dank and thick enough to smother. Greenish light dispersed from overhead, giving everything a sickly tinge. I recognized a few familiar faces in the crowd. None ones I needed to talk to. I ignored them and went straight for the bar.

I sat down on one of the scuffed leather-covered stools by the counter and waved the barkeep for a drink. "Same as usual." Didn't matter what you ordered here—all came from the same vile blend of engine cleaner and ethanol passed off as drinkable around Low Side.

"Been a while, Nettoyer," the barkeep drawled. Tarantino's was owned by Viv Coras, someone you better not turn your back to, 'less you wanted to end up with a knife in it.

Coras had a thing for old, pre-Empire action flicks, hence the name of their place and the layers of tattered black and white film posters covering the walls. One featured two guys, one black, one white, neither of them had ever been in an actual shootout, the way they were holding their guns. Lethal Weapon, my ass. Another set showed a woman who really wanted to kill Bill. Twice. Antiques, most of them: yellow and bubbly with age. A streak of white graffiti across some guy holding a gun to another guy's head read "Ezekiel 25:17." No clue what it meant, but I kind of liked it. Fit the mood of the place.

"You know how it is, Coras. Places to go, people to shoot." Or so I hoped.

Coras grinned and wiped a stray silver loc out of their lined, brown face, tucking it back into the multicolored updo on top of their head. "Good to know business hasn't gone to shit for all of us, eh?"

"Guess that's one way to look at it." I kept scanning the bar for any of my usual informants. Coras passed me my gin, and I downed it in one go. Less chance of chemical burns that way. I passed the glass over the counter. "Pour me another one. Actually, make it a double."

Coras slid my drink across the cracked countertop and lit a cigarette. If anything, it made the air a little more breathable.

"You gonna tell me what in the Seven Hells you're doing here, Nettoyer?"

"What, can't a guy come here for a quiet drink without getting his motives questioned?"

"Cut the crap, Nettoyer. We both know you don't come here for the drinks." Coras shot me a look over their red-rimmed cat-eye glasses. "Your pretty boy toy get tired of you yet?"

"His name's Aris, Coras. And no. 'Sides, not everyone's out collecting spouses to add to their marriage the way you do. And we're not—"

"What, married? Could've fooled me, the way you two carry on. Got the kid and everything, so why not make it official? You're sure old enough to start getting serious."

I almost choked on my drink. "Shit, Coras, don't ever let Jay hear you call her the kid." I downed the rest of it to get the mental image out of my head. Coras and their marriage might've been on their eleventh or twelfth kid by now, but I was honestly the last person thinking what we needed in this fucked-up world was more kids.

Gods, time to cut to the chase if for nothing but a fucking topic change.

Coras moved to pour me another glass. I waved them off and slid over a stack of credits.

They raised an eyebrow at the sum.

"I need some information, Coras."

"And you are doing a horrible job at getting it, don't you think, darling?" Raeyn said with a mocking lilt to his voice before he scooted onto a stool next to me. He slipped an arm around my shoulder, cool fingers brushing against the nape of my neck. Getting way too close, way too fast. I stiffened, reflexively wanted to pull away—punch him in the face while I was at it—but he didn't back off. Except part of me also wanted him to stay exactly where he was at and if that wasn't fucked up, I didn't know what was anymore.

"What are *you* doing here?"

"Oh, is that how you greet me nowadays? You wound me, darling." Shaded by the brim of his hat, Raeyn's expression shifted into something like disappointment. He was convincing enough, I almost bought it.

Coras raised a knowing eyebrow and looked away, pretending to be busy with the dirty dishwater that filled the sink behind the bar. Raeyn used that chance to lean forward toward me, his lips suddenly way closer to my ear than I'd ever want them to be. I flinched when they brushed against my neck.

"What the *hells* are you playing at?"

"Listen," he whispered. "There's Watch all around this place. Play along and I'll get you out of here." That got him my attention. Sure enough, I caught a glimpse of a red coat in the corner of my eye. Pretty damn sure he hadn't been there a second ago. One Red leaned by the door, casually smoking a cigarette, and another one waited outside, barely visible.

"Fuck."

"Indeed," Raeyn's voice became a low purr. He rested his head on my shoulder, his right hand trailed across my chest in lazy, languid circles. "Now, may I kiss you?"

"Um, yeah, but—" *Wait, what?*

"Oh, good," Raeyn beamed. "Because I'm fresh out of distractions otherwise." Before I could ask him what the hells that was supposed to mean, Raeyn's left curled around my neck, drew me close, and he kissed me. Mouth and lips and tongue and all.

He tasted minty with a hint of something herbal. Holy fucking shit. His mouth was a hot demand for surrender. I should've pulled away, but instead I clenched my hands into his shirt and dragged him closer, turning this from a kiss into a fight of lips, tongue, and teeth.

"Now you tell me who's not out collecting extra husbands," Coras trilled next to me before stepping away to take care of something on the other end of the bar.

I came up for air. Bit my lip against the twinge in my ribs.

"What the—"

Raeyn didn't let go, nuzzled my neck, paying special attention to the sensitive spot below my earlobe, his hand casually stroking my thigh.

"Trust me, I like it as little as you do," he said, eyeing me through silver lashes. His fedora blocked most of our faces from view. Raeyn leaned in and nipped a sensitive spot below my jaw, drawing a raw sound from somewhere deep inside of me. "Hm. Have to admit, you're not half bad at this. I may have misjudged you. Keep it up and you might just live. Now come with me." Raeyn's voice got louder and twice as insinuating with that. He'd wanted Coras to hear the end and lazily curled his hand around my belt buckle, dragging me with him as he slid off the chair.

I swallowed a curse and went with him, even managed to slide an arm around his waist. Almost made it look natural, too. Even Aris knew I didn't do public touchy-feely, least of all with the batshit son of the godsdamned president. But I also didn't want to die. So there.

I kept close to Raeyn, letting him touch me in that deliberately sensual way that'd better all be faked. Gods, I wanted to kill him. Definitely didn't want him to keep going, his hands having a weird way of anchoring me, keeping me from doing something truly stupid. Only his stunt worked. Coras still pretended to be busy, probably cackling their head off. Everyone else seemed too caught up in their card games and drinks to notice the two of us slip past and closer to the exit.

Until one heavy hand clamped down on my shoulder and whirled me around. "Damian Nettoyer? Valyr wants to see you." Yeah. Guess that made two of us. Except I was pretty sure I wouldn't like much how that encounter'd go or where it'd leave Aris and the rest.

"Hi there," Raeyn said brightly with that crooked smile of his. "You want in on this? There is always room for another—" The guy punched him, then turned on me, sending me flying into the counter in a crash of breaking glass and Coras snarling how we were fucking up their bar with our shenanigans.

"Aw. Now look what you've done to my pretty face." Raeyn spun around and roundhouse-kicked Big and Beefy into the ribs. Raeyn was fast and obviously knew what he was doing as he punched and kicked his way past the Red and made for the door. No idea how he could move like that and keep his damned fedora on his head. Must've had a lot of practice.

I was pretty fucked myself, cornered by two Reds in their civvies but with telltale buzzcuts and movements that spoke of military precision. I dodged a blow aimed at my head, but the next already lunged for me. He crashed into the counter instead, sending more glass flying.

"Honestly," Coras said, standing above him, crowbar in hand. "You'd think you government officials would be more concerned about violating personal property. Think of the paperwork." The guy tried to scramble to his feet and make a go for Coras. I grabbed a bottle of Tarantino's best from the shelf behind me and cracked it over his head. He dropped like a rock.

"Damn it, Nettoyer, did you *have* to use my last bottle of that? Stuff takes weeks to make." Coras scowled at the unconscious guy. "You *will* hear from my insurance."

"Hey Coras, how 'bout you quit whining and put that crowbar of yours to some use?"

Coras stiffened like I'd told them to cut out their own liver and fry it for breakfast. "Are you kidding? I raise as much as a pinky against a Red, they'll revoke my license before last call."

"Uh-huh. Then what d'you call braining one of them with that thing?"

Coras shrugged, flicking drops of red from the crowbar. "That was self-defense. It's different. Now, get the fuck out of my bar, before—"

They didn't get any further. Broken glass crunched underneath my boots, then bit into my back, scraped along the back of my head when the second Red rounded in on me and knocked me to the ground. It punched the breath right out of me, and for a second, I was convinced someone finally managed to completely shatter my ribcage. His boot on my chest pinned me as I tried to wriggle out from underneath him and tried to get my Colt, still hidden in my coat. I couldn't reach, could hardly breathe, let alone shake the Red's weight off my chest.

"Hey!" I yelled at Raeyn. "Wouldn't mind some help here."

But he was busy getting the shit pounded out of himself, his grin wiped off his face, twisted into a snarl. The Red's boot pushed down harder, something prickled against the back of my head, static scrambling my vision, making the hulky guy above me faze in and out like a bad holoscreen projection.

Additional Reds streamed in. Patrons pushed out, wanting nothing to do with this shitshow. A shot sounded, then a second. Both went wide, doing little more than put extra holes into Coras's walls. Whoever had shot didn't know shit from a target.

It must've been the gunfire that distracted the guy on top of me. Half a tick later, just when my vision flared white, he was off me and crashed back-first into one of the chairs someone'd tossed over. Not a second too late, either. I must've cracked my head when he'd knocked me over earlier because it felt like someone'd given it a serious clubbing. White flares mixed with red streaks as I staggered to my feet. Got a hold of my Colt in time to draw it point-blank at the Red's head as he picked himself up from the floor.

"Now listen," I growled. "Drop the gun. And back. The fuck. Off."

He froze and stared at me with the weirdest look on his face. "You! How'd you—Your eyes!" The guy's mouth snapped shut. He stumbled back, hands clamped white-knuckled around his gun, looking at me like I was the scariest fucking thing he'd ever seen.

"Look," I said, blinking past the starbursts Coras's lighting set off in my eyes. Fuck, like I needed another concussion. "I'd love to stay and chat, but what part of 'put down that gun' didn't you understand?"

The guy shook his head, finger trembling on the trigger. "Get the hells away from me, you abomination, you—" He didn't get to finish the sentence. He hit the floor with a bullet in his head, half of which ended up splattered all over the mismatched floorboards. Messy, but I sure as shit wasn't going to wait for him to finish his little rant and beat me to the trigger.

"Should've backed off when I told you to," I said and stepped over his outstretched arm to get to Raeyn. He'd managed to pin a Red of his own— this one without flying brain matter, but still. Not that it mattered because they had us surrounded by now. How many of them *were* there? A dozen? As good a guess as any. I went for the back door, Tarantino's excuse of an emergency exit, nodding at Raeyn to follow me, guns drawn at the Reds in front of us.

Talk about being outnumbered. I could barely see what I was aiming at anyway. Almost tripped over more pieces of furniture that'd become collateral, but Raeyn was fast enough to grab me by the arm.

"Are you all right?" he asked and dragged me behind the counter.

"'M fine," I grunted and wiped at a bloody nose, pushing his hands away. "Keep moving. You can play doctor on me once we're out of this mess."

"Promise?"

"Shut up and move, Nymeron."

We almost made it. Until the door opened. Enter Faelle Valyr herself, .45 pointed at me.

"Freeze," the commander of the Watch barked. She wasn't a tall woman, all brown curls and whipcord muscle concealed beneath a red coat. She sure knew how to fill a room, her glare made menacing by the eyepatch covering her left eye, accessorizing a face made of hard lines and angles with nothing soft about it. Her piece wavered between me and Raeyn, who was still moving but came to a complete stop.

"Well that complicates things," Raeyn said, voice light and calm just like anyone else would announce today's weather. The tightness in his face put a lie to that real quick. He didn't lower his gun but took in the Reds crowding in and Valyr blocking the door. Ignoring her, Raeyn took a step toward me, one hand curling into my shirt as he pulled me against him.

"I'm sorry, darling." Raeyn's lips suddenly got scarily close to mine again. Worse, part of me almost wanted him to kiss me again. He didn't. "I'll come back for you. Promise."

I never saw him pull the trigger.

I'd forgotten how much it hurt to get shot. Enough to momentarily block out my throbbing temple, my brain wanting to squish out the front of my skull. Pain cut through my left shoulder, burned its way through me. My mouth opened, closed again, no sound coming out. My Colt clattered to the ground. Raeyn let go of my shirt and shoved me at Valyr. Guess she'd been expecting this as little as I had. I crashed into her and took her down to the ground with me. Raeyn used his chance and made a dash for it in the middle of the whole mess, a black shadow whisking out the door. Traitorous bastard.

Something wiggled under me. Rough hands hauled me off one pissed-off looking Valyr.

"Cuff him, then get him out of here. Tosh, you and the rest go after the other one. He can't have made it that far yet," Valyr snapped from somewhere above me. "At least we have who we've come for, don't we, Mr. Nettoyer?"

Someone forced my arms back and something tore inside my wrecked shoulder. I didn't bother biting back the moan.

"Fuck you, Valyr." I would've been more convincing if I hadn't been shaking and sweaty with pain, my mind spinning with the possibilities. Did she know about my deal with Raeyn and Taerien? And what about the others? Was a squad of Reds already tearing through the *Shadow*? I focused on the pain, if only because it kept the rising panic down.

"Yes, speaking of." Valyr adjusted her eye patch that'd slid a little off-center in our tangle. "For future reference, I hear picking up your allies in a bar seldom makes for reliable backup."

No shit. The thought of my hands around Raeyn Nymeron's throat flashed through my mind, making me grin through the pain. What I'd do to him next time I got my hands on him would almost be worth having a hole put in my shoulder.

Then someone dragged a bag over my head and everything tipped into blackness.

8

I Always Wanted to Go Out with "Fuck You"

I CAME BACK 'round to darkness, pain, and the smell of cat piss. Better not question what they'd used the bag for before it'd ended up covering my head. Seriously, those things should be single-use only. But that was just like the Reds. Inconsiderate bastards.

A quick assessment got me right back to where I'd blacked out: still handcuffed, still bleeding, and my left shoulder felt like someone'd taken to it with a drill dipped in acid.

I was conscious, alive, and in complete fucking agony.

Aside from that, I hadn't the damnedest clue where they were taking me or how in the Seven Hells I was going to get out of this one. After bagging me, the Reds'd stuffed me into some sort of van—had to be one of those models with fuel injectors and all that fancy shit, because it wasn't nearly as loud as the things we drove around Low Side.

I figured there were at least two or three Reds in the back with me; they stayed silent during the ride, except for one who kept fiddling with something that sounded a lot like a butterfly knife, flicking it open and closed with annoying clicks and snaps that cut through the silence. Probably the same kid who couldn't tell a wall from a moving target. Someone finally told them to quit it. I almost thanked them, but kept my mouth shut, doing my best to pretend to still be out cold.

If nothing else, it'd give me a few minutes to think. This wasn't the first time the Reds'd hauled me off. Though I doubted this stint would involve recording devices and a conversation on the wrong end of a two-way mirror. Shape I was in and as pissed as Valyr was, I'd be lucky if it didn't end with my body floating facedown the East River.

Maybe it was the way the handcuffs twisted my arms behind my back or the blood loss, but my left arm slowly grew numb. To make up for it, I hurt everywhere else, pain pumping through my body like a second heartbeat. The van stopped and the throbbing in my shoulder spiked to a hot jolt. I couldn't smother a muffled grunt, which someone took as an invitation to start shaking me some more.

"Ah, you're awake." Laras's voice. 'Course she'd show up. Because I needed someone to make my day even worse. "Which means you will be able to walk. Good."

I didn't remember seeing her back at Tarantino's. Too busy getting the shit kicked out of me and being shot. Figured she wouldn't miss this. Laras took hold of my good arm and dragged me out of the van. I gritted my teeth against the hole in my shoulder stabbing hot knives down my spine with every step.

"Get your hands off me." I jerked away. Bad idea. More pain. Dizziness. And pretty damn pointless overall, cuffed and blinded as I was.

Laras took it as an invitation to get real close this time and grabbed a handful of my ass while she was at it. An involuntary flinch straightened my spine. The fresh slice of pain almost a welcome distraction from Laras's hands on me. It didn't last long enough to blunt Laras's grin burning at my back. I clenched my teeth, tried to breathe through the panic like Iltis'd taught me.

Laras's grip only tightened.

"I don't know what Aris sees in you," she whispered into my ear. "Tell me, do you make him scream like I do?"

I twisted away from her hand, my left shoulder shrieking in its socket. "Don't. Talk to me. Not about him." But I'd already said too much, given her what she wanted.

Laras sighed. "Sweetheart, that's your problem. You keep trying to protect Aris from everything when that's the last thing he needs."

I gnawed my lower lip, tried not to think of the mess she'd made of Aris, or how hard he'd gotten when I'd clenched his wrists.

"Did it hurt?"

"Yes."

"Did it help?"

"Yes. Damian, please."

The memory crumbled. My hands curled into fists. I breathed through the hot stab in my shoulder, helpless against the cuffs or Laras or the fact I knew she wasn't lying.

"Shut the fuck up, Laras. Those fucking drugs almost killed him. You telling me he needed that, too?"

That put a hitch into her step. "I didn't—" She let out a tight breath, the steel bleeding back into her voice. "No. Which is why I told him we were done if he ever did anything this reckless ever again."

"Yeah, like you'd give him a fucking choice."

Laras let out a low laugh. "Oh, but that's where you're wrong. Aris always has a choice. Everything I do to him I do because he *wants* it. Why else do you think he keeps coming back?"

I was almost grateful she spared me having to work up a reply as she hustled me inside a building. Probably some old factory, a warehouse or wherever else the Reds brought people they wanted to quietly do away with. Laras stopped, then elbowed me in the ribs, dumping me into a wooden chair before she ripped the bag off my head.

Fresh air was definitely underappreciated. Even if stale and kind of dusty.

I blinked, squinting against the bright halogens overhead, everything blurring together. Valyr stepped into the light next to Laras, and things started to clear up fast.

Laras's hand clenched in my hair, bending my head back.

"Word has it you feel like your current work arrangements aren't meeting your needs anymore. That you have decided to...branch out." The commander of the Watch cocked her head to one side, face set in tight, angry lines. "Now, why don't we have a chat about that? You know, since feelings have been hurt and contracts breached. The Empire does value good employee relations after all."

I snorted. "Employee relations. Right. Next, you'll bust out the paperwork and tell me I get off with a write-up. Or maybe a final warning?"

Valyr's smile didn't make it to her eye. "I'm afraid we're taking the paperless approach here." She nodded at Laras.

So, she'd be the one doing Valyr's heavy lifting. Laras's hand closed around my shoulder, fingers digging into the bullet hole.

I let out a strangled scream as her nails dug into my blood-drenched shirt. Everything turned white with singing, burning pain bleaching out everything else. Laras's fingers came away red. She made a face and wiped her hand on my shirt. It barely registered as I hunched over, gasping for breath, waiting for the colors to leak back into my surroundings.

Valyr watched me, expressionless.

"Now that we got the icebreaker out of the way, we can get to the core of things," she said. "Like what you were doing at our mutual friend Mael Taerien's, for example. Since it clearly didn't involve fulfilling your contract."

I laughed. It came out a dry, scraping sound. Should've known it'd end like this.

"Not much, honestly." Other than making a deal with some batshit-crazy wannabe revolutionary who played people like they were fucking poker chips. I should've made up some story about how I'd gotten delayed. That she shouldn't worry. I'd get the job done.

Except I'd known Valyr long enough to know she'd see right through my bullshit, so I said, "Taerien happened to outbid you."

"I see." Two words, clipped and icy, punctuated by a cheek-splitting punch from Laras.

I spat blood. Hoped my words didn't slur too badly. "Problem with hiring outside hitters."

It occurred to me I should keep my mouth shut and wait for them to rough me up and let me go. Unless they planned to shoot me outright, and there was pretty much fuck all I could do to stop that. Either way, any sense of self-preservation had been shot and thrown out of a three-story window that night over a week ago. Now it was all free-falling and waiting for what got me first: the bullet or the splat of impact. Either way, it'd be quick, without anything to trace this back to Aris and the others.

I'd done enough runs to know sometimes taking out the middleman was your safest bet. Even when the middleman was me.

Too bad for me Valyr wasn't one for quick solutions. Laras stepped forward and hit me hard enough to make my ears ring and the chair teeter, a hair from falling over.

Gods, this was going to be a long night. And she was only warming up.

A double jab to my ribs left me hunched over and gasping for breath. The jagged thought whether this was what Laras did to Aris, how he'd gotten those black and blue ribs, fractured the pain. Part of me almost wanted to ask her, if only to get Laras to stop long enough for me to catch my breath. To show Laras two could play this game. Except that'd give Valyr a clear line of access to Aris and I'd let Laras beat me to death before I let Valyr get to Aris.

My left eyebrow burst open next and started leaking all over my face, turning half of my vision dripping red. Times like these I couldn't help but realize how much this whole working for the Empire thing wasn't worth the paper my nonexistent contract was printed on.

"Look," I hissed, trying to keep a grip on things. "Can we speed this up and get to the point? Yeah, I fucked you over." I blinked, trying to fight the black spots dancing in my vision. "So, either shoot me or tell me what you want me to do about it."

Valyr scowled at me and not for the first time I wondered if she just wore that eye patch of hers to have exactly this kind of creepy Cyclops-effect on people. Didn't think even Aris knew how she'd lost that eye. Doubted anyone who wanted to keep all their important body parts had ever asked her.

"Leave us, Captain."

Laras opened her mouth as if to protest, her right fist already tense for the next upper right aimed at my face. Her shoulders straightened. She gave Valyr a curt nod and walked out.

Which left me with Valyr and four of her goons hovering by the doors, discreetly out of the way, but ready to jump if I made any move to off their precious commander. Fat chance of that, cuffed to a chair and bleeding all over the place as I was.

If I didn't hurt so much, I would've been flattered.

"Now, let's talk rehabilitation. Never let it be said the Empire isn't giving any second chances," Valyr said, her voice low. "Where is he?"

"Where's who?"

Wrong answer.

Valyr hit me hard enough the chair toppled over. Blood filled my mouth. My shoulder smashed into the concrete floor and didn't leave me enough breath to scream. The world tilted dangerously, flashing black for a second before it came back into focus and zoomed on Valyr's red fingers curled in my collar.

Something flickered in her eye, when she said, "You know exactly who I mean, Nettoyer. Where is my *son*?"

Ah. Wondered how long it'd take her to bring up Aris.

Her so-called parental concern was something fit to be filed under "Most Fucked Up Family Relations." Aris had turned his back on her years ago, just after he'd found out he was a Voyant, after he'd seen how Valyr intended to "help" people like him.

He'd been running ever since, dodging all those talks along the lines of "I'm so disappointed in you" and "Why don't you join the Reds like a good little minion?" and her attempts to snatch him back, promising him a safety she'd never be able to give him. I'd worked for Valyr for the past five years, keeping her eyes on me and away from the rest of the Shadows, all the while gathering as much dirt on the Empire as I could. I couldn't blame Aris for taking it up with Laras instead of asking Mommy Dearest to cover for him.

First off, she wouldn't ever keep him safe. Not when she could use him instead. And second, no, I wasn't even going to start thinking what she'd make him do. What she'd turn him into. Much as I hated to admit it, Aris fucking Laras might not be the worst-case scenario, all things considered.

"Fuck you, Valyr." The words came out mangled. I spat blood on the cracked concrete floor. "He stopped being your son a long time ago. I'd rather die before I hand him over to you."

"Are you sure of that?" She dragged the chair back up, her .45 inches from my head.

I licked my lips, the taste of blood thick and salty at the back of my throat. Valyr stood above me, hands tight around her gun, her red coat buttoned up all the way to her chin. Would hardly even see the blood spatters on it afterward. She looked at me like she expected me to cave any second. It would be easy, too. All I had to do was arrange a convenient time for her to run into Aris and me alone. Could even pretend I'd had nothing to do with it.

Aris would never see it coming.

"Forget it, Valyr. Go ahead and shoot me already." Then a thought hit me. "Just don't half-ass it like that bastard Raeyn Nymeron did. In fact, do me a favor, save a bullet for him?"

Blowing Raeyn's cover story was petty as hells, but I'd be damned if I didn't do whatever I could do to take that backstabbing shit down with me. Valyr was nothing but efficient at getting her goons to take out the trash. At least she'd wipe that smug grin off his face for a bit.

Apparently that one hit right home, too, because Valyr stared at me like I'd started babbling in some foreign language. "You've seen Raeyn?"

"Bit more than seen him. Unfortunately."

The blank look on Valyr's face morphed into a furious snarl. And like that, I knew I'd gone too far. "You are a Light-forsaken liar, Nettoyer," she snapped, pointing her piece at me.

So glad we were back on track with that bit, at least.

"I would ask you if you had any last words, but I prefer we cut the theatrics, don't you?"

"Well, I always wanted to go out with 'Fuck you,' but whatever," I said through my teeth and watched her pull the trigger.

9

Avenging Angel

PRETTY SURE VALYR only missed because right then the window high up to my left exploded in a shower of glass. Blinding white light swallowed everything. Shards of glass rained down. Something landed next to me with a heavy thud. Valyr's bullet grazed my left ear and set off a high-pitched, tinny ringing in my skull. I cursed, my voice sounding weirdly loud and muffled. A thin trickle of blood ran down the side of my neck.

"Shit, Valyr, I'm going deaf because you can't fucking aim!" I winced. Talking and moving my jaw hurt like hells. Not like Valyr was paying attention. Someone hurled her away from me and threw her back-first into the wall to my right. She slid into a limp slump.

Then I saw who'd jumped down from the window. If I'd believed in that kind of thing, I would've said Aris looked like an avenging angel. One who'd been to all Seven Hells and back.

The glow flooding the room was brightest around him. His scuffed brown leather coat flapped in the wind, a weird parody of wings. Only there was no wind, just the Voyance, hot, blinding, and wracking the air, with Aris the eye of the storm. His hair'd come loose. It shone almost white, blowing around his face in wild tangles, his jaw clenched, lips a tight line.

The Reds around me lost their shit. One rushed to Valyr, but Aris's gaze landed on him and he stumbled into me instead, clutching at my collar as his knees gave out. Not much I could do to shake him off, handcuffed to the damn chair.

The guy panicked, his mouth opening and closing in some mute plea for help. His face contorted, bones crunching, twisting into weird angles. Like a pair of invisible hands gripped his head and squeezed. Red spilled out of his mouth, half of it splattering my shirt before he toppled over and stilled. Dead. Blood oozed out of his ears. Usually a bad sign as these things went. Same thing happened to the other Reds hovering by the door. Now they lay crumpled on the floor, bleeding from their eyes, leaking onto the concrete. Yeah, definitely dead.

"What the fuck."

Aris turned to me, his eyes stark white. For a terrible moment, I thought he'd kill us all.

"Aris?" The same feeling as when he'd almost strangled me crept in. Like a face-off with a rabid dog: ready to tear your throat out at a wrong move. But he was still *Aris*. My eyes flicked across the room. Across the bodies that lay scattered around me. Aris didn't seem to notice. Just stared at me without blinking, without a hint of recognition.

I swallowed.

"Aris?" I asked again, hoping he'd get his grip back on things. "Come on, snap out of it." Trapped as I was, I tried to ignore the scrunched-in faces of the dead Reds scattered like broken toy soldiers. Eyes hollow, like they'd boiled in their skulls before they died.

Gods, I'd never thought I'd feel sorry for a bunch of Reds. Or be afraid of Aris.

"Please." The urge to reach out, to touch him became unbearable. "Come back to me."

It was like a light went out in Aris. The glow faded, his eyes turned back to normal.

"Damian?" His voice sounded distant, but even over the rushing in my ears, I could hear it shake. He sank onto his knees in front of me. "Are you okay? Did I—" His eyes darted from me to the dead Reds. He took in a shuddering breath. "Gods, did I do this?"

I squinted at him and forced a grin, trying to be reassuring and failing miserably. "Thought we'd talked about you letting me know you can do this kind of shit. Having someone around who can make people's brains melt out of their ears would make my job so much easier."

Aris flinched as if I'd slapped him. "I didn't mean to—" He licked his lips. "I saw her. She was going to kill you and I—" He turned away, his fists clenched against his thighs.

"Hey." I tried for calm and reassuring. "It's okay. You're okay. Look at me."

I could see the muscles in Aris's jaw move as he swallowed. When I looked at him—really looked at him—I saw how pale he'd gotten. Blood ran out of his nose. He didn't seem to notice it dripping down his chin, staining the collar of his shirt.

He took out a set of lockpicks and fiddled with my cuffs. First time he touched me, it felt like running into an electric fence, residual Voyance crackling across my skin.

My shoulder complained at being jerked around, and I couldn't quite stifle a groan.

"Sorry." Behind me, Aris breathed in and out deeply for a few seconds. When he touched me again, the charge was gone, but his shaky hands only managed to jar my shoulder and drop the picks. "You've been shot."

"Really, I didn't notice." I tried to laugh. Bad idea. It came out as a wheezy, dry sound and hurt like hells, setting off explosions of needling pain in my left arm and inside my head. "Your m—uh, Valyr's got the key," I said once I was done coughing and Aris kept fumbling with the cuffs.

"Right." He got up and stiffly moved over to Valyr clawing herself up into a sitting position. "Mother."

Valyr still seemed dazed but pointed her gun at Aris's chest. "Stay where you are."

If I hadn't known her better, I'd have sworn her voice shook almost as bad as her hands. Valyr was terrified of Aris. She'd gotten what she wanted. Her son. Going by the quiet tears sliding down her face, this wasn't how she'd imagined their reunion.

"Aris, please, don't do this."

Aris got his eyes from Valyr, same as the sharp, high cheekbones and the curls, though hers were brown, where his were blond. From my vantage point, handcuffed and bleeding, the creepiness of their similarity grew to a whole new level of fucked up.

Aris held out his hand. "The key, Mother."

They stared at each other until Valyr sighed and handed over a ring of keys. "You don't seriously expect me to let you go. You've gone too far this time."

"You aren't exactly in the position to stop me."

Valyr snorted. "Be reasonable. You can barely stand."

I felt the Voyance rekindling around Aris. "Are you sure?"

Valyr's mouth twisted into a thin smile. The eye patch made it menacing. "Please. You're making this too hard on yourself. Come with me. I'll even be persuaded to let your pathetic friend go." Changing course, her voice almost turned pleading for a second. "Aris, please. Just come to the palace."

Aris snorted, an almost perfect imitation of Valyr. "And do what? Hold still and wait for them to Cleanse me?" He laughed, the sound carrying a hysterical edge. "No, thanks."

Valyr looked like she'd completely forgotten the gun she'd aimed at him. "You don't honestly believe I'd let them do that. The palace can help you."

"Right. I forgot that's what you call it." Aris's fingers curled around the keys, careful not to touch Valyr. "I'll take my chances. I suggest you look for someone else to play your games with. We're done. Goodbye, Mother."

Aris's eyes stayed white as he staggered back to me, moving like he could hardly keep from falling over. He crouched down and unlocked the cuffs. My first impulse was to prop him up—not that either of us was in any shape to hold the other up.

His skin radiated warmth. Tiny licks of static crept up my arms when he dragged me to my feet. He brushed against my busted shoulder, and I had to bite my lower lip to stifle a scream.

"Sorry. I'm sorry. I've got you." He carefully slid his arm around me. "Let me."

In the end we had each other. Probably looked hilarious, both of us holding on to the other, unclear who was supporting who, stumbling to the warehouse's door.

A peek around the corner at the front of the building showed something an awful lot like a trench-war zone in one of those old black and white movies Coras loved so much. Jay's wide hover car barricaded the door against Laras and her two remaining Reds.

"Hey!" Jay shouted when a bullet left a deep groove in the hover's nose, avoiding her by inches. "I *just* finished the new paint. You lot are why we can't have nice things."

Next to Kovacz, Jay kept shooting, taking cover behind the hover's patchwork steel hull. Looked like Jay and the others had come around the corner and used the hover to block them from getting back in right after Aris had started throwing down with the Voyance.

Past the hover, Laras spotted me dragging Aris into a corner by the door where its concrete wall protruded enough to shelter us from stray bullets. For a second, she struggled to level her gun at Aris. The thought that maybe he was more to her than just someone she liked to routinely fuck beyond coherence wormed itself into my mind. It dissipated when she took aim at us. For a horrible moment, I was almost pathetically grateful her rank among the Reds outweighed whatever attachment she had to him.

"Hello, Dahlia." The way Aris said her name, like something dirty and familiar, way too familiar, made some primitive part of me want to kill them both.

After we got out of this.

I winced at his arm tightening on me. He lifted his right hand and stepped out into the clearing between the entrance and the hover. This time his eyes only got a tad lighter, the glow a shimmer, not blinding.

"Lower your weapons," Aris called to Laras and her Reds.

Whatever mindfuckery he pulled, it worked.

Laras's hand trembled, fingers twitching around her .45. She bit her lip, trying to fight it.

In the end, things happened quickly: Laras's gun clattered onto the ground. Aris ignored it, but held his position, somehow managing to hold both her and her goons frozen in place.

Behind us, Valyr shouted something from inside the building. She never made it past the doorframe, caught in Aris's Voyance like a fly trapped in a spider's web. It was brilliant. Totally fucked up, but brilliant. And pretty damn obvious Aris couldn't keep it up for much longer, swaying where he stood.

"Get him out of here, Orion," Aris called to Kovacz running toward us from the hover.

"Getting the hells out of here. Good plan." Kovacz popped up next to me and pried me loose from Aris, slinging my arm across his shoulder. It felt like he was ripping my shoulder out of its socket. The world momentarily flipped and bright stars exploded in my vision, leaving glaring afterimages trailing behind as I stumbled against him.

"Ah shit, Kovacz," I ground out past clenched teeth, waiting for the world to right itself.

Kovacz grumbled but did his best to keep me from falling over. "You know, 'thank you' would have been the appropriate thing to say, but whatever."

"Hurry," Aris hissed through his teeth. The Voyance crackled, threatening to fizz out whenever he as much as moved a few steps. A second later, he fell to his knees.

"Aris!" I lunged for him, but Kovacz held me back. Laras and her Reds, figuring out nothing pinned them anymore, moved in on Aris, vultures picking at a corpse.

"Don't. No use to him if you get yourself caught, too." Kovacz's grip tightened.

"You bastard, that's just like you to leave him there. Forget it."

"Go," a voice said to my left. I turned to see Raeyn Nymeron of all people step out from in between the tail end of the hover and cross over to Aris. He'd managed to knock out the guy who'd moved around the hover coming for Aris and held off Laras's remaining Red at gunpoint.

"Yeah," Jay shouted, doing her best to keep Laras in her sights. "Would be real nice if we could hurry this up."

"Yes, I think we've had enough blood and gore today," Raeyn said with a theatrical sigh at the befuddled Red. "But go ahead if you must. Pick a kneecap."

"*You*," I said. "Where in the Seven bloody Hells did you come from?"

Raeyn kept his eyes on the Red. "I told you I'd come back for you." A grin quirked up his lips, suddenly reminding me way too much of how it felt when he'd kissed me. He kicked my Colt over to me. "I even saved this for you. Now *go*." This time he sounded a notch more pissed off than before. "Just once, do as you are told. You've had your bullet for the day. Move and keep us covered. I've got him."

He turned to the warehouse and dragged Aris to his feet but froze midmovement when Valyr stepped into the doorway.

"Raeyn," Valyr said softly, all the hardness leaking out of her voice. She stared at him like he was a ghost. It made her look breakable, not like herself at all.

Raeyn's smirk wiped off his face, falling away like a mask he suddenly couldn't hide behind anymore. He opened his mouth as if to say something, his gun aimed right at her.

Laras and the other Red raised their guns, but Jay and Kovacz discouraged that real fast.

It'd be easy for Raeyn to do my job for me and kill Valyr right there. But he didn't. It was like Raeyn'd completely forgotten he was even armed.

"What the fuck are you doing, Nymeron?" I raised my piece. Took aim.

"No." Raeyn's voice cracked through the silence like a single shot. "Not like this."

Valyr used that hesitation and dodged out of my line of sight. Raeyn's jaw hardened as he turned and dragged a half-conscious Aris into the six-seat flatbed hover with him.

"About damn time," Jay called from the driver's seat when Kovacz and Raeyn dumped Aris and me in the backseat. "Damn, what happened? You two look fucked up."

"'S what happens if your boss wants to have a talk with you, Grasshopper." I grinned, weak and lopsided. I collapsed next to Aris.

"No shit." Jay gunned it. Not a second too late, because the air behind us filled with the black smoke of flash grenades she'd planted to cover up our retreat. Not that there was much of anyone left to follow us. Aris had made sure of that. Even Laras and Valyr knew better than coming after us clearly outnumbered. I'd seen a lot, but the images of those dead, eyeless Reds still sent shivers down my spine.

"Gods, that was...something else," I said after a while of tense silence. Then, "Um. Thanks. For. You know." Kovacz was right, being grateful had never been my strong suit.

"You're welcome." Aris opened his eyes and winced. He rubbed his temples. He looked dead tired, sweaty curls plastered to his forehead, skin the color of old newspaper bleached out by the sun.

He turned to me, his face carefully blank. "Next time someone blackmails you into killing my mother, fill me in from the get-go?"

I blinked. "You knew?"

Aris jerked his head toward Raeyn, then grimaced at the abrupt motion. He closed his eyes and pinched the bridge of his nose. "Raeyn told me."

"Oh."

"Yeah." He waved me off when I tried to explain. "Look, I'm not blaming you. It's not like I didn't see this coming, but..." Aris sighed. "Next time, tell me." A tight smile edged his mouth. "Personally though, I opt for not doing this kind of thing again anytime soon."

"Um, what the hells *did* you do? I mean you did your Voyance thing and it felt like...fuck." I trailed off, suddenly glad his eyes were closed so he couldn't see how freaked-out I still was.

Raeyn's head snapped around. "You're lucky it didn't kill you. Using the Voyance like that. Are you out of your mind?" He shook his head. "You're both hopeless, you know that? Barging in like that." He glared at Aris. "The fire escape was a lookout. You were supposed to wait for an opening. For the rest of us. Have you ever heard of organized recon? As in, the kind not likely to get you killed in the process? I'm honestly surprised you two made it as long as you did out here."

"Maybe that's because we don't turn around and shoot each other in the back?" I growled. "And while we're at it, what in all the Seven Hells was that with you not killing Valyr when you had every damn chance? What kind of fucked up game are you playing, Nymeron?"

Raeyn bristled. "The kind of game that doesn't start wars. Not that I've been the least bit successful from the looks of it."

Aris studied him through half-closed lids. "Thought you were the one saying we would have to improvise. Or did you expect me to calmly wait for her to shoot him?"

"I didn't think she would—" Raeyn flinched but recovered quickly. "That wasn't improvising. That was killing half a dozen members of the Watch and very nearly yourself and the rest of us while you were at it." Raeyn looked ready to explode. It almost made this whole thing worth it.

"No." Aris's grin was hollow. His hands twitched violently in his lap. "That was saving our collective asses."

"Yes," Raeyn said. "In other words, welcome to the Empire's most-wanted list. Congratulations."

10

Healthy Exchange of Blame

"WHAT FOR FUCK'S sake were you thinking? *Were* you thinking?"

The door to the *Shadow's* infirmary hadn't quite clanged shut before Iltis rounded in on Aris and socked him in the face. Aris stumbled back, caught on one of the white cabinets. On its counter, Raeyn had laid out a tray with scalpels, needles, and whatever else he called "surgical instruments." I thought they had a better place in any torturer's stash.

Aris would've swiped it right off the counter if Raeyn hadn't caught it last minute.

"I'd appreciate only having to stitch up one of you at a time," Raeyn said, his mouth a pinched, unhappy line. He shone a penlight into my eyes. It felt like he stabbed me right through a pupil. I scooted back, scrunched my eyes shut, waiting for the fireworks to stop going off behind my retinas.

"Gods, do you have to do that?"

Raeyn frowned at me, not saying anything for a change. At least he put the light away.

Next to him, Aris straightened, wiping his mouth with one sleeve, not taking his eyes off Iltis. For a second, I could've sworn I saw a faint white glow spark around Aris, a tiny bit of white flashing in his eyes in a murderous glimmer. And just like that, it was gone. Like it'd been nothing but some trick of light.

Aris stood strangely adrift in the glaring lights of the sickbay. Fighting to hold himself together, to keep from going for Iltis's wrinkly throat. His fingers twitched, gripping the cabinet.

"For Gods' sakes, boss, he can barely stand," I said when Iltis took a step closer, gnarled fingers white on her cane, ready to club Aris with it. I moved to slide off the metal examination table Raeyn had made me sit on, ready to get between them and tell Iltis to cut it the hells out. Raeyn's bony hand against my bruised solar plexus held me back.

"I said, *sit*," Raeyn said. "Didn't think I had to resort to basic dog training commands with you quite yet, but if that makes it easier for you: *stay*."

I glared at him, not quite suppressing a growl, but stayed where I was. Even held still when Raeyn pulled up a syringe and shot something into my shoulder that made my left side tingle.

"There's a good boy."

"Fuck you, Nymeron."

Raeyn smirked and went back to work, the sharp sting of disinfectant clinging to every movement.

Aris raised his hand, part defensively against Iltis, part directed at me. "I guess I deserved that," he said, the words a little thick past a split lip.

"Damn straight, boy," Iltis's hand remained tight around her cane. "Beating builds character. Not that it's done you a whole lot of good. You'd figure I managed to kick some sense into you by now, instead of wasting over a decade on you only to have you pull some stupid stunt that's going to get you and the rest of us in with the Reds real good. Congratulations. Might as well have pointed a signal beacon to lead them here."

"You're right. It's been enough." Emptiness crept into Aris's face. It was like watching a house of cards collapse, the moment stretching into slow motion, so you could see each layer topple and drag down the next, until the whole thing caved in on itself and the last card slipped away into nothingness. Aris didn't look at Iltis when he spoke next. He looked at me. "I'm going to take the Temple's offer. I'll leave in the morning."

He turned and walked out the door without another word.

Numbness broke. "You'll *what*?" I called after him, jerking upright fast enough for Raeyn's hand to slip and cut deeper than he meant to. "Shit, watch what you're doing!"

Raeyn cocked a silver eyebrow and he leaned back, his mouth twitching with annoyance. "You know, maybe we should leave the bullet where it is and see what happens."

"Yeah, you'd love that, wouldn't you? You put it in, you get it the fuck back out."

Raeyn rolled his eyes. "See, this is why we worked only on heavily sedated patients at the labs." Under his breath, he muttered something about how next time he'd aim a little lower and to the right.

"You wish," I growled, but forced myself to stay still as he started mucking about again, gritting my teeth against the bite of the scalpel in tender flesh. Fuck local anesthesia, the stuff didn't do much but take the edge off. Just as well. 'Least the pain kept my head clear.

I waited for Raeyn to finish cleaning the wound. His hands were gentle, wrapping me up and putting my arm into a sling until I looked like a one-armed mummy. It felt like way too much effort to half shrug back into clothes and go after Aris. Raeyn had to help me with my shirt, his fingers cool against my skin as he carefully fastened each button.

"He's doing the right thing," he said quietly. His hand lingered a little longer on my good shoulder than strictly necessary to close the Velcro of the sling.

I pulled away. "What in the Seven Hells do you know about doing the right thing, huh, Nymeron?" The name came out a curse. The way Raeyn recoiled, fingers drawing back and curling into themselves, it hit right home, too.

His eyes grew hooded and distant when he said, "Hardly enough, I suppose."

He turned back to cleaning up the mess of bloody instruments, spilled cotton pads, and bandages scattered across the examination table.

"Change of plan," Raeyn said. "Valyr knows we're on to her. Killing her now wouldn't just be stupid, it would be suicide. If we're lucky. But that doesn't mean we can't keep the Empire on its toes."

"And do what?" I gingerly got off the table. Topped off with a few of the better painkillers, the pain had dulled to a throb shoved behind gauze padding. "Bide our time, keep the Reds away while you and Taerien find the right people to scheme with until the time's right to overthrow the Empire?"

Raeyn paused what he was doing. There was no trace of humor in his words. "Basically, yes."

I shook my head, quickly regretting the motion. "Fuck, Nymeron, you're even more batshit than I thought. Gods, this is a fucking suicide mission."

"Not as long as you do exactly as you're told." He said it casually, like a reminder not to pick at my stitches.

"Right. What other choice do I have?"

He rolled his eyes. "Please. Don't pretend I'm asking you anything you aren't already doing. Taerien is doing you a favor. And he is paying you better than the Empire ever has."

"It's not about the money."

Raeyn met my gaze. Held it. "I know it isn't. That's why I picked you."

I glanced away first. His mouth curved into a faint smile as he went back to work.

"Face it, darling, we are on the same team."

"I'll never be on your team, Nymeron."

"Of course." I could hear the smirk in his voice. "Keep telling yourself that."

I didn't give him the satisfaction of an answer, especially with that tiny voice at the back of my head whispering he might be right. At least he left it at that and didn't look up when I left.

I found Aris in our room, staring at an empty bag on the bed in front of him, its zipper yanked open and gaping wide like a slash wound.

He didn't turn around when I came in, just stood there, hunched over, his arms braced against the bed.

"I killed four people today," he said. "Killed them, just like that, and I don't even remember. All I know—" He paused, his bent head framed with a spill of golden curls that'd escaped his messy ponytail. "All I know is it felt *good* and how fucked up is that, huh? It was easy, too. So easy." His arms wrapped around himself.

Standing there, he looked more broken than anything a couple painkillers and some bandages could fix. It drained the fight right out of me. I didn't say anything about him leaving or about Raeyn and Taerien's suicidal plan. Instead, I stepped behind him and with my free arm reached out and slipped the black band out of his hair, fingers combing through tangled curls.

"You'll be okay. We'll get you help, and you'll be okay, you hear?"

I felt Aris laugh, a naked, desperate sound. "You sound so sure."

"Hey, it worked out for me, didn't it?"

Honestly, I was full of shit on that one. Images of *L'Ecole* bubbled up. Ish's sneering face above me. Marten's knee in my back, hands clamped around my wrists holding me down, pinned on cracked tile floor.

Yeah, institutions sure had worked out well for me.

I clawed the memory away. Concentrated on Aris's hanging shoulders in front of me. His open vulnerability'd been what brought me around in the first place; now it was what made him draw away to some place I couldn't lure him out and do for him what he'd done for me.

I hated it. Hated having to admit that maybe the Temple was his best shot. Maybe they'd be able to glue the pieces back together where I couldn't even see them amid all the cracks.

I wanted to tell him to stay. Beg him. But this wasn't about me. This was about doing whatever I had to if it'd get the Voyance to stop tearing him apart. For that, I'd do anything.

Even let him go.

I swallowed the lump in my throat. Took a deep breath before I trusted myself enough to pull him close, for my hands to unclench when I tucked his shoulder under my chin.

"All I'm saying is I've got your back, no matter what."

"Thanks," Aris said. I could feel the warmth of my own sigh against his neck. He leaned into me, and we stood there, neither of us saying anything for a while.

11

The Right Thing

I SNAPPED OUT of my doze when Aris tried to slink out of the room.

"What do you think you're doing?" I flicked on the light by the bed.

Aris flinched against the sudden brightness. He stood by the doorframe, cornered, his bag clutched in a white-knuckled grip like some secret loot he was trying to steal away with.

"I—" he started, then took me in, sitting on the bed, fully dressed. "You didn't sleep, did you?"

"And let you sneak out like some kid dodging curfew?"

Aris bit his lip. "Damian, I—"

"Yeah, yeah. You're bad at goodbyes. Wanted to let me sleep in, yadda yadda. Bullshit."

I swung my legs out of bed and nearly fell when my body got back at me for that long, sleepless night, reminding me just how worked over I was. There wasn't an inch of me that wasn't bruised and aching. The shoulder sling wasn't helping my balance. I staggered stiffly to the sink and splashed some water into my face. It didn't do much to wake me up, only made the veins in my bloodshot eyes stand out worse. I rubbed my jaw, black stubble, way past its usual five o'clock shadow, prickly against my fingers. It did a piss-poor job hiding the bruises turning half my face blue and purple, something like those ancient abstract paintings that never got the nose in the right place.

"Um, what are you doing?" Aris asked, watching me shove my Colt into its shoulder holster and attempt to one-handedly strap a knife to each wrist. Might have to grit my teeth and lose the sling if I wanted to wear my jacket to cover it all up.

"What's it look like?" I said, debating the .22 that'd disappear into my pant holster or something bigger, just in case. "I'm coming with you, of course."

"Uh-huh." Aris nodded slowly. "But do you really think you need—"

There was a rap on the door. He went to open it.

"Don't even start, okay? I'm too damn tired for that kind of argument, and I'm not going to let you run off with that backstabbing asshole."

"Talking about me?" Raeyn said, leaning in the doorway. "For the record, I despise the term 'backstabbing.' If I'm going to stab you, I will be looking right into your pretty brown eyes, darling." He gave me a look as I slid a second knife into my bootstrap. "Are we preparing for a siege?"

"What?" I closed the strap and gingerly straightened, after securing the straps on my other leg. "This?"

"I was going to ask the same thing, but the Gods forbid I get a word in edgewise," Aris said, his bemused look ruined by the smile tugging at the corner of his mouth.

I snorted. "Yeah, right. In case it passed by you, but we're neck-deep in Reds lately. That and the Gods know what kind of religious nuts we're about to deal with at that Burner Academy of yours. Never can have enough guns for those."

And packing an extra clip couldn't hurt when Raeyn Nymeron of all people claimed to be on the same team as us. Gods only knew how he knew people at the Temple. At this point, I'd be surprised if there was anyone in the city he didn't have connections to. The guy was a spider. Ties fucking everywhere.

Raeyn raised his eyebrows. "Well, whatever you do, do me a favor and don't call them 'religious nuts.' At least not to their faces." He put on his fedora and tured to Aris. "Ready?"

Aris paused and gave me the strangest look and then stepped forward, closed his hands around mine, and took the reserve clip I meant to slip into my pocket away from me. He slowly put it on the counter, gaze never leaving mine.

He nodded. "Yeah." It came out a little hoarse and he let go of me, his face carefully blank.

Raeyn took him aside and whispered, "Is he always this paranoid?"

Aris didn't say anything. Behind his back, I picked up the spare clip and tucked it away with the rest.

The *Shadow* lay dark and quiet, the low hum of flickering green emergency lighting along the corridors following us out. The only real light came from Iltis's study, a bright slit of yellow that crept out from beneath her door. Not sure why the blind old bat needed light. Habit probably.

Wouldn't be the first time she'd fallen asleep with her hands on her reader, some oblong gadget that converted letters into Braille.

I pretended not to notice Aris's eyes lingering on her door as we went past. He and Iltis had another talk last night. Aris had come back pale and tense around the eyes. No idea what Iltis said, but I hadn't been the only one who didn't get a wink of sleep afterward.

The *Shadow*'s back door opened with its usual rusty screech. With an annoyed meow, Dust streaked inside, back from her nightly prowl for mice. Jay entered after her. She didn't say anything, just went up to Aris and hugged him tight, like she'd never let him go.

"Promise you won't forget us." Her words ran thick with tears.

Aris's smile almost crumbled. "Never."

"Good. Because the Gods help me, I'll get Damian and kick your ass if you do."

We left her standing there, petting her cat, and went out into the semidarkness of the Poubelle. The first red fingers of dawn already clawed at the horizon, breaking into a thousand tiny splinters reflected by the wire fence that separated the junkyard from the rest of Low Side. Clearly Jay wasn't the only one to pick first light to call it a night. On the bleached-out hood of one of the car wrecks piled up by the *Shadow*'s rear, Kovacz sat, a lazy parody of a night's sentinel, a red leather coat draped around his shoulders.

"Hey." I jerked my head at his coat. "Think it's a good idea sitting here with that on?"

Kovacz shrugged. "Not like there's anyone but you yahoos around this early." He reached for a flickering holoscreen he'd dropped by the car's flat front tire. "'Sides, anywhere but here seems like a red coat's the only thing helping you blend in." He flicked off the screen and waved into the direction of the Core. "Place is swarming with Reds. The news feeds are going crazy trying to cover it up, so it doesn't look like some Low Side street rat actually got a good shot in against the Empire."

His eyes narrowed at Aris. "Just how many of their guys *did* you deep-fry with your Voyance mojo? City's busier than a fucking anthill."

"Enough of them," Aris said, his tone clipped.

"Better get going then." Kovacz pushed a bent pair of reading glasses up his nose.

"We better," Aris said and walked past. He left the Poubelle without looking back.

In a place that never completely stopped moving, first light was as dead as Helos ever got, like the city was resetting. An icy wind whispering promises of a rough winter to come did its part to wipe the dregs of Low Side clean at this hour. It kept the usual riffraff tucked away, squatting in the burned-out ruins that'd once been part of the more illustrious shopping districts of Helos.

What wasn't usual at all were the scattered patrols of Reds wandering the streets. Kovacz had been right. There weren't a lot out here, two or three Reds at a time, nothing but scout troops. Errant dots of color, they stood out against the grays and browns of Low Side like blood stains on paper.

One of their tag teams nearly spotted us before Raeyn dragged Aris and me into an arching doorway leading into a brown sandstone building at the edge of Nightshade.

"You know what happens to stray Voyants?" Raeyn asked once the Reds passed us.

Aris stayed quiet before he said, "They die."

I tried to swallow past the coldness turning my insides into icicles.

We'd known, of course. Both of us. But there was a difference between knowing and Aris saying it out loud.

Raeyn licked his lips. "Yes, but." He fiddled with the brim of his fedora, then caught himself. "It's not that easy, I'm afraid." He added quietly, "There's someone I'd like you both to meet."

He obviously hadn't chosen this place as a hiding spot at random. Raeyn knew exactly where he was going. I almost wasn't surprised anymore. At this point, I doubted the words "random" or "coincidence" existed in Raeyn Nymeron's vocabulary. He stepped farther into the gaping doorway and knocked twice on the massive door. After a second and some muffled grumbling, a slit in the door opened and a dark pair of eyes peered out.

"Yeah?" a rough voice snapped.

"I apologize for the hour, Mistress Ferris, but we're here to see an old friend." Raeyn tipped his hat briefly and the eyes scrutinizing us widened. The slit closed, and the door opened.

The woman Raeyn had called Ferris was short and wiry, her cropped hair peppered with more gray than brown. The lines around her eyes crinkled when she greeted Raeyn with a smile.

"Pascal didn't mention you'd be dropping by. Good to see you, Sir—uh, Raeyn."

"Yes, it has been quite a while, hasn't it?" Raeyn said absentmindedly as he stepped inside. His smile had something bitter and forced to it, but Ferris didn't seem to notice, too busy switching back to her narrow-eyed glare when Aris and I followed Raeyn.

"And they are?"

"Right, where is my head?" Raeyn shook off that weird inward look and introduced Aris and me to Ferris, who was apparently part of some sort of Temple's-Own guard.

"Uh, pleased to meet you," I said in a hurry to follow Aris's example. Probably would've gone over smoother if I'd been better at this honest, open smile-thing Aris had with new people. Or if Ferris had taken the hand I offered to her.

"Not sure if I'd say the same," she said, eyes fixed on my jacket. "You gonna drop your stash here? Unless you fancy a frisk."

"You're kidding me, right?" I shot Raeyn a look. He barely could keep his face straight.

"Told you so," Aris said, fighting a grin of his own.

Ferris held out her hands. "Lose 'em, big boy, I promise no one's going to shoot you in the back while I'm watching."

Sure, because she'd be doing the shooting.

I glared back at her and started to unbuckle things, trying not to let her see me grimace when the movement tugged at my shoulder. Ferris blinked at the heap of guns, knives, and spare clips I piled in front of her. Aris gave me a look and a nudge. I sighed, adding a beat-up pocket knife on top of it all. Behind me, Raeyn coughed. Ferris's brows drew up and she let out a low whistle through her teeth.

"Damn, boy. Paranoid much? I'm not even going to ask what you'd need *that* for." She shook her head and piled the knife into a rusty locker with the rest.

"Well then." She waved us on. "After you." The outward hostility had left her voice, but I still caught how her right hand brushed over the hilt of a knife at her belt. I got the message.

Following Raeyn, we went up a flight of trodden-out wooden stairs that only added to the shabbiness of the place. Dim lanterns swinging from metal fixtures lit the narrow hallway. Going by the black stains covering most of the ceiling and walls, curling the faded brownish-yellow wallpaper, there'd been a fire up here. The faint smell of smoke still clung to everything; it mingled with old wood and molding patches of wallpaper, making it hard to breathe. In front of me, Raeyn stiffened, each movement tight and locked down, like he was fighting the urge to run the other way.

"What the hells is this place?" I asked, fingers itching for my Colt.

"We call it *L'Oubliette*." Raeyn cleared his throat. "The Temple set it aside for Voyants who are too far gone. They can be safe here."

"You mean the Temple sends them here to die." Aris wasn't looking at Raeyn, but at the locks on every door we passed. They shone a dim gold in the flickering light. I shuddered.

"That's one way to put it," Raeyn replied quietly. One of the doors to our right opened. A dark-haired kid in ripped jeans and a loose cream tunic, who could've been Jay's lighter-skinned twin, nearly ran into us. "Why, hello to you, too, Pascal."

"Oh! Hi!" The kid—Pascal—kissed Raeyn on the cheek with a smile that shone like a beacon in the dim light. "Should have told me you were coming. I would've made cookies or something."

"It's good to see you, Pascal." Raeyn smiled and turned to Aris. "I believe you've met them already?"

Aris nodded, an uncertain smile tugging at the corner of his mouth. "Initiate Pascal has been rather...vocal in their enthusiasm for me to join the Temple."

"Please, just Pascal's fine." Before Aris could step back, they hugged him tightly. "I'm so glad you made it! I started to wonder if Aemelia scared you away. She can be stuck up and condescending as hells sometimes, but once you get to know her —" Pascal caught themself and before I had time to get worried about more hugs, held out their hand for me to shake. "Anyway, welcome." Their face turned serious when they asked Raeyn, "You're here to see Gren, aren't you?"

Raeyn nodded. "How is he?"

Pascal bit their lip. "He keeps asking for you."

Raeyn's face turned unreadable, but I registered the faintest twitch in his hands as we followed Pascal to a room up the hall where the fire damage was worst.

"Pascal," Raeyn said, taking in the fire-scarred door. "What happened?"

Pascal squared their narrow shoulders. "He has episodes. Forgets where he is. Goes to look for you." Pascal exhaled. "We had to sedate and restrain him. I'm sorry, Raeyn."

"I see." Raeyn nodded, his gaze distant. Lost. "How long?"

Pascal shook their head. "It's good you came when you did." They opened the door.

Unlike the hallway leading up to it, this room was bright and freshly painted. The first rays of the rising sun fell in from a large arched window. With stacks of books haphazardly piled on top of a table and two comfortable chairs next to it, the small chamber could've passed as a miniature copy of Iltis's study.

The similarities stopped at the smell of disinfectant and sickness that filled the air and the narrow bed by the window.

If I hadn't known better, I would've said the sunken figure strapped to it was dead. If there was something like mercy in this world, he should've been.

The guy Pascal had called Gren was little more than a skeleton with tendons stretched over it, his skin the gray of old, wrinkled paper. The worst part was his face, covered in sores, as if whatever Voyance was left in him was trying to punch through his skin. A white bandage wrapped around his head, speckled with blood where his eyes should have been.

I took a quick step back and nearly tripped when an image flashed to life in my head: Gren, fingers twisted into claws, ripping into his eyes with the panic of the irreparably insane. Only tearing out his eyes hadn't made the images go away.

"What the hells?" I only got a glimpse of the things Gren saw, a flicker of the pain he had to be in.

I'd heard about some Voyants projecting things into other people's minds, especially when they lost control near the end. This was enough to make me want to turn and run like hells. The only thing that kept me anchored was Aris's hand, slipping into mine. He squeezed my hand, his grip cold and clammy, but he stood his ground and so would I, mental whiplash or not.

Whatever'd just happened, whatever I'd seen, thought I'd seen, I crammed it into the back of my mind. No wonder I got the jitters in a place like this.

Raeyn wasn't doing any better. At first, he merely stood by the bed, one hand raised to his mouth in what couldn't be read as anything but silent horror. He closed his eyes and let out a shuddering breath, then pulled up a chair. Carefully, he loosened the padded strap around Gren's right wrist and took the fragile, emaciated hand into his.

The muscles in Gren's throat moved as he swallowed, working out the syllable. "Raeyn." His voice was a fraying thread. His thin lips twisted into a parody of a smile.

"Gren, *mon cher*." Raeyn's voice was gentle but laced with sadness. He pressed a kiss to Gren's knuckles.

I suddenly wanted very much to trade places with Ferris, who'd waited outside. Much as I hated the sly bastard, watching Raeyn with this guy Gren felt like interrupting something private, something he should be doing alone.

Worse, watching them felt like staring into a mirror showing me a future I'd do my damnedest to avoid. I'd put a bullet into both Aris's and my head before it came to this. I knew it was what Aris wanted. We'd talked that one through years ago. And Aris'd expressly told me he'd haunt my ass if I took myself out after him. I'd take it up with his ghost when it came to that.

Except we both knew I mightn't get a choice. Raeyn sure hadn't from the looks of it.

Raeyn seemed to have forgotten Aris and the rest of us were even there. He reached out and smoothed back strands of ash-blond hair plastered to Gren's forehead.

"Gren, do you remember what happened? Where you are?"

"The fire! I can't—Can't stop it." Gren gasped, fear ringing in his tone. His hand closed around Raeyn's in a grip much stronger than what I'd thought him capable of. His mind slipped into incoherence. "Where's Raeyn? I have to find him. I—"

"It's all right." Raeyn leaned down, carefully took Gren's hand and placed it on the scar tissue that lined the left side of his face. "You got him out. Saved his life, remember?"

I noticed the bubbly trails of burn scars covering Gren's hands, running from his fingers down to his lower arms in raised pink and white welts. They looked about as old as Raeyn's. I wondered if they told the same story.

What in the Gods' names happened during that night the palace burned?

Gren took a ragged breath, his hand shaking as he felt Raeyn's face. "The Watch. They'll kill him if they ever find him."

"He will be fine. Nobody will find him," Raeyn said softly. The shaking in Gren's hand increased and Raeyn put it back on the sheets without letting go.

Gren went silent 'til I was sure he'd drifted off to sleep. "I still see them," he whispered under his breath. "Always see them. The fire, flames everywhere. They're all burning. The kids. Gods, Raeyn, they're just kids!"

Raeyn hissed as Gren's fingers dug into his wrist. Heat radiated off the man strapped to the bed. It smelled of singed hair and skin. I took a step toward him, but Raeyn's free hand motioned me to stay where I was.

"It's all right," he gasped. I wasn't sure whether he meant me or Gren, who had eased his grip until the heat went away and he settled into a fit of uneasy twitches. The skin of Raeyn's wrist stood out bright red and just shy of blistering beneath Gren's grip. Raeyn ignored it. "You should rest, Gren. Sleep."

"Can't. Screams won't let me. They know, Raeyn. Gods, they know *everything.*"

"It wasn't your fault, Gren. You couldn't have gotten them out. You know that. You merely did as I said. The fire was my fault, and if it hadn't been for you, I would have died in it."

Gren paused. "You hear them too, don't you?"

Raeyn nodded quietly. "Every day."

"Will you..." Gren licked his cracked lips. "Are you here to end it, *Somnifere?*"

I dimly caught the meaning of the word *Somnifere.* Sleep bringer. Some old-fashioned euphemism for doctors who put their patients out of their misery. I realized I'd never asked what kind of doctor Raeyn was. Gods.

"I want it to be over, Raeyn. Please. As you love me, don't make me beg for it."

Raeyn closed his eyes. Bent over Gren's hand. "If you are certain that is what you want."

Gren nodded, his thumb stroking slow circles over Raeyn's fingers. "I am. Please."

There was a long pause before Raeyn reached into the inside of his coat and pulled out a syringe along with a vial of clear liquid. Going by Raeyn's tightly shuttered expression, it wasn't just another sedative to help Gren calm down.

It strangely reminded me of the time he'd pulled out a similar vial before he'd dosed Aris outside of the Red Garter a few days ago. One to save a life, another to kill—he didn't seem to have any issues keeping them apart. Either he was used to carrying half a pharmacy around with him wherever he went, or he'd packed for the occasion.

A cold shudder ran down my back when I realized whatever Raeyn carried, it had to be as deadly as the arsenal I'd left out in Ferris's locker. The only drawback was Raeyn had to get close to people first. Real close. But in the end, a well-aimed needle killed as fast as a well-aimed bullet.

"Thank you," Gren sighed while Raeyn drew up the syringe. Raeyn's movements were smooth and efficient, like he'd done the same thing countless times before. Maybe he had.

It was Raeyn's voice, not his hands, that trembled when he asked, one last time, "Gren, are you sure you want this?"

"I'm sure."

Raeyn exhaled. Closed his eyes and bent over Gren in silent prayer.

Gren let out something close to a content sigh when the needle went into the bruised crook of his arm. "Raeyn, did you ever find him? Your bro—"

He cut off when Raeyn placed two fingers against Gren's cracked lips. "Shhh, don't worry about it." After a pause, he added, "I think so."

"Oh, good. That's..." Blindly, he fumbled for Raeyn's hand again. "Raeyn?"

Raeyn's fingers interlaced with his. "Hm?"

"Make sure your father won't find him."

"I will. Don't worry."

"Good." His throat clicked when he nodded. "If you see Raeyn, tell him, I—" Gren spiraled, lost his thread. "I think, I'd like to sleep a little now."

"*Bon passage, amour*," Raeyn whispered and leaned forward, gently kissing Gren's chapped lips.

A beatific smile spread over Gren's face, smoothing out some of the pain lines as he went. His chest fell once more before his hand slid out of Raeyn's and fell limply to his side. Raeyn sat frozen in place, eyes fixed on the still face. The syringe fell from his fingers and clattered to the ground.

Raeyn rose to his feet and left the room.

Pascal had hung back but now moved in like a shadow between the swaths of white curtains and the rumpled covers of Gren's bed. They gestured for Aris to help pull up the top sheet to cover Gren's mutilated face. Pascal fished two large coins out of their pocket and placed the silver where Gren's eyes had been, then lit a single candle on the nightstand. Its light was a small, pale thing compared to the sunlight that flooded the room, but they'd keep it burning for a day and a night just as people had done in the old days.

During all of it, I stood, useless and out-of-place. A piece of furniture someone'd crammed into a room already too full.

"Uh, I guess I'd better go check on him." I jerked my head toward the door.

"Good idea," Aris said. The gray tinge of his face put a lie to the thin smile probably meant to be reassuring.

Honestly, I would've preferred to help them with the body.

I found Raeyn outside perched on the stoop, knees drawn up, fumbling with a lighter and a cigarette. All the pompous arrogance had gone out of him as he sat there with empty, red-rimmed eyes, his black trench drawn close around himself. He looked awfully tired.

I took the lighter from his unresisting fingers. It flicked to life, the small flame chasing dark hollows across Raeyn's face. I lit the cigarette for him and he took a deep draw, watching the smoke dissipate in the cold morning air as he exhaled. None of us said anything for a while.

Raeyn flicked away some ash and I caught a flash of his wrist, his skin red and angry where Gren had burned him. "Should get that checked out."

Raeyn pulled down his sleeve. "It's fine. I've had worse."

My eyes narrowed when I took in his scars. "He didn't—" My mouth suddenly went dry. "Shit, he didn't do this to you, did he?"

Raeyn's eyes widened at the implication. He let out a dry, shaky laugh. "No, Gods. No. Gren saved my life. He came when I needed him, even after I ended things." He left it dangling there, let me try and put together the pieces. "He pulled me out of the fire that was supposed to kill me," Raeyn said finally, lighting his second cigarette. He'd tossed the first one, only half finished, and watched it slowly flare up red, then extinguish in a wisp of smoke.

"They had been testing Voyants, mostly children, in the Empire's labs for years. Snatched them off the street, all under the guise of giving them a chance to make it without ending up at one of those Low Side orphanages that would just sell them to Nightshade anyway. Or worse. You know."

I nodded. Fuck, I knew all about what "or worse" meant.

"They claimed they were looking for ways to control the Voyance," Raeyn said. "To find out where it came from, even cure it. It was madness. The Voyants all died. Heart failure, aneurysms, take your pick. The tests killed them. I saw a boy who—"

Raeyn shook his head, the cigarette all but forgotten in his hand. "I tried to get my father to end it. I thought if I'd get the kids out and get Gren to help me burn the lab, Father would stop. That it would save a few of them at least. I was so naive. He knew, of course. He had known all along." Raeyn stared off into the distance for a minute before he continued. "The detonators were rigged to finish me off with the rest. It all happened too fast. All I remember is Gren kicking that door in. I don't know how he got me out." A glimmer of despair crossed his eyes. "There were twenty-seven people in there that night. Most of them kids. I killed them. Thinking I did the right thing." Raeyn laughed, a dead, breathless sound. "I guess that total comes to twenty-eight now."

I swallowed. What did you say to that? Guess this was the more elaborate version of what the Empire passed off as the accident that'd resulted in the president's son's tragic death.

Of all the things that did pop into my head in the lingering silence, I said, "I killed a girl the Reds Cleansed that night you threw me into that river." Why the hells was I telling him this? What did it even have to do with anything? "I thought I was doing her a favor, that it was some kind of mercy." I cut off. The memory of those empty eyes made me shiver.

A bitter smile tugged at the corner of Raeyn's mouth. "Look at the skeletons in our closets. All covered-up under a heaping layer of good intentions."

He flicked away the last remnants of his dying cigarette and brushed the ash off his coat. "I'm babbling. I'm sorry. I didn't mean for you to see this." He fidgeted with his hat that'd fallen by his side. "I didn't think Gren would be this far gone already."

"Well, if you meant to show us how much the Voyance fucks you up, then yeah, you made your point."

Raeyn winced. "Gren held out longer than most. All things considered."

"And in the end, he's dead all the same. That what you meant to show us? That even the Temple's no guarantee?"

"That's just it. Gren never went to the Temple. He never learned to control it. He stayed with me until..." Raeyn trailed off. "I'm not going to lie to you. The Temple is a chance. No more. No less. I want you to know the Temple takes care of its own. Even in the end."

"Well, good to know." I didn't even try to keep the sarcasm out of my voice. "If all goes to hells, at least there's a place where they'll let you die. Sure Aris will appreciate that."

"He knows his options. The Temple has been very clear on this from the first time he contacted them." Raeyn watched me, his eyes hard like a frozen lake in winter. "It's you I wanted to come. I thought you needed to see for yourself. Pascal, Aemelia, and the rest of them, they're good people. They will do what they can to keep him safe."

I still pondered Raeyn's definition of "good people" when we went back inside to see Aris off with Pascal. That and how much I prayed I'd never have to make the kind of choice Raeyn'd just made for Aris when it came to it, because Gods, I knew I wouldn't walk away from it. I forced the thought from my head, forced myself not to hold on to Aris, not to cling.

"You better stay in touch," I said, my voice catching. "Remember, Jay's going to kick your ass if you forget us."

"How could I ever forget you?" Aris smiled. "Tell her not to worry so much, okay?"

Maybe Raeyn was right. It was a chance. In the end, what else could you ask for?

And yet here we were, both pretending this wasn't goodbye. Pretending we didn't know this was the end.

The thought followed me all the way back to the *Shadow*, lingering longer than that last taste of Aris's lips on mine before he'd disappeared with Pascal into the cold fog of an early Helos morning.

Part Two

Decoy

12

Witch Hunt

"WHY THE FUCK do I have to do all the body-dragging?"

"Because," Raeyn said, "to quote you, we fucked up. No, let me rephrase, *you* fucked up. And now quit whining and do your job."

I wanted to strangle him. Him and his pompous airs who'd gotten the Red to sneak up on him in the first place. And how did he thank me for saving his sorry ass by cutting the guy's throat before he got the chance to call his buddies? Figures.

Should've made this a solo run instead of taking up Raeyn's offer to fill in for Jay. This had gone from minor pickup of some gear from Staxx's vendors to major disaster thanks to Raeyn's tendency to mouth off and get noticed. Wasn't my fault it was easier to kill a Red than come up with something elaborate to distract them these days.

It'd been over three months since I'd dropped Aris off at the Temple and teamed up with Raeyn. After Taerien's plans to off Valyr'd gone kaput, he and Raeyn had to lay low for a while. My job was to make sure none of Valyr's flunkies got too close to either of them and their plotting. It didn't help Raeyn was terrible at sitting still and hiding like any halfway decent fugitive. Claimed he'd rather take whatever was out there head-on. Meaning he stuck with me. At least I could keep an eye on him that way and stop him from getting himself killed.

"Seriously surprises me you haven't stuck a Dumb Muscle label to my forehead yet."

"You want one? Why didn't you say so before?"

I growled something in Raeyn's general direction as I lugged the dead weight of the Red with me through this godsforsaken rain. He was a heavy bastard, even with his coat stripped off. Raeyn had put it on, not without complaining how he had to resort to cheap masquerade tricks. I stopped listening after a while.

The downpour that'd caught up on us had two benefits. One, the rain washed away our tracks from the riverside as we dumped the body. Two, it kept away any random bystanders. Said something about this part of Helos that nobody as much as raised an eyebrow at two guys quietly getting rid of a body by the East River.

Lately, most of Low Side had completely fucking lost it.

The place'd been swarming with Reds for months and things had gone down hard. People wouldn't go out more than they absolutely had to, what with the curfew the Empire put into place. The Watch arrested people left and right, for whatever flimsy reason they could come up with. The Place du Marché had shut down. Business had gone from shit to nonexistent.

"A shame how low the palace's standards must have fallen if they let individuals like this one join the Watch." Raeyn sniffed the high collar of the coat and wrinkled his nose. "This thing smells, and look at the man. I bet he hasn't even heard of a close shave."

"Yeah, whatever. You're just throwing a fit because you had to leave your trench and that ridiculous hat behind."

"Am not." Raeyn gave me a sour look and flicked a strand of wet, silvery hair out of his face. "Also, I have the best intentions of getting my clothes back, thank you very much. Do you know how much a genuine fedora costs?"

I didn't give a shit about his fancy headwear, but any retort I might've had died in my throat when we passed the gallows. The Empire hadn't hanged anyone since the Dark Days, the riots that'd ended with most of Low Side burned down decades ago. Now, three corpses hung, strung up on the scaffolding by the riverside. They must've been there for days, rotting entrails spilling from their slit bellies like too much stuffing out of a pillow.

I might've known them when they'd been alive. Death turned them into strangers, eyeless scarecrows after the ravens had their pick at them, the caves of their eyes and mouths gaping empty.

"Dear Gods," Raeyn whispered.

"The Gods got nothing to do with that," I said and walked toward the river, where the water was deep and the current strong enough to take the Red's body down and away. "Here looks good enough." I let go of the dead guy's shoulders. The body flopped into the water with a slurp. It didn't drift off right away, and I gave it a shove with my right foot for good measure.

"You don't weigh it down?" Raeyn asked. "Isn't that proper body-dumping etiquette?"

"Gods, you're kidding, right?" I laughed, couldn't help it, soaking-wet and aching from dragging some dead-ass carcass across town. Proper body-dumping etiquette. Bullshit. "Don't they teach you anything, growing up with all those Reds around you? You'd think this is your first time doing this kind of thing."

The corner of Raeyn's mouth twitched impatiently. "It may surprise you, but not everyone relies on murder as their primary source of income."

"Yeah, I forgot. You were born with a golden spoon. Up your ass."

Raeyn snorted and started covering up our tracks in the mud. "Aren't you worried the Watch will find him?"

I shrugged and crouched to clean my bloody knife in the stream. "They'll find him, all right. They always do. Doesn't really matter in the end. The river gives us time to get our asses back where we belong—a long way *away* from the body. That and the water will make sure they have a harder time finding out what the hells happened to the poor bastard. Ever seen a body that's been in the water for a while?"

Raeyn made a face. "No. And I don't particularly care to."

"Good for you. And ditch that coat. Can't risk anyone asking stupid questions."

For once Raeyn did as he was told without complaint, dumped the red leather into the river, and watched it sink, hugging himself against the cold.

I stood up and wiped my knife on my pants. It was still wet when I shoved it back into its sheath under my jacket. Aris would've given me hells about how it'd get dull and rusty that way. Knives had always been more his thing. Not like he needed them anymore. Not with the kind of shit he could do with the Voyance. He'd probably be able to vaporize the Red. Bye-bye evidence. I chased the thought away. Last time I'd heard from Aris, he was working for the Temple now and things were going great. That'd been a few days after we'd seen him off. For the last three months, it'd been radio silence. Better he kept his distance. Safer that way.

Least that's what I told myself.

"Let's get out of here." We wiped our tracks as best we could. The body had drifted downriver and would be well out of range until the Reds found him. The rain would take care of the rest. "Don't know about you, but I need a drink." Or three.

Anything to blur the memory of those bodies, gently turning in the wind.

Raeyn flashed me a grin and I tried very hard not to notice the tight stretch of already rain-soaked fabric across his chest and arms. "I thought you'd never ask. But first, we're getting my coat and hat."

Which would've been fine if Raeyn hadn't stopped in front of every godsdamned light pole along the way to rip off the holosheet election posters the Empire'd hung.

"Shit, would you quit it already?" I grabbed his wrist as he was about to tear down the corner of the second poster to join its twin in the gutter. The rain made it spark red and black before it went down the drain. "That one Red wasn't enough for you? You'd almost think you *want* to get caught."

The muscles in Raeyn's jaw clenched as he stared at the holosheet like his eyes could burn a hole through its transparent glare. Like hundreds of copies scattered all over Helos, it featured close-ups of the president's stylized face, gray eyes piercing in a face framed by silver hair and a matching silver beard, the gleaming sun symbols of the Empire decorating the collar of his red coat. A bobblehead on posters and holoscreens reminding people of their duty to cast their votes as citizens of the Empire in the upcoming elections.

"You know, Father has always had a knack for crowds. Called it his special gift."

"He's the president. He damn well better be good with that stuff."

"Not what I meant." The sheet crumpled in Raeyn's fist. "It's a farce. All of it."

I shrugged but didn't let go of his arm. His skin felt impossibly soft against mine. "'Course it is. Tell me something new, Nymeron."

"Farce" pretty much summed up the whole bloody Empire since it'd been founded nearly thirty years ago. Not exactly long ago as far as governments went, the Empire'd been a long time in the making till it just seemed like the next logical step: drawing together a world that was already pretty much one nation. Consolidation to end conflict. One Nation to govern all. All that bullshit. Old slogans now, but back then, it'd made sense, what with the world falling apart and everyone fighting over the few scraps of resources left.

At some point, sides became irrelevant. All came down to who carried the biggest stick. 'Course they never passed it off that way. There was the pretense of adhering to democratic principles and regular "free elections" to avoid pissing off all who'd scream for revolution otherwise. Calling their central government "Empire" had been a stretch, but people'd let it fly and kept casting their votes every five years, never mind there was only one party on the ballot.

"Nothing you can do, 'side from getting your ass arrested and how well's that going to go over, huh?"

"Hm." Raeyn's voice didn't match the hard set of his mouth. His eyes went distant, when he said, all silky smooth, "As a matter of fact, I have an idea or two."

"Why did I know you'd say something like that?"

Always surprised me how much Raeyn hated his father. He never talked about what'd happened. He didn't need to. Raeyn's face never gave anything away for free. The way it shut down at the mere mention of his father told me everything I needed to know and then some.

I shook my head and realized I was still holding his wrist, his pulse beating against mine. I let go and looked away. Just being around Raeyn made a headache build between my eyes.

"Anyway, now the Empire's property is safe from you for the moment, how about that drink?"

I barely caught Raeyn's nod. He snatched his hat and trench from where he'd left them, dangling from a tree branch outside of the Dregs. Not like they'd do him much good, drenched as they were, along with the rest of his clothes. He still donned his hat and wrapped his coat around himself tight like armor. Out of the corner of my eye, I saw him twist the piece he'd ripped off the second poster in his hands. He stared at it for a good minute before he finally tossed it into a puddle by the wayside and followed me through the rain.

The old neon sign in front of Tarantino's was switched to Closed. I knocked on the door. The sign flickered with a staticky sound. The door slid open with a tinny screech and one of Coras's bouncers gave me the hairy eyeball. "We're closed. Go home."

"Right," I drawled and tipped him two hundred credits. Standard cover charge these days. Coras knew how to milk those desperate for a quiet drink. "I'm sure Viv will make an exception."

The bouncer grunted and shoved the door open wide enough to let me and Raeyn through. It shut behind us and we traded the cold and rain outside for a thick stew of sweat, smoke, and alcohol. Some things hadn't changed; no matter how bad it got, Coras's bar still stayed the same divey shit hole. At least it was a dry, divey shit hole.

The barkeep was new, not one of Coras's kids who usually helped out. This kid had freckles and greasy hair somewhere between red and brown. She slouched behind the bar, eyeing us and the water we trailed behind with even less enthusiasm than the bouncer. Good thing we weren't here for the hospitality. I plopped down on one of the scuffed seats and ordered two of whatever Coras had managed to smuggle past the Reds.

"I didn't know you wanted to lose your eyesight along with all your brain cells," Raeyn said, his fedora drawn deep into his face, rain dripping on the counter. He frowned at the clear content of his glass.

"It was good enough for you last time, wasn't it?" I said. "Or maybe you didn't notice, because you were too busy groping me."

Shouldn't've brought it up because with it came the memory of how soft Raeyn's lips had been and part of me desperately wanted to do it again. Preferably without getting shot. Gods, shit must've been getting to me worse than I'd thought if I was sitting here fantasizing about the way he'd smelled, all wrapped around me, bringing on a want I knew fuck all what to do with.

"Oh, that." A crooked grin tugged at the corner of Raeyn's mouth. He gave me a slow once-over, making it feel like he was peeling back my black pants and shirt clinging to me like a second skin, brushing over slick black hair plastered to my forehead. Fuck, guess I wasn't the only one who'd noticed how wet clothes left little to the imagination. Raeyn took in all of it with an expression sparking a warmth in my core that rapidly traveled lower. "I'm afraid there isn't much to get distracted by. Other than an appallingly loose tongue."

"Whatever." I knocked my drink back in one shot, hoping the stuff wouldn't eat right through my esophagus as it went down. If anything, it might warm me up a little and dull the nagging headache that made even the soft greenish light a little too bright as it painted flickering shadows against the patchy walls.

"How about a chaser?" I asked the barkeep, who glared at me with the same scowl she'd given me when we'd first came in.

"Tap's closed." Before I could turn to the voice behind me, a hand landed on my shoulder, yanked me away from the bar, and smacked me into the wall behind me.

"Shit, Coras, talk about a friendly welcome." I spat blood from a split lip. Coras stood above me, Squinty Eyes from the door at their side, another one of their female bouncers holding Raeyn pinned at the counter. Raeyn got a leg up, tried to claw her off him, but only managed to get himself slammed back down, hard enough I could've sworn I heard his ribs crack.

"Sorry," Coras looked like they meant it. They shoved me back at Squinty Eyes. "You lost the privilege of a friendly welcome when you trashed my place last time, remember?"

Coras stalked over to Raeyn and yanked his hat off. "And *then* you come back and bring a fucking fugitive into my bar. Any idea what the Reds would do if they found him here after what you and that Burner of yours pulled? Sure as shit won't be friendly, Nettoyer."

"Since when do you give a damn about the Reds, Coras?"

"I don't." Coras sauntered over to the bar and drew a knife out from under their counter. "What I do care about is getting things back to normal. Might've slipped past you, but some of us make a life out of normal. Even if it's a shitty one. It takes care of spouses, kids, fixes the shit you like to break whenever you turn up. And I wonder how I can get that back?" Coras stepped behind Raeyn and turned the knife over, a gleam of light flashing through the semi-darkness of the bar. "Got a feeling that pale-eyed friend of yours might do the trick. Nothing personal." They nodded to their two goons. "Take him."

"You fucking wish."

No way was I going to break Squinty Eyes' grip on me. I wasn't exactly short, but the guy was the human equivalent of an anvil. Lucky me, he was also slow like one. Before he could haul me forward and crack my head open on Coras's countertops, I twisted and rammed the heel of my right hand into his nose. It broke with a crunch. Howling, the guy jerked back far enough for me to get a hold of my Colt and empty half my clip into him. Distracted by her buddy being filled with lead, the woman holding Raeyn slipped up and bent double when Raeyn's knee drove into her abdomen.

"And here I thought we could have made friends," Raeyn ground out between punches. "I think I'm beginning to see why they say bars aren't the right place for that." He spun around to me, his face alight with fake exasperation as he dodged another hit. "Why is it every time we come here, we end up having to shoot people?"

"Do me a favor and try not to shoot me this time," I pushed past a set of overturned chairs, trying to get a fix on either Coras or their barkeep. Just in time to get a glimpse of black swishing through the backdoor, a battered mammoth of a cell phone cradled to her chest. The cracked screen lit up green. Shit. The kid was calling in the troops.

The smoke hanging low in the air made my eyes water. I blinked to clear the white and gray swirls away. Not that it did me much good. The kid was gone in a flash. Smart enough to get out while the getting was good. As for Coras—

"Raeyn," I called. "Let's—Shit, watch out!"

"What?" He stopped kicking the shit out of the bouncer who was clearly too stubborn to lie down and quit already. Still, Raeyn moved a tick too late and suddenly Coras was behind him, one hand yanking his head back, the other holding their knife to his throat. "Oh."

"Yeah. That." My breath hitched. I aimed my Colt at Coras. They weren't impressed.

"Ah, a classic standoff," they said with a small grin. "Guess my line in this would be 'freeze and drop your fucking gun or your friend here is toast,' but I like you, Nettoyer, so why don't we wait until Lem comes back with the Reds instead?"

That confirmed where the kid had slunk off to. Shit.

Raeyn stood perfectly still. Drops of red clung to the blade where Coras had nicked him.

"Since when do you keep Red spies on payroll, Coras?" I kept my Colt on them, just lowered it a bit, because their head was getting blurry and when in doubt, aim for the core. I didn't want to shoot them, but I'd be damned if I missed and took Raeyn out by accident.

I blinked. Fuck me, since when was missing even an option?

Sweat trickled down the back of my neck, and I fought the urge to wipe my sleeve across my forehead. When had it gotten so hot in here?

Focus.

I barely heard Coras over the rushing in my ears. I saw their lips move, but only caught the tail end of what they said. "...after that shit storm you, your boy toy, and Pale Eyes here cooked up with Valyr. By the way, did I say thank you for that yet?"

"Only about three or four times in the last five minutes." I squinted. My head felt like it was stuffed with cotton balls. "Anyway, go ahead and kill him if you want," I nodded toward Raeyn staring at me, eyes wide. "Don't expect me to wait around for it. I'm out. Have fun with the Reds, Coras."

My voice sounded hollow, my steps muffled as I slowly backed toward the door.

"*Damian*," Raeyn hissed through his teeth.

I didn't look at him. Kept my eyes, and my aim, on Coras. Surprise flickered across their face. "Wouldn't've taken you for the kind of coward who leaves his people behind, Nettoyer."

"See, there's the thing. He's not my people."

I almost sounded like I believed it.

Gods, I wished I did. Then I could leave Raeyn, have Coras and the Reds take care of him. Wouldn't even break my contract, strictly speaking. After all, I'd tried. 'Course Taerien would never see it that way. That, and Raeyn'd saved my ass one too many times for me to just ditch him. I owed him more than that.

Talk about hells of a shitty timing for my conscience to come knocking.

I took another step toward the back door before the room tilted sideways. I caught myself at the corner of the counter.

Coras frowned, or I thought they did, because their face blurred, stretched like a piece of gum someone'd peeled out from under their boots.

"You okay, Nettoyer?" Coras asked from very far away. "You don't look so good."

I scoffed. It came out as a choked-off cough. "Worried I'd miss, Coras?" I let go of the counter and used both my hands to steady my Colt. I left a sweaty handprint behind. "Should know me better by now."

I could hit Coras with both eyes closed. If the room quit wavering for a second. Something thumped against the door at my back. Sounded more like a boot trying to kick the door in than a knock. Fuck me if that traitorous barkeep didn't have the Reds on speed dial or something. It all drifted to the background at the look Coras gave me. Their nails stood out white around the knife against Raeyn's throat.

"You know what I think?" Coras's smile melted into a grimace, their dark eyes glinting like cut glass. "I think you're bluffing."

Specks of light caught on the edge of the bottles lining the shelf in the back of Coras's bar. In the whole place, they were probably the only things not covered in dust or grime, most of them empty save for fading labels in scrawled handwriting. The gleam became blinding, a supernova of broken reflections.

Coras brought the knife down in an arc of silver across Raeyn's throat.

"No!" The shout was out before the blade bit into skin. The pounding between my ears almost drowned it out. It turned outward, a sound like a gust of wind whooshing through a narrowly cracked door. The bottles behind Coras's bar exploded in a sparkling scatter of glass, drenched in alcohol and splatters of red.

I barely saw Raeyn twist away from Coras in a trail of red. Coras's head snapped back, and they crumpled to the floor in a boneless heap. All I could make out were sketchy outlines and bright streaks of negative images. Then all the color leached out of them and everything around me whited out.

The front door flew open. The fall of heavy boots echoed across the wooden floorboards.

Eventually the white cleared out, and I found myself curled up on the ground, the steel-toed boot of a Red only inches from my face.

Well, fuck.

Didn't help that I'd dropped my Colt or that my head felt like someone'd worked it over with a jackhammer. I tasted blood at the back of my throat. More gushed out of my nose, dripping on the floor. A pair of leather gloves fisted in the collar of my shirt and yanked me to my feet, backed me against the counter.

"Well, I'll be damned if I didn't show up in time for things to get interesting," Orion Kovacz drawled, his jaw set in a hard curve, the collar of his red coat nearly brushing against half a day's worth of blond stubble.

A few months back, Kovacz had made good on one of his rather ambitious ideas and joined the ranks of the Reds. For connections, he'd claimed. Infiltration, being a step ahead of them by being one of them and whatnot. Looked like he had way too much fun with the real deal.

"Never thought I'd say this about a Red, but damn, I'm glad to see you, Kovacz," I said.

Behind his glasses, Kovacz's eyes were cold as glaciers.

"Don't even fucking talk to me, Nettoyer." Kovacz's voice was a hiss underneath his breath. "How long's this been going on?"

I blinked at my arm, lifted to wipe my bloody nose, now hanging limp and forgotten by my side, blood trickling onto the collar of my shirt. "What?"

A breathy laugh rippled through Kovacz's anger. "Clever move, really. Getting Aris out of the picture and make everyone think it'd solve our little Burner problem, when you were one of them all along."

"What the—" I shook my head. Bad idea. It set off the jackhammers again. Kovacz's face blurred. Then it hit me where I'd seen the look Kovacz gave me before. I almost puked on Kovacz's shiny boots.

It'd been here, a few feet away. Right before I'd put a bullet into that Red's head. Before Valyr had crashed Raeyn's plan to hump my leg just enough for any overzealous Reds to turn their backs while we snuck out.

"Get the hells away from me, you abomination."

"Your eyes!"

It'd been months ago, but it all came back to me now. Things had happened too fast for me to even think about back then, but I remembered how it'd felt. Like I was ready to lose it. Pass out. Anything. The rushing in my ears, like some amplified heartbeat. The way everything had turned white for a second, like some reversal of a drunken blackout.

My stomach dropped about ten stories.

No. No fucking way.

Finally, I translated that look on Kovacz's face. It clicked like the safety coming off right before someone fired a slug into your skull.

It hadn't been Kovacz who'd knocked Coras out and burst all those glasses and lights overhead. It'd been me. I'd used the Voyance. All Kovacz had done was kick that door down and gotten a front row ticket to the show. This was just the fucking grand finale.

Oh Gods.

Shards of glass scattered around me, broken reflections of Kovacz's cold stare. My throat closed up, panic worming itself to the top, making my stomach lurch like the telltale signs of a terrible hangover. Instead of letting it spill to the surface, I locked it down, tried to keep my face blank the way Raeyn always did.

"I have no idea what you're talking about, Kovacz."

Kovacz choked out a dry laugh, his lip curling when he pushed me away. "If I had any sense, I'd turn you in along with that fucker Nymeron, you know that?"

I kept my mouth shut and pretended not to notice how he wiped his gloved hand on his leather coat as if the Voyance was contagious and he'd catch it just by touching me.

Kovacz shook his head. "Yet here I am, saving your worthless ass."

And like that, the world went back to normal speed, like Kovacz's whispered little interval had been nothing but a blip on a holoscreen. One of those dots flashing in the corner of the screen, gone so quickly you wouldn't notice unless you stared right at it and it'd leave a glaring imprint whenever you blinked.

"I'll take it from here, kid," Kovacz said aloud and stepped over to where the wide-eyed barkeep was back, pointing a gun at Raeyn. Her grip was steady enough, but I'd bet she barely knew which end to point. Also, it was my fucking Colt she was holding. Sneaky little shit.

Raeyn could've easily knocked it out of her grasp. Instead, he watched the chaos with a look of mild interest bordering on amusement. He kept his hand pressed to his throat, red leaking through his fingers.

"I'll take that as well," Kovacz said and took my Colt from the kid's unresisting fingers. "If you want to be helpful, go see to your boss and stay out of my way."

Kovacz didn't need to ask twice. The kid shuffled over to Coras, who was still out cold next to one dead bouncer and another who'd probably wish she was, once she woke up from the beating she'd taken.

"Don't stand there, Nettoyer. Move." Kovacz shoved my Colt at me, careful not to touch me. "We don't pay you for standing around twiddling your thumbs." His own gun was out and aimed at Raeyn's chest. "Make sure he doesn't drip all over the place."

Not sure what Kovacz was playing at, giving up my former cover to the kid who was busy leaning over Coras. Guess it was only fair for Kovacz as a fake Red to lure Coras's little spy with my fake cover. Whatever kept them from wondering why Raeyn was the only one leaving this place in handcuffs.

I wasn't going to argue. Instead, I snatched one of Coras's cleaner dish towels from the bar and dabbed at the gash across Raeyn's throat. He watched me with steady eyes, no reaction even when Kovacz forced his arms back to slap a pair of handcuffs on his wrists.

"Just tie it off," he hissed when a piece of cloth caught at the edge of his wound. "I promise I will try to restrain myself from fainting into your arms from blood loss, *darling*."

I tried to find some sort of sign Raeyn had put two and two together. Had he seen what I'd done? Damn me if I could read anything in that carefully blank face of his. Nothing but faint amusement at my awkwardness. I loosely tied the towel around his throat, the fabric already staining red, then turned away and followed Kovacz who shoved Raeyn at the door.

"Hey, what about my money?" the kid asked, crouching on the balls of her feet. The girl's face was even more freckled and scrunched up from that angle.

"Right," Kovacz said and tossed her a stack of credits. "Well done, uh, Lem, wasn't it? Next time make sure your boss keeps to curfew."

Lem bobbed an eager nod, her fingers visibly itching to count the money right then and there. I hadn't noticed how skinny she was before.

No wonder the Reds didn't have any shortage of spies if all they had to do was pick starving kids off the street.

"You owe me two-and-a-half thousand credits," Kovacz whispered when I followed him and Raeyn outside.

It'd stopped raining, so we merely trudged through puddles and overflowing gutters for a block or two until Raeyn stopped in his tracks in the middle of one of the narrow back alleys leading down to the Poubelle.

"All right, we can quit the charade." He held out his hands to Kovacz. "The handcuffs, if you would."

Kovacz snorted. "What makes you think I'll let you go, Nymeron? All I need to do to get you off my and Damian's ass forever is hand you over to the president. Now that's a reunion I'd want to see. Wouldn't you?"

Raeyn froze, the tendons of his wrists standing out taut against the handcuffs. "You wouldn't."

"Try me." Kovacz shoved the tip of his gun against the base of Raeyn's neck. "Unless you prefer to get it over with right here and now."

"Cut the bullshit, Kovacz," I cut in. "If you think I'm going to stand here and let you shoot him or hand him over to your Red friends, you better fucking think again."

"Oh yeah? What are you going to do about it?" Kovacz tracked me like he expected me to use the Voyance to cook his brains in his skull or something. His expression made the contents of my stomach curdle.

Instead I drew my Colt on Kovacz, barrel shoved underneath his jaw. "How 'bout settling it the old-fashioned way?" My voice dropped to a whisper. "Unlock his cuffs, Kovacz."

"Why? What's he to you, huh? Damn it, Nettoyer, I'm doing you a favor here."

I wondered if Kovacz knew he was pretty much echoing what I'd said to Coras before. Maybe part of me should've agreed with him. It didn't. "I gave him my word, Kovacz."

Which wasn't exactly true. My deal was with Taerien and on grounds of some serious blackmail. Still didn't mean I'd stand here and watch Kovacz blow Raeyn's brains out.

Raeyn mightn't be my people, but fuck me if he wasn't my responsibility.

"I said, let him go."

I could see the muscles of Kovacz's jaw jump as he bit off a reply and opened his hands, slowly lowering his gun before shoving it back into its holster. He unlocked Raeyn's cuffs and tossed the keys. They fell into a puddle, neither of us bothering to pick them up.

"Well," Raeyn said, his voice still a bit rough around the edges as he rubbed his wrists and fingered the cloth I'd tied around his throat. By now the front was soggy with blood. "Thanks. I suppose."

I waved him off. "Let's get back to the *Shadow* and patch you up, because if you fall over, I'm not going to carry you."

Kovacz snorted. "You go ahead. Some of us have some honest spying to do."

He'd already turned away before he stopped and pulled something out from the inside of his coat. "Speaking of, thought you might like to see this."

He handed me a folded holosheet. It wasn't even half the size of one of those presidential election posters, the corners half ripped off from where it'd been stapled, the edges fritzing and damp from the rain. In the center of it was Aris's face. I made out enough of the text shorting out across the page to get the Empire was looking for him and they'd posted a hefty reward for pointers to his whereabouts.

My blood ran cold.

"These went live a couple hours ago," Kovacz said and pushed his glasses up his nose. "Three months and they've finally made it official. Looks like someone really wants to find him if they're willing to admit what happened. And here we thought things were calming down. Wonder how long it's going to take them to toss that Temple of his."

13

In Plain Sight

FIGURED ARIS WOULD pick a brothel as his perfect hideout. Not sure what I'd expected the Temple to be like after what I'd seen with Raeyn and Aris at *L'Oubliette*. Some ramshackle ruin with airs of grandeur, maybe something with catacombs. Something more...templish.

Sure as shit nothing like this.

Outside, the place called *La Maison* looked like any other warehouse crouching at the edge of Nightshade in a patchwork of sagging roofs and flaky brick walls with boarded-up doors and windows. There was a small copper plaque by the door, the surface so scratched the writing was almost illegible. It was the only thing that marked this place as *La Maison*, a small number underneath claiming it had been established sometime in the last century or so.

A bald black guy in a gray suit leaned against the wall, pretending to smoke a cigarette while giving me the once-over. He acknowledged me with the barest nod. The Temple kept their bouncers on the down low. Interesting.

The front door clashed with the run-down warehouse image. It was massive, shaped like a gate, a black arch outlined with iron studs, its handles shaped into heavy knockers. I lifted one, creaky with rust, and let it fall against the solid dark wood.

One wing of the door opened inward. A white girl in similar clothes as the bouncer on the street smiled at me brightly, waving me through to the lobby.

I fought not to stare. It was as if someone had stripped the presidential palace and threw the façade of some Nightshade dump over it, covering it like one of those white sheets protecting furniture from dust.

The floors and walls were white marble; in the glow of the glass chandelier dangling from a vaulted ceiling, they shone like something carved out of ice.

Yeah, this was definitely Aris's kind of place.

I caught myself before running my fingers over the smooth stone when one of the girls in what I now recognized as livery piped up. "Sir? Your invitation and I.D., if you please?"

Sir? Seriously? Shit. It had to be the clothes. I felt ridiculous.

Raeyn had nearly gone into apoplectic shock when he'd seen me in what I thought was perfectly acceptable whoring attire. Which was exactly what I was already wearing: black, practical, wouldn't show blood too obviously.

"You have got to be kidding me," Raeyn said when I stitched him back together a couple hours earlier. "Are you trying to get thrown out of *La Maison*?"

His chin was smooth under my fingers, but I could tell by how tense he was, his shoulders all stiff angles, that he didn't much like me touching his scars. Tough luck. Coras had cut him deep enough, just gluing the skin of his throat back together wouldn't do. It'd take stitches and a lot of touching neither of us was too happy with.

"It's a brothel, Nymeron. Pretty sure Nightshade's all about taking your clothes *off*."

Raeyn raised an eyebrow, amusement sparking in his eyes. Up close, they were way too pale, gleaming like the edge of a knife. "Well, if this is what you wear whenever you frequent Nightshade—oh, wait, I forgot, you don't. Maybe that's your problem. Which would explain your abysmal mood since Aris left."

"You're pushing it, Nymeron," I growled. We were so not having this conversation.

"More than abysmal," Raeyn corrected, visibly trying not to wince as I pushed the needle through his skin. "Which reinforces how badly you need to get laid, darl—" He hissed. "Gods, you're not supposed to stab me with that thing."

"And you're supposed to keep your mouth shut." I glared and pulled the thread tight. Good thing his neck was already webbed with scars, they'd cover up the piss-poor job I was doing with this one.

"All right," Raeyn said through his teeth. "I'm much more interested in hearing you talk anyway. Let's start with how you almost got me killed."

The silence lasted long enough for me to get the last stitches in, then I said, "Maybe Coras was right, Nymeron. Maybe I was bluffing. Too bad you'll never know."

Except we both knew I'd never have left him behind. Not anymore.

Raeyn gave me a long look, like he could see right through me. "I'm actually quite curious as to what exactly happened that made all those glasses explode while also knocking Coras out. Awfully fast reflexes on your part. I could have sworn I didn't even see you move."

Raeyn's eyes steadied on me, calculating. My mouth went dry. He knew. He fucking *knew*. I stopped in the middle of taping a gauze pad to his throat, my hands still, waiting for him to state the obvious. For the word Voyance to come out of his mouth.

"Of course, I was rather busy getting my throat cut at the time." Raeyn took the tape from my numb fingers and fixed his bandage.

He knew. Clearly. But he was holding back on purpose. Very much like him and the rest of the Empire to sit on everyone's secrets until they were useful to them. But Raeyn already had me where he needed me. What else could he possibly want?

Jay interrupted my train of thought, pushing through the door, dragging a heavy leather trunk behind her. It landed on the greenish linoleum floor with a heavy thud.

"There you go," she said to Raeyn. "Costume chest. I dare you to find something that'll work in there. Double points if it's something sparkly."

Raeyn flashed me a grin. "Now there's an idea."

I didn't dignify that with an answer, just left them to dig through years' worth of disguises, some of them with bloodstains and scorch marks to show for it.

Pacing the small room, I caught my reflection in the mirror above the corner sink. I squinted at the face staring back at me, my eyes their usual dark brown. A bit more bloodshot than usual, but other than that there wasn't a speck of white in sight. I squinted harder, trying to get a grasp on the tingling in my hands, the lurching queasiness that'd made my stomach flip at Tarantino's, right before—

Something flashed in my eyes, and I nearly jumped out of my skin before realizing it was just the lid of the heavy chest thumping shut, the gleam of its hinges sparking in the bright neon light of the *Shadow*'s infirmary. I jerked away from the mirror, fingers aching from their clench around the porcelain sink. I forced them to relax.

Fuck me if I started losing it now. I could freak out later, once I got Aris safe.

Scattered piles of clothes covered every available surface around me, many in shapes and colors I wouldn't be caught dead in. Raeyn and Jay were grinning. This couldn't be good.

"This is perfect," Raeyn said.

I guess it could've been worse. I ended up in a dark blue button-up shirt, silk of course—trust in Raeyn to insist nothing less would do. At least the pants were a gray dark enough to almost be black. Made of soft material that, according to Raeyn, "showed off my assets." A jacket of the same fabric finished off the look. At least I talked him out of adding a matching tie.

Jay whistled through her teeth once I was all done, my curls tamed with some goo that apparently came out of Raeyn's personal stash.

"Damn, boss, you clean up good."

"Yes," Raeyn purred with a small smile, his eyes glued right on my tight-pants ass while I bent down to pull on the black boots he'd lent me to go along with the rest of this silk and pinstripe nightmare. "He'll do."

Looked like he'd been right.

I handed both my fake invitation and I.D. to Livery Girl who gave it a cursory glance and waved me through with added perkiness.

"Have a pleasant evening, Mr. Crane."

Right.

I entered the lounge and the scent of incense loaded with something more potent clogged my senses. Going from the handful of Nightshade brothels I'd been to, I'd expected some sort of bar or club setup. This place was both and neither.

Deep, plushy couches and cushions clustered around low tables. The fluff was a Nightshade standard requirement, but *La Maison* clearly found its niche by not just being high class, but given my first look at the kind of people crowding the lounge, also by catering specifically to Reds and Core clientele. Whoever ran this place was either a bloody genius or completely batshit, trying to hide a gaggle of Voyants right under the Reds' noses.

And Aris was smack in the middle of it, his face likely on every holoscreen all over Helos by now. I stifled the fluttering panic twisting my stomach into knots. Nothing to do but try to look normal, like I was looking for a score, not like I was feeling completely naked without my Colt on me.

There was a bar out back, but most of the drinks were served by people who made up in glitter and metallic body paint what they lacked in clothing.

All wore elaborate masks covering the upper half of their faces in swirls of gold, silver, and gemstones. They broke the low light of colored lampshades into a kaleidoscope of gleaming slivers.

Out of the corner of my eye, I caught a streak of silver hair. Just as I was about to whirl around and ask Raeyn what the fuck he was thinking following me here, I realized it was one of the servers. He was close to the right height and same slender build, but Raeyn probably had a good five years or so on him. The silver hair was a dye-job or maybe a good wig, his eyes hidden behind a mask of silver swirls that gleamed like they'd been painted on. The design trailed down the left side of his face, spilling over into black and silver body paint writhing down the side of his pale torso and curling down his legs, the pattern only broken by a sparkly binder hugging his chest and a pair of black briefs.

The eyes behind that silver mask were blue and crinkled when he caught me staring.

"First timer, hm?" He shot me a bright smile and sidled up to me, handing me a bubbly drink from the little silver tray he was balancing. He regarded me from beneath long lashes and slipped an arm around me, warm breath tickling against my ear. "I'm off in half an hour, Handsome. Find me at the bar. Ask for Kip."

He sauntered off, a glint of silver swirling into the small crowd gathered around the bar. The spot beneath my ear felt hot where his lips had touched my skin.

Where in the Seven Hells was Aris? The folded-up holosheet with his face on it was an iron weight in my pocket.

I found him sprawled in a plushy couch toward the back, playing poker with three Reds. I stopped dead where I stood. One of the Reds, a white guy with brown hair and eyes, was pawing all over Aris with a blissful grin on his face like a cat who'd gotten into the cream.

I already hated him. Would've even if his hands hadn't been all but down Aris's pants.

Among all the pretty boys, girls, and nonbinary people of *La Maison*, Aris outshone them all. He didn't just look good. He looked fucking splendid. The shadows under his eyes had disappeared and he'd filled out. He wore faded blue jeans along with an unbuttoned white shirt displaying the flat, smooth planes of his chest. With his blond curls unbound and slightly ruffled hanging past his shoulders, every bit of him radiating an air of being positively fuckable.

Obviously, I wasn't the only one who thought so.

The Red twirled a copper chain hanging around Aris's neck to pull him closer. Something cracked inside of me at Aris's fluid, catlike movements. The Red's mouth crooked around a scar slightly twisting his upper lip, like someone'd taken a chink out of him. He whispered something into Aris's ear with an insinuating smile that made Aris's mouth curve a little wider before it brushed against the Red's. The kiss only lasted a few seconds, but it was enough.

I should leave. Had no business being here. Get the hells out while I still could.

This was exactly why I'd always stayed out of Aris's runs.

Gods, I wanted—

No.

I forced my fists to unclench, my shoulders to relax, and put on a smile that was hardly more than a baring of teeth. Concentrating on taking deep, even breaths, I strolled over to their merry little poker table, trying my best to pretend I wasn't crashing their party.

"Care if I join next round?"

Four pairs of eyes fixed on me instantly. Aris's eyes widened a fraction, his face stunned, before it slid back into place and melted into a crooked smile. It made him look like he had back when things hadn't been all complicated.

Gods, I'd missed him.

"Of course," he said brightly. "I insist."

The Red who'd been all over him a second ago snorted. "Only if you don't value your wallet. Aris cheats."

Aris laughed and disentangled himself from the Red's grip. The chain around his neck slid down his chest, weighed down by some sort of heavy-looking brass pendant.

"No need to cheat if you let me see right into your cards, Jon," Aris said mildly, his eyes never leaving mine. "Poker is all about bluffing. And I learned from the best." His eyes softened for a moment, lingering on mine.

I wanted nothing but to get him the hells out of this, but Aris stayed where he was, one finger tapping against the polished cherry wood of the table in front of him before he patted the couch gesturing for me to sit.

I threw down a sizable stack of credits and sat down on one of those plush seats that couldn't decide if it wanted to be a chair or a cushion. "Well, then, show me what you got."

The Red who'd been with Aris took over the deck of cards and began to shuffle it while his two companions seemed to be distracted by a guy and a girl walking by, both obviously attractive, obviously half-naked, and obviously with the house. If they kept those two occupied, all the better. Two down, one to go.

"Well then, welcome to your bankruptcy, Mr—"

"Marten Crane," I said, quietly surprised how easily a dead man's name rolled off my tongue. Guess the years proved I could own Marten after all, and by now I wore his name like any other mask. I studied the Red's face closely. Pleasure to meet you, motherfucker. Maybe I'd add his name to my list of cover I.D.s someday.

"Jon Sykes," the Red said. And with a pointed lilt to his voice, "You already know Aris?"

"Intimately," I replied, pretending I didn't notice Sykes's hand on Aris's thigh. Aris didn't say anything, but a spark of amusement danced in his eyes.

The round went over quickly, and to say it didn't go as I'd expected was the understatement of the year. Wasn't even like my hands were shit or useless, but Aris managed to strip me clean five rounds straight. This wasn't cheating. Whatever he was pulling here, I hadn't taught him that. Which made me wonder who the fuck had.

"Okay, I'm out." I glared at Aris. He shot me a slow grin.

"Excellent." Aris got up in one fluid motion and laced my hand into his, leaving his cards scattered on the table. "I was starting to get bored. Winning does get tedious, you know." He snaked an arm around me and whispered, "I need to talk to you. Alone."

You too, huh? What I said was, "Um, sure," and let him pull me to my feet. Was about damn time. The incense was giving me a buzz.

"Excuse us," Aris said to the others with one of those smiles of his that could melt a rock. Damn, he was good at this.

Sykes opened his mouth—as if the disappointed kicked-puppy look on his face didn't speak volumes—but shut it again and scowled at me.

Aris's cool fingers curled around mine as he hooked arms with me and led me out of the lounge that opened into a wide corridor lined with doors to private rooms.

We passed them and once we'd reached the end of the corridor, Aris turned to make sure the hall was empty before he slid out one of the cherry wood panels and motioned me through the gap. It opened to a stairwell that looked like it'd been part of the original warehouse that hid the Temple, all concrete and red paint chipping from iron railings. We went down two flights of stairs and in through what must've once been an emergency exit, leading into a dim-lit hallway that smelled of wood paneling and old books.

Aris opened a door to his left and waved me inside. Light flashed to life, and I got a brief glimpse of a big four-poster bed of the same black wood as the row of bookcases lining the room's opposite wall. Then Aris pushed me against the closed door and kissed me.

It was more of a bite than a kiss. Aris's lips trailed from marking my mouth to the hollow of my throat, the buttons of my shirt a scatter beneath his hands. I didn't have any room to complain. My breath was hot against Aris's shoulder, hands on his hips, pulling him closer, getting busy with the button of his tight jeans before he tore himself loose to gasp for air.

"What in the Seven Hells are you doing here, Damian?"

Something snapped inside of me, and I shoved him away, the fabric of his shirt bunched in my fists. "Fuck, Aris. What am *I* doing here? What are you playing at, disappearing and—" And not letting me know if you're okay. Not coming back.

I swallowed and what I got out instead was, "You're fucking a Red."

Aris blinked. A defensive note crept into his voice. "Jon is a friend."

"Oh, great. You're friends with a Red *and* you're fucking him. So much better."

Aris sighed and ran a hand through the tangle of his blond curls. "You know, after all those years, the one thing I didn't expect from you anymore was jealousy." He lowered his hand and took a step back.

"I'm not jealous!" Obviously. Gods, this wasn't going how I'd planned at all. I forced my fists to unclench. "Aris, I—"

The words died in my throat when Aris's eyes blazed white.

Shit. I scrambled back but couldn't go anywhere with the wall against my back.

It was over in less than a second and there was something broken in the way Aris studied me.

"Damian." His hand was cool on my cheek when he leaned forward and kissed me, gently this time. I could still taste the tingle of the Voyance on his lips.

"You worry too much," he said against my mouth. "I know why you're here. To warn me, because the Watch are after me. There's a crumpled holosheet with my face on it in your pocket, and you think Jon and his friends are going to hand me over to the Empire first chance they get." His cool fingers stroked my cheek, ran through my hair. "You're right. That's what they want, but it doesn't matter, because I know, and I was faster. I won't let them ruin things. Not this time."

I stared at him, trying to unscramble my brain. "What the— How do you— You *knew*?"

That sad, lopsided smile was back when he let go of me and moved a step or so away so I could get a good look at him. He looked different. Still incredibly good, incredibly hot, but beneath that veneer, he was tired and dangerous. A cornered dog ready to bite off the hand trying to put him on a leash.

"The Voyance has its uses, you know," he said. "And despite Celebrant Aemelia's best efforts, I've learned quite a few things. Among them, ways to keep the Reds too busy drooling all over themselves so they forget all about who they're looking for in the first place. Oh, and ways to beat even you at poker."

"You didn't." It's possible my jaw dropped just a little as it dawned on me. "No way. You used the *Voyance* right in front of the fucking *Watch*?"

Aris flashed me a grin, then leaned in to kiss me again. "Trust me, those poor bastards have no idea who they are messing with."

"Hm, seems like you got it all covered. You don't need me then."

"Don't be silly." Aris smothered whatever else I was going to say with his lips and didn't let up until he'd dragged me over to the bed. Under his lips, everything dissolved into a tangle of panting breaths and scattered clothes. Damn him if he thought fucking would fix everything. As if it could rewind the clock. Fucking wish it were that easy. Just shut the door to our bunk behind us and forget the world.

"Aris." I tried to swipe his hands off my shoulders, but the attempt was half-hearted with Aris on top of me pinning my wrists above my head.

"Shhh." He nipped my lip. "I can feel your brain running. Stop. Let me help."

And he did. His mouth trailed down my torso and lower until I couldn't protest, even if I'd wanted to. Fat chance of that with Aris's hands stroking any tension from my body. His breath grew hot between my legs, a teasing whisper against the stiffness of my cock a second before he took me in his mouth. From there, it was Aris's show, the sheets his stage, and my body the instrument he knew to play all too well as he wiped any coherent thought right out of my head.

We got lost in each other, taking care to rediscover every sensitive spot, relish each moan, draw out our releases until we collapsed in a sweaty tangle of pleasant exhaustion.

It took some time until we both felt like paying attention to the world again.

"Better?" Aris murmured against the hollow of my throat, gently nipping sensitive skin.

The bed was a complete mess. Rumpled sheets twisted around my legs with the warm weight of Aris's body against my chest kept me trapped in a warm, contented haze, so all I managed was a lazy, "Mhmm."

I combed my fingers through the golden mass of Aris's hair, breathing in the smoke and sandalwood smell of incense that clung to it. "Couldn't you have, I don't know, called? Stayed in touch somehow? Be all cliché and write letters, sneak out, anything?"

As soon as the words were out, I hated how needy they sounded.

Aris turned against me, one hand brushing a strand of black hair out of the way before he kissed the side of my neck. "I'm sorry. I wanted to, but I thought it best if I disappeared for a while without giving Raeyn and that corporate who funds him even more reasons to get to you."

I snorted. The sound didn't hold a scrap of humor. "I'm actually working for them full-time now. Sort of. The Gods know Nymeron needs any muscle he can get to keep his ass safe."

Aris quirked an eyebrow. "Does he now?"

"What's that supposed to mean?"

"Nothing." I could hear the damn grin in Aris's voice when he nestled back against me, the long brass chain around his neck sliding sideways, its pendant brushing against me.

I picked it up and turned it over in my fingers. "What's this anyway?"

The outside felt old, worn, if not quite tarnished. A little mechanism flicked it open to reveal a pocket watch inside.

"It's the symbol of the Temple," Aris said. "A mark, if you will. Every initiate gets one the day they enter. Once they've learned to control the Voyance and stop using it, they stop the watch and become full members of the Temple."

I looked at the watch's white face with its golden hands and cogs slowly ticking away the seconds. "Yours is still ticking."

Aris's tense smile confirmed what I was thinking. "And I don't intend to stop it."

"But why the hells not?" The image of that poor bastard Gren rotting away at *L'Oubliette* flashed back to the surface. I tried to suppress the goose bumps rippling my skin despite the warmth of Aris's room. That's when I noticed how bright Aris's eyes were, how his skin seemed to glow in the dim light. It wasn't the same blinding white I'd seen before when he'd drawn on the Voyance; more like an afterglow, as if—

"Gods, you're using the Voyance *right now?*"

"Damian—"

I was glad Aris chose that moment to disentangle himself from me to reach for a stack of books he kept in a crooked pile on his nightstand. That way he didn't notice how I flinched away from him, recoiling into the pillows as if the sheets of his bedding were some protective wall I could hide behind. He dropped a heavy leather-bound volume on the covers. The title was something vaguely Latin-looking.

"They used to call it magic, you know?"

"Yeah, back when people died before they hit thirty and didn't notice it was melting their brains," I said. "Fuck, Aris, you can't just—"

His face took on a dangerous streak. "I can't just *what?*"

Aris caught me tensing up and sighed, long fingers uncurling until they lay flat on his naked thighs.

"Look, it's not that easy. I studied the Voyance. Read anything I could find on it over the last three months. There's little enough as it is and what sources exist are contradicting each other. Sure, abstinence is one way to go. Until the backlash catches up with you." Aris's arms wrapped around himself. "I've seen the ones the Celebrants take to *L'Oubliette*, Damian."

He shook his head and hugged himself tighter. "The thing is, it doesn't matter in the end. That's how the Voyance works. It's like a parasite, a virus, whatever you want to call it. It uses you up bit by little bit, whether you draw on it or not. Until there's nothing left."

I shook my head and pushed myself up onto my elbows. "So, you're going to keep using it until it gets you? That's a fucking addict talking, Aris, and you know it."

"Damian." Aris tried to reach for me.

"No." I held up a hand and nearly hit the headboard, scooting back as far as I could. "Don't. Just don't, okay?" I lowered my hand. "Damn it, Aris, you were supposed to get help here, not, not—"

The sad smile that tugged at the corner of his mouth nearly broke my heart when he said, "This is going to kill me, Damian. But I'm not going to wait for it, you understand?"

I squeezed my eyes shut. Nodded. Damn, but I understood. "Yeah," I said, voice hoarse. "Yeah. Fuck."

"Hey." Aris gently brushed my arm. "Are you okay? You're shaking, and your aura is all—" Something crackled at his touch on my skin, like built-up static, magnified ten times. I caught the reflection of a white glimmer in his eyes.

Aris pulled back his fingers, his eyes wide. "Oh Gods," he whispered, staring at me. "Why didn't you tell me?"

"There's nothing to tell." I scrambled out of bed. Dove for my clothes. "I've got to go."

Aris was after me in a flash, his hands hot on my bare shoulders, pinning me to the wall. "No," he said, ignoring the fizzling zap running through both of us as his skin touched mine. "You don't get to cut and run, damn it. Talk to me. Damian, please."

"Don't know what you're talking about," I ground out between clenched teeth.

"Right." Aris's eyes glazed over in a murky white. "Just like you don't feel this either."

His Voyance hummed in my ears like an electric current. He didn't touch me directly, but I could still feel his hands on me, brushing against naked skin, like a velvet glove that made my whole body tingle, leaving me hard and panting like some fucked-up version of foreplay.

"No," I choked out, throat tightening with the panic of being trapped. "Aris, stop. *Stop.*"

He didn't. "See? You feel it, too. No 'nothing' about it. You didn't seem to mind earlier."

Aris had always been home to me, his touch the first I'd learned not to flinch away from after Marten and *L'Ecole*. He'd taught me how to trust again, shown me it was worth the risk to want again. Now it all cracked under his unrelenting hold. Betrayal laced with something sharper than fear dug its claws into my heart and squeezed. I knew only one way to get out of this.

I clocked him in the face. He stumbled back. I got a knee up into his abdomen and he went down with a wheezing cry, knocking over stacks of books on his way.

"I said *stop.*"

"Damian, I—" Aris's voice was thick past the blood gushing from his nose. Behind the red, all color drained from his face. "Oh, Gods, Damian, I didn't mean—" He reached for me. I stumbled back, my hands raised in a defensive shield.

"Don't ever touch me like that again. You said you never would, remember? Or did you forget that, too?" I fought down the panic, buried it along with the grief of having lost something I knew I'd never get back, and blinked the white fog away from my vision. I shrugged into my pants and shirt. My fingers shook so badly, I didn't bother with the buttons. "If you're too fucking strung out to go cold turkey on the Voyance, that's your problem. But don't think for a second you can use me like, like—"

Every word felt like another punch. Like I was choking on them, spiraling to a place I swore I'd never return to. The worst was part of me still tried to desperately hang on to Aris. To patch things up. Stay with him, take this on together, like we always had.

But the truth was we'd passed the point of no return a long time ago.

My head pounded in time to my heartbeat, fingers numb and slippery around the doorknob, when it opened, and I came face to face with the kid I remembered from *L'Oubliette*.

"Hey Aris, you okay? I heard shouting and—" Pascal froze when they caught me standing in the doorway, their eyes wide at my bloody knuckles. They rushed inside and to Aris who winced, pulling himself off the ground. "Aris, what happened?"

"I'm fine, Pascal." Aris brushed their arm off and tried to scramble after me. "Damian and I were just talking."

"Yeah, and we're done talking now." I stepped through the door. The concrete floor sent cold chills up my bare feet, but I was more worried about getting the hells out of here than about Raeyn's boots I'd left behind somewhere in Aris's room.

It nearly tore me apart to walk away from him, to treat him the way so many Reds had before. Like he was just another Burner. Uncontrollable. Dangerous. Those times it'd been easy. I could deal with that with a good, old-fashioned ass-kicking where we always had the *Shadow* to go home to if we needed to lick our wounds. This was different. This we couldn't fix, because that'd need one of us not to be broken.

"Good luck with the Reds," I said. "Looks like you'll need it."

And Gods, I hoped he stood a chance.

14

Distractions

THE GLASS TOWERS of corporate Helos glowed like they'd been dipped into liquid fire. Here, the streets were wide enough to easily navigate with a hover, not like Low Side where you'd have to worry about clipping every corner or random pedestrian that might be underfoot. In the Core, the worst-case scenario was getting a traffic ticket for flooring it.

The last rays of dying sunlight tickled the back of my neck. So much for making the meeting with Raeyn and Taerien on time. That's what I got for playing stand-in at runs that should've been Kovacz's business. After the thing at Tarantino's, he'd pretty much gone AWOL, patching holes with his Red friends while I was running my ass off to cover for him.

Fucking par for the course, the way the last couple of days had been going.

Aris's last note was burning a hole into my pocket where I'd shoved it, crumpled and unread. It'd been the third one in as many days since I'd left him there. I was fiddling with the wrinkled paper, trying to push past Aris and his ridiculous idea everything would be right in the world if we just talked it out, when I saw the pillar of smoke half a city away.

"Oh, shit." I gunned it.

Minutes later, I brought the hover to a screeching halt outside the gate to Taerien's mansion. Or what was left of it after the Reds had turned it into the largest Sunfest bonfire Helos had ever seen. Smoke billowed from shattered windows, orange flames licked up the whitewashed walls trailing black soot and planting crackling nests of fire under the roof. Sunfest and the Election were still weeks away, and the Reds usually didn't make it a habit of torching the homes of their Upstanding Core Citizens. That and the place was too quiet, no one making the slightest move to get the fire under control, not with the East River blocking Taerien's off from the rest of its expensive neighborhood. This was a controlled burn.

Which meant the Empire was onto Taerien.

Ah, *fuck.*

Of course, they'd attack now, months after Valyr'd found out Taerien was gunning for her. Very fucking like her to bide her time and wait until Taerien let his guard down the tiniest fraction, enough to give the Reds an opening while he and Raeyn were sitting ducks.

Gods, of all days, why'd I have to be late today?

One of Taerien's guards drifted facedown in the river, their uniform jacket tangled up in the weeds by the riverside. A second slumped against a tree, her throat cut ear to ear. I left the hover behind a hedge, far enough away to avoid any Reds stumbling over it and scaled Taerien's wall to get a better look at things. Crouched behind the cover of some tree branches, I blinked the smoke from my eyes.

No sign of Taerien, but I spotted Raeyn right away.

Looked like he'd really pissed off the wrong Red this time. That, or they'd decided to finish the job, what with him supposedly having been dead for years and the Empire not needing this kind of publicity.

Hands cuffed behind his back, Raeyn stood on one of Taerien's fancy chairs someone'd dragged outside. Half a dozen Reds circled him, one standing on an overturned box and slipping a noose around Raeyn's neck.

"About time someone put a leash on Taerien's dog," someone sneered. The rope wound around the lower branch of one of the trees by Taerien's front gate. Raeyn swayed on his feet, bruises covering his face where it wasn't all scarred up already. He was barely recognizable. His hair hung down in red strands, the front of his shirt dark with blood. Fighting to stay conscious, he drew himself up when the Red tightened the rope and said something I couldn't make out.

I recognized the guy. It was Jon Sykes. Aris's fuck-buddy.

Under all the bruises, Raeyn's face'd been set like stone. Now he gave Sykes that trademark arrogant grin of his as if he wasn't barely able to stay upright, bleeding, and set to star in the Reds' favorite pastime aside from Cleansing little girls.

Shit, Raeyn, you should've run. Why didn't you run?

Because he wouldn't. Not when he knew he had another ace up his sleeve. Not when—

He'd been waiting for me. The sudden realization twisted something deep in my chest.

Right then, it felt like he was looking straight at me, those light gray eyes of his on the exact spot he knew I'd be hiding. It only lasted a second.

Raeyn's mouth twisted into a sneer at the Red. Whatever he said in reply earned him a brutal crack across the face.

I could leave the Reds to it, get rid of Raeyn Nymeron once and for all. The thought left my brain as quickly as it'd entered. Because fuck me if I could still pretend I didn't give a shit about him. That somewhere in this mess that'd started the night of my botched hit on Taerien Raeyn hadn't become one of my people.

Sykes kicked the chair out from under Raeyn's feet and the rope snapped tight. I hoped it wasn't Raeyn's neck snapping with it, but I was already off the wall and running.

I had to work fast. Raeyn had minutes. At most.

I dashed back to the hover, and, once inside, almost tripped over the toolbox in the back, cursing as I busted my knee. With flying fingers, I yanked open the lids of the stabilizing containers that held Jay's portable stash of explosives. Trust the Grasshopper to always pack enough to make hells of a big boom. Like, say, blow up a hover to create a diversion.

Two bags of acetone peroxide from Jay's kit and some duct-tape should do the trick.

Trying to shoot a gas tank would just make the fuel leak out. Shoot it with a few bags of acetone peroxide taped to it—different story.

Jay was going to kill me. I'd face her after I got Raeyn out of this.

Speed over delicacy, I taped the plastic bags to the hover's tanks in messy lumps. I kicked the hover into autopilot, hoping it wouldn't pick today of all days to take a dump on me. Randomly blowing myself up was the last thing I needed.

I'd parked out of view of the Reds who were watching Raeyn slowly choke to death off to the side of the building. I needed to get them away from him, even if it was just for two minutes. Wouldn't need more than that to get him and make a run for it.

I needed this to work.

The hover whirred to life, and I floored the accelerator, aiming it straight at Taerien's front gate. Good thing it was blown wide open.

Thanks, Reds, for making my job easier.

I angled the hover so they wouldn't notice what was happening until it was too late.

Then I jumped.

And remembered exactly why stupidly throwing myself off any vehicle at full speed was a really bad idea: there was no good way of hitting asphalt full-on. Hurts like a motherfucker. Strategic falls, my ass.

I set my jaw and tried to ignore the ten thousand or so tiny rocks ground up into the skin of my hands, the impact numbing my entire left side as I scrambled in the dirt. The Reds who'd lagged behind to watch Raeyn die ran toward the hover. If I wanted to get a good shot at the hover, I'd have to kick things up a notch.

"Ah, fuck it all," I snarled and did just that, firing from my crouch. Once. Twice.

The hover exploded in a burst of flame before it crashed into the façade of Taerien's mansion and went up in smoke and flying parts of rusty engineering.

Damn. I'd *liked* that hover.

All that mattered was it worked. The impact of the explosion knocked the Reds flat on their asses, limbs flailing like a bunch of red beetles that'd fallen onto their backs.

The whole thing had maybe taken two minutes. I hoped it hadn't been two minutes too long. My distraction wouldn't keep the Reds away long, so I cut through the smoke filling Taerien's yard and got to Raeyn while the getting was good.

There were only two complications.

Complication number one was taken out with a couple of silenced shots. Sure, shooting Reds from behind was low, but I didn't have time for honor codes.

Complication number two was a tougher one. Raeyn had stopped kicking, his body hanging limp, gently swinging by the rope around his neck. Panic tightened my throat. Seeing Raeyn this silent and still felt...wrong. Worse than the blood and the beating he'd taken.

There was no gentle way to cut down a body dangling from a tree by yourself. I settled for climbing on the chair the Reds had left behind and tried to hold Raeyn up while hacking through the rope. I managed to ease his fall to the ground, where his body lay collapsed on itself. I loosened the rope, and something loosened inside of me with it. Raeyn's throat was black, but he was breathing. Barely and in shallow gasps, but it'd have to do.

"Okay, you're not quite dead yet, so hang on."

I slung him across my shoulder, staggering under all his gangly dead weight, but managed to half run, half stumble out of Taerien's and stay ahead of the Reds, their shouts and heavy footsteps echoing in the streets behind me.

We made it nearly a block, cutting corners, trying to get as much ground between us and the Reds as possible. I stopped behind what used to be a department store but now had become a hulking concrete ruin with blind windows and crumbling walls that cast long shadows to hide in.

I put Raeyn down on the cold concrete floor, trying to be gentle even though every muscle in my body was screaming at me. It all faded into the background when it hit me Raeyn'd stopped breathing. I frantically felt for a pulse or a heartbeat but couldn't find one. The front of his shirt was soaking wet, dripping red everywhere.

"Fuck, don't do this to me. Come on, Nymeron."

I cupped his jaw, made sure his swollen tongue wasn't blocking his throat before giving him my best shot at CPR. His lips were blue and felt like cold rubber against mine as I tried my damnedest to get air back into his lungs.

"Come on, Raeyn, you asshole, you're tougher than this." I lowered my face to his again. Raeyn's eyes flew open. His body convulsed in a shock of harshly indrawn breath and pained coughing.

"Easy," I said as he dry-heaved and clawed at his battered throat. "Just breathe."

Once he'd stopped coughing, Raeyn collapsed, his chest heaving with ragged breaths. His face twisted up when he opened his mouth and his voice came out as a hoarse croak.

"You're late." He sounded awful, each breath a scraping wheeze. But he sounded alive.

I laughed, too fucking relieved to be properly pissed. "Gods. And for you, I blew up a perfectly good hover."

Raeyn gave me a weak grin, but his eyes were already glazing over.

"Hey. Stay with me. Come on. Look at me. You like looking at me, remember?" And I'd be happy to let him, long as it kept him from dying on me.

I ripped his shirt open. He hissed. His chest was black with bruises and I recognized the outlines of at least one or two boots against his ribs. The Reds had worked him over before they'd tried to kill him. Most of the blood came from a stab wound under his ribs. Reds could've saved themselves a whole lot of trouble if they'd just waited for him to bleed out.

"What the fuck happened to you?" I took off my shirt to rip it into a bandage. I wrapped it around him with trembling hands, my arms red to the elbows. "Can't I leave you alone for a few hours? How the fuck did you survive on your own before? Gods, you're bleeding everywhere."

Why did my voice sound so panicked all of a sudden?

"Stupid," Raeyn mumbled. "Stayed too long. Should've left. But I knew you'd—" His hands fumbled for mine. I held on, tried to work some warmth back into his fingers, and reassure myself he was in fact alive. "Thanks. I— You didn't have to—"

"You're babbling," I said, not ungently. Gods, it hurt listening to him. Almost as much as him thinking I could've abandoned him. "And I should clock you for even thinking I would've left you there. So how about you stop talking, just for now and keep those hands busy holding your insides in, okay?" I captured his hands and pressed them against the makeshift bandage.

Raeyn nodded, eyes drifting shut. All the bravado leaked out of him. He groaned drowsily as I tied off the wound. The shirt was already soaking through.

"Hey!" I patted his clammy cheek. "Come on, stick around. Can't have you dozing off. Not before we get you somewhere safe." Problem was I didn't have the slightest clue where to take him. The *Shadow* was closest, but we didn't have the kind of doctor Raeyn needed.

"Temple," Raeyn mumbled already half asleep. "Taerien's at the Temple."

I sighed. Of course he was.

"Well peachy. 'Cause that's where we're going." I squeezed his hand. "You're not going to stop breathing again, are you?"

"Tempting," Raeyn croaked.

"Well, don't," I said and got him onto my shoulder in a poor imitation of a fireman's carry. "Hold on and try not to grope me."

15

Second Son

RAEYN MADE GOOD on his promise and kept breathing.

By the time I got him to the Temple, I was covered in sweat and blood, my black T-shirt sticking to me in wet patches. Raeyn was out cold, a dead weight across my shoulders. *La Maison*'s back door wasn't much more than a slab of spray-painted steel, blending in with the rest of the Temple's warehouse front. Last time, I'd been too busy getting the fuck out of this place to pay much attention to any guards posted out back. Now I ran into the same sourly scowl that'd given me the hairy eyeball back at *L'Oubliette*.

"You." Ferris swerved toward me, the glare of her flashlight making my eyes water. "What d'you—" Her eyes widened recognizing Raeyn. "What did you do to him?"

I took a deep breath. It didn't do anything for the stiffness or the burning in my shoulders. "Look. Ferris, was it? I didn't do anything to him, but I swear to all the Gods, if you don't move your ass away from that door and get me Aris and Initiate Pascal right this fucking instant, I'm going to take him in from the front. Wonder what all those Reds will do when they see him."

Ferris's scowl deepened. "Wait here."

She must've broken some record, she got back so fast. Pascal was a dark shape against the bright doorway, their lips pressed together in a thin line.

"Get him inside." I gave them credit for not asking what happened. Behind Pascal, Aris melted out of the shadows. Seeing him brought back everything that'd happened the last time I'd seen him, reminded me of the way my knuckles stung after I'd hit him and worse. He didn't say anything. Just gave me a hand, and together we carried Raeyn down a flight of stairs and put him on a cot in a tiny room lit by two gas lanterns. The bare, whitewashed walls gave me a flashback of *L'Oubliette*. A shudder skittered down my spine.

Didn't help that Raeyn looked like death warmed over. His skin was almost translucent where it wasn't covered in a patchwork of bruises, a ring of black and purple digging into his swollen throat like the collar of a choke chain. He opened his eyes when Pascal unwrapped the makeshift bandage I'd tied around his chest. The shirt was soaked red, but they held it in place to staunch the bleeding while Aris got the Temple's med kit. Pascal said something to Raeyn, their voice low and smooth, but his eyes stayed glassy and unfocused.

Pascal worried their lower lip between their teeth and wrestled their coils into a messy bun to keep them out of their face. They nodded at a tall cabinet across from me.

"IV bags are in the top right. He needs fluids to make up for all that blood loss."

By the time I got the bag of fluids, Pascal had tied off Raeyn's arm. They started an IV and motioned me to hold the bag up while they dragged a stand to hook it from. Pascal secured the bag and adjusted the drip. I tried to step away, but Raeyn's long, pale fingers curled around my hand, holding on.

"Stay," he whispered. "Please."

Um. Okay. Clearly someone needed a godsdamn teddy bear or something.

I nearly extricated myself in time for Aris to come back with the Temple's extensive med kit and an IV bag of warmed synth blood. Thought I saw a spark of something awfully close to jealousy in his eyes. I sat, giving in to my tired muscles, grateful for the chance to rest, if only for a moment. I perched on the edge of the cot, Raeyn's fingers threaded through mine, his breath calming a bit, keeping me anchored.

And almost jumped up anyway at the figure who'd sneaked in after Aris, lugging a bucket of hot water and towels.

"Well if it isn't Mael Taerien. Looks like someone ran fast enough from the Reds."

Taerien's nostrils flared and he drew himself up straight. "It looks like it, doesn't it?" he said in all the condescension of his cut-glass accent. Then he got a good look at Raeyn and his façade cracked. "How bad is he?"

"What's it to you?" I cut in, suddenly furious. "You let the Reds string him up."

Taerien's eyes went cold and flat, like a snake's. "Don't you dare. Do you honestly think I would leave him there?"

He was about to close in on me when Pascal stepped between us. "Okay, that's it. Both of you, either make yourselves useful or leave this room."

Taerien opened his mouth but snapped it shut and backed off without further comment. I tossed him the bloody rag that'd once been my shirt. He caught it and gave Pascal room to work.

Aris handed them extra clean cloths, blond eyebrows crinkling in a frown as he watched Pascal clean the wound.

"I can fix this," Aris said, his eyes intent on Raeyn's chest. The bleeding had slowed down some, but red still trickled out with every ragged breath. Aris glanced from Raeyn to Pascal, like he was asking for permission. "I can fix him, Pascal. Please."

Of course. All his talk of using the Voyance for good. Like healing. Oh hells.

Pascal shook their head without looking up. "Forget it," they said, in a clipped voice. "Aemelia will kill you if she gets wind of you even suggesting this. Hells, she'll kill both of us. Right after you're done killing him."

"Pascal," Aris cut in, but they turned, face set in hard angles.

"Look," they said. "I get you're trying to prove something here, but that's not how it works, okay? The Voyance isn't some magic cure."

"It's been done," Aris insisted in that same stubborn voice he used whenever he decided to be a particularly giant pain in the ass about something he'd gotten into his thick head. Like wanting to talk to me about the Voyance. I shoved that thought down as far as it'd go.

"I can do it, Pascal."

"Aris—"

He'd already brushed past them. He reached for Raeyn, his eyes sliding to white.

"No." Raeyn couldn't have been all that out of it after all. He let go of me and snatched Aris's hand, quick as a cat and only a little shaky as his grip closed around Aris's wrist. Shit, he was going to yank out his IV if he kept on like this.

"No, you won't." Raeyn sounded like someone'd taken his vocal cords and strung them over a cheese grater. "I'll heal myself. 'S all I'm good for anyway."

Aris let go of Raeyn, hazel seeping back into his eyes. "What do you mean, heal yourself?"

Raeyn's mouth curled into a thin smile. "Not all the family's Voyance genes went to you, little brother."

Aris stared at him. "What?" The word cracked his blank facade. "What did you say?"

"Sorry," Raeyn whispered. "Weren't supposed to find out like this."

"You're lying," I said, because someone had to say something, and Aris stood there, still, looking like something inside him had snapped and was rattling around in empty space.

Aris'd gone sheet-white, but his voice was eerily calm. "He's telling the truth. He knows lying to me would be pointless."

Right. Aris had his Voyance mind-reading thing. Shit. It made my skin crawl. Aris cast me a sidelong look, and I concentrated on thinking blank thoughts. A humorless smile tugged at the corner of his mouth and it suddenly hit me how alike he and Raeyn looked. The same high cheekbones and high foreheads, even their eyebrows had the same slant.

"Gods, you're serious."

Raeyn nodded weakly. His eyes never left Aris's. "'Fraid so."

Fuck, there were conspiracy theories about this. Spread by people who clearly had an overabundance of imagination and a lack of anything better to do. Hells if they hadn't been on to something.

"How come he doesn't have the whole white hair and pale eyes thing going on?" I asked, unable to take Aris's shocked silence anymore. "I mean, aren't you all supposed to be some sort of inbred clones of each other?"

"There's a theory." Raeyn laughed. It was a raspy, broken sound that caught on a cough. At least he'd stopped bleeding. Whatever he was doing worked. "Glamour. Got you out early. Father never knew."

Aris shook his head, staring at his hands. "Why? Why go through all that trouble when I could have grown up—" He stopped and took in Raeyn and the layer of scars that covered him like a set of pink and white spiderwebs. Some of them were way older than his burn scars.

"Oh," Aris said in a tiny voice.

Raeyn didn't quite manage a smirk. "Correcting past mistakes," he croaked. "Father needed a successor. A Voyant. Not..." Raeyn's fists clenched in the sheets and his voice faded out, stumbling over mangled words.

"Wait a minute," I cut in. "The Empire fucking *Cleanses* Voyants. Hunts them down and all but bloody kills them. And now you're telling us our oh-so-perfect president wants to raise mini-Voyants? With all the pitter-patter of little batshit Voyant feet?" Out of the corner of my eye, I caught Aris and Pascal shooting me dirty looks. "Uh. Sorry, but you let me know if any of this starts making sense to you."

Raeyn tried to protest, but Pascal wasn't having any of it.

"Okay, that's it," they said, frowning at Raeyn. "He needs rest. More later."

Both Raeyn and I tried to protest, but at one look from Pascal, Raeyn backed down and sank into the pillow that kept him propped up. He nodded at Taerien still hovering by the door.

"Tell him," Raeyn rasped, his eyes already drifting to half-mast.

Taerien sighed. "Of course. Leave it to me to disclose the Empire's most guarded secret." Taerien's eyes lingered on me and Pascal, obviously not convinced he could trust us.

Raeyn gave him the tiniest nod. "'S what I pay you for."

"You what?" The words were out before I could stop myself. Everything slid to a stop, rewinding that whole fucked-up night when all of this had started. Raeyn throwing me into that damn river. Taerien cutting me a deal. Raeyn clinging to me like a second shadow. Fuck me. "Taerien's been a *front? A fucking flunkie?*" I stared at Raeyn. He didn't even have the decency to look guilty.

Taerien scoffed. "Really, Mr. Nettoyer, I'm incredibly relieved he merely pays you for the shooting and not for tactical matters. Also, I prefer the word business associate."

Taerien made a face. "Be that as it may. About the Voyance. In case you haven't noticed, this Empire is founded on control. And how better to control the masses than with the Voyance where it takes but a blink to instill a thought or even sway a political vote with no one being the wiser? It's the perfect model of tyranny, neatly wrapped in a democratic disguise."

Next to me, Aris stayed motionless.

"Okay," I said into the silence. "Our president is a megalomaniacal bastard. Fucking news. Still doesn't explain why he's making chasing down Voyants public sport number one. I mean, if he's one of them, why doesn't he—Oh." I stopped. It clicked.

Taerien snorted. "Why doesn't he publicly admit he considers the Voyance a gift from the Light itself and it's his personal key to undermining democracy? Please."

"He wants to control it," Aris said in that small, quiet voice that seriously gave me the creeps. "Probably even wants to fix it, but there's no way to fix or control a mob of unpredictable Voyants. It's like defusing a bomb. Cut the right wire in time, or watch it explode."

Everyone fell silent, chewing on that.

"Speaking of collateral." Taerien turned to Aris. "Congratulations on completely giving yourself away. Or did you think killing half a dozen of Valyr's men was particularly subtle?"

"Valyr," Aris said, staring at Raeyn. "She's your mother, too."

For once Raeyn wouldn't meet his eyes. "Yeah. Not that you'd know it."

Well, fuck me, that explained how weird Valyr'd been when I mentioned Raeyn's name. Or why he wouldn't let me shoot her. At least not while he was watching. Gods, talk about family issues. Shit.

Aris opened his mouth. Closed it. "No wonder you didn't want me to come along when she took Damian."

Raeyn's mouth curled into a pained smile. "Not like it stopped you."

"It was all a set-up, wasn't it? Mother trying to talk me into coming to the palace, after everything. She wanted to make sure I'd run the other way. Tried to protect me." Aris's fingers curled into fists, reaching for a lifeline, but grabbing nothing but thin air.

"Looks like the other shoe finally dropped," Taerien said in a tone that made me want to strangle him, just so he'd stop talking. Couldn't he see Aris was ready to crack, damn it?

"Anyway, the short of it is the Watch caught on to us knowing who you were." His head swiveled toward me, brown eyes glinting. "Thank your friend Kovacz for burning down my home, by the way."

I took a deep breath. Guess that answered the question what Kovacz had been up to those last few days. Gods.

"You can stay at the Temple," Pascal said as they finished rewrapping Raeyn's chest. "At least for now. The Gods know we have enough empty beds."

Raeyn shook his head, his eyes fluttering open. "Can't stay. Need to run. Should've told you earlier." His eyes flicked to me at that last part. "My mistake."

Aris shook his head. "I'm not going to run off with you." He squeezed his eyes shut, rubbed his temples like he was fighting a headache. "I have to think about it."

Raeyn nodded. "Don't take too long."

Aris laughed. "Or what? I can pick between the Reds Cleansing me or dragging me off to become Nymeron's—Gods, *Father's*—personal toy? I don't have all that many options to consider. Unless you count waiting this out and slowly going insane."

Aris paused and there was a sharp edge to his words when he spoke again. "Tell me this, what's to say if I go with you, you won't use me the same way he would, *brother*?"

Raeyn was silent for a moment too long. "Aris—"

But Aris was already on his way out. "I'll let you know." He closed the door behind him.

Apparently, that was Pascal's cue to kick us out, telling Raeyn in no uncertain terms he wasn't going to run off anywhere with anyone if he didn't rest up first. I moved to get up and follow Taerien, but Raeyn's fingers brushed my arm, stopping me.

"Thanks. I owe you. You didn't have to—" Raeyn's eyes were strangely intent. I had to look away. "I'm sorry, Damian."

"Not sure if I want your kind of favors, Nymeron," I said quietly. "You telling me you wouldn't've handed us all over to the Reds if it'd given you the least bit of an advantage?"

"Damian, I—"

"Save your breath, Nymeron." Anything else drained away, making room for a bone-deep tiredness that hit me like a truck as soon as I got up.

I left Raeyn with Pascal and went after Aris.

He'd left the Temple and stood outside, his body haloed by the light of a flickering lantern where he sat on the curb of the street, watching *La Maison*'s late-night customers stumble back to their bunks in the palace's barracks. I sat down next to Aris, just shy of touching him where he sat with his knees drawn close to his chest.

"So. It's Aris Nymeron now, huh?" I said and immediately wanted to kick myself for not saying something else. Something better. Like that, I was sorry things had gotten so fucked up, for hitting him the other day. That I knew he hadn't meant to force the Voyance on me. That I didn't want him to run off and leave. Instead, my throat locked up and no words came out.

I really sucked at this whole comforting thing.

It took me a second to figure out Aris's shoulders were shaking because he was laughing. "Isn't it ironic. You hear all those stories about orphans dreaming of secretly being the child of some rich king." He shook his head, blond strands falling into his face as he sat there, hunched over, hugging himself against the cool night air. "I always hated fairy tales."

"Makes two of us," I muttered and cautiously slipped an arm around him, his body warm against mine, his head on my shoulder a reassuring weight. Almost felt like old times when I would always have Aris's back and he had mine. When our biggest worry was dodging the Reds and life hadn't gotten all complicated.

"I'm so sorry," Aris said. "The other day, I—"

I silenced him with a finger against his lips. "Let's...not. Not right now, okay?" I took a deep breath. "What are you going to do?"

It'd been the wrong thing to say.

Aris all but flinched away from me. The image of reassurance blurred like one of those ancient black and white photos that faded over time until you could barely make out what had been on it, to begin with.

"Look, I need to think." Aris rubbed his eyes. "Alone."

I got to my feet slowly, trying not to show how much his brush-off stung. Used to be there'd been nothing between us we couldn't talk out. Now nothing was left but loud silences.

"Um. Sure. Got to take a shower anyway." I took another step away, so I wouldn't accidentally brush against him. "I'll see you later." Then, before I could help myself. "Promise you won't run off without me?"

Aris gave me a tight smile. In the washed-out shadows of the Temple, it turned into a gray caricature. "You're not getting rid of me, remember?"

16

Loyalty

THE *SHADOW* LAY dark and silent, a tomb encased in steel—the faint hum of the ship's generators the only thing animating its hulking carcass. I slunk inside, not bothering with light switches, my movements sketched out by the flickers of green emergency lights. Instead of going down to my bunk, which shared way too many memories of sharing it with Aris, I padded upstairs to the bridge and what used to be the cockpit. Now it was nothing but a circle of rusty dashboards gathering dust and cobwebs between cracked buttons and levers jammed after decades of disuse.

It also had the two most comfortable leather chairs in the whole ship. No wonder this was Iltis's favorite spot to think—or, as was the case more often these days, for a quiet nap. I eased into the chair to the left, feet up on the dash, imagining how it would've been back when the *Shadow* had been flying, before lack of basic things like fuel had permanently grounded her, rusting away buried under heaps of junk.

Up here, you got a pretty good look at *La Poubelle*, Helos's very own trash can, dump for unwanted machinery and people alike.

The junk would outlast the people inhabiting it. Depressing thought, but in an odd way it was comforting that even if I did run off with Aris and Raeyn, there'd be a place to come back home to. Even if half the Core was out to kill me. Even if Aris looked at me like I was a stranger. Everything could go to shit, but the *Shadow* would still be home.

I didn't notice I'd dozed off until the warm fingers of morning sunlight tickled my forearms as it broke through the twisted web of starred glass and bent steel surrounding the cockpit. Going by that and hells of a crick in my neck, I must've slept for at least a couple of hours. It also explained the smell and why my shirt chafed at the back of my neck, the collar stiff and scratchy with Raeyn's blood.

I needed a shower. Badly.

The bathroom next to my bunk was like anything on the lower deck of the *Shadow*: tiny and utilitarian. It also constantly smelled dank and musty, thanks to whatever engineer thought it was a great idea to put the shuttle's trash chute right next door and have it share the same ventilation duct. No air freshener was strong enough to get decades of reek out of the walls.

I had to hunch to keep from braining myself on the ancient shower head that screeched in a rising pitch as soon as I turned the water to its highest setting, which was lukewarm at best.

It felt fucking wonderful.

Would've been even better if I'd gotten longer than a few minutes and hardly enough time to get the dried blood out of my hair before the shower curtain ripped open with a whoosh.

"What in all the Seven Hells—" Jay's eyes cast daggers. "—did you do to my hover?"

I stood there, acutely aware I was butt-ass-naked and Jay didn't give a damn about it. Not sure if her modesty switch had broken that one time she'd walked in on Aris and me and she'd never bothered to fix it, or if she never got one to begin with. She just stared me down, knowing full well she'd backed me into a corner.

"Um." I turned my face out of the spray of water before turning the water off with a squeal of rusty piping. I fumbled for a towel and took cover. "Pretty sure parts of it are still somewhere around Taerien's place."

Jay's hand yanked the towel away from me. "Parts of it." She looked ready to implode.

"Yeah." I decided to make it quick and painless. "I sort of had to use it as a distraction." I gave her the rundown of the crazy stunt I'd pulled to save Raeyn's ass, while snatching back my towel and trying to get as many layers of clothing between her and me as I could.

"You blew up my Bonnie to save Raeyn Nymeron."

I hid a wince by pulling my shirt over my head.

"Look, Grasshopper, I know you're pissed, and I'm sorry, okay? But I couldn't leave him. He would've done the same for me."

It dawned on me I meant that last bit. My parting words to him aside, Raeyn had gotten me to trust him. Well, trust him to the point of shooting me and saving his own hide before calling in the cavalry. Still. Raeyn could've left me hanging many times, but he hadn't.

I shrugged. "Pretty sure he'll buy you a new one. Guy's got enough money squirreled away to drown in."

Not sure how true that was, especially after the Reds had torched Taerien's—guess that made it Raeyn's—mansion, but I'd leave that for Raeyn to sort out.

Jay grumbled. "Better make sure your new boy toy pays up. I want a new hover, pronto."

"He's not my—" Upstairs a rap of gunshots cracked.

Pretty damn *close* gunshots. Coming from the main deck.

Cold dread settled into my bones. My head whipped around to Jay. "Tell me that's Kovacz doing target practice."

She shook her head, her eyes so wide they seemed about to pop out. "Orion's been gone all day."

Which only left one option. The Reds found us.

"Oh fuck. *Fuck.*" I dove into my bunk, grabbed my Colt, and shoved a bunch of spare clips into my jeans. I tossed Jay a semi-auto before grabbing another one for myself.

"We gotta get to Iltis."

The shots came from the main deck. We weren't the only ones with that plan. Fuck, but I could've used Kovacz right now. I gritted my teeth. I'd have to worry about him later. There was a pause between shots. I listened for steps coming downstairs. Nothing. I pressed myself flat next to the door, gesturing Jay to follow me.

"Stay back!" I whispered. "Whatever you do, stay back."

"Sure," Jay cocked her head, pulled out her own gun and clicked off the safety. "Lock. Load. Watch your back. Got it."

"Sounds like a plan."

I dodged around the corner. Stairs were clear. Which didn't mean they weren't waiting for us to come up, laying low for the right timing to shoot. Not a risk I was going to take.

Jay darted to the slitted cover of the ventilation duct inserted in the wall. It was bent and stiff with rust like most of the *Shadow*, but with some prying, it creaked open.

"You're not serious, Grasshopper. No way we're going to fit—"

I heard something clatter and hiss down the stairs.

"Close your eyes," I hissed. Jay pulled me after her. A second later, both of us were crammed into the duct with the lid jammed shut. Just in time for a flash to go off and the first wisps of smoke to start crawling through the slits.

"So glad we got an understanding here," Jay whispered in front of me. "I'll take a rain check on you thanking me for saving your ass with my engineering genius."

"Smartass," I grumbled but followed her lead.

They'd built cargo ships like the *Shadow* bulky back in the day, allowing enough room for some sneaky modification of the ship's ventilation system. 'Course all the extra room Jay'd carved into the ducts with a blowtorch and some clever rewiring had been meant to quickly hide cargo in a pinch, not to be used as an emergency escape route. I barely had enough space to squeeze through the crawl space between the walls. My nose pressed into a hundred years of dust and cobwebs, I forced down claustrophobic thoughts of dying here, stuck in some hollowed-out air vent, and kept inching forward.

Two more gunshots rang out, the clank of combat boots dulled by half an inch of steel. Through the slits of another vent cover, I caught a glimpse of red leather.

Reds. 'Course, who else would raid a place like this in the middle of the fucking day?

Except this wasn't just any place. This was our fucking home and if I found out who'd brought them down on us—I squeezed my eyes shut. Focused on the task ahead. Get to Iltis. Keep her and Jay safe. Find Kovacz. Kill whatever Red tried to get into the way of me getting them the fuck out of here.

We kept moving slowly, careful not to give ourselves away by clanking and scraping against the walls that seemed to close in on us. White smoke drifted through the vents, making my eyes water, my breaths a wheezing echo in my ears. I choked down a cough, dragged up my shirt, and fought down panic threatening to bubble up before blindly fumbling for some corroded lead piping that opened to a shaft going up. Sweat pooled at the small of my back. Panting breaths condensed on the wall in front of me. I dragged myself up and felt something with way too many legs skitter down my shoulder. I fought the impulse to lash out, to smash it but didn't let go. I kept my eyes on Jay ahead of me, her easy, certain movements keeping me grounded. Hand and footholds were few and far between, but we managed to shimmy up to the main deck.

Down on hands and knees now, we stopped at the infirmary right across Iltis's study. I rolled out of the duct and straight under the bed by the wall, back pressed against the cool white tile. Jay gave me a reassuring nod, both of us gulping for air and taking half a second to work the kinks out of our arms and legs. The room was empty, though someone'd nearly ripped the door off its hinges. The contents of the med cabinet littered the floor, broken glass glinting in the neon light.

I got to my feet, Colt ready, and squeezed flat against the wall by the door, waving Jay to cover me as I slunk around the corner.

Iltis's study was surrounded by Reds.

At least half a dozen clustered by the door, red beetles scuttling over a corpse. Even so, Iltis, being Iltis, gave them a run for their money, going all blind ninja on their assess.

Anyone who says you can't shoot if you can't see had never met Iltis. I'd learned never to mess with the blind old crow years ago when Jay and Kovacz set me up on a dare that ended half a second in with Iltis's .38 shoved under my nose. She'd dragged me to the firing range and for weeks afterward had me do target drills blindfolded with the *Shadow*'s scratchy PA blaring music overhead. She'd made me wear that damn blindfold until I could do anything from wiping my own ass to stripping and reassembling a gun in perfect darkness.

The issue of how Iltis managed to shoot the way she did never came up again. Neither did the fact books weren't the only things she hoarded in her crammed study.

Bullets pelted the wall. The ricochet turned the hallway into a death trap, shots clanging like pebbles rattling around in an empty tin can. One Red outlier scouted the surroundings, probably waiting for one of us to hop in front of her .45. I put a bullet into her head. She went down in a red smear, blond ponytail fanning out in a sticky pool around her head.

One down, the Gods only knew how many to go.

I signaled Jay to stay back while I slunk out of our little hiding spot and took out the middlemen between us and Iltis. Two Reds went down almost simultaneously. They hadn't stopped twitching before another one followed and it hit the rest how fucked they were.

We kept them pinned for maybe five seconds before the first wave of reinforcements stomped down the hallway to my left. Another minute tops until they'd turn things around on me and I'd be the one trapped like a fly on sticky tape. Fuck.

"You idiots! Get out of here!" Iltis shouted. I only got a glimpse of her crouching behind her overturned desk, the dark wood riddled with bullet holes. She tossed the gun she'd been using and reached for another. For once, Iltis wasn't fast enough.

The bullet hit her in the chest. Everything slowed, chopped into still-frames of Iltis falling. She didn't make a sound, just stumbled forward, flailing like someone'd shoved her. Red spread across her chest, and she slumped over, bloodless fingers hugging the corner of her desk.

Behind me, Jay screamed Iltis's name, the sound blotted out by the single shot from her gun taking down the Red who'd ducked into Iltis's study and killed her.

The rushing between my ears grew into a deafening storm.

Iltis scrabbled for a book amid a whole stack knocked over along with what'd once been on her desk. Iltis's hands left shaky red streaks on the book's covers. For a second her milky eyes seemed to be looking right at us, her lips forming one single word.

Run.

Then Iltis lunged forward, hurling herself at the remaining Reds by the door, the book clutched close to her chest. Her bloody grin was the last thing I saw of her. I was already running, yanking Jay with me, when out of the corner of my eye, Iltis flipped open the pages.

The study exploded.

The shockwave threw us back. Jay's hand slipped from mine. At least three Reds stood close enough to be ripped apart by the explosion, their screams swallowed in the flames.

We got away from the worst of it before Jay went perfectly still next to me, the fires eating up what was left of Iltis's study a flickering reflection in her wide, dark eyes. I grabbed her arm and tried to drag her along. Jay didn't budge. Wherever her mind had slunk off to, didn't look like she meant to come back anytime soon.

"Fuck, Grasshopper, we don't have time for you to go all catatonic right now, okay?"

I exhaled, then took her face in my hands.

"Jay. Look at me."

The smoke filling the corridors made my voice rough and my eyes water. "Damn it, Grasshopper, you got any idea how fucking pissed Iltis is going to be when she finds out she blew up half the *Shadow* to buy us time to get the hells out of here and we wasted it?"

A hysterical giggle fought to choke me off, but something seemed to get through to Jay and the blankness cleared out of her eyes, giving way to something colder.

"Let's go and kill the fuckers who got her."

My smile felt like a broken grimace. "You bet, Grasshopper. Let's go."

We turned another corner and almost made it to the stairs when I caught something glinting on the bridge above us.

"Down!" I slammed into Jay, landing on top of her as we both smacked into the ground. A line of fire licked across my shoulders. I grunted through clenched teeth. The sniper shrunk back into the shadows before I could get my Colt up.

"Shit, are you okay?" Jay wriggled out from underneath me. Her forehead crinkled in a frown. "You're bleeding."

I got to my feet. "Fine. Just a graze."

"Oh, in that case, let me fix that," a voice above me said. I got a good look at Kovacz right before he lifted his rifle and shot my left leg out from underneath me.

I went down with a scream, writhing with my leg a bleeding ruin. I tried to roll away, tried to get a hold of Kovacz and bring him down with me, but he was faster. The butt of his rifle smashed into my face, my nose giving way with a bloody crunch and a moan. Blood rushed into my mouth, clogging up words I tried to get out. The rifle swung away from my vision, replaced by the cold muzzle of his .45 against my jugular.

"Orion, what the *fuck!*" Jay yelled, echoing my thoughts, jumbled and blurry with pain. Kovacz grabbed a fistful of my hair and yanked my head up. His eyes were cold and flat. He shoved Jay away from me.

"Go," Kovacz said. "They don't want you. This is between me and him."

Jay shook him off and stayed where she was. "What do you mean, it's between you and—" Her dark copper skin turned the color of ash, and she stumbled back as if he'd hit her. "Oh Gods. It was you. You called in the raid."

No need to look at Kovacz to know Jay was right. My insides turned hollow and brittle.

"It wasn't supposed to be this way, you know?" Kovacz shook his head. His gun never wavered. "I thought I could save you. I thought—"

"Kovacz," I croaked.

The barrel of his gun smacked into my mouth. I tasted blood between loose teeth.

"*Shut up,*" Kovacz's face twisted into a grimace, the gleam of his gun mirrored in his eyes. "You fucking Burner, you *abomination.* You—Gods damn it, I *trusted* you!"

"Orion, what the hells are you talking about?" Jay's voice sounded shrill, my head pounding in time to the blood gushing wet and warm down my leg. I strained to listen for the telltale footfalls of heavy Red combat boots. None came.

"Oh, he didn't tell you either, did he?" Kovacz's face turned fuzzy around the edges, his leather gloves creaking as he held me by the back of my collar, like a kitten by the scruff of its neck. "Well, then I suggest you look real close at his eyes. Right about now."

Kovacz flicked his wrist and the next thing I heard was the zap of a shock stick. It hit the back of my neck and my world drowned in white.

Colors seeped back into things a moment later. I lay on my side, broken nails clawing at a crack in the floor, the pounding in my ears a buzz of white noise filling my head. The smell of scorched hair and skin grew overwhelming, even before I felt the burn seared into my neck.

"See?" Kovacz said on his knees next to me. "They said it takes a bit more than a love tap with the stick to bring out the Voyance, especially with the fickle ones. Got to crank up the heat to go for a full on visual. No wonder the Empire doesn't go for this in public."

He pulled me into his lap, his hands gentle, cool fingers brushing against my forehead. The back of my neck felt like it was on fire, rubbing against the coarse material of his pants. I tried to get away from him, but all I managed was a weak wriggle that sent a streak of burning pain down my leg. Kovacz held on tight, his gun against my neck a cold reminder to stay put.

Above me, Jay's eyes were dark and very wide. I couldn't read the look on her face, floating somewhere between shock and fear. Something clenched inside of me when it hit me she might be afraid of me.

"Damian. Your eyes. How?"

"Don't know." The words felt raw in my throat, as if I'd been screaming. "I don't know."

"Shhh," Kovacz said, his voice soft, hands cool against my face. "It's okay. I'm going to take care of you." His tone sent a shudder down my spine. "Remember what Iltis said that night I came back from the Marché without you and Aris?"

I nodded. Couldn't fight him. "I remember."

It'd been a few months after I'd gotten out of *L'Ecole* and Iltis took me in that I'd had one of my worse breakdowns thinking I'd seen Ish Vereux's face in the crowds at the *Place du Marché*. Aris had spent all night talking me back down, both of us squatting in the abandoned ruins of an old school house. When he came back without us, Iltis had beaten Kovacz black and blue; he couldn't sit or walk right for days. Sure, it'd been Aris and my turn the next day, but Kovacz hadn't forgotten the lesson she'd beaten into him that night.

"Always have each other's backs," he said now. "No matter what."

"No matter what," I echoed him, numbly. Sweat trickled down my scalp.

Gods, I wanted to get Jay the hells away from here. At least keep one of us safe, but I couldn't fucking move.

Kovacz nodded, patting my cheek. "That's it. Don't worry. The others just want Aris. I'm not going to let them have you. Know you wouldn't want that."

"No," Jay whispered. "Orion, don't."

Kovacz acknowledged her then. "Go. You don't have to watch. I promise it'll be quick."

His finger tightened on the trigger. I closed my eyes.

A single shot tore through the silence. I blinked in time to watch Kovacz's gun fall from his fingers, slick with his own blood where Jay had shot him. He didn't have time to start screaming and clutching his mangled hand before Jay was on him and cracked the butt of her gun into the side of his head once, twice. Kovacz sagged sideways with a low moan.

Jay stood above him, eyes hard and cold. "I said no." Her voice boiled with rage. "You—" She swallowed. "You fucking traitor. You killed Iltis. I'm not going to let you have him, too."

She crouched next to me. "Better move it before the Reds are done turning the rest of the *Shadow* over looking for us. Come on." She pulled me up, one arm sliding under my shoulder to steady me. My knee buckled underneath me. She somehow managed to stay upright.

"Jay, I don't think I can—"

"Yeah, don't think." From somewhere she got my Colt and pushed it into my numb fingers. "Run. Point and shoot. No brains required."

My leg was a mess of white-hot pain, bad enough to blur everything into a haze. Clinging to Jay and leaning onto the wall to my right, I made it to the stairs in a mad stagger.

"Down the stairs." Jay's voice sounded strained and tinny, like an echo thrown back through a long tunnel. "They probably surrounded the ship. Can't use any of the regular exits."

I didn't make sense of her words, just followed her blindly. Around me, the world started to wobble. I barely registered lifting my right arm to shoot at two red streaks in the corner of my eye. I must've hit them because they fell away before my ears stopped ringing.

I clutched the metal railing like a lifeline. I lost my balance twice and would've fallen, if not for Jay's hands digging into my shoulder and side.

"Hey," she said when I was ready to say fuck it all and give in to the impulse to lie down on the cool metal tile. "Don't leave me hanging. Almost there."

I nodded, trying not to think about the endless corridor still lying ahead of me. Footsteps fell somewhere behind us, and I picked up my pace. The pain washing up my leg jerked the world back into sharp focus. If I clung to that, maybe it'd keep things from tilting again.

The running steps closed in. Someone shouted for us to stop, his voice cut off by two more shots firing into empty space over my shoulder. At this point I didn't even try for an accurate aim anymore, the shots nothing but a feeble attempt to buy us a second or two. Three rounds before my Colt would click on empty.

Not sure how many of them were there or if Kovacz was one of them. Either way, there were too many and no way for us to outrun them.

We'd almost made it to the lid of the *Shadow*'s trash chute, Jay's plan B since the Reds had closed off all other exits, when Jay stumbled.

"Grasshopper?"

She made a surprised little sound, somewhere between a gasp and a sigh. "Oh," she said, eyes fixed on the red stain spreading from the center of her tank top. "Shit."

I was still trying to make sense of all the blood and how fucking wrong it looked on her, how this wasn't how things were supposed to go, but her hand tightened around mine and yanked me forward.

"Jay, let go. Let go for fuck's sake."

She shook her head. "The hells I will." Her lips pressed into a hard line that felt almost as wrong as the blood soaking her shirt. "Told you, I'm not going to let them have you. You're going to fucking live through this."

With one hand, she hit the button that opened the hatch to the trash chute, with the other she pushed me against the wall. Behind her, I saw the flurry of oncoming Reds. We had seconds, if that. Jay didn't pay them any mind. Instead her hand was warm against my cheek.

"Grasshopper, what the hells are you doing?"

Jay's face lit up in a bright smile. It made her dark eyes dance with mischief, only dulled by the sob that caught in her throat.

"Damn it, let me take care of you for once."

She hugged me, tight enough for both of us to wince in pain and yet neither of us let go.

"Jay—"

"Shush. Now get out of here and let me deal with them." Jay's eyes welled up as she pulled away, but she smiled at me through her tears. "Oh, and one more thing: Avenge me."

That last bit clicked into place too late. "No, Jay—"

No, this wasn't how this was supposed to go. This wasn't how any of this was supposed to go.

Jay's smile peaked to a copy of her usual grin. "Here's the thing. I learned from the best."

She shoved me back hard enough I lost my footing and tumbled into the opening behind me. The last thing I saw of her was her hand slamming the lid shut behind me and I went down.

The quick rap of machine gun fire was a hollow echo following me as I fell.

Everything happened too fast for me to even hold my breath against the rank smell of decades of garbage ingrained into the walls. I landed in a messy heap behind one of the *Shadow*'s landing struts. My vision went white with pain and I just lay there, the jagged gravel biting into my hands and the back of my neck.

"*Jay!*" It might've been a scream or nothing but a whisper. Either way, silence was the only answer I got. Above me, the chute stayed closed. "Gods damn it, Jay!"

La Poubelle was baking in the afternoon sun. I distantly felt the hot metal burning my skin when I hooked an arm around some rusted tubing of the *Shadow*'s struts to pull myself upright.

"Oh, don't get up," Valyr said from behind me. She clicked off her safety, casually pointing her piece at me from where she stood in the shade of the *Shadow*'s bulk, leaning against one of the wrecked cars shoved against the ship's second strut. The Gods alone knew how long she'd been there. Behind her rose the outlines of at least three of her flunkies.

"You should have used the front door." Valyr pushed a pair of dark sunglasses up her nose. They almost managed to cover up her eye patch. "Your friend might even have made it. Such a shame, really. You Low Siders do have a thing for pointless melodrama."

I didn't hear most of what she said. Just her standing there, all smug and aloof brought everything back. Iltis's bloody grin, the mad glimmer in Kovacz's eyes, the way Jay's mouth had opened in that little oh of surprise when she'd been shot. I completely fucking lost my shit.

My Colt had three shots left. Two more than I'd need.

It was over before I could as much as drag myself to my knees and take aim. The sad part was it didn't even take any of Valyr's lackeys to bring me down. All she had to do was get behind me and aim a kick at the back of my left knee and I lay in the dirt, gasping.

Valyr kicked my Colt out of my shaking hands.

Fuck, I was a mess.

"Honestly, Nettoyer. I thought better of you." Gods, she had the same look on her face as Aris did when he tried to be reasonable with me. It made me want to puke.

"Fuck you, Valyr."

"Predictable too. Good thing my expectations were low, to begin with. Although I have to admit, I thought you would think to pick someplace a little less conspicuous for your hideout. It's a miracle we didn't find you years ago."

I spat blood. It trickled into the gravel before Valyr grabbed a fistful of my collar and pulled me to my knees. Part of my weight fell onto my left leg. I bit back a scream, squinting against the blinding sunlight overhead.

"Oh my." Behind her sunglasses, I could see Valyr's eyes narrow in a wince. "Looks like someone took out a bit of a personal grudge on you."

"Anger management issues run in the team," I said. Only there wasn't a team anymore. Iltis and Jay were dead, Kovacz had sold us out and Aris... Gods, if I was ever grateful for him far off, hidden away at the Temple, now was the time.

That's the part that didn't make any sense. If Kovacz hadn't lied out of his traitorous ass and Aris really was who the Reds had come for in the first place...

Why? I wanted to ask. Why the death squad? Why now?

Instead, all I said was, "Come on, Valyr. Get it over with already."

Valyr shook her head. "See, that's the real tragedy. You always seem to think everything is about you. When you don't matter at all."

She crouched down, balancing on her heels.

"Did you seriously think I hired you for your skills? You, when I could have had anyone? You were a tracker, Nettoyer. Always reliable to tell me exactly where he was. Always keeping him safe."

No need to tell me who "he" was. Aris.

More softly, Valyr added, "Thank you for that. But I'm sure even you can see I'm the only one who can protect him now."

"No. No, *fuck you*." Instinctively, I fumbled for my Colt. The Colt I didn't have. It didn't matter. "Go ahead and kill me then, because he isn't here, and I'd rather fucking die before I tell you where he is."

Valyr breathed a sigh and gave me a pat on the cheek. "You know what your problem is?" Her hands were freezing, but I didn't have the energy to jerk away. "Loyalty. It's a quality you share with my son. It's also how you are going to lead him straight to us. And for what it's worth, I am sorry for this."

She shot me.

Two rounds into my chest. The pain choked off all sound. It soaked through my body like the wet stain that grew on my shirt. My hands came away red when I touched it. The skin underneath the fabric already started to feel like it wasn't mine anymore. And still, I stared at my fingers like I was surprised. Like I didn't know Valyr had finally made up for past misses and killed me after all.

Everyone's luck runs out some day. Iltis had told me that, when? I didn't remember.

Avenge me, Jay's whisper came as an overlay. *Sorry*, I thought. *Grasshopper, I'm sorry. I fucked up.* Pretty sure she'd get to kick my ass for that sooner rather than later.

You're not getting rid of me. Aris's voice a promise, his smile a gray veil over everything before it fluttered away with the rest.

I folded in on myself, taking Valyr's twisted smile with me as I sagged back against the *Shadow*'s three-pronged strut.

"Don't worry. Your friend Kovacz made sure Aris got our message. I'm sure he's already on his way to try and save you," Valyr said. "Too bad all he'll find is your body. And, well. Us."

She melted back into the shadows, leaving me to drown in my own blood.

17

In My Time of Dying

WHOEVER SAID TAKING a few rounds of lead was a quick and easy way to go was full of shit.

Time had a fucked-up habit of slowing to a drip when you're in pain. Every breath felt like I was trying to breathe in a handful of nails scraping down my throat, punching through meat and cartilage before they turned into steel shrapnel buried in my sides and under my ribs. They shredded deeper every time my chest rose and fell.

Above me, the sun was a ball of bright light stabbing my eyes. I couldn't feel its warmth. Everything warm was leaking out of me, staining the dirt around me a muddy red. Figured I'd die in bright fucking daylight. I turned my head into the shade.

A crow perched high on some of the *Shadow*'s rusty piping. Its head cocked to one side, then it slowly righted itself again as it stared at me with flat, beady black eyes. From my angle, the beak looked huge and menacing, gleaming in the sunlight like a blade made of black steel. I remembered the eyeless scarecrow bodies of those poor bastards the Empire'd strung up by the river, crows pecking at their soft bits, pulling out entrails like oversized worms.

"At least wait 'til I'm dead, damn it." The words brought more stabbing pain and the taste of blood rising at the back of my throat. "'S bad manners. Staring at your food while it's still twitching."

I must've passed out for a bit because I woke to someone shouting my name. It sounded like the crow cawing, all rough around the edges. I cracked my eyes open. A face framed in pale fire loomed above me.

"Damian, can you hear me?" Aris touched me, hands shaking worse than his voice.

He did something to my shirt and pressed his fingers to my chest. As if that'd keep the blood inside. I couldn't quite bite back a moan.

"Aris." His name came out frothy with blood. "No. Go. Go, damn it."

"And Scene." I caught the gleam of Valyr's .45 before she'd fully stepped out of the shadows and aimed it at the back of Aris's head.

At her signal, two of her goons materialized and grabbed Raeyn who stood behind Aris. Should've figured Aris would bring him. It scared me that part of me was glad he'd come.

"Ever heard of the term innocent bystander?" Raeyn spread his hands. With his right foot, he casually kicked away the gun he'd been holding. "What?"

Valyr barely acknowledged him. "Now everyone come quietly and no one else gets hurt."

Aris stayed where he was. "I'm not leaving him."

"Oh, please." Valyr rolled her eye. It made her look strangely lopsided. "Can we cut the dramatics? He's dying. There's nothing you can do."

Aris's eyes flashed white.

"I suggest you leave that to me." He jerked his head toward the guys holding Raeyn. "And him. You let him go. You let him help Damian. After that, I'll come with you."

Valyr snorted. "Will I now?"

"Yes," Aris said simply. "Unless you prefer me to torch your little death squad."

He smiled at one of the Reds lurking behind the guys latched to Raeyn and his grin turned wolfish. The Red was little older than a kid, eyes wide like fucking dinner plates as he caught Aris's stare. "I think I'll start with that one. I hear taking them out one by one while the rest are watching is great for morale."

The white in Aris's eyes sparked. The kid shrank back with a frightened whimper.

"For Gods' sakes, stop it," Valyr snarled.

"Do we have a deal, Mother?"

"No," I choked out, squirming against Aris. "Don't. Jus' kill them and go."

But he'd never be able to take them all by himself. Not without getting himself killed. The Reds'd trapped Aris and Raeyn like they'd trapped the rest of us.

"Run," I whispered, though I wasn't sure there was anywhere to run anymore. Not if the Reds knew where the Temple was. I tried to say more, but everything came out mangled, drowned in a fit of bloody coughing.

"Shhh, don't talk." Aris slid an arm underneath me and propped me up against him, my head resting against his shoulder. "Stay with me, okay?" A faint tingle brushed against my skin when he smoothed back some hair that'd been stuck to my forehead. His hands were sticky but warm. So were his lips when he kissed my forehead.

"It'll be fine. Just stay with me." Aris's eyes never left Valyr's. "So?"

Valyr's lips pressed into a tight line. I could see her jaw muscles work, but she lowered her gun and stepped back. "You have two minutes."

Someone else dropped to his knees next to me. I almost didn't recognize Raeyn, my vision had become so blurry. For once he didn't say anything at all. I wondered if maybe all that blood had washed away all his smart-assery and snarky comeback lines. His hands were warm and so very careful when he touched me. It didn't take long until he shook his head.

"I'm so sorry," Raeyn said, eyes on me, his voice strangely thick. He turned his face away, but not fast enough for me to miss the flash of silent despair washing over his face.

Oh, fuck me.

"No," Aris whispered. His grip tightened. "No, there has to be something you can do."

I wanted to tell him, weirdly tell them both, it was okay. That it was bound to end this way and wasn't this how these things were supposed to go? Dying in the arms of the guy you love and all that bullshit. Pretty sure I could hear Iltis and Jay crack up beyond the grave at the sappy stupidity of that idea. Fuck, if I hadn't hurt so much, I would've laughed with them.

Raeyn didn't look at Aris but at me, his guarded expression a veneer doing a piss poor job hiding the cracks beneath.

"I can give you something for the pain, if you'd like. It would make it easier." He broke off. Swallowed. Dug into the pocket of his trench.

I snatched his hand. Held it. "No." I shook my head feebly. All it did was make Raeyn's face look all streaky. "I need you." I squeezed his hand tighter, fought for every bit of breath I could get through my collapsing lungs because this was important. "Need you to get him out."

Behind me, Aris said something in protest. I ignored him.

"Keep him safe. You both safe. Good at that."

Raeyn gave me a shaky smile, his eyes flicking to Valyr and her Reds. "I'll—"

"No." I dragged him back down to me. "Promise me."

Raeyn brought my hand to his lips and kissed it. For once, I didn't mind. "I promise." He lowered it gently back to my lap and got to his feet. He turned to Aris, but his eyes lingered on me, when he said, "You heard him. We need to go."

I couldn't see Valyr, but I knew she was there, waiting to pounce. My breath whistled through my nose; the nails tearing up my insides turned into ice-cold spikes. Not long now.

And I'd never let the Empire have Aris. Never.

"Damian," Aris started to argue. I didn't let him finish.

"'S your fault."

I couldn't have hit Aris worse if I'd put two slugs into his chest. "What?"

Gods, forgive me, but I'd do whatever it took to get him out of here.

I tried to lick the copper taste from my lips, but all I managed was bring up more blood gagging me, squeezing my voice into a quickly fraying thread. "Reds jus' wanted you."

All color drained out of Aris's face, but he only gripped me tighter. "No. Don't do this. Don't push me away when you think you're--"

I hated that raw brokenness in his voice even more than I hated how well he knew me.

"Doesn't change the facts." The icy spikes inside me twisted. Red welled up, trickling down the corners of my mouth. I couldn't breathe. Damn it, I couldn't—

No. Not yet. Damn it, *not yet*.

I forced the cough down and air in. The nails of my right hand were digging into Aris's arm, leaving bloody gouges around his wrist. I made myself relax.

"Jay and Iltis are dead," I wheezed. "Don' make it completely pointless."

It took all I had left in me to push away from him. I slumped to the ground in a boneless heap, like someone'd ripped out my skeleton and squished the rest of me into a tight plastic bag, the way they used to sell chickens at the Marché Noir. No bones, just pieces of meat sloshing around in too much red. Something in my abdomen flipped, and I wondered if I was going to piss myself before I died.

"Damian. Stop. Please." Aris tried to reach for me. I brushed his arm away when all I wanted was to hold on to him until it was all over.

"Go," I mumbled into the dirt. "Should've never come back in the first place."

The worst was I actually meant that last bit.

Aris didn't move. Just stared at me, dazed, like something'd snapped inside him. I bit my lips to keep from taking it all back. Gods, why wouldn't he *leave*? He could do it. Blast his way through the Reds with Raeyn as his backup. If he'd only fucking *move*.

Raeyn stepped forward and took Aris by the wrist. "Come on. It's what he wants."

"I know," Aris said and let Raeyn pull him to his feet, his eyes never leaving me.

I would've heaved a sigh of relief if I could've breathed right. As it was, I lay on the ground, too weak to lift my head. Bits of gravel dug into my hands, the side of my face. I barely felt it. Everything fell away, narrowed into a tiny blip of light.

I wasn't even cold anymore.

Aris and Kovacz had been wrong. If I was a Voyant, I'd heal. I'd walk away from this.

Aris didn't budge. His body had become nothing but a shadowy outline against my dimming vision, but I still saw him tear himself loose from Raeyn.

Oh, for fuck's sake.

"Damian?" Aris's voice hovered above me. "Damian, don't you d—"

The blip of light winked out.

18

Wayfare

MY FIRST BREATH felt like liquid fire burning down my throat. It also felt absolutely fucking wonderful, once I was done hacking up bits of dried blood that'd clogged up my lungs. It wasn't until I saw Aris on his knees above me, his eyes stark white, that I freaked the fuck out.

"You really thought I'd let you die."

Aris's smile was a skeleton grin. His hands shook, cupping my face, his skin dry and rough like old paper. Blood ran from his nose, a trickle of red ink that stained his teeth.

I reached for him. Feeling crept back into my fingers, blood flow chasing away the numb tingling. My breaths came flat and fast enough to strangle me.

"How?" I squeezed my eyes shut. Forced myself to relax before opening them again. "How in the Seven Hells—"

Okay, shit, so much for trying to keep my calm. I bit down on my lower lip, let out a deep breath and squared my shoulder blades. Only paused for half a second to be amazed I could; the icicles twisting my insides were gone.

Never thought something as simple as breathing could feel so... Oh Gods.

"You brought me back with the Voyance."

Aris's grin widened a fraction. There was no humor in it, just borderline sanity.

"Told you I'd fix you," he whispered, and the white seeped out of his eyes. He shuddered, hugging himself in a white-knuckled grip. "Think my two minutes are up."

His eyes rolled back, and he went limp.

"Aris!" I lurched forward but couldn't get a grip on him. My muscles turned to jelly and nothing was working.

Valyr was faster anyway.

"There, there." She gently caught Aris and brushed a few blond locks out of his face. "I always knew there was something special about you." The look on her face was almost...motherly. It gave me the creeps.

"Be careful with him," Valyr said to her two flunkies appearing at her shoulder.

"No." I clawed myself upright, ignored the tug inside my chest. "You're not taking him."

I fumbled for my Colt, but someone held me back.

"Don't." Raeyn's voice was a low whisper at my ear, his grip tight on my shoulders.

Valyr pretended not to see him, her eye narrowed at me. "I'm only letting you live because I gave him my word, so I suggest you don't push it."

More quietly, she said, "I'm only taking him where he belongs, Nettoyer."

"Oh yeah? How 'bout you let him figure that one out for himself?"

Valyr's smile quirked with something dangerously close to pity. "But he already has."

She turned and left, her two flunkies and Aris nothing but red dots flickering in the heat.

Behind me, Raeyn exhaled. "Well, damn." His hands around my shoulders relaxed.

"You bastard!" I whipped around and took a swing at him. "You godsforsaken bastard, you promised! Why didn't you do anything?" My punch would've had more of an effect if it hadn't been so weak, my fist squishy like a sponge soaked with water. Raeyn caught it easily.

"And what do you suggest I could have done?" he asked calmly. His hands tightened around mine. "Other than getting myself valiantly killed, of course."

Raeyn's voice was still hoarse, like it scraped past a handful of gravel shoved down his throat. Something about it made my rage boil over, reminded me how much less complicated it was to hate him.

"Damn convenient for you, isn't it? Just let Valyr snatch Aris and you get out clean."

Raeyn's face shut down. He grabbed a handful of my collar and dragged me close enough our faces were only inches apart. Then he yanked off his hat and pulled his hair back, so I got a close-up look at the scars etched down the left side of his face.

My first impulse was to turn away, but his hand whipped out and cupped my jaw, gripping hard enough to bruise. His voice was sharp like a whiplash. "Look at me."

I did. I'd seen his scars before and I knew he hated when people stared at them. His hair and eyes weren't the only things he tried to cover up under that fedora and high-collared trench. Deep craters and ridges were burned into his skin, dragging his mouth slightly off center, giving him a crooked look, especially when he smiled.

He wasn't smiling now.

"Those are the finishing touches." Raeyn pressed his lips together in a thin, bloodless line. "Father burned me for the first time when I was eleven. Back then he used the Voyance, so it wouldn't leave any visible scars, but it felt—" Raeyn shook his head. "It was a test. He said all I had to do was use the Voyance and make it go away. I failed. In the end, he managed to give me scars all the same. It's what he does."

I swallowed. Hoped he wasn't waiting for me to say something. Nothing could erase the trauma his father'd burned into Raeyn's skin. I wasn't about to make an ass out of myself by trying.

It was the flatness in Raeyn's eyes, the frozen rage, that hit home, tugged at my own share of baggage, reminded me we weren't that different when it came to pushing away our lived nightmares.

It'd been a long while since I'd last let myself think of the first time Marten and Ish taught me how I was going to pay for the friendship and protection they offered.

I slammed a lid on all of it, crammed the memory back into its tightly locked box, and buried it. One panic attack at a time. I refused to think of Marten and Ish now, not when my friends lay dead a few feet away. Everything that'd held me together after I'd gotten away from *L'Ecole* dead and gone.

No, not all of it. Aris was still out there, and I'd get him back. I gritted my teeth.

Fuck Raeyn Nymeron for making it so damn hard not to trust him.

"If you're looking for a pity party, better start looking elsewhere, Nymeron. I'm busy."

"I don't want your sympathy. I want—" Something flickered across Raeyn's face. He let go of me, like I'd zapped him. "Just understand I would never, *never* hand anyone over to my father. Least of all my brother."

"Then help me get him back," I said before I could think twice.

"I will." Raeyn's words held a dark edge. "I promised you, remember?"

"Yeah." I was so tired and worn out, I didn't bother pulling my hand out of his. "I know."

"I'm sorry, Damian."

"Don't," I said, my voice barely a whisper. "Please. Don't."

I couldn't deal with the way his touch made me feel and everything his "sorry" said but didn't say. Not now. Probably not ever.

"Right." Raeyn finally broke our silence. "Let's give your friends a proper sendoff, shall we?" He got to his feet and pulled me up after him.

I felt him wince and watched him go a little gray at my added weight. "Shit, you okay?"

Less than twelve hours ago, Raeyn'd been all but dead and it was honestly beyond me how he was out and about and snarky already. Okay, maybe not the snarky part. Raeyn would mouth off to Death itself given the chance.

"Fine," Raeyn said through his teeth, his free hand pressed against the spot underneath his ribs where the Reds'd almost gutted him. He didn't let go of my arm. "What about you?"

"I'm not dead." I tried to ignore the nervous flutter in my chest as I thought back to the cold and darkness and Aris's blazing white eyes. Even so, my arms prickled with goose bumps. "Okay, I guess. Feel like someone ran me over with a fucking hover, but other than that." I took a step just in time for my left leg to give out underneath me.

"Careful." Raeyn's grip on my arm kept me from pitching over. "Take it slowly."

I nodded and let him park me with my back against the *Shadow*, my head and shoulders resting against the sun-warmed steel.

It took me the better part of a minute to work up to the question. "I really died, didn't I?"

Raeyn nodded. "You were gone for over five minutes. No pulse, no heartbeat. Nothing." He looked down. I noticed his hand had slid to my wrist. Right to where my pulse was, beating steadily against his fingers.

I remembered the flash of desperation that'd streaked his face when he thought I was a goner. Except we couldn't talk about that. Talking about what happened after was much safer.

"Mother—Valyr—tried to take Aris, but he wouldn't let anyone near him. Near you. He—" Raeyn licked his lips. "I don't know how he did it. It should have been impossible. It *is* impossible. No one could have brought you back at this point."

"But Aris did."

"Yes. I don't know how, but he did."

Well, that sure explained the way Raeyn was still looking at me like he'd seen a ghost crawl out of its grave and start walking. I swallowed, trying not to think about how much Jay would've gotten a kick out of this. The Grasshopper loved old zombie movies. The gorier, the better. *Had* loved them. Past tense. I closed my eyes.

"He should've let me die."

"Nobody ever listens, do they?" Raeyn's crooked grin died. He reached out. "May I?"

I shrugged. Wasn't like he'd asked for permission to feel me up before.

"Purely scientific interest, I promise."

"Sure." I rolled my eyes. "Have at it."

I tried not to watch him pulling aside the blood-crusted tatters of my shirt to reveal nothing but tender pink scar tissue where Valyr'd shot me. Too fucking freaky.

Raeyn crouched down to check my leg. "I suggest you rest that knee for a few days. The Voyance may have brought you back, but it doesn't mean it healed everything without scars."

"Right, not like it's some miracle cure." I couldn't keep the bitterness out of my voice.

Raeyn continued his checkup. "Let me know if anything changes. Shortness of breath, tightness in your chest, fever, bleeding, anything."

"What if I gotta take a piss? You want to know that, too?"

Raeyn pursed his lips. "Just be careful."

"Will do if I get the chance," I muttered and pretended I didn't need to lean on the rail, limping up the *Shadow*'s ramp to take care of my friends' bodies.

From the outside, the *Shadow* looked like the shell of a crash-landed dragon, parts of it still smoking where the explosion in Iltis's study had torn a big chunk out of its side.

The inside was worse.

The *Shadow* had turned into something out of one of those old pre-Empire history books Iltis kept around. A burned and blackened relic. Another Low Side ruin. A patina of soot dulled everything in the entrance and holding bay. Walls were dented and bent out of shape, doors unhinged or completely gone where the worst of the explosion had blown everything outward. The smell of smoke stung my nose and eyes, mingled with the stink of charred flesh.

The emptiness in my stomach clenched into a tight knot.

"Hey." Raeyn stopped by my side. "You don't have to do this. Not right now."

"I'm fine," I lied. "'Sides, no knowing when the Reds get back, so." I pushed onward.

Iltis's study was a gaping hole littered with blackened debris. A dead Red slumped against the remnant of one of Iltis's towering bookshelves. Their face was gone. The leather coat had molded itself to the torso, chest caved in, everything above the collar melted into a mass of seeping holes and crusted-over furrows. I shuddered and almost stepped on a hand that reached out from under the ruin of Iltis's desk. Only it wasn't attached to anything. Just a hand, its long fingers gray and curled into claws.

For a horrible second, the image of Iltis's hand on the leather-bound book came back to me. Long fingers caressing the book's thick spine as she held it to her chest, like a mother would hold a small child. The memory curled away like a piece of paper held against a candle flame.

Someone touched my shoulder, and I nearly jumped out of my skin.

"Are you all right?" Raeyn's voice behind me.

I nodded and waited for my heart to slow down.

I'd convinced myself Iltis had gotten away somehow. That maybe she'd made it to one of the study's hidden panels, opened an escape hatch, anything. But standing here, it was painfully clear no one had made it out of this alive.

I turned away from the study, away from that hand.

"I've got to find Jay."

Down by the bunks, the light flickered, chasing ragged shadows across the walls. Shooting must've messed up some of the circuitry. Damn, Jay'd be pissed if she found out someone'd messed with her wiring. I could almost hear her going on about how the rest of us were nothing but clumsy idiots who shouldn't be let nowhere near delicate electronics. 'Course half the time she'd already fixed it before we even knew it'd been broken.

I found Jay at the end of the corridor, leaning against the trash chute, head slumped forward. A step or two away from her lay the body of a Red, tossed into the corner like a discarded wrench out of her toolbox. Jay always worked in chaos; cleaning up after herself never more than a derailed afterthought.

"Hey, Grasshopper, what'd I tell you about sleeping on the job, huh?" I crouched down in front of her and gathered her in my arms, her curly head heavy against the crook of my shoulder. "Thought I taught you better than that."

Jay'd hated the first time I took her on a run. Quarter of an hour in, she'd started nagging me about when the action would start happening and criticized the lack of doughnuts and caffeine to make up for all the boring waiting. I'd carried her to her bunk that night, her body warm with sleep in my arms.

I didn't notice how cold she was or how some of the blood soaking the front of her tank top was seeping into my shirt until I felt Raeyn's fingers brush against my arm.

"Damian," he said gently. I didn't look at him or at Jay huddled in my arms, her dark eyes blank like marbles. I stared at the floor where Raeyn's footsteps trailed smears of ash against the tile. His hand tightened on my shoulder. How could his fingers be so warm when Jay was so cold? "Damian, she's gone."

"I know." The words came out mechanically, grinding against each other like a set of rusty gears that didn't quite fit. Finally, I managed to close Jay's eyes with one trembling hand and got to my feet, only staggering a little under her weight.

"What are you doing?"

Raeyn tried to give me a hand, but I shoved him away with a growl. "Don't touch her."

"Okay." Raeyn took a quick step back, hands raised. "Okay."

"Can't leave her down here," I muttered. But where else was I supposed to put her? It seemed wrong to carry her to her bunk, like I'd done so many times before. I knew I wasn't going to come back. Couldn't leave her with Iltis either. Jay'd hated being alone in the dark.

I took her up to the bridge instead. My bad leg dragged and throbbed at each step, but I didn't stop or accept Raeyn's help until I put her down in one of the seats in the *Shadow*'s cockpit. Jay's body looked ridiculously small and fragile in the big leather chair.

"She always liked it up here, you know. Her and Iltis had this idea of fixing the *Shadow* up. Making her fly again."

I got a blanket out of one of the closets. It was old and smelled a little musty, but it was clean. Something sharp poked my hand when I wrapped it around her. I reached past the blood splattering her shirt and pants into her pocket to get it out.

When I saw what it was, I laughed, the sound catching on a sob. It was a set of wings Jay'd taken off an old flight suit she'd found somewhere in the *Shadow*. The thing was bent and tarnished, black gunk hardened in its crevices, but Jay'd carried it with her for years.

"Never seen a plane in the air her whole life and the girl was obsessed with flying."

I finished tucking her in, fastened the pin to hold the blanket closed around her neck and kissed her cool forehead.

"You shouldn't've done this, Grasshopper," I whispered, my voice thick, remembering what Jay'd said right before she'd shoved me down the trash chute to save my life. "Promise I'll get the fuckers." Except there was fuck all that'd do to bring her back or make this even the tiniest bit less unfair. "Sorry I couldn't do more for you, kiddo."

Then, before I lost my nerve and lay down with her, I tore myself away and got the canister of kerosene from the cockpit's emergency supplies.

"Damian, what are you—" Raeyn asked, then caught on. "Oh."

"We've gotta burn it. Can't leave them to the Reds."

Behind me, I heard Raeyn swallow. "Right. Um, are you sure you—"

"I've got it. Go downstairs. Second door to the right. Grab whatever you can fit into a couple of bags. Leave the rocket launcher. It's out of ammo."

Raeyn let out a shaky laugh. "You have a rocket launcher stashed away with your—" He shook his head. "Never mind. Of course, you do. I'll be right back."

He bounded down the stairs, and I was suddenly, inexplicably glad for it. Seemed if you had to pack up your life in five minutes' notice, it was almost easier to have someone else do it. Less personal that way, because I'd had all the personal I could handle.

I made sure the blanket around Jay got soaked all the way through before I dragged the canister out onto the bridge, trailing clear, sharp-smelling liquid behind. By the time I'd gotten the rest out of the *Shadow*'s cargo bay and sloshed it all over the main deck and below, Raeyn trudged up the stairs, panting under a load of black duffle bags slung across his shoulder.

"You failed to tell me you're keeping an arsenal in your closet."

"Always be prepared. Isn't that how it goes?"

"Yes, if you were a boy scout back in the old days. I highly doubt this qualifies."

I shrugged and took two of the bags off him. That's when I noticed the gray bundle of fur he'd tucked into the inside of his trench coat. Dust's green eyes stared up at me menacingly, her tail batting against Raeyn's chest.

"You found the cat."

"She found me," Raeyn replied. "She seemed to take exception to being burned with the rest of the ship."

"I bet." I smiled, despite myself. "Anyway, let's get this over with."

I walked out without looking back. Out of the corner of my eye, I caught the glint of two large silver coins on the ground next to the clawed hand buried under Iltis's desk. Raeyn had put two just like them on Jay's closed eyes before he left. Wayfare, he'd called it, for the Gods to safely tide them over. Wherever "over" was, I hoped it was better than the cold and darkness I remembered.

For a while, I stood outside the *Shadow*, a scratched-up hurricane lighter in my hand, staring at the wreck that'd been my home. Now it'd become my friends' funeral pyre.

I flicked the lighter open and threw it into the rainbow-colored puddle of gasoline pooling at the bottom of the ramp.

"*Bon passage, mes amis,*" Raeyn said softly.

I said nothing. Couldn't trust whatever'd come out of my mouth not to be screaming.

Instead, I made a silent promise to Jay and Iltis to avenge them. To get Aris back. And to tear this godsforsaken Empire apart. I'd light its ruins on fire and watch it burn.

The *Shadow* went up in flames.

19

Personal Guard

"YOU'VE GOT TO be fucking kidding me. *This* is your plan?"

"Brilliant, isn't it?" Raeyn smoothed the collar of his black uniform shirt. The Gods only knew where he'd gotten two full sets of Red gear in the first place.

Not that the uniform was my biggest problem at the moment.

"You turned me into a fucking underwear model!"

I couldn't tear my eyes from the mirror. There was no escaping it.

At least they were still *my* eyes staring back at me. Bit wide right now, set in a face that'd fit right on the cover of some holomag with cheekbones sharp enough to cut glass, and a nose that'd never been broken before. Never thought I'd miss my scars, but staring at this smooth, airbrushed version of myself—myself as a gym-obsessed blowup doll because no way those arms came naturally—made me feel naked. More naked than I currently was, dressed in nothing but boxers and too-tight pants. Nothing fit right anymore. Even my hair was wrong, still black, but shoulder-length and relaxed until it was bone-straight.

Gods.

Thought it couldn't possibly get any worse, holed up in Raeyn's rooms at the Temple for nearly a week, going stir-crazy laying low, waiting for the Reds to burst in any minute and finish us off while Raeyn worked out the details of his completely batshit plan to get Aris back.

A headache pounded against my temples, chipping away at my skull.

I scrunched my eyes shut, half expecting it to all go away when I opened them again. To be back in my own body. Nothing happened. I pulled on my boots and stifled a hiss at the stab of pain that shot through my leg. Even after Aris's Voyance healing stunt, my knee didn't like to bend. Guess some things were still the same.

Small favors. Wouldn't have felt right to get out of the *Shadow* scot-free when Jay and Iltis hadn't. Not that I needed the reminder with every step. Burning the bodies of your friends was pretty hard to forget. I hadn't slept in days and as much as I tried to convince myself this was just another nightmare, all the pinching in the world wouldn't wake me up.

"Do you have any idea how completely fucked up this is? You can't put people into whatever body you want them to be in and pretend it's normal."

"I'm sorry." Raeyn cringed. "Saffron wasn't thinking." And quietly, "I wasn't thinking."

"Yeah. You don't have to." I clenched my fists, took a deep breath to keep from punching him. "If the Empire had its way, we'd all be the same. Obedient fucking copies."

"That's not what I—" Raeyn bit his lip. He wouldn't meet my eyes. "I should have told you. Saffron's glamours are only second to what the Empire's labs can do. Clearly, they took my instructions to make sure you wouldn't be recognized too far. I'm sorry, but did you expect we would go infiltrate the palace and the president's personal guard wearing a pair of wigs and fake mustaches? Maybe colored contact lenses? Please."

Yeah, and erasing much of what made me *me* was such a better plan.

Not for the first time I thought how I'd be better off if I'd ditched him and done this solo. Get into the palace, get Aris, and get the fuck out. Would be nice if it were that easy. Even I had to admit that wasn't much of a plan. I'd never even get in. All I'd end up with were my brains splattered against the palace walls, like a bug squashed against a windshield.

Much as I hated to admit it, getting into the palace called for Raeyn's more weasely skill set. 'Sides, he was all I had left.

"I look like I should be in some action holoflick, crushing people's skulls between my thighs."

"Bit generic in my opinion, but it'll do," Raeyn said dismissively. I'd expected his eyes to linger, but he'd barely looked at me. "I much prefer the real you. Especially when we're talking about being between your thighs."

I snatched up my shirt and yanked it on. "Fuck you, Nymeron."

Raeyn smirked.

The glamour he wore was as inconspicuous as you could get: medium-height, medium-build, medium-brown hair and brown eyes in a face that belonged to a guy so obviously meant to be overlooked, it almost seemed like he was trying too hard.

"How come you're going all Mr. Average?"

"That's Captain Rhys Emerson to you, Lieutenant Crane," Raeyn said, his accent suddenly all blunt consonants and drawn-out vowels. "Staff Recruiter of the outer perimeters of the Empire. Regular guest at the palace."

I quit fiddling with the cufflinks of my shirt to stare at him. "Wait a minute, you do this kind of thing on a regular basis?"

"Quality intelligence is so hard to come by these days." Raeyn straightening my cuffs in brisk, efficient movements. I noticed he hadn't looked at himself in the mirror even once. He wore his glamour, and the uniform that went with it, like a pair of ratty sweats; something you shrugged into and left the house in, without giving a shit about appearance. Only Raeyn would never be caught dead in sweats. Something about it just rubbed me the wrong way.

"Either way," Raeyn went on, "I'm your perfect cover. Nicely low profile."

I snorted. "Don't think I'd call posing as one of Aris's personal guards low profile."

"Well, *I* am staying in the background. You are getting all the brownie points for staging a glorious rescue and saving the damsel in distress." Raeyn pinned the silver sun crest of the Emperor's personal guard onto my left lapel. "Trust me. Nobody will even look twice at you walking off with him. It's what bodyguards are for. Lots of muscle, very few questions. You'll have him out of the palace and back here in no time. No death or destruction required."

"Right. And for that, you had to stick me into *this*." I spread my hands. Even my fingers felt bulkier. "It's temporary, right?"

Raeyn nodded. "Don't worry, Saffron will take it off as soon as we're back. In the meantime, make sure nobody touches your skin."

"What happens if anyone does?"

Raeyn reached out and touched my cheek. As soon as his bare fingers brushed against my skin, his glamour began to ripple and change until his real face broke through it like through a curtain of water.

"Oh," I said as the glamour slid back in place. "That why you don't wear this kind of thing more often? It'd make for a better cover than that hat and coat of yours, wouldn't it?"

Raeyn's smile died. He pulled away from me, his face slammed shut behind a mask tighter than the best glamour. "I have my reasons."

It wasn't until I glanced up from tugging on my gloves that I saw Raeyn standing in front of the mirror. One hand went up to touch his face, jerking back almost instantly.

That's when it hit me what his problem was and what I'd said. Ah, shit.

"You know, you spend way too much time worrying a few scars might ruin your pretty-boy looks, Nymeron. Get over it."

Raeyn looked at me as if I'd punched him.

"Don't." His voice was husky and broke off. He drew his red leather coat around himself like armor. "We should get going."

Neither of us said much on the way to the palace and once there, we let Raeyn's fake paperwork do the talking. The Palace of Light ringed in by two concentric circles, an outer and inner wall with the palace itself in the middle like the bullseye of a target. Along the walls, there were three checkpoints. They took my fingerprints and retina scans at all of them.

Raeyn had told me this would happen, but the first time I put my finger on the touchpad, I knew that this was it. Any second now the pad would turn red and there'd be flashing lights and alarms going off. The spot right between my shoulder blades started itching. I could all but feel the red dot of a laser sight burning a hole into the back of my coat.

Brilliant and simple plan, my ass. This was a suicide mission.

I kept staring at the smooth wall in front of me, wondering if the Empire hired some poor bastard to keep all that stone at a polished shine. Even the cracks were white and spotless. Pretty sure I'd ruin that guy's day if I got shot, splattering blood and gore all over it. Then again, maybe he was used to that kind of thing and would just go straight for the bleach.

With a short blip, the pad turned green. The glamour held like a glove, changing my fingerprints and retinas along with the rest. Creepy.

"Welcome to the Ice Palace," a light-skinned guard said. Her brown eyes smiled at me. She gave me a once over and didn't stop there. I could swear she was only half looking at whatever she was checking off her clipboard. "Hey, in case you need someone to show you around. Or, you know, want to get together for a drink—"

I stared. "Uh." I was still trying to wrap my head around the fact that I'd gotten hit on by a Red before I'd even made it two steps into the palace, when Raeyn came to the rescue.

He glared at her. "Lieutenant Falk, we don't have all day."

The Red's smile dropped dead. She drew back her shoulders and gave Raeyn a stiff salute.

"Of course, Captain Emerson, sir!"

Raeyn nodded impatiently and all but ripped a clipboard out of another guard's hands, checking off boxes and filling in blanks in a series of sharp scribbles and slashes.

Falk grimaced.

"Didn't know you were with Captain Frostbite," she whispered and passed me a stack of papers to sign. Her eyes darted to Raeyn. "I swear, the guy's so cold he shits ice cubes."

Too late, I managed a cough to cover up my laugh. Shit, Reds had a sense of humor. Guess they were human after all.

Raeyn cleared his throat and jerked his head for me to follow. The guy closest to the door hurriedly pushed in a panel that opened the gate. He looked like he was worried Raeyn was going to eat him.

"Captain Frostbite, huh?" I murmured stepping through the gate.

Raeyn's eyebrows drew together. "Excuse me?"

I bit down a grin. "Never mind."

Behind us, the door snapped shut like a mouth full of sharp teeth. The palace was a monster made of glass, marble, and chrome, swallowing the shuffling drag of my steps. Raeyn obviously knew where he was going. He led me down a wide corridor with a floor checkered in black and white, a life-size chessboard and us just the pawns pushed forward. I got why Falk had called it the Ice Palace. Everything was made of glass. Most of it was a milky white, turning walls that should've been see-through into something that reminded me of those mirrored interrogation rooms where you couldn't see who else was watching.

The twitch between my shoulder blades was back. I fought the impulse to wipe my sweaty palms on my neatly creased uniform pants.

Raeyn stopped in front of a door made of heavy black wood to go with the place's chessboard theme. He gave me a look that asked if I was okay without as much as moving his head. I replied with a not-quite nod, and he squared his shoulders before knocking with two sharp raps.

"Enter," Valyr's clipped command came from inside.

Not sure what I'd expected Valyr's office to look like, but it sure as the Seven Hells wasn't this. Valyr's office was...cute. In an old-fashioned, homey way that clashed ridiculously with the hard-ass Valyr I knew. The first thing I noticed was the cup she was holding. It was one of those small, dainty ones, with gold trim and painted in a blue flowery pattern. Way too fragile to fit into a hand I mostly remembered curled into a fist.

Even her desk had fallen to the invasion of the knickknacks with lacy bits clinging to every corner like sticky spider webs. Valyr liked *doilies*. And I thought I'd seen it all.

Then the guy sitting in one of the chairs in front of her desk turned around.

Aris was a statue carved of ivory and ice. His hair had turned white, long curls framing his face in a silver halo. He'd always been pale, but now his skin nearly seemed to glow, his jaw and cheekbones standing out at sharp angles.

Something cracked deep inside me seeing him like that.

Gods, what have they done to you?

"Sir." Somewhere behind me, Raeyn snapped into a stiff salute. I should've copied him, but it didn't track. I felt my mouth shape Aris's name, but no sound came out.

I remembered Raeyn talking about the glamour Valyr'd put on Aris to hide him, but I'd never put much thought into it. Never thought they could just take it away, the way you'd take an outfit off a doll before putting on another.

They'd even changed his eyes. The hazel was gone, replaced by near-colorless gray gemstones that blinked at me with a hint of confusion.

"My, looks like the help needs someone to show him the ropes, doesn't he?" Orion Kovacz sauntered over to Aris's side, teacup and saucer in hand. "Pretty over brains, that it?"

He made it all of two steps before my gun came out. "Freeze." The word came out between teeth clenched around the impulse to scream at him to get the fuck away from Aris.

Valyr shot to her feet, but Kovacz held up a hand for her to stay where she was.

"He speaks." Kovacz carefully set his cup down on the corner of Valyr's desk. "Do you always start conversations by pointing your piece at people, or are you just happy to see me?"

The rushing between my ears blotted out his words. Around me, the office broke up into snowy static. The only clear picture was Kovacz standing way too close to Aris. And Aris sat there, watching with nothing but mild interest, as if this was all entertaining enough, but didn't really concern him.

"I'm here to weed out a traitor," I bit out, trying to keep up appearances and failing miserably. "And look at that, I found one right here."

Kovacz let out a breathy laugh. "Is this supposed to be a joke? Because you might have noticed no one is laughing." He glared at Raeyn. "Call off your dog or I will put him down." Kovacz didn't even look at my gun. Instead, he watched me drag another limping step toward him. His eyes narrowed. "What happened to your leg?"

"Traitor shot me." The rushing grew into the deafening sound of waves crashing down on me, pulling me under. I felt my face drag itself into a grin. "Just here to return the favor."

"No, you won't."

A metallic click and the muzzle of a .45 pressed against my skull. Raeyn's voice grazed the back of my neck sharp as a whiplash. "Put down your weapon, Lieutenant."

Well, fuck.

I was still wondering how serious Raeyn was about blowing my brains all over Valyr's lace doilies when she cleared her throat. "Someone explain to me what in the Light's name is going on here."

I ignored her. Standing in Valyr's office, in the middle of the fucking palace, Raeyn's piece cocked against my skull, the fact I'd spectacularly blown my cover—all that should've been screaming at me to keep my mouth shut. But between that first shot coming from Iltis's office and the moment the *Shadow* went up in flames, nothing quite mattered anymore.

I kept my eyes on Kovacz. "The Shadows send their regards."

All color leaked out of Kovacz's face. "You. How?"

The knife slid into his hand in a smooth streak of silver. I expected him to lunge for me, but he didn't. He went straight for Aris.

"No!" My scream faded into background noise.

The waves crashed with a roar. Valyr's office drowned in white light.

The lamp on Valyr's desk flickered and died with the smell of fried wiring. I knew I was in deep shit. It barely registered. I snapped into movement. The barrel of Raeyn's gun fell away, Raeyn's and Valyr's shouts nothing but white noise, shoved into the background.

Even if I'd had time, no way I'd hit Kovacz in close quarters like this without risking Aris getting hit, too. So, I did the next best thing and took a direct approach. I slammed into Aris and knocked him aside. Kovacz's knife came down, and I threw my arm up in time to block it from stabbing into the soft, fleshy spot where Aris's throat met his shoulder.

The blade slashed a streak of fire across my palm, cutting through my gloves and down my forearm. My grip was red and slippery, trying to wrangle the knife from Kovacz's hands.

"You're never going to learn, are you?" Kovacz bit out between clenched teeth. The knife was suddenly very close to my eyes, the tip gleaming with my blood. "All he'll do is get you killed. I'm doing you a favor."

"Right. Like you did to Jay and Iltis?" I grated. Numb fingers clamped around his wrist. "I burned their bodies, you bastard."

Something flickered across Kovacz's face, and I got a grip on his shoulder. There was a crash and the sound of breaking glass and china as we toppled sideways into the cabinet that lined the wall. Splinters and sharp edges dug into my back and shoulders. I barely felt it. Rage beat behind my temples like a second pulse. I rolled out from under Kovacz, kicked the knife from his hands and closed my hands around his throat. Kovacz made tiny frantic noises, tried to kick out at me, but I held him down. Warm blood leaked out between my fingers and made a collar around Kovacz's throat. I kept squeezing and it tightened like a noose.

Kovacz had been with me the day we'd picked Jay off the streets. The Grasshopper always said it was her who'd picked us, following us home, going on about how we'd stiffed her out of the money she'd charged for fixing up our hover. 'Course she'd won it right back, cheating Kovacz dry at poker. They'd stuck together ever since.

Nothing but bleached-out memories now. A flash of white caught in the reflection of Kovacz's glasses. His eyes rolled back, lashes fluttering like a pair of panicked little birds shoved out of their nest. White fog swallowed all of it.

I didn't notice I was shaking until a pair of hands pulled me off Kovacz. Raeyn yanked him back and away from me. The click of handcuffs cut through the sound of hoarse coughing. Someone was talking to me, a low string of words I couldn't make out. Warmth trickled down my arm and the side of my face where I lay twitching on Valyr's carpet.

The fog lifted slowly. I recognized Aris above me.

"Hey." My voice lagged a bit, and I had to try twice to make it past the bitter aftertaste that clogged the back of my throat. I clawed myself into a sitting position, my head heavy and pounding. I rested it against the wall to stop the world from tipping over. "You okay?"

"Fine," Aris said in a strangely clipped tone. Keeping up the act. Right. He dodged my hand when I reached for him. "Hold this, you're dripping."

For a broken second, I thought he was holding out one of Valyr's doilies for me to stop my nose and arm from gushing blood all over Valyr's rug, but it was just a bunch of napkins he'd gotten out of the ruins of the cabinet we'd trashed. I choked back hysterical laughter and used my good hand to press the napkins to my nose.

"I hate to repeat myself," Valyr said, glaring at the mess that'd once been her office. Her eyes settled on me. "But what in the Light's name happened here?"

"That's what I would like to know," a voice by the door said. I could've sworn someone'd seriously hit me on the head and I was seeing triple. Either that or this really was Sirius Nymeron, the president and Big Bad himself standing in the middle of Valyr's office, shards of broken china crunching underneath the soles of his shoes.

Oh. Fuck.

Nymeron nodded at Valyr. "Commander."

Could be just me, but I thought I heard a slight stiffness in Valyr's "Mr. President." Both of them sure as shit kept up pretenses they were nothing but business relations. Guess thirty years or so of practice made pretty fucking perfect.

In real life, Sirius Nymeron looked older than his holoscreen shots. Then again, there was a difference between seeing the face of the Empire on screens and far away during public appearances and having him stand within three feet of you. I got a good look at the deep lines that ringed his milky gray eyes and the sagging skin underneath his chin even his closely cropped white beard couldn't quite hide. Still, steel infused every movement, his eyes flat like a snake's. They only softened when he spotted Aris crouching over me, wrapping a towel around my arm.

"Are you all right, son?"

I hated the concern in his voice. It made him sound so harmless. A father worried for his son. The same guy who sent his goons to hunt down little girls in the streets and who'd all but killed his other son. The one who currently stood across the room doing his damndest to blend in with the furniture. I couldn't see Raeyn's eyes, but I saw the way his knuckles stood out, while holding on to Kovacz, keeping him upright so no one could see his hands shake.

"I'm fine, Father," Aris said. The smile he gave Nymeron, the guy who'd fucking kidnapped him, made me want to puke. "Lieutenant Crane saved my life."

Valyr opened her mouth but shut it at a hard look from Aris.

Nymeron's eyes pinned me down with invisible needles, an insect fixed on a corkboard, to be dissected layer by layer. Something brushed my mind and I focused hard on thinking empty, loyal Red thoughts. I fought to keep from throwing up all over his expensive loafers.

"Good work, Lieutenant." Nymeron gave me a nod.

I wanted to run screaming. Instead, I clenched my teeth, tried not to flinch when he patted my shoulder, absurdly grateful for the several layers of stiff fabric between his skin and mine that kept my glamour intact. "Get yourself stitched back together. We need more of your sort around here."

Right. "Um. Thank you. Mr. President. Sir." *Gods*, just let me get Aris out of here.

Lucky me, Aris pitched in to save me before my stammer-fest went overboard.

"I'll get him to the infirmary. It's the least I can do." He regarded Valyr, challenging her to say something, to admit in front of Nymeron exactly how spectacularly we'd broken her shiny security system. Twice. Valyr glared at him and said nothing.

Aris offered me a hand and drew me to my feet, his finger brushing the gap between my glove and my wrist. His face went slack in recognition. He let go of me so fast I nearly dropped back to the ground. My heart kicked up in my chest.

Aris stayed silent, but his eyes darted to Nymeron, who'd started exchanging words with both Valyr and Raeyn, who kept his eyes down, his sentences short and to the point.

Nymeron hadn't noticed. No one had. Still, I needed a few seconds with the wall until my legs stopped shaking.

"Father." Aris looked like he was staring right through Kovacz, his face so perfectly blank I wondered if Raeyn'd given him lessons. "I believe it's time we show the people of Helos what we do with traitors, don't you think?" The casualness in his tone made me shiver. I almost felt sorry for that bastard Kovacz.

Nymeron's lips curled in approval. "You're a fast learner, son. He'll be dealt with appropriately." He nodded at Valyr to follow him out the way someone'd call their dog to heel.

Raeyn prodded Kovacz to the door when he shook that vacant look off his face and found his voice again.

"No traitor," Kovacz called after Nymeron, pupils wide, beyond focus. "Traitors all around you. That son of yours. Lieutenant Crane. 'S all a lie. Traitors. All of 'em."

My heart skipped a beat, long enough for Valyr to turn back around. "That's quite enough from the knife-wielding lunatic." She tipped her head to Raeyn. "Remove him, Captain."

"No!" Kovacz's voice shrilled. "You don' get it, you—"

Raeyn shoved him into the wall. "Now. You heard the commander. You can either come quietly or I can fix that for you with some duct tape. What's it going to be?"

That seemed to wake Kovacz up. "You can't do this! I have my rights, you can't—"

He thrashed in Raeyn's grip, but Raeyn was faster. He slammed Kovacz into the doorframe and slapped a piece of silver tape he'd swiped off Valyr's desk over Kovacz's mouth.

"Oh yes, I can. And I will," he said quietly. "I'd say next time think about who you're going after with a knife, but I don't think there will be one, do you?"

He ignored Kovacz's muffled sounds of protest and hauled him out into the hallway. Before he left, Raeyn gave me a quick jerk of his head, his eyes darting to Aris. I'd see him again on the outside. I was on my own now.

Aris waited till we were in and out of the infirmary and he'd personally patched me up safely away from prying eyes until his stony silence cracked.

"Are you *completely* out of your mind?" he hissed and pushed me into the alcove of an abandoned corridor. "What in the name of all the Seven Hells are you doing here?"

I blinked at him. "What am *I* doing here? Maybe you should've let that doctor check your head. Might've shaken something loose there. I'm getting you out of here, of course. Come on."

I took his hand, held it long enough to check whatever the Empire'd done to him wasn't going away and for a part of my heart to shatter with that realization.

Aris stepped back. "I'm not going anywhere, Damian. The only one leaving here is you."

His words hit me like a punch in the gut. "What? You're—No. You're kidding, right?"

The Empire's labs hadn't managed to get rid of that frown line carved between his eyes whenever he was really serious about something. No. I shook my head, the nails of my unbandaged hand digging into the crevice by the windowsill, glad to have something to hold on to.

"You're not serious." The words sounded small and broken, like shattered hopes.

"Gods, if you could see your face. I'm sure Raeyn and you had it all planned out, didn't you? You'd sneak in, get through to me, and we'd walk right out together to live happily ever after, is that it?" Aris shook his head. "Sorry to ruin your pretty plans. It's not going to happen."

"Damn straight, it isn't," I snapped, anger taking over. "I'm not going to leave you here."

"Funny how you always seem to think it's all about you. It's not, you know."

Aris tried for gentle, but all I could think was if he'd always had that hard streak around his mouth or if it was just part of his new make-over.

"This is my part to play. I'll make sure Kovacz gets what he deserves for what he did to Jay and Iltis. For what he did to us. But after that—" Aris's breath was a sigh against my ear. His lips touched my skin. They felt like ice. "I've made my choice. Please, Damian. Just go."

"Why?" The question was out before I could stop myself. "How can you choose this after everything that happened, everything we've been through?"

"How could I choose anything different?" Aris said, all softness wiped from his eyes.

I wanted to shake him off, but two could play this game. My good hand curled in the collar of his shirt, pulling him almost close enough to kiss.

"Have you looked at a mirror lately? You don't even look like yourself, so quit bullshitting me. You're fucking crazy if you think you can get rid of me like this so you can play house with daddy dearest. Forget it."

Aris's face shut down completely, his voice a velvety smooth parody of his father's. "Who said I was giving you a choice?" A flash of white danced across Aris's eyes. I smothered a gasp when his hand clenched around my taped-up arm.

"Oh no, you're not. You're not—"

"You're right, I'm not." Aris let go of me. His smile didn't reach his eyes. "I don't need the Voyance to get you out of here. Not when this is so much more efficient. I'm sorry, Damian."

He called out for his guards.

"I suggest you start running."

Part Three

Dead Draw

Burning

THEY BURNED KOVACZ three days later.

"I don't know about you, but I really don't want to see this," Raeyn said, hunched into the high collar of his trench.

"Told you, you didn't have to come."

I kept my eyes on the press of people bunching in. The Empire sure knew how to draw a crowd. With the elections coming up, this became a fucking spectacle. Not even noon and the Place du Marché was bursting at the seams. People kept bumping into me: hips and elbows, the dangling legs of children riding on their parents' shoulders to get a better look. The smell of caramel popcorn hung in the air, thick enough I could almost taste it. It was like someone'd screwed with time and decided to stage the Marché Noir in bright daylight. Except instead of black market goods, this peddled campaign slogans and fear mongering.

"And leave you without supervision? I don't think so." Raeyn reached inside his coat and unfolded a pair of black sunglasses. Between his trench and the fedora drawn deep over his face, they fell into place like the last soldier taking position in a shield wall bracing for attack.

"I don't need a fucking babysitter, Nymeron. 'Sides, shouldn't that be the other way 'round?"

He shrugged and tucked a stray strand of silver hair under his hat, out of enemy lines. "You honestly expect me to watch you throw yourself at Aris first chance you get? Sorry, darling, that's a risk I can't afford."

Whatever I grumbled in reply drowned in the gurgle of water as I hunkered deeper into the shade of the fountain we'd made our lookout spot. Pretty sure I wasn't the only one who appreciated the irony the Empire'd gone through the trouble to fix a fountain that'd been bone-dry since I could remember for the very day they'd publicly torch someone. Now there were children splashing water everywhere, leaving wet footprints scattered across the hot tarmac like the imprints of a stampede. A little over, two girls perched on the cracked marble, laughing behind cupped hands. An old woman pushing a faded blue stroller glared at them through squinty eyes. No better way to get a good view without being spotted right away than hiding in the heart of the crowd.

The Reds had built a makeshift stage at the south end of the square, two seats elevated and off center. I kept my eyes on those two empty chairs and avoided the pyre. It still lurked in the corner of my eye, a pile of jagged wooden planks and hacked-apart furniture, like the Reds gutted some Low Side ruin and dumped its interior out with the trash.

If I looked closely, I could almost make out splintered pieces of Iltis's desk along with broken remnants of her bookshelves, crumpled book pages ripped from their bindings and shoved between the gaps like tinder, the clawed fingers of an out-flung hand reaching for me—

A shriek cut through the buzzing masses. I jumped and halfway got my Colt out of its holster before it clicked the sound came from one of the girls after the other'd pushed her into the fountain. Now her friend pulled her back out in a tangle of soggy pink skirts and blonde hair plastered to her forehead, both laughing in that too loud, too high-pitched way of Core girls who didn't know any better.

Fucking tourists. I waited for my heart to stop trying to punch a hole through my ribcage.

"Hey." Raeyn's fingers were a warm flutter on my arm. "Are you okay?"

I squeezed my eyes shut, chasing away the images. The *Shadow* was gone, nothing left but rust and scraps of blackened steel.

"Fine."

Sure you are, the quirk of Raeyn's lips said, but he didn't call me out on it. He reached into the inside of his coat and passed me a silver flask. "You look like you could use it."

I took it by reflex. It felt more than half empty already. Raeyn stood close enough to me now I could smell the whiskey on his breath.

"Shit, you're drunk?"

"Unfortunately, no." His lips twitched on the edge of a smirk. "I hope to be very soon."

"Uh-huh.", I took a swig. The whiskey left a pleasantly burning trail down my throat. "Well, at least you're packing the good stuff."

"Oh, darling, do I ever."

I didn't comment on that one or shrug off his hand, still curled around my arm, because right then the president and his son took the stage.

Aris moved with the mechanical precision of a wind-up toy, eyes forward, a set of glinting mirrors. In the sun his hair shone bright like fiberglass. Didn't think I'd ever get used to Aris looking like a younger version of Nymeron.

He took the seat to Nymeron's right. Going by the murmur going through the crowd, the symbolism wasn't lost on anyone. Valyr and a dozen Reds formed a protective half circle around the president's back, their dress uniforms gleaming like fresh blood. Laras and Sykes stuck to Aris's side, two trained dogs standing guard. Aris sure knew how to pick them.

It took a minute or so for the sting to dig in, right when I noticed I was looking for something, anything, to crack that icy mask Aris had shut himself behind. It never as much as slipped an inch.

I reached for Raeyn's flask again when they brought Kovacz out.

The Place du Marché fell so silent I could hear every clink of the manacles clasped around his ankles and wrists scrape against pavement as the Reds prodded him up the stairs and toward the pyre. Kovacz took each step slowly, carefully, like someone blind, who had to feel out every inch in front of him. Iltis had never walked like that. Kovacz made it without stumbling.

The Reds chained him to the stake. Kovacz didn't put up a fight. They'd stuck him into an oversized shirt and wide drawstring pants, white and hanging from bony shoulders and hips. Kovacz's body was nothing but a bunch of sticks waiting to be tossed in the fire. I probably was the world's greatest coward, but Gods, I prayed he wouldn't turn his head and see me watching.

If this was what revenge was like, it could go fuck right off.

Nymeron stepped forward, and I tried to get my teeth to unclench, my jaw already aching, but all I managed was to bite down harder. Pressure built inside my head. My ears popped, the way they sometimes did when Jay decided to take the hover for one of her crazier spins.

It was gone in a flash, a trail of goose bumps rippling down my suddenly heavy arms.

I could barely look at Nymeron without squinting against the sunlight reflected off his crisp white suit. A few days ago, he could've passed for an old man in the right light. Harmless.

Now the president was a bolt of silver lightning, something the Gods had sent down to the world to smite it.

"Orion Kovacz," he said, every syllable ringing out clear into the hushed square. All eyes were on the pyre waiting to see how badly the stick figure chained there would go once they lit him up. "For your acts of treason, you have been condemned to die by burning, sentence imposed by a jury of your peers. May the Light have mercy on your soul and may it save the citizens of its Empire. Do you have anything to say before the sentence is carried out?"

Might've been just me, but behind him, Valyr appeared a bit pale around the nose. Probably because she knew as well as at least half of Helos that everything Nymeron had said was a heaping load of bullshit. "Jury of your peers," my ass. Those frilly "acts of treason" were nothing but a cheap stand-in. With Daddy's stamp of approval, Aris was making this personal.

I couldn't even blame him. Not after Jay's body'd gone cold in my arms.

Still, it wasn't supposed to end like this. Nothing should.

"Save you?" Kovacz's voice was quiet but steady. Nothing like the raving lunatic he'd been at the palace. He didn't turn his head when the two Reds flanking the pyre stepped forward and lit their torches with a crackling sputter. The wind carried the smell of burning oil strong enough to make my nose itch.

"You honestly expect someone will save you from a monster you've let in all by yourself?" Kovacz stared straight at Nymeron and jerked his head toward Aris. "Bit late, don't you think, with you Burners right in front of everyone's noses?" Kovacz snorted. "Speaking of, you're burning the wrong guy. Should start with you and that 'son' of yours. Think people will keep voting you into office if they know what you really are, Mr. President?"

The Place du Marché exploded like a kicked hornets' nest. Voices started buzzing past each other, one over the other. The words "Voyant" and "Burner" were on everyone's lips like a prayer or a curse no one was sure they actually believed in.

Next to me, Raeyn whistled through his teeth. "Your traitor friend has guts."

Something like that. 'Course they'd torch him anyway. Trust in Kovacz to cook up hells of a shitstorm before he went.

And Aris would make sure it'd be the last thing Kovacz ever did. He'd been sitting unmoving, a marble statue while Nymeron was talking.

Now he got up and yanked the torch from the Red closest to him.

"Light it," Aris snapped and stepped in front of the pyre.

Against the light of the torch Kovacz's eyes were glowing embers over a trembling skeleton grin. "I'll save you a seat in all the hells."

"I'm counting on it," Aris said. Thought I saw him add, "Jay and Iltis send their regards."

He threw the torch.

The pyre lit up with a whoosh that pushed out all the air in a wave of heat and black smoke. I smelled gasoline. The Empire sure didn't half-ass things.

Kovacz waited until then to panic. He jerked against the chains holding him, his mouth opening and closing in a series of breathless gasps, like he was trying to scream, but couldn't get enough air for the sound to carry. The flames nipped at his scrabbling toes, licking at the hems of his pants and shirt when his thrashing suddenly stopped and his eyes tracked me.

Through the fire, I saw his lips shape words, but all that came out was screaming. The blaze caught on Kovacz's arms and legs until his whole body was a writhing pillar of flame. His screams turned into high-pitched screeches. There was nothing human in those sounds.

I didn't remember when Raeyn's hand slipped into mine; I just held on to it and somehow didn't completely lose my shit.

The rational part of my head kept telling me Kovacz must've passed out by now, that there was no way he could still be screaming. It took forever until he stopped, his body crumpling in on itself as if it'd melted around the chains keeping it upright. Someone once told me it could take hours to die burning like that, but that was way too fucked up to be possible.

I swallowed past the bitter taste of smoke at the back of my throat and tried not to think about how the whole place smelled like someone'd fired up a big barbecue. Bit heavy on the coals. My stomach twisted. Bloody Gods.

The Reds left him to roast a little longer before they moved in with fire extinguishers to put out the rest of the guttering flames. There wasn't enough of Kovacz left to even call it a body. Just a charred ruin of blackened crusty skin and weeping flesh. Specks of white fire extinguisher foam clung to it like soap bubbles.

Raeyn's hand clenched around mine in a vise-grip. I tried to wriggle my fingers out before they got mashed to a bloody pulp, but he only clutched harder. Under the sunglasses, his skin was the color of smudged chalk; his scars stood out in a curdled gray.

"Hey. You okay?" No response. Even in the bright sunlight and under layers of trench coat, I could feel him tremble. "Raeyn?"

His breaths came in shaky, flat gasps that didn't get enough air to be choked-off sobs.

Oh, hells.

"Hey," I said, and, because I didn't know what else to say and Raeyn swayed, like he was about to fall on me. "C'mere. Sit down, okay? Breathe. Listen to my voice and breathe."

Raeyn slid down bonelessly, his back against the cool stone of the fountain, dragging me with him until I crouched right in front of him. With his knees pulled tight against his chest and his head down, Raeyn looked very small. Like something had finally snapped behind the cocky front, and I hadn't the first clue of what to do with him like this.

I tried to let go of his hand, give him a minute to put himself back together, but he shook his head.

"Don't." His fingers laced through mine and dragged me closer. "Please."

His free hand brushed his fedora off his head; the sunshine made a silver beacon of his hair. Before I got a chance to say this was a bad idea, what with all the people around us, he sagged forward and rested the top of his head against my chest.

Oh.

I swallowed, not sure what to do with my free hand, so I awkwardly put it on his shoulder and hoped it was enough.

People'd started to clear out around us by the time Raeyn took a deep breath and rocked back on his heels.

"I'm sorry," he said. "I didn't think it would be this bad. But the fire, and—" Raeyn's hands almost touched his face before he caught himself. "Can we go now? Unless you prefer me to lose my lunch all over your shoes."

"You mean that lunch you haven't had yet?"

Raeyn cracked a pale smile. "Point."

"Well then, let's fix that for you."

"You're *hungry*? After—" Raeyn paled even further. He didn't look at the smoking remnants of the pyre.

I shrugged. "Alcohol has calories. Pretty sure there's a bottle or two with our names on it back at the Temple. C'mon."

Raeyn snorted but tugged his hat back on and let me pull him to his feet. He didn't comment when I took a detour away from the Place du Marché before merging onto the street that'd get us back to the Temple. And I didn't comment when he waited till we were at the door to finally let go of my hand.

Whatever'd been in Raeyn's flask, turned out he had two bottles of it stashed away.

He put both on the table. I raised my eyebrows. "Don't have any other plans for the day, huh?"

"Do you?" A smirk tugged on the corner of Raeyn's mouth, and I was relieved he'd started to look like himself again. "Start drinking, darling."

Raeyn poured two doubles, and for a while, we let the whiskey do the talking.

Afternoon sunshine spilled in from a window overhead, chasing golden flickers across the table. Raeyn tossed his hat and sunglasses in a clatter, long fingers raking through hair plastered to his head on one side and sticking up on the other. The shadows under his eyes looked as if someone'd punched him. He buried his face in his hands, his half-empty glass forgotten at his elbow. I wondered when he'd slept last. Not like I was one to talk.

"Why're you doing this?" My words cut through the silence like a series of gunshots.

"Doing what?" Raeyn lowered his hands and started to peel the brownish label off the whiskey bottle. He didn't look up. The corner came off in flaky layers. "Sitting here, feeling sorry for myself while slowly but steadily drinking myself into a coma?"

"Not what I meant." I took the bottle away from him before he managed to completely shred the label and tip over the bottle while he was at it. It was either that or cover his hands to make him stop fidgeting, and we'd already more than filled today's quota for handholding. I snatched his glass and poured us both another shot. "Why are you still here, Nymeron? If I were you, I would've been running for the hills soon as those Reds torched that fancy mansion of yours. But you keep sticking around. So, why?"

Raeyn stared into his glass, made a face and pushed it away. Half a second later, he changed his mind and downed it in one go.

"I already told you. I want my brother. I want to get back at my father. And you are my best shot at that, never mind you're volatile and homicidal and will doubtlessly get us both killed."

He made another grab for the bottle, but I was faster and closed my hand around his. "Bullshit."

Raeyn blinked. His eyes turned flat, fingers trapped under mine. I watched his Adam's apple bob as he swallowed. "Oh, really?"

I let go and shoved my chair back with a screech. "Fuck, Nymeron, if I know one thing about you, it's that you don't do anything 'less you got your own ass covered first. So, what's in it for you?"

Raeyn's knuckles tightened white around the bottleneck. He stood hunched over it, shoulders shaking. It took me a second to figure out those breathless, wheezing sounds he was making were laughter. Never would've thought Raeyn would be the giggly type.

His face was dead serious when he straightened up again. He only wobbled a little bit. Two long strides and he'd pushed me back, cornered me against the door, hands curled in the collar of my shirt, his face less than an inch from mine.

I could make out the tiniest flecks of blue in his eyes.

Raeyn's breath was hot against my throat. "You want to know what I want?"

"Hit me."

I halfway expected him to do just that when he pulled back. Instead, he shoved me hard against the door, grabbed a fistful of my hair, and kissed me.

What really came as a surprise was that I pushed against him and kissed him right back. Raeyn obviously hadn't expected that. His eyes flew open wide, he made a low, hungry sound in his throat and dragged me closer, his mouth opening under mine.

It was one of those hard and bruising kisses, the kind that left marks you'd regret later. The kind where you asked yourself what the fuck you were doing and why you kept doing it and the only answer was it felt way too fucking good to stop.

"That," Raeyn said, panting once I let him up for air. "Exactly that."

Somewhere in between, we'd switched positions. My body pinned him to the wall, pressed against the hard planes of his chest and stomach, his hands on my waist, mine buried deep in his hair. Underneath the whiskey and smoke, Raeyn smelled like lavender soap and expensive aftershave. His heartbeat was a frantic pounding against my chest.

I should've torn myself away then. I needed to sober up, get moving, bust some ass, and get Aris back. Not make out with his batshit brother. Who I hated. And didn't want and—

"Oh, damn it all to hells." I kissed him again.

Didn't matter how fucked up this whole thing was. For a while, I lost myself in Raeyn's ragged breaths, his lips hot against mine as I kissed him, invaded his mouth with my tongue, all but bit him whenever he made the slightest move to draw back. My hands were rough when I untucked his shirt, fingers sliding up against the smooth skin of his stomach. I brushed against a ragged patch of scar tissue spilling down his hip and he locked up.

"Damian." Raeyn gasped for air only to kiss me again. *"Damian—"*

I rolled my eyes and nipped at his lower lip. "Gods, Nymeron, stop talking. Thought this's what you wanted."

Raeyn's lips curved against my mouth. "Darling, I'd love to tear off all your clothes right here and now, but from the sounds of it we're about to have an audience."

Shit, I hadn't even heard the knocking. It sounded like someone was hells-bent on kicking the bloody door down any minute. "Ah, fuck."

"Later?" Raeyn asked with a hopeful smirk. "I might want to buy you dinner first."

"You're hopeless, Nymeron." That's when it hit me what we'd just done. And how much I wanted to do it again. My mouth went dry. I stumbled to the door. Anything but look at Raeyn, all rumpled, with his shirt missing buttons where I'd all but ripped it off him. Bloody Gods. Shit.

I tore myself away and yanked the door open. And nearly ran into Pascal.

"Finally. What were you—" One look at Raeyn and their eyebrows raced toward their hairline. A wide grin split Pascal's face. "About damn time, boys!" They winked at Raeyn. "I so want details later."

Pascal reminded me so much of Jay, I couldn't even glare at them. Damn, the Grasshopper would've liked this one.

Pascal's face turned serious. "Now, one of you tell me what in the Seven Hells Commander Valyr is doing in our lounge? She says she's not going to leave until she's talked to both of you."

I froze. "Valyr is *what*?" Panic clenched my throat. Should've figured whatever'd happened in her office was just a pause. That it wouldn't be long until the Reds came kicking the place down.

"Oh please," Raeyn let out a long-suffering sigh. "Very much like Mother to pick the worst timing ever."

Least Likely of Allies

"I NEED YOUR help."

Just when I'd been thinking things couldn't possibly get any more fucked up, Valyr had to show up and say something like that.

"You're kidding me." My voice rang a bit hollow. Late afternoon meant the lounge of *La Maison* was all but dead. A few of regulars lingered by the bar, hunched over their glasses, but between the three of us, we had the place pretty much to ourselves. Good thing, too, that way no one was going to freak out about the gun I pointed at Valyr.

Her lips twitched as she watched me. "You can put that down, you know."

"No, you can't." Raeyn sat down on the plushy couch next to me.

He was positively disheveled, hair all messed up and shirt only half tucked in. Had to admit it was a nice break from his usual fastidiously neat looks. A faint bruise was forming at the corner of his mouth. I barely stopped myself from reaching out and running my hand through Raeyn's hair, ruffling it where it stuck up in the back.

Gods. Stop it.

'Sides, Raeyn probably wouldn't appreciate me going all gooey right now. He sat stiff and closed off. I could feel the tension crackle in the air.

"This is about Aris, isn't it?" Raeyn made no effort to keep the bitterness out of his voice.

Valyr nodded but turned to me, her expression suddenly haunted. " I thought I could protect him, but you saw what his father is turning him into. The execution—" The fragile edge in her voice felt completely out of sync with her usual hard-assery. As wrong as the black turtleneck and gray slacks she wore. Most of her face hid behind big sunglasses; I spotted the tiniest hint of gray at her temples where she'd pulled her curls into a tight ponytail. No makeup or jewelry. Valyr even wore her civvies like a uniform.

She glanced down and picked invisible lint off her slacks, a tick she shared with Raeyn. "Aris isn't himself."

I clenched my fingers around my Colt. "Like you even know him, Valyr. Wasn't this what you wanted all along?"

Valyr leaned forward, hands curled into claws on the table. "I wanted to protect him," she bit out. "Aris didn't leave me a choice. I thought he would at least be safe at the palace. Not be turned into a monster."

"Touching," Raeyn said. He rubbed his temples as if fighting off a headache. "I most definitely need more wine for this."

He waved over one of the servers, the same skinny guy I remembered from that night I went to the Temple to warn Aris about the Reds. This time he was a little less glittery, wearing a shimmery purple shirt over faded, ripped jeans and a dish towel slung over his shoulder. He balanced a tray with a bottle of red and some glasses.

Raeyn gave him a radiant smile. "You are a lifesaver, Kip."

"Anytime you need me." Kip sauntered off, the low light bringing out streaks of leftover silver dye in his brown hair. Valyr scowled after him.

"Really," Raeyn swished wine around his glass, cold eyes fixed on Valyr. "You almost had me for a minute. Which is saying something given how you spent the last twenty-nine years turning your back to everything Father did."

"Raeyn." Valyr could barely look at him. Still, her eyes darted across the room as if afraid the wrong people could overhear.

"Please." Raeyn held up a hand. "Spare me the melodramatics. They will help Aris as little as they helped me, so I would appreciate it if you could stop wasting our time."

I never realized his voice got that extra-prissy edge when he came unglued.

"In fact, I will leave you to it." Raeyn got to his feet and murmured to me, "Fetch me before you shoot her. I might bring popcorn."

Raeyn grabbed his glass, when Valyr said, "I want you to help me kill him, Raeyn."

The wine glass shattered in Raeyn's fist. He didn't seem to notice the shards cutting into his palm. A breathy laugh cut through the silence.

"*You're* going to kill Father." Raeyn swallowed past the hoarseness in his voice. "That's rich. Oh, yes, that's *good,* Mother. After all the years you've spent groveling, always coming back to him no matter what he did to you, no matter what he did to—" He closed his eyes and brushed the bloody glass off on his pants. It fell to the ground in a cluster of crystals. "You're never going through with this. I don't need your help, Mother."

Valyr took off her sunglasses and slid them across the table, next to her untouched wine. Without them, I could see the deep lines carved in her cheeks, around her mouth. She looked old.

"I couldn't get you out," Valyr said, voice thin. Her fingers flexed, as if wanting to reach for Raeyn. His hand hung forgotten by his side, red droplets hitting the table steady like a clock counting the seconds. Valyr's left hand dropped into her lap. "He would have found us if we had run. I wouldn't have been able to protect you. At least this way I could—"

"Could what?" Raeyn's mouth thinned into a tight line. "You stood there while he *burned* me, Mother. And then told me he wasn't always this bad. That it would get better if I only *tried*."

His face twisted into a sneer. "Face it, *Mother*, he never even acknowledged you as his partner. For him you were nothing but a willing dog, always by his side, ready to take commands, eager for any scraps of affection he'd throw your way no matter the cost—"

Valyr slapped him hard enough to split his lip.

I rose to get in between them, but Raeyn held up a hand.

"No. I deserved that." And more quietly, "But it doesn't mean I'm wrong."

"I tried to cover for you!" Valyr's voice rose before she caught herself. "For you and your brother both. You were always my first priority. I thought he killed you, Raeyn! But when I found you, I made sure he would never lay a hand on you again."

"Yes. Well done. Better late than never." Raeyn gingerly wiped his bleeding lip. "Good luck, Mother. For Aris's sake, I hope you won't fail him as you failed me."

He picked up the wine bottle with his good hand and walked out.

I moved to get up and go after him, but Taerien slipped into the room and stopped me cold.

"Leave him be. He'll come around." He reached for a glass from a nearby tray. "We need to talk to you." He tucked himself into his seat, neatly folded, like a spider ready to leap.

"We." I did a double take between him and Valyr and it hit me. "You're in on this."

Taerien didn't even have the decency to look fazed. "Mutual death threats," he said mildly, pretending to sip his wine. "The perfect cover.

People don't expect secret conspiracies if you're busy killing each other. Messily. In public."

"How convenient for you." The wine turned sour in my stomach. "And I've been nothing but your tool, something for you to point and shoot." My hand tightened around my Colt.

"Oh, you've been most useful," Valyr cut in. Butter couldn't've melted in her mouth. After she'd fucking killed me. After she'd killed Iltis and Jay.

Taerien held up a hand. "We had to make sure you were the right one for the job."

Yeah, no need to point out "the right one" meant expendable; all the while they'd watched me like a rat chasing through a maze, trying to outrun the other rats. Either win or get cornered and torn to pieces. Never mind the collateral. Details, I remembered Taerien saying. Iltis. Jay. Aris. Even that godsdamned traitor Kovacz. All just *mere fucking details.*

I stared past my Colt at the cluster of broken glass bleeding red Rorschach patterns into the carpet. My thoughts came to a screeching halt, a derailed train crashing full-speed into a brick wall.

"Does Raeyn know?"

Valyr shook her head and a weight slid off my chest. "He always knew he had sympathizers inside the Watch. If he had known it was me—"

She choked off when I shoved the barrel of my Colt against her jugular. Taerien sighed.

"Boo-hoo," I drawled. "It's getting old, so let's change gears, okay? That's the problem with tools you can't quite control, they might accidentally go off in your face."

Valyr watched me, unblinking. "I meant it when I said I needed your help." Her throat dented around the muzzle. "I need you to shoot the president."

"You keep saying that." I laughed; couldn't help it really. "Sure. I'll go right ahead. Maybe I'll take care of world peace while I'm at it. Oh no, wait, that was Nymeron's gig. Right before he went evil overlord on our asses and now no one can kill him."

"Wrong," Valyr said. The dimmed lights hid half her face behind a veil of shadows. Now she leaned forward, and I felt myself involuntarily inching back. "You *can* kill him. Election Day is in three days. That's when we need to act."

"What in the Seven Hells are you talking about, Valyr?"

"You have seen how the president is with crowds," she said and laced her fingers in her lap. Sure, that explained it all.

"Um. He's good. I guess. A people person. Stage hog. Loves to hear himself talk. Thought that's supposed to be a politician thing."

"Yes." Valyr gave me an irritated flick of her wrist. "But that's not all there is to it." She took a deep breath. "He gets a boost from crowds. Specifically, Voyant crowds. I suppose you could say he leeches energy from them."

I almost dropped my Colt. "He *what*?"

And then I remembered. The way Nymeron almost seemed to glow with energy. The popping in my ears. The pressure. The chill.

"Holy shit."

Valyr gave me a grim nod. "There's a reason why attendance of public events is strongly encouraged for citizens in good standing. Think of how many Voyants his election speech will draw out, desperate to be on their best behavior, to stay under the radar of the Empire." Her lips twitched in distaste. "It will be like an all-you-can-eat buffet."

And none of them even realized they were being nibbled on. Bloody hells.

A sick dread burrowed in my stomach. So, our president wasn't merely a megalomaniac, he also was a Voyant who leeched juice off other Voyants while conveniently also staging a godsdamned witch hunt against them. Fucking perfect.

"We're getting to the part where you're telling me how exactly this is supposed to make things easier, right? Because right now we're right back at un-fucking-killable."

Valyr gave me a tight-lipped smile. "That's the catch. To let it all in, he has to lower his defenses. Open himself wide up."

"You will have anywhere from three to five seconds," Taerien cut in. "Plenty of time."

Yeah, "plenty of time" to get myself conveniently killed for their cause.

I leaned back. "I keep hearing 'you' here. What makes you think I'll do it? Way I see it, this is an express ticket to the next pyre." I could still smell the smoke clinging to my clothes, Kovacz's screams a ringing echo in my ears. Just thinking about it made me want to run like hells.

Then Valyr said the one thing that'd make me run the other direction. "You want Aris back. You take out the president, you end whatever hold he has over him."

It was a simple statement of fact and damn it if she wasn't right. If that's what it took to erase those hard lines from Aris's face, to get him to come back, I'd climb on that fucking pyre myself. And Valyr knew it, too. I saw it in that glint of her eye, the way she knew she had me even before I lowered my Colt.

This was a long shot where getting myself killed almost seemed like the best-case scenario. I'd need some fail-safes in place to avoid that. Never mind making sure she wasn't going to throw both Aris and me to the wolves to get what she wanted.

"Two things," I said in a flat voice. "One. If you turn tail on us, I *will* kill you. I want your people to get me in and back out, are we clear?"

A nod from Valyr. "Two?"

"Two," I took a deep breath. "Aris. I'm all for Nymeron biting it, but I'm going to get Aris out before the shit hits the fan."

Valyr snorted. "And you want to accomplish this how?"

I gave her a wolfish grin. This was a last-ditch effort, but I had nothing to lose.

"I need to talk to him. Alone." My Colt shoved back into its holster, I clasped my hands in my lap. "So. Here's how it's going to be. I put a bullet into Nymeron's brain and you get me some alone time with Aris before it all goes down, because unlike you lot, I believe in giving him a choice in what happens."

I reached for my drink and gently clinked it against the rim of their glasses.

"I take it we have a deal."

22

Slipping

ARIS SIGHED AS I wiped Sykes's blood off my knuckles. "Please tell me you didn't kill him."

For someone with my Colt aimed straight at him, he sounded awfully calm.

Valyr had made good on her promise. Less than twelve hours after our little chat, she'd gotten Aris right where I needed him: out of the palace, off to stand in at one of Nymeron's campaign remotes that broadcasted the end-all that was the Empire. Pretty sure the president was going to get a nice bump on votes out of it. People loved sappy stories of reunions with lost sons and all that bullshit. Even trumped the rumors about the presidential family's connections to the Voyance, even some anti-Empire propaganda cropping up in places. Had to give him that, Nymeron put on a good show. Might not even have to rig results this year.

I'd caught up with Aris and his personal pet Red outside an abandoned metro station, the stairs leading down to the old subway tunnels, a black hole behind me. It cast shadows deep enough you could barely see Sykes slumped against the rusty metal railing, his head lolling onto his chest.

"What, worried I broke your boy toy?"

"Is that what this is about?" Aris's hand twitched and he took a step toward Sykes before he caught himself. If not for the uniform, complete with the silver sun crest of Aris's personal guard or the trickle of blood down the side of his head, the Red could've been just another street rat, passed out drunk right where the smell of piss and stale graffiti was worst.

"He'll be fine." Out for a while, given the tranqs I'd dosed him with, and would wake up with one hell of a headache, but fine.

I'd promised Valyr I wouldn't kill any of her people. Didn't say anything about not kicking them when they were already down.

Aris rubbed his eyelids; in the late-morning sun, they looked bluish and hollowed. Maybe I wasn't the only one who hadn't slept since the Empire'd taken him.

I hated how something so little made me hope so much.

Aris's lips thinned, his face all tight lines and hard angles. "Damian. What are you doing here?"

"Nice to see you, too."

The tightness across Aris's shoulders had nothing to do with the Colt I kept aimed at him. He looked worn to the bone—a skeleton puppet, walking, talking, and slinging the Voyance around whenever Nymeron tugged on his strings.

"You look good," I lied, playing over the catch in my voice.

Aris let out a deep breath, tension draining out of his body until he almost seemed like a bleached-out version of his old self. Before I could stop myself, I put a hand on his shoulder. For a fraction of a moment, he leaned in, his head lowered, watching me through white lashes. The heat of his body was only inches from mine, teetering on the edge of closing the gap. Then he stiffened and stepped back, his eyes hard like slate.

"Can we speed this up? I really don't have time for this."

"What? Too busy being daddy dearest's errand boy? Looks like that's going great for you. Burned anyone else lately?"

The old Aris would've flinched at that, but now he just stood there, cold and unblinking, as if something cast in iron. "What do you want, Damian?"

Anger burned brighter than the sting. "What do I want?" I bit down on the urge to scream at him and tightened my grip around the Colt. "I want the old Aris back. But that's obviously not going to happen as long as Nymeron's still holding you by a fucking choke chain. So, I'm getting you the hells out of here, that's what." I waved my Colt. "Let's go."

Aris didn't move. "I'm not coming with you."

"Funny how you say that like I'm giving you a choice." I nudged him forward. "You're coming with me. Either walk or pick your least favorite kneecap and I'll drag you. Your call."

Aris's eyes narrowed at my Colt, silver brows crinkling. "You wouldn't."

There was so much conviction in his voice. He was *sure* I wouldn't hurt him.

Once I never would've. Shit sure had changed.

I swallowed past the dryness in my mouth. At the back of my mind, a tinny voice kept yelling at me how fucked up all of this was. This was *Aris* in my sights, for Gods' sakes. I cocked the hammer. The voice choked off and died.

"Try me."

Cold understanding dawned on Aris's face. He took a step toward me, and I knew I had him. He'd come with me. I'd get him the hells out of here, far away from Nymeron's mindfuckery. Things would be okay.

For the first time since the *Shadow* burned, I almost believed it.

Aris's words were a low whisper. "I wish you wouldn't make me do this."

"Make you do wh—"

The Voyance flashed to life in Aris's eyes.

My head exploded in white-hot pain that nearly drove me to my knees. A tight-knuckled grasp of the iron railing was all that kept me standing, hunched over, too breathless to scream.

"Just let me go, Damian."

Some traitorous part of my brain brought back the memory of lazy mornings spent in bed, his head warm on my shoulder, hair fanned out, spilling through my fingers in golden strands.

"You're not going to hurt me." Aris's words from what felt like a lifetime ago, coming back to me now, mangled into a faded echo with my own assurances. *"There's nothing I'd do to you if you don't want me to, you know that. And not just because you could kick my ass with the Voyance."*

Of course. I should've known better. Just never thought he would.

"No," I hissed through gritted teeth. Somehow, I managed not to drop the Colt. I clenched it in a death-grip, blinked through the pain dragging me to the ground. My aim was shaky at best, but it held. "You're not going anywhere."

"Damian, please." He closed in. His fingers brushed against my face, cupping my jaw. His touch took away the pain and I leaned into him. Couldn't help it. Of course, I wanted to let him go, to do whatever he wanted. What was I doing here anyway? I needed to let go and we could go back to tangled sheets and his hands warm on my face, his lips a soft whisper against the side of my throat. We could get back to all of it, back before there'd been any thoughts of him leaving, when it'd just been the two of us. All I had to do was—

The image shattered into a million shards.

I shook my head and bit my lip hard enough to draw blood, chasing away the fog that settled on my mind wrapped in pain. Something warm and wet ran down my upper lip, dripping down my chin. The pressure inside my skull skyrocketed; it felt like a balloon someone'd pumped full of too much air, past the point where it'd burst. Fuck, it *hurt*.

"Forget it." I ground out the words. "I won't let you. You hear me? I won't let you."

A whimper cut off anything else. Stabbing pain needled my eyeballs; I tasted blood at the back of my throat.

"Damian. Be reasonable. I don't want to hurt you."

"That's the thing," I spat a mouthful of blood, a splash of red against dull concrete. "*You* never would. But this isn't you, is it."

Aris became blurry, fuzzy around the edges. The only thing I could see clearly were those hard, stark-white Voyant eyes. Nothing else.

I'd been so stupid. Thinking the Aris I'd known was still in there.

I was wrong.

That Aris was gone. Stripped away by something that went deeper than silver-white hair and pale eyes. It still looked like him. Just like that little girl the Reds had Cleansed at the Place du Marché.

This was nothing but a Shell.

The realization laid me open to the bone.

Something between my ears gave with a pop. Everything around me drowned in white.

Aris's eyes widened; for the first time, I could see real fear flickering across his face.

"Damian, don't." A flash of white illuminated him, like the sun had come out from behind a cover of clouds.

Only this time it wasn't his Voyance that lit the place up like a New Year's light show.

It was mine.

And inside me, the Voyance screamed.

I could see Aris's lips move but couldn't hear him over the noise. He took a staggering step forward. I didn't notice I'd started shaking until he was pressed against me, holding on tight while the Voyance burned through me.

"Hey. It's okay." Aris's mouth was warm against my ear, the tip of my Colt crushed against his chest, forgotten. "I'm sorry. You're okay." His hands shook as he dragged me closer; my head tucked underneath his chin, body curled against him as he slowly walked me backward, cradling me all the way. His lips brushed a kiss against my forehead before he pulled back, taking the Voyance with him, and my head became painfully clear.

The distant thought that this was bad, bad, occurred to me, but I couldn't remember why. Something about the Empire. Something about Nymeron—

Too late, I picked up the surge in the Voyance around Aris or the way his hand clenched around my shoulder.

I got my Colt up in time to hear Aris say, "I'm so sorry, Damian."

He shoved me backward. His Voyance lashed out and threw me down the stairs into the tunnel gaping below.

The brief, panicked feeling of falling only lasted a second.

Then my body hit the concrete stairs.

The impact knocked the screams right out of me. I scrambled for something to hold on to, anything to stop my fall. The shove of Aris's Voyance was stronger. All I could do was throw up my arms to try and protect my head on my way down. My knee slammed into a hard edge, bent at the wrong angle. A red haze overlaid everything. My shoulder smacked into an iron post. Something snapped. I tried to make a grab for the railing, but my arms weren't working. More crunching. Finally, the thud of my body hitting the ground hard enough to crack tile.

The Voyance imploded behind my eyes.

Black bumped it off to the side before my body finished skittering to a halt.

Green emergency lighting cut into the darkness, splattering jagged patterns across the walls and ceiling. Overhanging wires dangled like tentacles of a monster lurking in the shadows, the mouth of the tunnel wide open, waiting to pull me in. My entire body felt like someone'd stomped on it and decided to mop the floor with what was left. I let my head fall to the side with a moan that sounded altogether too weak and broken.

I squinted. Too bright. The Voyance turned everything into searing negative images. The pain. The light. Everything was too bright.

I missed Aris coming down the stairs until he stood over me, the Voyance still burning in his eyes.

A sound dangerously close to a whimper snuck out of me. I tried to move, broken fingers fumbling for the Colt I'd lost on my way down. Pain tore into me with iron claws, keeping me pinned to the ground. All I managed was to smear more blood across the tile.

"Stay away from him!" someone shouted to my left. Raeyn? How did he—

The click of the safety on his semi-auto cracked the silence. Against the aftershocks of the Voyance, Raeyn was nothing but a hazy outline with a gun trained on Aris's head.

"I suggest you leave while you still can."

Aris froze. "I— Raeyn, I didn't mean to." His voice broke. "Damian."

He stared down at me, hands opening and closing, one verge of reaching out, but Raeyn grabbed his arm.

"Get out." He bit off the words. "Or so the Gods help me, I *will* shoot you."

Whatever he was about to say, Aris seemed to think better of it. With a silent nod and a last glance at me, he vanished up the stairs, and I finally let myself collapse.

"Damian?" Raeyn dropped to his knees, cool fingers against the back of my neck and the side of my face, trying to stabilize me against his knees. Inside of me, all the pent-up Voyance kicked and my head snapped back at the jolt, leaving me gasping for air.

Raeyn cursed. I must've zapped him or something, but he didn't let go. "Easy. Easy." I heard him grit his teeth, trying to keep his voice calm as he held me through the shakes. "Listen, I need you to relax, all right?"

The Voyance rattled my bones. For a while, the only thing I heard was the soothing stream of Raeyn's voice against the frantic gasps of my breath and the sound of my feet scrabbling on the floor. It seemed to take half of forever until I got myself to stop. Slowly, the world returned to its normal colors. I felt myself go limp, fighting the sudden urge to curl into the warmth of Raeyn kneeling by my head. I might've done it, if I could've gotten myself to move. My left side felt like someone'd taken a jackhammer to it.

Raeyn's face hovered over me. "Gods, you are so *stupid!*" he said with passion.

He moved me carefully, shrugged out of his coat, bunched it up, and shoved it underneath my head with practiced efficiency.

"What were you thinking going after him alone? He could have killed you. Easily."

His anger drained away like water through a sieve and something softened in his eyes. "Can you feel your legs? Toes?"

"Yeah." My voice came out as a hoarse croak, but I was dead set on showing him Aris hadn't managed to break me completely. "Feel 'em all right. *Fuck.*" I bit my lip. My left knee was pounding with bursts of pain in time with my heartbeat. I coughed. Bad idea. Felt like someone'd broken off my ribs and turned them into chopsticks to jab at my insides.

Raeyn made a noncommittal noise. "You are a mess, darling."

"Thanks, Captain Obvious." I winced and closed my eyes. Didn't need him to tell me my knee was busted. And my shoulder. Add a couple broken ribs and a sprained wrist for good measure. Wish he'd stop poking at me already. Not that I had enough breath left to argue.

I let him go at it and tried not to stare at the spot where I'd seen Aris disappear. The memory gaped like a dark abyss dragging me toward it.

I'd lost him. Gods, I'd lost him.

I squeezed my eyes shut. All I could see was white. Bright white burning inside me. And I remembered how good it'd felt. Raw power tearing through me. My fingers still tingled with it. The Voyance hovered out of my grasp. I only needed to reach for it, and I could do anything.

The realization hit. I was a Voyant. I was—

My stomach lurched up.

No. I kept my eyes closed and tried to breathe through the reflex. Puking was nothing but tension. That's all it was. And I couldn't lose it right now. Not here. Not in front of—

I'd enough time to roll over before my post-hangover breakfast splattered onto the floor. It was mostly watery bile, but it hurt like fuck. Broken ribs skewered my innards. I couldn't get enough air through to stop the retching. Probably would've fallen over and face-first into the stinking mess if it hadn't been for Raeyn's arm around me, anchoring me.

"Relax." Raeyn's voice seemed to come from very far away. "Breathe."

"'M fine." Would've been more convincing if I could've gotten my hands to stop twitching. I wiped my mouth on my sleeve. "Just get me the hells out of here."

Raeyn rocked back on his heels. "Not to sound discouraging, but how exactly do you think I am going to carry you up four flights of stairs? You may not have noticed, but super strength isn't one of my amazing powers. I'll get help from the Temple. It won't take long."

He tried to get up, but I grabbed his wrist. "No." I clenched my teeth and stretched my leg, slowly and without looking at it. If I didn't look, it couldn't be so bad, right? Right.

"I can make it," I said at the doubtful expression on Raeyn's face. "Please. Don't leave me alone in this godsforsaken tunnel. Please."

Raeyn gave me a sidelong glance, but he nodded and gave me a hand. It took him two tries and me lots of bit-back cursing to get me up and park me against the wall. The pain kept me hunched over, my breath coming in quick pants, twisting like knives beneath my sternum.

"Ready?" Raeyn asked after a while. Made me wonder how long he'd been standing there, watching me try not to fall over.

I nodded, surprised how much effort the movement took.

"Well then, do you suppose you could let go of the railing?"

Oh. I focused on my hands. Hadn't even noticed I was holding on to it tight enough to make my knuckles pop. "Uh. Sure."

I took a step toward Raeyn. My knee held for half a second before it gave way.

Raeyn caught a rough handful of my shirt and slid his shoulder under mine; the quick save sent a fresh stab of pain into my side and left me gasping, clinging to him as the tunnel tilted and threatened to slide away.

Raeyn took on my full weight and winced.

"Yes, you are perfectly all right, aren't you? You—" I turned my head into his shoulder and his breath hitched. Somewhere in the back of my head, I knew I shouldn't have, but I couldn't remember why. Didn't matter. He was warm. Much warmer than the cold floor dragging me down and I knew he wouldn't let me fall.

"I have to admit, this isn't how I pictured you clinging to me, all sweaty and...well." Raeyn sighed and his grip on me tightened. "Hold on."

He snaked my arm over his shoulder and started up the stairs.

Raeyn had to all but carry me. I tried to help, to hold on to the railing, but my fingers were numb, my whole left side a broken, useless mess. My knee screamed with every dragging step. It felt like climbing the side of a cliff, darkness swirling in the corners of my eyes like dark waves crashing against rock.

Twice the stairs almost won. Each time felt like slipping. In the end, Raeyn pulled me through and we made it to the top.

For a horrible second, I thought we'd be running right into an ambush of Reds, circling the exit like vultures biding their time. But the sidewalk was empty. Aris was gone, and he'd taken Sykes with him. Relief washed over me, and my eyes drooped, suddenly heavy.

The world darkened at the edges.

I could almost let go.

Just a few more steps.

"You so owe me." Raeyn's harsh breaths were a ragged echo of my own as we stumbled over cracks in the pavement toward the Temple's hover, glinting silver in the sunlight.

"Anything you want." Just get me a bed and all the painkillers in the Temple.

"I'll remember you said that. Lucky for you, I accept rain checks."

23

Stay

"YOU SHOULD HAVE shot him."

Taerien's voice cut through the haze of codeine and whatever else Raeyn'd given me to dull the pain from a flare to a constant full-body throb. Not sure if it was the drugs or Taerien's pacing that set the room spinning. He hovered at the outer edge of my vision. I wanted to swat him away like a fly.

Through droopy eyelids, I caught Raeyn shooting him a warning glance. "Leave it, Mael." Judging from the steel behind Raeyn's words, Valyr's reveal of their plans hadn't earned Taerien any bonus points in the trust department.

The room was bright enough to make me squint and wonder if there were any lamps left in the Temple Raeyn hadn't dragged in here. The harsh light didn't hide the twitch of Taerien's jaw muscles as he clenched his teeth.

"Don't 'Mael' me, Raeyn. Look at him. He's a mess. The elections are in three days, and if he can't—"

"Okay, two things." I clawed myself upright through the painkiller fog. My ribs didn't like the idea of sitting up at all. Neither did my shoulder or the rest of my left side. "One, don't talk about me like I'm not right fucking here. Two—" Pain snatched at my breathing. I fought the urge to curl around it. "Two, stop stressing about E-Day. I'll be fine. Ready to point and shoot like a good little soldier. Don't you worry."

Taerien scowled. "I wouldn't *have* to worry, if you hadn't been so heedlessly stupid. A tête-à-tête with the president's prodigal son. And the elections right around the corner. I cannot help but wonder how far your inclination to 'get him out' went." Taerien leaned in, rigid with pissed-off fury. "If he's a Voyant worth his salt, he could have plucked everything right out of your head. Hells, for all we knew, you went right ahead and told him everything."

I got up and my fist smacked into Taerien's nose with a satisfying crunch. It would've been much more impressive if I hadn't crashed to the floor as soon as my knee gave, my body reminding me painkillers only went so far.

"Don't you ever—" I squeezed my eyes shut. Taerien's bloody nose zoomed in and out in front of me and the room dimmed. Shallow breaths. Shallow breaths were my friends. "I didn't tell him shit. Yeah, I fucked up. Trust me, it won't happen again."

Taerien nodded, too busy clutching his nose for his glare to carry much weight.

"Good," I said through clenched teeth and fought the urge to roll over and stretch out on the floor. The Temple had nice carpets. I could fall asleep right here.

Raeyn hauled me back into bed.

"I suppose I should thank you for being considerate enough to punch him before I started setting any bones."

I looked down at the throbbing knuckles of my right hand and decided now probably wasn't the time to point out at least I'd used my good hand to punch Taerien.

Raeyn sighed. "Now, lie still, or I swear by the Gods, I *will* tie you to the bed."

His scowl swiveled to Taerien. "And you. Out."

Taerien opened his mouth, but the ice in Raeyn's voice shut him down. "Have Pascal take a look at your nose."

Lips pressed into a pale line, Taerien grabbed a wad of tissues from the counter and strode out of the room. Kicked out to the doghouse. Served him right.

Raeyn opened drawers in a rolling cabinet, neatly organizing things on metal trays. I settled back against the pillows and tried not to look too closely at the gleaming edge of the scalpel he'd laid out. The next stage of painkillers kicked in and the glare of the light above me softened and got fuzzy around the edges. Felt like my body was packed in Styrofoam, nothing quite coming through. Even my thoughts turned sluggish, slowing to a trickle as if coming through an IV drip.

"You didn't tell him I'm--" I said, stumbling over the words as if saying them out loud made them even more real. "I'm a Voyant."

Aris had always healed freakishly fast. Couple hours of sleep and he'd be right as rain. Fucking Voyance perks. Meaning Taerien's little hissy fit could've been easily prevented.

Raeyn didn't look up from a syringe he was prepping. "And give him even more ammunition?" His lips quirked into the beginning of a tense smile. "No, Mael is already overeager to toss you back into the fray. Let's keep him on his toes for a change."

I tried for a nod, but it seemed too much work.

"How come I'm only feeling it now?" I asked instead. "Shouldn't the Voyance have kicked in years ago?" Aris had been seventeen when he'd first fried one of the *Shadow*'s circuits. I chased the thought away. I hurt enough as it was.

Raeyn lowered the syringe. "Everyone is different. Something may have triggered you." He gave me a small smile. "Or maybe you are just that good at repressing things."

"Very fucking funny."

Raeyn's smile withered. He went back to work. "It may very well have kept you alive."

It hit me then that it mightn't be the drugs that made me feel better, but the Voyance patching me up from the inside. My breath hitched against broken ribs. I bit back a hiss.

"But like you said, it's not a miracle cure." Raeyn's gloved fingers were warm against my arm as he stretched it out and tied a dark green strap around it. "The Voyance will help you heal faster, but you'll still scar. You can still—" He drew his hand back from where it'd hovered above the healed-over bullet holes in my chest where Valyr had shot me. I knew what he meant. I could still die. Already had, if only for a few minutes. Next time I wouldn't have Aris to yank me back.

I swallowed past the tightness in my throat and focused on the present.

"How bad is it?" Broken bones weren't any news to me. That shoulder would be a pain for a while, so would my ribs, but what worried me were the tight lines that'd appeared around Raeyn's mouth as soon as he'd cut away my pants and taken a good look at my leg. Even with the painkillers, the damn thing was pounding.

Raeyn wouldn't look at me. "Well, I'm afraid it looks like I owe you a new pair of pants." He tightened the strap around my biceps. "Make a fist."

I did, and he shot something into the crook of my arm.

"This will put you under for a while. Count down from ten."

"You're a cheat, Nymeron," I said, my tongue suddenly thick in my mouth. "'M serious. Need to know if I got to look for a new line of work. This gig's short-lived if you can't run."

The lines in Raeyn's face softened. He leaned forward and left a blurry white streak in the air behind him.

"Let me worry about that for a while, all right?" His eyes shone like silver mirrors. "Start counting, darling."

I closed my eyes and did what I was told, no juice left to argue. Sleep settled over me like a warm blanket. My toes and fingertips started to tingle, impossibly heavy to lift. I made it down to seven before Raeyn's fingers touched the side of my throat to take my pulse.

He flinched just a little when I turned my face into his palm. "Raeyn?"

"Yes?"

"Don' go."

He took a deep breath and almost pulled away, but then he brushed a curl out of my face, his hand curved against my cheek.

"I won't. Don't worry."

"Good. Tell Jay if that cat of hers sleeps on my face again, 'm goin' to kill it."

Something softened and broke in Raeyn's face, but if he said anything else, I didn't hear it, because I slipped away right when my lips shaped the word "four."

WHEN I WOKE up, the brightness had leaked out of the room. All those extra lights Raeyn had hauled inside were gone, along with the trays and equipment from the infirmary. The only light still burning was a dim glass lamp on the nightstand off to the side. It blended in with the orange fingers of sunset that clung to the windowsill, painting everything in streaks of fire.

Raeyn was asleep in one of the plushy chairs he must've pulled up from across the room. He sprawled in it with one leg slung over the arm of the chair. Jay's cat Dust was a purring ball of gray fur asleep in his lap. Raeyn's head was turned to the side, his scars hidden against the high back of the chair. At that angle, he'd wake up with hells of a crick in his neck. The fading light outlined him in a warm glow, like a statue cast in pale gold. Exhaustion had carved dark hollows underneath his eyes. I wanted to reach out, brush them away like smudges of ink.

It still took a scary amount of effort to sit up. The stabbing pain underneath my ribs had disappeared and given way to weakness that'd settled in my bones like lead. Still, the mattress creaked as I shifted around stiffly and Raeyn's eyes fluttered open, dark and hazy with sleep. I put my hand down quickly.

"Hey." Raeyn's mouth curved into a slow smile. It twisted into a wince as he unfolded himself from the armchair and rubbed the back of his neck. Dust let out a pissed-off meow at his movement and stalked out the cracked door. "How are you feeling?"

I wanted him to sit back down so I could put my head where that damn cat'd been a moment ago and go right back to sleep.

But what I said was, "Okay. I think." Even though pulling myself up to a sitting position had felt like an incredible feat, I wasn't lying. I felt weak and a little stiff, like I'd slept for a hundred years, but the pain was gone. "Voyance healing is creepy as fuck."

The corner of Raeyn's mouth twitched into a half smile. "I suppose it is, a little."

"How long've I been out?" I remembered drifting in and out for a while and dimly remembered eating, a lot. Still, my stomach felt hollow, like I hadn't eaten in days.

"A little longer than a day and a half."

"What?" I started up sharply. Bad idea, I thought, prepared for the kick to my ribs. It didn't come.

"You needed it." Raeyn slid off the sling he'd tied around my shoulder. "Lots to repair."

"Mhmm." I leaned into him, didn't care where he touched me as long as he kept doing it and I didn't have to worry where all those touchy-feely ideas came from. The scrapes and bruises were gone, nothing but a bump in my shoulder where it'd separated. All set and healed.

Carefully, I took a deep breath, still not quite used to it that I could.

"Holy shit, it's like nothing ever happened."

"Hm." Skepticism furrowed Raeyn's forehead. "I wouldn't go that far. The Voyance may mask some of it, but that knee of yours is going to give you some trouble for a while yet. You should take it easy for at least a few days."

Easy. Right, what with E-Day looming just around the corner.

He was starting to make up excuses to keep his hand on me. The covers had slid down to my waist and I wasn't wearing anything but boxers and the elastic around my ribs and knee.

I wasn't the only one who noticed. Raeyn let his hand fall to his side. "You should rest." His fingertips left a tingle on my skin that quickly turned into goose bumps. "And eat. The Voyance makes your metabolism burn through calories."

He stepped back, but I was faster and snatched his wrist before he could leave. "Stay."

Raeyn looked at me, stunned. His voice cracked a little. "I should go."

He tried to wriggle out of my grip, but I held on.

"No. Stay," I repeated and brushed my lips against his fingers. "Please."

Before I could think twice about it, I dragged his head down and kissed him. Whatever doubts I had were shoved back into the farthest corner of my mind, buried deep under the feel of Raeyn's mouth hot and hungry against mine and the thrill that kissing him sent through me. It was like a shock of electricity or lightning, like a fight that could only be won once there wasn't a gap between us, just skin against skin.

I pulled him down to the bed. Raeyn went after me like a man drowning, helpless against the current that dragged him out to sea.

"There," I said, a little breathless against his mouth. "Better."

"Are you sure you are all right?" Raeyn said once I let him up for air. The back of his hand touched my forehead. "Hm, no fever. A concussion maybe? Wouldn't surprise me if you hit your head and didn't even notice. So very typical. Your pupils *are* a bit dilated."

I brushed his hand away. "Stop that. Is it so hard for you to believe I..."

"You, what?" he asked, carefully pronouncing each syllable. Very fucking like him to make me say it. Bastard.

"I—" I swallowed against the sudden tightness in my throat, the flutter in the pit of my stomach. The words came out in a rush. "Oh, for fuck's sake. I like you, okay? I really like you. A lot."

There. Out it was. Bit on the shitty side, but wasn't like I had practice at these things.

With Aris, I'd never needed to. With him, everything'd been easy. Until it hadn't been.

Shit, just thinking about Aris sent a pang deeper than guilt through my gut.

Raeyn stared at me as if I'd slapped him. He pushed away and out of the bed.

"Don't humor me. Anything but that."

I blinked. "What the fuck? Shit, you don't think I—"

I reached for him, but he held up a hand. "Please." His eyes reminded me of the big silver coins the Celebrants of the Temple laid on the faces of their dead. "You don't want me. You can't even stand me. And about the other day. When I kissed you." He trailed off. For a split second, I thought he was ready to reach out, close back in on me, but he took a step back. "I shouldn't have pushed you."

"You weren't the only one pushing." I remembered how I'd shoved him against the wall, my hands in his hair, under his shirt, his lips hot on mine... Fuck, but he confused the hells out of me. A few days ago, he'd all but jumped my bones and now this.

"I'll say it again, if you want. I *like* you. Never thought I'd say that, but I do. I want you." I took a deep breath, very aware of how completely fucking pathetic I sounded, especially when I added quietly, "Thought you wanted me, too."

Raeyn gave me a shaky smile. "I do."

"Then what in the Seven bloody Hells is your problem?"

"My problem is I want you to want me for *me*. Not for whom you see in me."

"For who I, wait, *what*?" I could've kicked myself. Right after I got done kicking him. "You think I like you because you look like *Aris*?" Ah, Gods.

Raeyn wouldn't meet my eyes. Just stared at the empty stretch of carpet between him and the bed.

"I trust you understand I'm fairly tired of living in the shadow of my little brother. I'm not him and I refuse to be his substitute." Two steps got him across the room. He leaned his forehead against the door. "Gods, this is embarrassing." White knuckles closed around the doorknob. "I should go. Let's pretend this never happened, okay?"

"Like hells."

I hauled myself out of bed and staggered to him. My body took less than two seconds to remind me I wasn't entirely out of the woods yet. I stood shaking, my fists curling into Raeyn's shirt.

"I said, stay." The words were muffled against his neck, and I had to fight for the breath to get them out. My knee felt like someone shot spikes of fire through it, but it held. "Don't leave. I mean it." Not that he'd much of a choice with me clinging to him.

I thought he'd push me away, but then all the tension drained out of him and he leaned into me instead, his breath a whisper against my ear.

"Dear Gods, what will it take for you to stay off that leg? I meant that part about tying you to the bed, you know."

"Whatever you want."

I let Raeyn drag me back to bed. "You know this would be easier if you let go of me."

"Not a chance."

Raeyn snorted, but he didn't let go of me either.

"It's okay." I pulled him down with me and kissed him again. "Don't worry."

"I'm not worried!" He sounded breathless. "I simply refuse to be your rebound fling. Contrary to popular opinion, I do have standards."

"Prove it." I leaned in close enough to see the pulse jump under his skin. "Fuck me."

Silence. "You—" Raeyn cleared his throat, but it didn't get rid of the croak in his voice. "You want me to—"

"If you're so worried about me comparing you to Aris, then come here and fuck me." I watched him, distracted by the way his hair curled around his ears and against the side of his neck and then decided to hells with it and licked the taut line of his throat. "The Gods know he never did."

Raeyn let out a strangled sound, trapped somewhere between a gasp and a moan, hands clutching at the sheets. "Are you sure?"

"I'm sure." I grinned and nipped at his earlobe. "Unless your stamina isn't up to snuff?"

"Please." Raeyn's eyes glinted in amusement. Then he was on me, one hand on my good shoulder, the other buried deep in my hair. He pulled me up into a harsh kiss.

I gasped, smile etched with a wince. "Take it easy on me."

"Sorry." Raeyn pulled back. "You aren't well. We shouldn't—"

"I'm fine." I hooked a hand around his belt, already busy untucking his shirt. "'Sides I'm going to lie down and let you do all the work."

Raeyn gave me a crooked grin. "If that's what you want."

"Hells, Nymeron, I've wanted this since you kissed me to get me out of Coras's bar." And Gods, I had. It didn't hit me until just now how much. Shit.

Raeyn breathed a soft laugh. "I suppose that was before I shot you to save my own hide." He winced and glanced at the puckered scar he'd left in my shoulder. "I'm sorry for that, by the way. I—"

I put a finger to his lips. "Oh, let's be clear: you owe me for that one." I traced his lower lip with my index finger. "With interest."

He nipped at me. "In that case, I'd like to pay you in installments."

Raeyn kicked the covers out of the way and kissed me again. Never would've thought his lips would be so warm and eager, his breath hot and ragged when I bit his lower lip. I let him go and he kissed my throat, my shoulder, my collarbone. All aches and twinges faded as his mouth found my right nipple and then trailed down toward the waistband of my boxers.

"Raeyn." I barely got his name out. Suddenly it was hard to breathe, with Raeyn's fingers dragging down my last piece of clothing. "Gods, Raeyn, slow down."

He arched a silver eyebrow. "I can do that." He bent down and licked me, setting his mouth to work with tantalizing slowness.

I had to bite my lip to hold back the whimper, but that only encouraged him, and Gods did I want to encourage him.

Raeyn pushed himself on his elbows to watch me. "Gods, but you are gorgeous."

Heat burned up my throat. I swallowed. "Right, Nymeron. Pretty sure you say that to every guy whose dick you just had in your mouth."

Raeyn winked. "Not all of them. Only you." He closed his mouth around me again.

I let my head fall back and allowed myself to come apart under his mouth and tongue.

"Hm, not yet." It took two tries to get myself under enough control to draw him back up so I could get him out of his clothes. I made a total mess of Raeyn's shirt, buttons flying everywhere. As I was about to pull his shirt off, I noticed how he'd gotten completely still and wouldn't meet my eyes. Instead, he kept sneaking glances at the lamp on the nightstand and tried to turn his left side away from me.

"Hey." I caught his arm before he could pull away. "Told you, you're worrying too much about those scars. C'mere. Tell me to stop if this is too much, okay?"

Gently, I slid my hands under his unbuttoned shirt and slipped it off. The low light made shadows dance across the scars covering the left side of his body. Like the ones on his face, they'd healed to pinkish-white lines and welts spilling across his arm, back, and torso, twisting his skin like melted candle wax.

I felt him tremble when I touched the scarred side of his face. I paused. "Okay?"

"Yes." Raeyn watched me through fluttering lashes. He bit his lip. Nodded. "Yes."

"Okay," I said and turned over his hand in mine. "Just relax. How's that?"

First, I kissed his palm, then the inside of his wrist where the first tendrils of scar tissue started lapping at pale skin. Raeyn's breath turned more ragged the farther I inched my way up his arm. I grazed his collarbone, licked across the jagged hangman's scar that circled his throat, and lingered at the underside of his jaw.

"*Damian.*" Raeyn made a low, broken sound when I kissed the scars on his face. I took my time to get to the corner of his mouth, finally his lips. Long fingers ran through my hair, curved against the back of my neck as if he was afraid I'd walk away. As if there was a chance.

"Turn over," he breathed between kisses. "Please."

"Thought you'd never ask." I grinned and did as I was told.

There was the clinking of his belt, the sound of a zipper coming undone, skin shrugging out of fabric and the rip of foil and the roll of latex, until Raeyn straddled my thighs, naked and hot against me. A warm shudder rolled down my spine when he leaned down and kissed the nape of my neck, but I still twitched when his fingertips trailed across the tattoo on my right shoulder, skimmed the scars that mapped out most of my back. By now, I'd long forgotten which of them had been put there by Marten at *L'Ecole* and which had come later, layered on through training or my own special skill for pissing off Reds.

Raeyn's hands on my hips sent a flash of memory and my breath caught with a brief stab of panic. I squeezed my eyes shut to chase it away.

"Damian, are you all right?"

"Fine. Shit. Don't—" My heart beat in my throat. Stuttered when he let go of me.

"No," Raeyn said softly. "Turn around, please. Let me see you."

I exhaled. Rolled over, half terrified to find pity or worse in his eyes.

Raeyn studied me with calm patience. "We don't need to —"

"Fuck, Nymeron, I swear if you're going to quit on me now, I might have to kill you after all."

Raeyn laughed. "Can't have that, sorry." He dragged a pillow close and slid it under my hips. "Lie back. Let me take care of you."

And he did. Kneeling between my legs, Raeyn's hands and tongue traced tingling patterns onto my skin, chasing the past away. Probably shouldn't've been surprised the lube he'd snatched from a drawer smelled faintly like the lavender soap he used. He carefully lifted my legs, propping them against his shoulders in a way that wouldn't jostle my knee.

"All right?" The question came with a kiss along my calf and a lube-slick finger at my taint.

I nodded, voice sliding into a groan when he slipped first one, then two fingers inside. He worked me thoroughly, touching me in places no one'd touched in far too long, stretching me with a third finger until I couldn't think of anything but him, hot and hard against me and how much I needed his cock in place of his fingers.

"Raeyn. *Raeyn.* Gods, quit being such a tease and fuck me already."

I felt him laugh and withdraw his fingers. "I suppose this means you're still sure about this."

"Fuck yes, I'm sure. Just, please. Go ahead and—"

Everything else caught on a moan when he pushed into me.

Raeyn took it slow, gently moving against me, pushing burn into pleasure, a string of low words murmured into the soft spot where my neck met shoulder. Wrapped around him, I forgot all about *L'Ecole*, Aris, my tired body, or how very out of practice at this I was.

All I had to do was let myself fall, knowing Raeyn'd be there to catch me.

24

Crackdown

I WOKE UP to darkness and an empty bed. Around me, the covers were a tangled mess, the hollow where Raeyn'd slept cool to the touch. The memory of his body warm against mine, naked skin growing warm with sleep, already started to fade like a half-remembered dream.

Fuck and run. Great. I hated the twist of disappointment deep in my gut. What the fuck had I expected? Fuzzy feelings and all that bullshit? I stared at the ceiling. Gods, I had to get over myself.

On the upside, I almost felt human again. Still felt stiff and bent out of shape, but the pain was gone. I made it as far as sitting up and throwing back the covers until the door bumped open with a faint rattle.

"Don't you dare get up yet," Raeyn said and dragged the door shut. "Getting up would defeat the entire point of breakfast in bed."

"Breakfast. In bed." I wondered if maybe I was still strung out on painkillers because he was carrying a tray complete with two mugs of coffee and two plates stacked high with eggs and what smelled an awful lot like pancakes. "Are you serious?"

"Dead serious. Breakfast is the most important meal of the day." Raeyn grinned and put the tray on the bed. He wore a robe, black silk lined with fancy silver designs. It slid up to his knees when he sat down and crossed his legs.

"And well, I have to admit I found myself a bit at loose ends." The corners of his eyes crinkled when he smiled. It opened up his whole face like shutters thrown wide to let in morning sunlight. "I couldn't go back to sleep and I didn't want to wake you. So, I found another outlet."

"You *made* those?"

"Don't look so surprised. They're good. I promise." He licked a speck of chocolate off his fingers. "You should try them before they get cold. I figure you'd be hungry by now."

I stared at the pancakes on my plate. They were layered with slices of what I was pretty damn sure was banana, chocolate drizzled all over in a gooey mess. It sent a signal right to my stomach, and I realized I was starving.

"Good?" Raeyn asked after I'd had my first bite. I must've made some sort of noise because, behind the rim of his coffee mug, his grin widened.

"Fucking fantastic," I got out between chewing. "Is that real chocolate?"

"Of course. I take my sugar seriously."

"No shit."

By the time we'd finished eating, Raeyn was positively preening, which may have been because after I was done with my plate, I polished off the rest of his as well. Even then I barely stopped myself from licking the plate clean.

"You weren't kidding when you said the Voyance burns through calories."

Raeyn nodded and moved the tray out of the way. "Let's just say you should plan on twice, possibly triple your regular food intake, especially with your level of...activity. The Voyance speeds up your metabolism as needed to keep its host alive."

"Ah." I exhaled. "Peachy."

Raeyn reached out, his fingers laced through mine. "Hey. Okay?"

"Yeah." I kissed the corner of his mouth, tasting chocolate. "Mm. You missed a spot."

Raeyn didn't complain when I pushed him back into bunched-up covers, my hands running through his tousled hair, down the side of his face, memorizing the line of his throat, the hollow of his collarbone, the planes of his chest. The front of his robe gaped open, a cool stream of silk running through my fingers untying the belt around his waist.

The tiny trail of white hair that ran down from Raeyn's belly button shimmered silver in the first fingers of dawn. I bent down and traced it with my tongue. His hands in my hair tightened and he pulled me back up for a kiss.

"And here I was half afraid you'd be gone by the time I got back."

"Sorry." I nipped at his lower lip. "Not a fan of one-nighters." As soon as I said it, I wanted to take it back. "Um, I mean, it's okay if you don't want me to stick around. We've both got shit to do. I can go. Find another room somewhere if you want."

Raeyn shook his head and cupped my face. "Darling, you have the most ridiculous, ideas."

The next kiss along with his lazy, possessive grip dragging me back down to him ended that discussion. I took up where I'd left off, licking and teasing till I got Raeyn right where I wanted him: clutching at me, arching his back, making all the right noises at all the right times.

"Gods, think I'll have to give you sugar first thing in the morning regularly," he said once he'd caught his breath again.

I grinned and licked my lips as I came back up. "Hm. Good plan."

With a crackle, the Temple's generators cut out and plunged everything into darkness.

"Okay, what the hells was that?"

The windows overhead let in enough bluish predawn light to make out Raeyn holding up a hand. "Shhh." He listened for a second, frowning. "That's odd. The emergency generators should have come on by now." He got out of bed and wrapped his robe around himself, tightening the belt before he headed for the door. "Stay here."

"What?" I scrambled out of the covers and bit off a wince at the twinge in my leg when I straightened out my knee. Even with the elastic cast still on, it wobbled when I put weight on it, but I gritted my teeth and it held. "I'm not going to let you go out there."

Raeyn gave me a sidelong glance. "You can barely stand. And as much as I would love to see Aemelia's face when she sees you wandering naked through the halls, you might want to get dressed first." He tossed me a bundle of clothes. "Relax. It's probably just a popped breaker."

Except we both knew better.

Gods, we'd been so stupid, thinking we'd be safe here.

"I'll be right back." Raeyn made a grab for his gun and slipped out the door.

"Raeyn!" It was more of a whisper than a shout and I was too busy fumbling into my clothes while trying not to fall over anyway. "Wait." I'd struggled into my pants and pulled my shirt over my head before the shooting started.

My blood ran cold. I was back on the *Shadow*. Iltis's bloody grin became a glint in the window pane, Jay kissing me a ghost tingle against the memory of Raeyn's lips on mine.

All gone now. I could still smell the smoke of the burning ship on my clothes.

Not again. Please, not again.

I gave myself two seconds to freak out. Spare ammo scattered to the floor in a shower of brass because I couldn't get my hands to stop shaking. Then I curled them around the familiar weight of my Colt, took a deep breath, and pushed out into the corridor.

"Raeyn?"

It was a hissed whisper, carrying through the hallway, a ragged echo thrown back by emptiness. Another series of shots upstairs. A high-pitched voice cut off midscream. Running footsteps followed by a heavy thud. At the end of the hall, the door opened; someone tumbled down the stairs in a clatter, came to a halt with a choked-off moan.

Cold bricks dug into my shoulders. The wall against my side kept me upright as I stumbled along the corridor, one uneven step at a time. The generator came to life like a crack of lightning, bright white flooding the hallway before it winked out again. Its normally constant hum died down to an intermittent purr like the sound of a sleeping dragon.

It left enough light to make out the shape of someone huddled at the bottom of the steps. I caught a glint of silver hair and started running.

And nearly pitched over twice by the time I got there, my knee a knot of pain, white-hot needles stabbing through it. I pushed it away and let myself fall, hands trembling as they closed on narrow shoulders, turned them over against the concrete steps.

"Hey," I said, heart beating in my throat. "I've got you, okay? I've got you."

I realized my mistake as soon as I touched him, hated the flood of relief that swept through me when I saw the hair beneath my fingers wasn't silver, but a dull brown, patches of leftover dye still clinging to the roots and tips.

Kip's eyes were dark and huge with pain, skin clammy to the touch. He shivered in my arms.

"Damian?" A pale hand reached for me, but the movement must've torn something inside and he crumpled against me with a whimper. I carefully checked Kip over and winced. Stomach wound. At least the bullet had missed his spine. Small mercies. Still, no idea how he'd even made it out the door, let alone down the stairs.

I swallowed and made myself focus past the blood and his shaking body, burrowing deeper against me, seeking warmth. "Kip." My hand found his, already slick with blood. "Hey kid, I need you to tell me what happened, okay? Where's Raeyn?"

"Lounge." Kip's voice was thready and flat. "Reds everywhere. Just started shooting and—" His face twisted in grief. "They're dead. Aemelia, they— They're all dead."

"I'll believe that when I fucking see it." I tried to pull away, but Kip wouldn't let go of my hand.

"Don't. Don't leave me here." Kip's slight body pressed closer. "Please." He bit his lip and his voice broke. "I'm scared. Gods, please, I'm so scared."

Oh hells. Oh bloody, fucking hells.

I prayed he couldn't see how I closed my eyes because I couldn't stand looking at him, eyes wide and panicked. I remembered that girl at the Place du Marché, how small and terrified she'd been, trusting me to make it all right. In the end, I'd let her down all the same.

Not this time. Not after—Gods damn it, I wouldn't let myself think of Jay. Not now.

I took a deep breath, swallowed, and hoped my voice held. "It's okay. You'll be fine, I promise. But I need you to trust me, okay?"

A nod. Kip's lashes fluttered closed, dark arcs brushing against pale skin.

"All right." I took his hand and pressed it hard against his wound. "I need you to stay here and hold on. Tight. I'll find Raeyn, get help, and we'll get you out of here, okay?"

"Promise?"

"Yeah." Gods, don't make a liar of me. "I promise."

I left him there. Kip's blood was still warm on my fingers, the railing slippery as I dragged myself up the stairs.

The lounge was silent as a crypt. Glass crunched underneath, the ruins of a chandelier scattered all over the thick carpets in shards that gleamed like teeth. I barely noticed them biting into the soles of my bare feet. Everything was too quiet. The carpets soaked up the sound of my steps like they'd soaked up the blood that stained dark patches where people'd fallen, where they'd tried to drag themselves out of the line of fire.

The Reds had turned the Temple into a house of the dead but forgot to bury the bodies. Where there should've been tombs marked with marble statues, looking like they'd fallen asleep or bravely fought in some battle, there were nothing but shadows. Huddled in corners, slumped against doorframes, draped over a broken table, faces frozen in terror or surprise. No one'd died in their sleep here. The battle had been one-sided, a butchering of people who hadn't even been armed.

Gods, why? Why now?

The sharp crack of a safety sliding back snapped the silence. I froze where I stood, leaning against the wall for support, finger on the trigger of my Colt. And very nearly dropped it when Raeyn stepped around a post, gun pointed straight at my head.

"Drop it."

Relief drained out of me like a gush of blood. "Raeyn?"

He didn't look at me. "I told you to wait." Blood spattered his right side; it clung to his jaw like paint smudged on paper. The blank mask of his face didn't leave any room for his usual crooked grin. "Get out of the way, darling."

I caught on just fast enough to twist to the side before Raeyn put a round into the Red who'd snuck up behind me. The Red went down screaming, clutching his leg.

Raeyn kept his piece on him. "Sorry, did you want to pick a kneecap? I'm afraid I'm fresh out of polite negotiations."

"Bastard." The Red curled up on his side. "Lightforsaken bastard."

"What, you want an even number? I can do that." Raeyn flicked his wrist and put a second slug into the guy's other knee. "Happy?"

No reply other than the Red's harsh gasps, muffled by the thick carpet against the side of his face. That's when I recognized him.

"Fuck me, that's Pyr. He's one of Laras's guys."

"Oh, I know who he is." Raeyn's tone was so even, it flatlined. "In fact, I know who sent him."

He yanked Pyr up by his collar, ignored his howls of pain, and ripped something from the lapel of his coat.

"Does this look familiar to you?" He tossed it over to me. A silver pin in the shape of a sun. The insignia of the president's personal guard. Aris's personal guard. Its weight burned my palm like ice.

"No. He wouldn't." My fingers curled around the silver, pointy edges digging into my skin. A hollow thumping filled my ears, too fast to be my pulse. A freight train on a collision course.

It made a horrible sort of sense. Aris knew the Temple better than anyone. He'd picked the perfect time for an attack, the gray hours of morning when most of *La Maison's* clients had left and business quieted down for the day.

Doing whatever it took to squash even the thought of standing up against the Empire.

I just never thought he'd go this far. Not after all the Temple'd done for him.

'Course, I'd never thought he'd hurt me either.

I could still feel Kip shaking in my arms, bright red leaking through my fingers. When I first met the kid, his smile'd been so bright it'd spilled over into his eyes. Aris had smiled like that once. Back when he'd been one of them, when he'd belonged to this place made up of light and laughter and glittering masks. Now, the low light drained the color out of death, even the brightness of all the red dimmed down to shades of gray.

Gods, Aris.

"Does it hurt?" Raeyn asked softly. Pyr turned his face into the carpet and said nothing. "Hm. Let me help you with that." He pointed his semi-auto at Pyr's navel. "See, that's the problem with spinal cords. They make you feel your legs."

"Please." The Red's jaw trembled, eyes huge. "Please don't."

Raeyn stared right through him; his smile didn't hold one ounce of humor. "They didn't beg, you know. Didn't say anything. You killed them too fast for that."

I stared at the blood on Raeyn's hands, his face. The tangle of bodies. They'd become faceless in death. Just shapes with too many limbs and slightly familiar hair. Behind Raeyn, I could make out Pascal, kneeling over a body wearing flowing Celebrant's robes now drenched in red, their eyes wide and shocky.

Shit, we had to get them and Kip out of here.

Raeyn's voice cracked. "This place was a Temple. A safe space. No one here was a fucking threat to you. Well, no one except me." His knuckles stood out white around his gun. "This might sting a bit."

He never got to pull the trigger. Two shots hissed past. One popped Pyr in the chest, a second in the head. Classic double-tap. The Red was dead before he could make a sound.

"Don't stand there!" Taerien's voice echoed across the floor, winded with running. "Move! Now!"

That's when I heard it. Overhead, the thumping from earlier had grown into a roar. A dragon's shriek that rose to a deafening pitch.

Next to me, Raeyn had turned sheet-white. "No. Father wouldn't."

"Wouldn't what?" I had to yell to be heard over the noise.

"Airstrike." Raeyn bit off the word. "They're condemning this place."

No time to ask what the hells he meant. Taerien grabbed Raeyn by the arm and pulled him forward. "Run!"

Fuck. I turned to Pascal, my voice barely carrying. "Kip! Downstairs!"

Looked like Pascal caught my meaning because they snapped out of their daze and took off for the stairs. I prayed I hadn't sent them and Kip both to their deaths. Then again, they'd probably be safer downstairs, given how the entire place was about to come down on us.

"Come on!" Raeyn's hand slipped into mine, dragging me along. Running felt like ice picks driving between bone and cartilage. I didn't make it even halfway through the room before my knee gave and Raeyn caught me. Taerien shouted something, but the howl of the jet engines, loud enough to rattle the windows, swallowed it up. Taerien kept running and burst out the door into the gray light of morning while Raeyn put his shoulder under mine, our fingers laced tight.

"Get out of here!" I yelled at Raeyn.

His grip on my hand tightened in response. Thought I heard him say, "Not this time."

We didn't quite make it to the foyer before the first bomb hit.

Plaster rained down. I could taste the ashes at the back of my throat.

Above, a surge of fire roared to life, a monster ready to eat us.

The walls collapsed in an avalanche of bricks. I threw myself against Raeyn, took him down with me, my body curled over his.

Fuck me, the Empire had a secret fleet of bomber planes. If Jay'd been alive to see this, she would've been so pissed.

The world caved in and silence fell.

Election Day

HELOS WAS BURNING.

A day after what the Empire'd dubbed the Great Intervention, smoke still rose from the ruins. The bombers had left nothing but a crater where the Poubelle'd been. The Temple was gone, along with the Place du Marché. Overnight, they'd turned half of Low Side into black marks—cigarette burns on gray carpet, tracking survivors like sooty footprints through a city covered in ash.

There'd been riots and good old-fashioned looting. People decided to take up where the Empire'd left off. Shop fronts went up in flames, the skeletons of burned-out hovers lined empty streets. The dust was still settling when Election Day dawned. Against the orange glow of morning sunlight, it looked as if the air itself had caught fire.

Our stakeout was an old brownstone by the waterfront. A creaking fire escape zigzagged up three stories in the back, making for easy roof access. Or it would've been easy if I didn't have to take a second between each flight of stairs to catch my breath. By the time I reached the third floor, I left sweaty handprints on the rusty railing, the strap of my duffel bag digging into my bruised shoulder. My left knee felt like someone was using its tendons as a stretch band.

Even if the Empire hadn't dropped a whole building on me, my body felt stomped on. Like an aluminum can crushed under the soles of heavy combat boots, too many dings and dents in it to pop back into shape. Even Voyance mojo could only go so far. Should've taken the cane Raeyn'd gotten me. Had to admit, the idea of being a hired gun felt kind of badass. If nothing else, a cane made for a great way to beat the shit out of people.

Iltis would approve the hells out of this.

"Need a hand up, Nettoyer?" Laras called from the roof.

"Fuck off, Laras," I climbed the last few steps. "Shouldn't you be with your boy toy?"

"Please. You're still hung up on that?" Laras lounged against a cooling unit. With her face turned into the sun, she reminded me of a cat on a windowsill, basking in a pool of light. But when she turned to me, her smile was a tad hollow and something bitter lurked behind her porcelain doll eyes. "Congratulations, Nettoyer. I'm your tactical support."

I snorted. Immediately regretted it at the twinge of my still-bruised ribs. "Is Valyr trying to be funny, sending you? Speaking of, thanks for warning us the Empire was gearing up to fire-bomb us all."

"We would, had we known." Laras ground out and sauntered over. There was a tension to her movements, like a wild cat pacing the confines of her cage. "And no, this merely is the commander of the Watch getting the last bit of use out of a captain slated to be dishonorably discharged."

I set my duffle down on the concrete and unpacked my gear.

"Dishonorably discharged, huh? What, Valyr finally find out about you and Aris?"

"Oh, it wasn't all that dramatic." The corner of her mouth twitched. "All it took was a quarterly check-up and a positive pregnancy test."

I nearly dropped the telescope sight I'd been screwing onto the stock of my M82. "You're." My mouth went dry. "It's not Aris's."

Laras's laugh didn't hold a sliver of humor. "Aw, look at you. So sure. It's almost cute." She turned and instead of saying anything else on the issue, nodded at my rifle. "Pretty big gun."

"The bigger the gun, the bigger the hole," I said, still trying to wrap my head around the possibility Laras wasn't lying. That Aris was—The thought of mini-Nymerons snuck into my brain and I had to bite my lip to choke back a hysterical laugh.

If Laras noticed, she ignored it and eyed my box of .50 cal shells. "You know it's illegal to use those against human targets, right?"

"So's shooting them in the first place. Pretty sure the rest falls into some sort of legal gray zone." They used this kind of ammo to take out tanks. One of those would go straight through a vanilla human. It'd do for a power-hungry Voyant on steroids.

"Does Aris know?"

"Not yet." Laras kept her face perfectly blank. "Political assassinations tend to take precedence over personal drama." She pursed her lips and pulled her own piece out of her hip holster, checking it with quick, practiced movements. "For the record, you're not the only one who wants to get him out. Don't miss."

Laras took cover by the cooling unit, leaving me to crouch by the ledge and wait. Fucking irony Valyr'd chosen Laras of all people to guard my back. Or maybe that's why she'd chosen her. Because Laras wouldn't hesitate to shoot me if I'd made a wrong move.

Guess I'd have to make all the right moves and hope.

The sun baked the flat roof, radiating off the concrete and the streets below. All around Lightsquare, the early crowds had snatched away every inch of shade. The rest bunched along the sidelines, hunched under umbrellas scattered along the riverside in bright dots of color. The sharp rap of clubs against steel cut through the constant buzzing of the masses as Reds in brushed dress uniforms pushed people back behind riot gates.

Part of me hadn't expected that big of a turnout, given what the Empire'd done to Low Side. 'Course, nothing got rid of the "Don't vote for Voyants" and "Enough" posters cropping up all over Helos better than an airstrike to scare voters straight. This was surrender, neatly hidden behind a front of celebrating ideas no one believed in anymore.

I sighted in on the stage at the center of the square where Nymeron'd give his presidential acceptance speech. Handy thing about thirty years of rigged one-way elections: when noon hit on E-Day, the computers would've already counted out a solid majority. Just in time for pompous speeches in full sunlight. Endorsed by democratic vote, the Light itself and all that bullshit.

I scanned the crowds for Raeyn. He'd keep my exit clear. And hopefully stay safe without doing anything stupid. As long as he stayed the hells away from the Reds and his father. Taerien'd about ripped me a new one after he'd dug us out of the rubble. If Raeyn'd let him, he would've left me buried under tons of brick and concrete. Like it'd been my fault the Empire'd nuked half of Low Side.

I didn't let myself think that maybe it was. That it'd still be standing if we'd lay low, plotted quietly. Instead, we'd pissed off Aris with my delusional attempt to save him. I should've known better.

A whoosh snapped through the air and the Core went up in flames. "Holy shit!"

The words drowned in the gasp that went through the masses already pushing away from the gates between them and the fire. It took a second for the initial panic to die down.

Then the clapping started. Hesitant at first, before it broke into full-blown applause as people caught on. Didn't hurt that there were plenty of Reds around, encouraging proper behavior, so things looked pretty for the cameras.

The fire, if it was real fire, wasn't spreading. Instead, flames nearly half a foot high snaked along the streets, burning in pools of liquid blocked off by narrow rows of charcoal. Along the river, large braziers lit up. The applause peaked, leading up the stage in the middle of Lightsquare like a signal beacon until it too was surrounded by a ring of flames lapping at the flickering air.

My hands clenched around the aluminum stock of my rifle and I tried to shut out the image of the burning pyre in the middle of the Place du Marché. The memory brought back the smell of roasting flesh, the echo of Kovacz's screams. I took a deep breath. It tasted of smoke and ashes.

Speakers blared the first notes of the anthem. Huge floating holoscreens flashed to life, broadcasting the election and thirtieth anniversary of the Empire of Light all over Helos and through the newsfeeds out to the rest of the Empire.

Across my vantage point, a screen cast the presidential parade moving through the Core. Last time they'd gone for light shows and tech turning everyone into flickering holocopies.

This year Nymeron decided to play God. Literally.

The whole thing was one huge reenactment of an ancient victory train. Dancers behind golden sunburst masks twirled burning torches and rings of fire. Whorls of gold and copper body paint wreathed their skin in living flame.

Nymeron stood on a hover surrounded by Reds wearing silver versions of the dancers' masks. Behind the metal and their stiff uniforms, they looked like angry robots out for brains. Someone'd given the president's hover a makeover, turning it into one of those ancient chariots they always pictured in old paintings of the Gods. Only this thing didn't have any horses to pull it; it floated. In the sunlight, it shone like a silver beacon with the Empire's sigil wrapped around the outside. Nymeron stood in front, dressed in a white suit that gave him a haloed glow.

Got a headache just looking at him.

A faint din started nagging at my ears. It rose in pitch as the president's hover closed in. Aris stood behind him. In his white and silver uniform, he'd dressed every part Nymeron's son. A bright shadow at his father's back, Aris stood as if he'd never known anything else.

As if he belonged.

Could almost pretend it'd always been this way. That the Aris I thought I'd known hadn't been anything but an idea that'd never stuck, never made it past its original rough sketch. Something Kovacz once said flashed back to me. About how much longer I'd be making up excuses for him.

Past Aris, Nymeron, and the crowds putting up a happy face at the Empire's bullshit propaganda, I could still see smoke carve a gap into the horizon where the Temple'd been. Remembered the fear and pain etched into Kip and Pacal's faces when we'd finally dug them out from where they'd found shelter in the half-collapsed infirmary in the Temple's basement. Quick thinking on Pascal's part to get Kip where they could patch him up and keep him mostly stable until help arrived. They'd been among the lucky ones. The newsfeeds had stopped reporting body counts somewhere around two hundred. Through Raeyn's channels, I knew the number'd probably be closer to two fifty before the day was out.

Two hundred and fifty reasons to be done making excuses.

I gave myself two seconds to take a deep breath and rest my forehead against the rough concrete. To pretend I could still hide from this. That it wasn't all on me now.

I slammed the magazine home and lined up my shot.

The president climbed the stairs to the stage and the applause grew to a roar. More braziers lit up until I recognized the sigil of the Empire, a sun made out of flames spanning the whole of Lightsquare with Nymeron at its center. The din grew to a screech, the sound of radio waves clashing. I gritted my teeth against the urge to clap my hands over my ears. Nobody else seemed to hear. In the middle of it all, Nymeron drank in the crowds. If he'd glowed earlier, now he radiated energy.

Hells, Valyr'd been right.

I swallowed against the pressure building up in my skull. It felt like someone was holding me under water. No sound but the droning in my head, everything around me blurring into bright jagged lines, the light show of an oncoming migraine.

From far away I remembered Raeyn's voice telling me to wait. *Hit him when he starts his speech. By then he'll be too far into it to stop. He'll never see it coming.*

Right. I forced my hands to unclench. Deep breaths. Couldn't hit shit if you didn't breathe. Through the haze, I could make out Valyr taking position at Nymeron's left, Aris at his right. Everything shrank to the tiny space between my crosshairs.

Nymeron stepped forward, arms spread in a gesture of welcome. "My fellow citizens, tragedy has brought us together today."

You fucking got that right, I thought and pulled the trigger.

The gunshot shattered the world.

It hit Aris in the center of his ribcage. Tore a huge hole into his shining uniform.

If he made any sound at all, I didn't hear it. Everything around me plunged into silence. Time slowed to a drip, split into the still frames of one of those old black and white silent movies I'd always thought Iltis only liked because they creeped the fuck out of the rest of us.

Aris stumbled. Valyr darted forward, tried to steady him as he swayed on his feet, but she wasn't fast enough. Aris's hands opened and closed, fumbling for something to hold on to.

My first instinct was to run and catch him. Tell him it'd be okay. Tell him I was sorry. I should've used my chance to tap Nymeron. Finish what I'd come here for. But I couldn't, even if I hadn't given my chance away. Everything faded into the distance. Numbness kept me pinned to the ground. The concrete threw back the echo of the gunshot, an endless ringing in my ears.

All I could do was watch Aris fall.

The front of his shirt bloomed red within seconds. In the sunlight, it was bright and shocking, like someone'd tossed a bucket of red paint against a white wall. Valyr got a shoulder under him, but Aris was slipping. He sagged to his knees, his mother's hands all over him like a pair of frightened birds. No point. This was a kill shot and I hadn't missed.

For a second, I could've sworn Aris looked straight at me. Already his eyes grew dull, his lips formed something that could've been my name or just him trying to drag in another breath through ruined lungs. Then his body crumpled in on itself. Too many Reds crowded in and I lost sight of him in the chaos.

Around me, all hells broke loose. The crowds erupted in panicked shrieks, stampedes pushed through the riot gates, trampling out the rest of the guttering flames that'd lined the parade. Braziers toppled over, scattering coals and burning embers. Close gunshots fell.

Gods, let Raeyn make it out before it all went to hells.

Gods, Raeyn.

I closed my eyes.

Gave myself three seconds to breathe through the temptation to let myself shatter.

I'd known this day would come. Had known for years, long before I'd ever sat on L'Oubliette's steps, alone with Raeyn and the knowledge I'd do anything to keep Aris safe. Even this. Problem was I never thought I'd live long enough to see the other side of it.

I needed to move. Get off the ground, but my hands were shaking too badly to pull myself up. I managed to crawl into a corner, wedged against cold concrete, as far away from the spot where I'd shot Aris as I could get. The M82 still lay there, a dead thing gleaming in a pool of sunshine. Should've tossed it over the edge, sank it in the river below, but I couldn't bring myself to touch it again.

Three stories down, Lightsquare gaped. Empty now except for Aris's blood all over the wooden slats and the echo of the gunshot lingering in my ears. Around me, the world tipped. Inside my head, Aris's fall was a never-ending replay loop, the image grainy and skipping as if it'd been recorded on one of Iltis's old projector tapes. Maybe if I got moving, I'd wake up and this wouldn't be real anymore.

I'd wake up and Aris would be fine. He'd come around the corner laughing with that big grin that'd make his eyes dance because of something Jay'd said and Iltis would yell at us how she wasn't paying us for fucking when there was work to be done. But Jay and Iltis were gone, nothing but dust at the bottom of a crater. And Aris wasn't going to come back laughing, because I shot him all to hells.

Even a Voyant couldn't heal a .50 cal slug to the chest.

Now there was nothing left. Nothing to keep all those loose parts and broken angles from rattling around my insides as I sat shivering in the noonday sun, trying to work up the resolve to get up and collect whatever pieces of this revolution I still could.

Fuck, I'm so sorry, Raeyn.

When the shadow fell over me, I'd been expecting it. Laras stood above me, the bluish glint of her gun so bright it stung my eyes. Somewhere behind me the fire escape screeched. Someone shouted my name. Didn't matter.

"You were supposed to get him out." Laras's jaw trembled, dark eyes burning holes in her pale face. Her hands shook. "You were supposed to save him, Nettoyer!"

But I did, I wanted to say. *I did, the only way I know how.*

"Damian, no!"

It all happened too fast.

Laras fired and something smacked into my side with a harsh gasp, punching the air out of me. Next thing she was on the ground and Raeyn's body on top of me, one hand pressed against his side, red leaking through his fingers.

"Raeyn?" I wriggled out from under him, frantic fingers trying to find where he'd been hit. Panic spiked when he didn't move. "Shit, Raeyn!"

"Why?" He squinted through the pain. "For fuck's sake, why, just once, couldn't you follow orders and do what you're told?" Roughly he pushed my hands away and dragged himself to his feet. "Gods damn you, I hope he was worth it." The look Raeyn gave me turned my blood to ice. I knew I'd break into a million pieces if I as much as dared to breathe.

Still, I tried. "Raeyn," his name came out strangled. "I couldn't. I—"

He held up a hand. Had to catch himself, swaying on his feet, leaving a red smear against the hood of the air duct. "Can we do the postmortem later? Jump."

"Jump?"

"Or fall if you'd like." He pulled me forward and shoved me over the ledge.

Three stories rushed past in a flash, the river below a wide glittering ribbon. We hit the surface with numbing force. Then the water closed over us and the current dragged me under.

Brackish water crammed its way down my nose and throat before I came back up to the surface, coughing and sputtering. "Gods. What's it with you throwing me into rivers?"

"Thought you'd cherish the memory," Raeyn gasped. Around him, the water clouded a murky red. He tried to brush me off but stopped when I got an arm around him to keep his head above water. Together we inched toward the shore.

"'Least it's not freezing this time."

Raeyn shook his head weakly. "Just get us out of here and I promise I will refrain from saving your life ever again."

"About that." I jerked my head to the riverside already lined with Reds drawing a tight ring around us. Search beams flared to life. The red dots of laser scopes flittered across the water, clustering all over our chests like a swarm of angry hornets.

"Ah." Raeyn swallowed, his jaw a taut line. "Well, fuck."

Endgame

I SHIFTED AGAINST the wall, trying to find a position that didn't make every inch of my body scream. They could've at least cuffed my hands in front of me. Or not cuffed me at all. Hands and feet were overkill. What the fuck was I supposed to do, locked down here in the deepest pit of the Finger of Light?

The cell was dark, a black hole swallowing up all light, not even leaving hazy outlines to go by. Nothing to shut out the images of Aris falling. Of Raeyn getting shot, taking a bullet for me. I huddled around the memories, tried to smother them in excuses about how it'd been the only thing I could've done, how Aris hadn't left me any other options, how he would've wanted it that way if he'd still been himself. It didn't help. None of it made it past the ringing of the gunshot searing my eardrums. None of it painted over the red spreading across Aris's chest like a bird unfolding its wings. In the dark, his eyes almost looked hazel again right before they broke.

The wall at my back was the only solid thing, the only thing that held in the black. It threw back the low mumble of the air filter that was probably the only reason we hadn't suffocated yet. Over it, I could make out the sound of ragged breathing.

"Raeyn?" I hissed at the hot stab of pain through my left leg as I dragged myself off the floor. In the dark, the cell seemed huge. The restraints around my ankles were so tight, there was no way I could stand up without falling right over again. I shuffled forward on my knees, one side against the wall. Every move drove a rusty nail through my kneecap, but I pushed on.

"Raeyn, where are you?"

The opposite wall found me before I found him. I nearly fell on Raeyn with a grunt and the dulled clatter of chains against the concrete flooring of the cell.

"Damian?" Raeyn's voice was a fraying thread.

"Hey." I awkwardly reached for him. I could feel the heat coming off his skin. Raeyn was curled up on his side, the chains binding his hands and feet rattling faintly as he shivered. "Shit, you're burning up."

"'M fine."

"The fuck you are." I fumbled with the front of his shirt. It was in tatters, stiff with dried blood. My fingers came away sticky.

Raeyn tried to turn away from me. "Leave it." The rest caught on a cough.

"The hells I will. C'mere, we've got to get you off that floor." Easier said than done with our hands and feet tied and Raeyn pushing me away as soon as I got close.

"Don't touch me." It stung. The ice-cold look he'd given me back on the roof etched into memory, an acid burn at the pit of my stomach. I forced it to roll off me like droplets of water.

"You can hate me later." Somehow, I got a shoulder under him without falling over. "And you should. I fucked you over. If I hadn't shot Aris..." *Killed Aris*, a small voice at the back of my head corrected me, but I still couldn't think of that. Not yet.

Raeyn shook his head. "Don't hate you. Knew you couldn't leave him. Should've figured. Not who you are."

His head fell against my shoulder and my mouth went dry. "Raeyn..."

"You know you only call me that when we're fucking or in trouble?" He made another feeble attempt to inch away. "Anyway. Can't touch me. It's important."

The heavy metal door at the end of the cell screeched open and everything flooded with bright light. I blinked, eyes watering.

"Ah, Gods."

I knew that voice. By the time I recognized Taerien, he'd already made it across the cell. "Raeyn?" Taerien crouched in front of him. "Raeyn, can you hear me?"

He unlocked Raeyn's handcuffs. The Gods only knew how he'd gotten the keys.

"Mael?" Raeyn's voice sounded like two sheets of sandpaper rubbing together. In the bright light, his skin was gray, eyes dark bruises in a face hollow with pain. The hole in his side still oozed red; a ragged smear stained the concrete beneath him.

Taerien got rid of Raeyn's ankle restraints and gently stretched him out on the ground.

"What happened to you?"

"Got shot."

"I see that." He ripped open what was left of Raeyn's shirt and sucked in a harsh breath. "I *told* you to stay out of it." Taerien's lips tightened to a pale line as he examined Raeyn's wound. His eyes burned into me. "This is your fault."

I wanted to tell him to go fuck himself, ask him where he'd been, why he hadn't kept Raeyn out of this instead of covering his own ass. The words shriveled and died.

Taerien stalked over and opened my cuffs. "Stay out of my way. For once."

He turned back to Raeyn and dug a knife out of his coat. Numb tingles in my wrists and ankles staggered my movements, but I was at Raeyn's side in an instant.

"What the fuck are you doing?"

"What does it look like?" Taerien fished for a lighter, flicked it and let the orange flame dance along the blade. "That bullet needs to come out."

"What?" Panic tried to strangle me. "You can't just—Do you even know where to cut?"

"He will heal. He won't if the Voyance kills him, trying to heal around that."

It only took one look at Raeyn to know Taerien was right. His chest rose and fell in short, harsh breaths, skin burning with infection. The wound in his side was a mess of blood and pus, all red, ragged edges like something tried to claw its way out from the inside.

I swallowed hard. "How can I help?"

Taerien gave me a calculating look. "Think you can hold him down?"

Oh Gods.

My face must've given me away.

"Forget it. I'll manage."

"No." I almost choked on the words. "I'll do it." I reached out before I lost my nerve, but Raeyn flinched and tried to twist away.

"Don't. Damian, please." His eyes gleamed dark with fever. "You can't. Please. You don't understand. I'll—"

"Shhh." My thumb brushed Raeyn's cheek, stroking a sweaty strand of hair out of his face. "You'll be fine." I glanced at Taerien. "He'll make it quick."

No point waiting for my heart to slow down and my hands to stop shaking, so I set my jaw and pinned Raeyn down and then nodded at Taerien to start cutting.

Raeyn couldn't get enough air to scream. His body seized against my grip, and I had to lean in hard, hands digging into his shoulders. It took my full weight to try and keep him still.

"It's okay. You're okay. I've got you." I was babbling, but I had to say something. Anything to cover the gurgling sounds of Raeyn's wet breaths, of the knife sawing through flesh.

I didn't know if Raeyn could hear me. His eyes glazed over, pupils tiny pebbles sinking into lakes of silver. Raeyn's hands clamped around my arms in a vise-grip, fingers digging into tendons till I thought I heard bones crack. I didn't make a sound, just held him as he turned his face into my forearm, his breath searing gasps against my skin.

Rushing filled my ears, the sound of waves crashing against rocky cliffs. I let it wash over me, carry me away like the tide. My head was killing me. Like someone was holding me under water, pressure built between my ears until sparks lit up my vision. It felt like someone was jabbing an icepick between my eyeball and the bone behind my eyebrow.

Took me a minute to realize whatever was happening, Raeyn was doing it. Leaching the strength right out of me. I couldn't have let go even if I'd wanted to. Something warm wetted my upper lip, a steady red drip trickling on my hands. I stared at it, hypnotized. Better than to look at Raeyn's face with no one in it, his mind somewhere the pain couldn't reach him.

Off to my side, Taerien's knife scraped against metal. He cursed. I could barely see the bullet in all that red, but he got it out and Raeyn let out a sigh. The waves swept it away with everything else. Raeyn finally let go of my wrist and all color drained out of the world, leaving too much white space and nothing to hold on to.

"Damian?" His hand brushed against my cheek, but I was trembling so badly, my arms buckled underneath me. Raeyn's fingers twisted in my hair, the touch soft like feathery wings. "Gods, Damian, I'm sorry. I'm so sorry. I couldn't stop."

He faded before I could move my mouth enough to ask him if he was all right. Tell him it was okay. The waves closed over me and the current dragged me under.

More cursing. Rough hands rolled me off Raeyn. I could still feel the waves lap at the tip of my nose, at my fingers and toes, but the world slowly swam into focus again.

Taerien dragged Raeyn to his feet. Raeyn looked like death warmed over, thin and pale, the new bandage wrapped around his chest already spotted with red.

"We have to get out of here before shift change," Taerien said.

Raeyn leaned on him heavily but locked up at Taerien steering him toward the door. "We're not leaving him."

"Watch me." Taerien tugged him along.

I knew I needed to get off the floor, get moving, but my body felt like it'd been broken into a million pieces, and whoever'd put it back together had gotten all the angles wrong. My head throbbed in time with my heartbeat. It weighed a hundred pounds, but I managed to turn over, clinging to the floor as it tilted and I almost slid off.

Raeyn pulled free of Taerien's grip. He stumbled and nearly fell before catching himself on the wall. "I'm not going without him."

Struggling to my hands and knees, I couldn't see Taerien's face, but I caught him clenching his fists at his sides. "Have you lost your mind? We are never going to make it out of here with him."

"Yes," Raeyn said, wheezing only a little. "Made sure of that, didn't you?"

"He *owed* you that much. For Gods' sakes, he got you in here in the first place! He ruined everything. Everything we've worked for, everything I've done for you. It was supposed to end today, and now you're going down with him, just because—"

"Because, what?" Raeyn slid back into his old sharpness. "Because I'm fucking him?"

"It certainly never stopped you before. What's different this time?"

"I am." Raeyn let go of the wall and took a wavering step toward me. "This isn't before." He made it to me without stumbling, but I could hear his breath rattle in his chest and his hands were clammy when he and grabbed me by my sleeve, clearly not trusting himself to touch my skin. Sweat beaded his forehead. "Come on, darling. Let's get out of here." He helped me to my feet and froze at the sound of footsteps coming downstairs.

"Looks like we'll have to hurry." Raeyn's voice was calm, his eyes steady on Taerien. "I take it you're armed?"

"Of course." Taerien reached inside his coat. "And it looks like that will solve two of my biggest problems right now."

He pulled out his .45 and pointed it right at me.

"Don't!" Raeyn moved in time for Taerien to line up his shot.

The figure in the doorway cut both short.

"Trust me, your problems are only just beginning." Aris stepped into the cell, a skeleton grin lighting up his pale eyes. "Surprise."

27

Checkmate

"ARIS."

His name tasted like ash in my mouth. Blood rushed from my head to my feet. Raeyn's grip on my arm was the only thing that kept me standing and I was painfully aware how pathetic we looked, one leaning on the other, cornered with no way out.

"You sound shocked." Aris's mouth twitched, one corner lifting in a parody of a not-quite smile. It sent a shudder of goose bumps down my spine. "Voyants are hard to kill. Thought you of all people would remember that."

He moved like a broken stick figure, one stiff step toward me, his palm a light touch against my chest where Valyr'd shot me months ago. Underneath Aris's fingers, I felt the cold burn of the bullets as they'd ripped me open. Nothing but a phantom echo, a memory of bleeding into the dirt while the world grew dim. It still tore a soft, strangled sound out of me. Cold concrete pressed against my back before I'd even noticed I'd backed away.

"Leave him alone." Raeyn pushed forward, but Taerien held him back.

Aris's smile didn't touch his eyes. "Oh, I'm not the one who nearly killed him, brother."

Raeyn didn't reply, but I watched a muscle jump in his cheek as he gritted his teeth. Aris wouldn't even look at him. His eyes were fixed on me.

"I told you not to get involved." Aris let out a sigh that caught on a wince. His hand went halfway to his chest before he stopped himself. Sweat shone on his forehead. "We need to get you out of here," he said. "And by the Gods, let's hope you didn't just fuck up everything."

Aris cast a quick glance to Taerien. "If either of them tries to run, you shoot them."

What the fuck? Since when was Taerien in cahoots with Aris? Fucking spider. He—

Aris kicked my legs out from underneath me. I heard the cold snap of handcuffs closing around my wrists before I even registered he'd slipped behind me.

"Trust me," Aris whispered against my neck.

Trust him. Right. Like we'd done so well with that so far.

"Fuck you."

"Thanks, but it looks like you picked my brother."

Something tightened in my throat. Out of the corner of my eye, I caught Raeyn glaring.

Taerien yanked Raeyn's hands back and whispered something to him that made him quit struggling fast. Aris shoved me out into the hallway, and I nearly lost track of Raeyn in the chaos.

A gaggle of Reds swarmed us, prodding us up the stairs. Laras's hand fell on my shoulder, her thin, bony frame pressing against my side.

"I always wondered if you were a screamer, Nettoyer," she said dreamily. Her gloved hand was a vise around the back of my neck. "Looks like we're about to find out."

Lightsquare'd turned into a caricature of itself. Sunlight had bleached away the fake brightness of the Election Day celebrations. Crumpled flyers and trampled garlands littered the waterfront. Clumps of spilled coal crunched under boots trailing soot across the white marble covering Lightsquare like a tomb.

The square was lined with Reds. The Empire must've pulled all its reserves for this one. Reds in riot gear formed a solid ring around the Finger of Light and the palace, walled in the crowds pressing along the sidelines and the riverside, spilling over into surrounding streets.

They might as well've soundproofed the place. Everyone stood with their heads down, voices low. Scattered laughter echoed across the hushed square, nervous, high-pitched sounds.

The Core'd gone into duck and cover mode, listening for the roaring of incoming bombers. No one'd forgotten how last time Nymeron'd leveled most of Low Side to make a statement. The Gods only knew what he'd do after I'd all but offed his son.

At first, I thought I was having flashbacks, the panicky kind that filled my nose with smoke and scraped at the back of my throat whenever I thought of the day the Empire'd burned Kovacz. They'd walked me across the square and halfway to the pyre before it finally hit me.

This one was for me. Nymeron was going to burn me.

I locked up. Started to panic. They were going to burn me. They'd make me get up that pyre, tie me down, and watch me roast like a fucking feast day lamb.

Aris would throw the torch.

I squeezed my eyes shut so tight stars sparked. My knee trembled, this side of giving out. If I fell now, Laras would only drag me the rest of the way. I'd make her day.

No one'd dragged Kovacz to the pyre.

I kept walking before Laras had to nudge me.

Next to me, Raeyn didn't blink. He'd slammed the shutters tight, his face locked behind his usual blank mask, so nobody saw how fucking terrified he was. I would've done anything to be able to touch him then, would've let them burn me three times over if it'd spare him.

But this'd stopped being a world with room for wishful thinking a long damn time ago.

The president stood at the same spot where he'd been about to announce his perfectly faked victory the day before. Valyr hovered in the background. Off to his side, I could still make out the huge dark stain where Aris's blood had leaked through the slats.

Aris's hand closed around my shoulder, the grip possessive, a dog pissing up a tree, marking his territory before another bigger, scarier dog got the chance.

"Father." Aris's head tipped just shy of a bow.

Nymeron nodded. Aris steered me onto the pyre. My stomach dropped. I wanted to dig my heels in, lose my shit, anything, if it meant staying alive for another minute or two longer.

I climbed the pyre without stumbling.

Aris stepped in front of me, gently pushed me back so he could tie me to the stake before he stopped. His cool fingers cupped my cheek, the touch old and familiar. I flinched when his lips brushed against mine.

Nymeron cleared his throat. "This really isn't the place, Aris."

"You're right, Father. It isn't. I should never have let it come this far." A fierce grin lurked behind Aris's eyes. "You know, you completely ruined my timing," he murmured against the side of my throat. At a flick of his wrist, my handcuffs clattered to the ground. "Sorry about this. I would have spared you the drama if there'd been a quicker way to get you out of the Finger. Anyway." He slipped my Colt into my hands. "Run."

His eyes lit up white.

A rustle went through the crowds, everyone close to the stage suddenly very busy getting the hells out of Lightsquare. Only the ones too curious to book it kept lingering by the river.

"And that's our signal," Raeyn said next to me, his hands uncuffed and pulling me with him. "Time to get out of here. Mael's driving the getaway hover."

I didn't move. Just stared at Aris and Nymeron, a Voyant shitstorm ready to hit the fan.

Raeyn sighed. "Well then. He better keep it running."

"Aris. What do you think you are doing?" Behind his pasted-on smile, there was a razor edge to Nymeron's words.

"What I should have done for months." Around Aris, the Voyance became a second pulse. The air hummed with it, a coil of power wound tight enough to snap.

It hit Nymeron square in the chest. He stumbled. Caught himself on the podium. The Voyance burned white in his eyes. The hum of power grew to a vibrating roar.

Nymeron smiled. "'Et tu, Brute?' Is that how it's going to be? I'm afraid you're harboring delusions of grandeur, son."

"I'm not your son," Aris said. "And I'm not alone."

Valyr met her son's eyes. Aris nodded. The Reds in riot gear put their shields up. Around them, the air blistered with power. Shit, guess the rumors about some Reds being low-key Voyants were true. And Aris had made an army of them.

The Finger of Light exploded in a shower of glass. Windows blew out. Concrete walls caved. The shockwave was deafening. I hit the ground before I even noticed I was falling. Raeyn's knee smacked into the small of my back, his weight keeping me pinned. The Finger's steel frame groaned but held. Fires flickered behind gaping windows. A hailstorm of metal and glass hammered down on the square.

Aris stood in the middle of it as if it was nothing but a mild spring rain.

He towered over Nymeron. "I'm not the only one tired of your lies."

My ears were ringing so badly I could barely pick out the words. Nymeron's face was gray, staring at the dust settling over the ruins of what used to be the hallmark of his Empire.

Aris didn't hesitate.

The Voyance curled around Nymeron's throat like a noose made of live wire. Nymeron's eyes widened. He tried to claw it loose, but Aris didn't budge. "To you, I never was anything but a windup toy. Something to show off and point at people when it was convenient." Aris pulled the noose tighter, trembling with the effort.

"Two can play a game, Father. See, I thought if I played my part, become the prodigal son you made me out to be, your poster child, the perfect successor, it would all be worth it." Aris's nose had started to bleed, a steady red drip down his upper lip. "I did everything you asked me to. I switched sides, became your puppet, killed without looking twice at the bodies."

His voice cracked, and he couldn't even look at me. "I turned on everyone around me. All for the off chance you'd let me in enough to turn your back on me just once, so I could—" Aris shook his head. I saw him draw the knife, the gleam of the blade a searing afterimage in front of my eyes. "I'm done playing, Father."

"Are you now? Well, that's a relief."

Nymeron struck without warning.

A brief flicker in the Voyance was all he needed to smash Aris's offensive. Aris's Voyance shattered into a thousand pieces. The blast kicked up a whirl of dust and fallen glass. I could smell fried wiring. Downed cables were striking sparks.

Aris staggered. He couldn't catch himself before Nymeron lashed out again. The strike hit him like an oncoming train. Sucked him under and ground him into the dirt before he even got the chance to scream. The knife slipped from his fingers, and Aris fell half a second behind, a bundle of rags collapsing at Nymeron's feet.

He didn't get up again.

"Aris." Valyr moved toward Nymeron, piece pointed at his chest. "He's your son." Her voice shook, but her hands were steady. "He's your *son*."

Nymeron's hands clamped down around her throat. "We'll talk about this later."

The Voyance snapped. Valyr made a small sound in the back of her throat and went limp. Nymeron tossed her aside like a broken doll.

"It's a shame." He shook his head. "So much potential. Wasted." Nymeron crouched, glass crunching underfoot. Long fingers brushed Aris's hair out of his face. Nymeron picked up the fallen knife and weighed it in his hands.

"Don't touch him." I got to my feet, ears ringing with a surge of Voyance boiling to the surface. I dragged my Colt up. "Don't you fucking touch him."

"Damian, don't."

I didn't notice I was shaking until Raeyn tried to tear me away, the Colt an impossible weight dragging on my arms. My eyes were glued on Aris lying on the ground in a crumpled heap. He'd played me. He'd told me he wasn't going to leave the palace when I'd tried to get him out, he'd thrown me down four flights of stairs into a subway tunnel. Gods, he'd launched a fucking air raid, killed dozens of people, people who'd been his friends, just to keep me far enough away from him and this batshit plan of his.

He once said he'd set the world on fire for me if it came down to it.

"You godsdamned bastard." I had to fight the urge to kick him. "Fuck you."

"Yes, all that." Raeyn's hand clenched around mine. "Anyway. Do you think we could save the wallowing in sudden but inevitable betrayal for later?"

I put two right between Nymeron's eyes.

"Or you could shoot people. If it makes you happy."

Might as well have poked Nymeron with a toothpick. He moved so fast, the slugs didn't as much as scrape him. His fingers burned white-hot, curling in my collar, pulling me close.

"Hm." Nymeron checked me over. "So, you are the new one."

"What the fuck do you mean, the new—"

Nymeron kicked me through the floor. Something creaked and gave where his boot hit my chest. The ground opened beneath me. Raeyn shouted something, but the words ripped away. My back slammed into concrete so hard, it dented, cracks spiderwebbing outward. My skull exploded into bursts of light. Dust and splinters rained down the hole my body'd punched through the stage.

Nymeron towered over me, tall and still as a statue, blotting out the light.

His lips twisted. "Disappointing."

"What?" I croaked. "Sad I don't do tricks for you? Want me to roll over and let you pet my belly?" I tried to pick myself off the floor. My stomach lurched. Pain sank its claws into my abdomen and yanked.

Nymeron put his boot on the small of my back and leaned. "Down."

I choked on the dust, dragging in breaths through bruised lungs. Glass shards dug into my palms, into the side of my face. Spots of color flittered in front of my vision. The Voyance tingled in my fingers and toes. Nymeron stomped it out like the guttering embers of a dying fire.

Nymeron clucked his tongue. "He almost drained you dry. Pity. And wasteful. Given he can't use it for anything other than to heal himself. Like a cockroach. Always coming back."

"What—" I fought for air, harsh gasps catching on kicked-in ribs. "—are you talking about?"

"Let him go." Raeyn was a silver streak in the corner of my eye, staring down at his father, my Colt glinting in his grip. "Leave him out of this."

"You didn't tell him." I could hear the shark-smile behind Nymeron's words. "Well, full disclosure never was your thing."

Raeyn's voice dropped to a growl. "I said leave him."

Nymeron's left hand fisted in my hair. He hauled me up fast enough I felt something tear. I hissed, the knife dug into my throat, the blade already warm and sticky with my blood.

"Yes, it's all talk with you, isn't it?" Nymeron pulled me close, effectively turning me into his meatshield. "I thought you had learned from last time. You were so broken up about Gren. Gren *was* his name, right? You go through them so fast, it's hard to keep up."

"Don't." Raeyn almost choked on the word. His finger tightened on the trigger. He'd shoot me. Anything to get to his father. This close, the bullet would go right through me before it'd take down Nymeron. I should probably be worried about that, but all I could do was stare at Raeyn because I'd finally drudged up the reference.

"Gren. That guy in *L'Oubliette*. You," I fumbled for the words. "You did this to him?"

I remembered Gren's ruined face, the bloody bandage wrapped around his eyes, his fingers digging into Raeyn's wrist, desperate to hold on. The images overlapped with Raeyn clutching at me after Laras shot him, the rushing of the waves dragging me under. Afterward, Raeyn'd been better. A lot better.

"So that's what happened." I was cold. Would've shivered, if I'd had room between Nymeron and the knife against my throat. "You said he saved your life. Guess he did."

"I never meant to hurt you." Raeyn's eyes bore into me, pleading. But he didn't deny anything his father said.

"That's why you didn't want me to touch you," I said. "Why didn't you tell me?"

The desperation in his eyes was all the answer I needed. Looked like I wasn't the only one with issues admitting things to himself.

"I'm not like him," Raeyn said. "Damian, please."

"Really, son." Nymeron shook his head. "Hypocrisy doesn't suit you. It played right into your cards that Aris ended up at the palace to keep me preoccupied while you could go about planning riots. Assassinations."

Raeyn recoiled like he was going to be sick.

Nymeron patted my shoulder. "You even got your very own Voyant to leech off. Impressive."

I froze over. Stared at Raeyn. "I led you right to Aris. To him and everyone else."

The thoughts came so easy, falling into place like puzzle pieces.

"No." Raeyn's face turned gray. "I didn't. Damian, I swear to you, I had nothing to do with the raid on the *Shadow*."

The cold carved into me. I couldn't think. My head was pounding. Even the Voyance burned like ice. Hollowed me out and lined me with cracks. If Nymeron as much as flicked a finger at me, I'd shatter.

Instead, he lowered the knife and handed it to me.

Nymeron's white Voyant-eyes sliced into me. "Kill him."

"What?" My broken fingers closed around the handle and I'd taken two steps toward Raeyn before the word was even out. "No. No, wait!" I took another step.

"I'm sorry, Damian. I should have told you." Raeyn didn't move. My mark. The presidents' son-turned-revolutionary. Aris's brother. My partner long before I'd woken up in his bed. Just stood there, pointing my own Colt at me.

"No." This wasn't how this was supposed to go. "He's in my head. Fuck, Raeyn, *move*."

I tried to stop. Dig my heels in. My Voyance flared, but it was like holding a candle to a wildfire. Nymeron swallowed it all up. I tasted blood. Felt it running down my upper lip, dripping off my chin. I trembled, fighting him every inch. Nymeron kept pushing me forward. To him, I was nothing but a piece on his chessboard.

Two steps. One.

You were a tracker, Nettoyer. Nothing more. Valyr's words echoing past the pressure building between my ears. I tried to drown them out, tried to remember it wasn't actually me thinking them. That they weren't true. I *knew* Raeyn.

As much as anyone could know him. Which wasn't much at all.

I closed the gap, knife angled at Raeyn's ribs. No. *No.*

"Tell me you didn't just use me."

He'd slipped his hand into mine the day they burned Kovacz. I remembered Raeyn's lips hot on mine, the soft sounds he'd made when I kissed his scars. Remembered pancakes in bed, how he'd taken a bullet for me even after I let him down.

"Raeyn, please." Move. Don't let him make me do this.

"I didn't lie to you." Raeyn's pale eyes were fixed on me.

He dropped the Colt.

"What are you doing?"

"I never lied to you," he said again. The tip of the knife sliced into the fabric of his shirt. It nicked his skin. Raeyn didn't flinch. "I want you to know that."

He leaned in. The blade dug in further. His breath hitched. "For once, I told the truth." Raeyn's palm was warm against my cheek, melting some of the ice. A crooked grin ghosted across his face. "And now I need you to do what you've come here for." Raeyn held my eyes. "I know I have no right to ask this of you, but do you trust me?"

"What?" Blood spattered my fingers where the blade slid between his ribs.

Raeyn didn't seem to notice. "Do you trust me?"

"Yes." I shouldn't, but I did. Fuck me, I did.

"Thank you." Raeyn closed his eyes in relief. It lasted for half a second. Then his hand clamped down on the side of my head. It was scorching hot. "And I really hope this works. Because it would be a horrible plan B if it didn't."

"What—" I tried to jerk away, but Raeyn didn't let go. His eyes were white and filmy, the Voyance crackling at his fingertips.

"You see, the Voyance works two ways. If I can take it from you, I can give it back."

The current hit me. It flushed Nymeron right out of my head. The knife slipped from my fingers. My knees gave out under me, my body jerked, trapped in a high-voltage circuit that wouldn't let me fall. Raeyn's Voyance poured into me; everything he'd stored up and that'd gone unused building up, rushing through, filling me up until I was sure I'd run over. Pressure pounded between my ears, behind my eyes. My heart fluttered, shocked into overdrive. Even my fingers and toes were throbbing with raw energy.

"There." Raeyn was breathing hard, wavering on his feet. His hand fell away.

"What." I gasped. Stumbled. "What did you do to me?"

"I may not be able to do anything with all the Voyance in the world. But you can." Raeyn swayed. His eyes were dull, his hair stringy with sweat, but he grinned through clenched teeth. "Fry him, darling."

I nearly tripped over Aris, his body a sudden, solid warmth at my back. "Damian?" Aris took a groggy step forward, reached, but didn't touch me, as if he was worried I'd shock him.

"Are you okay?" He squinted. Blinked. "Thought I told you to run."

"Yeah." I fought down a hysterical laugh. It was either that or scream. I could barely see him against all the white bleaching out everything around us. "Bit late for that, don't you think?"

Nymeron's eyes brushed over me, weighed and measured me before settling back on Raeyn.

"Honestly, son. Look at him. Trembling like a leaf." His mouth quirked at the corner. "You have got to stop betting all you have on one horse. It makes you look desperate."

Raeyn's face was an exact mirror of his father's when he said, "Someone once told me not to worry so much about how I look. You may want to give it a try." He sauntered forward. "Also, I never made a very good bystander."

Raeyn caught his father's hand.

Nymeron's eyes widened. Tried to shake him off, but Raeyn latched on tight.

"I'm not like you." Raeyn's lips pulled back into a fierce grin. "In all ways but one." He squeezed. The Voyance danced behind his eyes as he drained his father like a juice box. "Damian, *now!*"

Raeyn's voice was my signal shot. I turned to Aris. "Are you with me?"

"Always."

"Good." I swallowed the crack in my voice. "You heard him. Let's fry the fucker."

I took Aris's hand.

The Voyance screamed.

The world turned white.

Everything tilted. I would've fallen if not for Aris's fingers laced through mine, holding tight. I thought I saw him smile. The Voyance tore through conscious thought, a firestorm of burning energy racing through my veins.

It burst outward like the mushroom cloud of a nuclear explosion. Raeyn's hand tore from his father's and he flung himself to the side. The blast knocked him down hard. Wood splintered. Fallen glass turned to shrapnel cutting through the air. Raeyn lay unmoving.

Nymeron never had time to get his shield up before the Voyance hit him head-on. He staggered and dropped to his knees, mouth opening in a scream ripped away by the roar of the Voyance. It wrapped around him in a shroud of living flame. He tried to fight it, but whatever Raeyn'd done, on top of the load we threw at him, it was as if we'd popped a breaker. Nymeron's Voyance clicked on empty, nothing but sparks sizzling against the gale sweeping him up, burning him from the inside.

Aris and I burned with him, the Voyance around us flaring bright like a dying star. It fused us together, our skeletons melting. I felt my fingernails peeling back, curling away from the heat. The smell of scorched hair and charred skin stung my nose. Even my lashes felt singed.

Between us, the air burned. We sucked down liquid fire with every breath. I couldn't keep this going much longer. The Voyance'd hollowed me out, a pillar of ash about to crumble and blow away with the wind.

Just a little while longer.

Finish winning first. Then I could fall.

The backlash hit with a teeth-grating jolt. The Voyance shorted out, kicked back a half second later. Through the haze, I felt Aris slip away, his fingers slide out of mine, the Voyance around him spider-webbing before it broke and fell away.

"Oh no, you're not."

Aris's eyes fluttered shut when I caught him, yanked him back from wherever he'd been about to go. Bits of glass dug into my arms, slashing lines of fire through skin and tendons. My hands were raw and slick with blood, too slippery to hold on.

"Damian, let go."

"Forget it." I tightened my grip. The Voyance flickered, a light bulb before it burned out.

Nymeron took his chance. His strike nearly swept me off my feet, his Voyance crashing against mine.

I hit him with all I had left. The Voyance cracked down in a bolt of lightning.

Hairline cracks lined my skin. The pressure in my skull skyrocketed. Something wet trickled down my cheeks, from my lips, too warm to be tears.

The ground dragged me down, Aris's body radiating heat against my chest.

I barely made out the blurry figure moving toward Nymeron, the knife he'd picked up a glimmer in a bone-white hand. Raeyn moved through the flames like a ghost, as if they couldn't touch him.

He didn't hesitate. Just brought the knife down at the center of his father's chest. It cut right through Nymeron's Voyance. Silence fell; the only sounds the crackling flames and the soft sigh that escaped Nymeron when Raeyn pulled the knife out. He let go of the hilt, the blood on the blade sizzling, Raeyn's hand blistered with burns.

"You." Nymeron choked, blood bubbling at the corners of his mouth, running down his chin. He slumped forward, pale fingers snatching at Raeyn's shirt.

"Me." Raeyn lowered him to the ground. "May the Gods forgive us both, Father."

Nymeron made a wheezing sound that sounded like a laugh. "Proud of you," he whispered past the blood. "In the end. Exactly like your old man."

Raeyn froze. Shook himself loose. "I don't want your pride. Or your Empire. I just want you gone."

Nymeron cracked a red grin. "You think it's that easy? Kill me and that's it?"

"It's a start," Valyr said behind Raeyn. The side of her head was caked in blood, her hair wild, uniform in tatters.

Nymeron's face lit up at the sight of her, suddenly hopeful.

Raeyn's grin turned fierce. "Hello, Mother."

Valyr smiled at him. She picked up the knife. I tried to shout a warning at Raeyn.

Too late.

She kept smiling as she stabbed the knife into the base of Nymeron's throat. Nymeron's eyes bulged. He tried to scream, but all that came out was a mangled gurgle drowned in a gush of blood.

Valyr laid a finger against Nymeron's bloody lips. "All those years you thought I'd never turn on you."

She leaned in and pushed the knife down, sawing through bone and cartilage in a soggy crunch. Stilettos were made for stabbing, not hacking people's heads off.

Valyr managed.

A final spasm shuddered through Nymeron, then he lay still.

"You were wrong," Valyr said to his severed head. Her fingers left a red smear where they brushed against a slack cheek. *"Bon passage, mon amour."*

She put the head down. Drew herself up straight and nodded at Raeyn, who stood frozen, staring at Nymeron's headless body. No one made a move to stop Valyr when she turned and disappeared in the smoking ruins of Lightsquare.

At the edge of the stage, Nymeron's head rolled over, empty eyes staring at the palace, watching it burn.

I must've made some sort of noise rolling Aris off me because Raeyn snapped out of his stupor and staggered toward me. "Damian? Are you—"

"Gods," I croaked. "If you're about to ask me if I'm okay, I might have to punch you."

I wanted to take back the words as soon as they came out.

Raeyn stopped in his tracks. Reaching out for me, his hand fell before he got even close. I couldn't bring myself to look at him, the rawness in his face harsher than the spatters of his father's blood clinging to his jaw, soaking the collar of his shirt. The wound in his side'd torn open again, a growing red stain to match the rest of him. Didn't think he noticed.

Raeyn knelt in front of Aris, a puppet with his strings cut. "Just." He licked his lips. "Let me help. Please?"

I tightened my arm around Aris, his breathing ragged, but steady. "Think you helped enough."

Raeyn flinched as if I'd slapped him. I trusted him, but I hadn't forgiven him.

Either way, not much he could do. I'd felt Aris's Voyance burn out like an old fuse, leaving nothing but soot and rattling pieces on the inside.

He'd survived. Barely. Now it was on me to keep it that way, never mind I hadn't the slightest idea how.

I shook him. Aris made a weak protesting sound. "C'mon, gotta get up." I pulled his arm over my shoulder. "Time to get out of here before the Reds get their shit together and send in the cleaning crews."

I dragged Aris off the floor and almost keeled over, my whole body feeling as if someone'd torn my spine out and ground the rest of me to mush. I sucked in a sharp breath and ignored the twinge in my knee, pretending I didn't see Raeyn fidgeting, looking like he was torn between wanting to reach out and not daring to.

"I better do the same," he said. "I have a feeling people aren't the biggest fans of Nymerons right now." The corner of Raeyn's mouth twitched into a hollow almost-smile. "Can't blame them, really."

"You don't have to go." The words were out before I could stop myself.

Raeyn met my gaze and it was like watching a tower crumble and fall behind his eyes. "Best I disappear for a while. Divert attention. Let the dust settle."

My nod felt hollow. This wasn't how things were supposed to end, Gods damn it.

Pretty sure we were both running a mental recap of the same things: bodies strung up by the river. Reds raiding bars, torching houses. Iltis's charred hand curled against the floor of her study. Jay's body growing cold and heavy in my arms. All overlaid with the sting of smoke and Nymeron's body a mangled shadow off to the side.

"I'm sorry, Damian."

"I know," I said because it was the only thing to say. "Me, too."

I left him standing in the middle of the rubble. With Aris leaning on me, I limped out of Lightsquare. Around us, the fires guttered out and the world turned gray.

We'd won.

Fuck me if I had any clue how we'd even start picking up the pieces.

Postmortem

THE NEW PRESIDENT met me outside a small café by the riverside six weeks later.

I'd gotten there early and picked a table flooded with sunlight where the crowds were thickest and the chances of catching a bullet the slimmest. The family at the table next to me paid up and cleared out in a hurry before I'd even ordered my coffee. I pretended not to notice; just leaned my cane against the table, hunched behind the shades of my sunglasses, and scanned Lightsquare for hidden snipers.

A month and a half after we'd killed Nymeron, I could still smell the smoke.

Didn't matter how busy the interim government'd been scrubbing any traces of what'd gone down here, or how loudly they kept going on about drastic changes, new directions, and all the other bullshit politicians liked to promise. They'd even elected someone who was a complete nobody. Or at least that was the card the new president ran with. Spouting fancy words of change and rebuilding wouldn't fix shit. I mean, they'd made Taerien Minister of Internal Affairs. The Gods help us.

The new president of what we were now supposed to call the Republic made our meeting right on the dot. Just as well, because I'd been ready to put a bullet or three into the ancient, brightly colored ice cream truck that sat by the river, blaring music from crackling speakers.

Carol Stern had a thing for purple suits. She probably owned an army of them, her face on every holoscreen, trailing headlines and a landslide victory in her wake. She was in her early sixties, average height, with a short crop of iron-gray hair; people might call her plump, except there was nothing soft about Stern.

"Mr. Nettoyer." She held out a hand. "It's a pleasure to finally meet you."

"Right." Instead of taking it, I put my elbows on the table, barrel of my Colt level with Stern's head, finger on the trigger. "Wish I could say the same."

Someone screamed. One turned into many. Chairs toppled. People kicked back from their tables and burst apart like a flock of frightened birds. A red dot appeared on my chest. Two more, circling like vultures. Well, that took care of the whole hidden sniper problem. I made a mental note I'd been right about that ice cream truck.

"So," I said, watching her past the glint of my Colt. "Now it's just us, who do you want me to take out for you?"

Stern's holoscreen smile never slipped. "Do I get to have cake with that question?"

"What?"

She pursed her lips. "Are you going to shoot the waitress if she brings me cake? We are in a café, after all. It's only polite to order something."

"No! I mean, go ahead." Gods, whatever proof I needed that all politicians were completely batshit, I had it right there. Fucking cake.

"Good."

Stern waved a waitress over and calmly ordered coffee and chocolate cake. The girl was so terrified, she nearly spilled the coffee. She also looked so much like Jay, something clenched in my chest. I kept my eyes on Stern.

"Back to your question," Stern said, between two bites of cake. "That's not how we are doing things anymore. The Republic doesn't just kill people."

"Yeah. Heard that one before."

"Not to be nitpicky, but I'm not the one holding a gun to your head, Mr. Nettoyer."

"Call it insurance."

"And they said recruitment would be boring." Stern shaved off a bit of cream. "I want to make you one of our federal investigators."

Okay, that was new. "You want to what? *Why?*"

Instead of answering, Stern took out a handheld screen and held it out to me. It played back footage of Low Side after the bombs. Ruins where there'd been houses, the Temple a pile of rubble, bodies crumpled along the debris, whatever might've been familiar about them now smudged with ash. The last bit was a shaky clip of Lightsquare exploding in a burst of white flames, the Voyance a signal flare painting bright afterimages into the sky.

I stared at it long after the screen turned black again. "Forget it."

Stern put the screen down. "You misunderstand me, Mr. Nettoyer. I won't pretend someone with your abilities wouldn't be a tremendous asset, but this is about more than that. We have a nation to rebuild." She made a sweeping gesture, taking in Lightsquare and the gray ruins of what used to be the palace.

"All this isn't going to change overnight. We need the people on our side."

"Yeah and I'm such a people person." I snorted. "You've got the wrong guy, Stern."

"You are one of them," she said. "A link. You've worked with Low Siders and the Watch and, from what I understand, both sides, excuse my language, royally fucked you over."

"You've got that right." My aim never wavered. "'Course, me being a Voyant and giving you an in to everything you could get out of me about my former boss doesn't have anything to do with this at all."

Stern's lips crinkled. "It helps." She handed me her card. "Think about it. We could use people like you. As could they."

I bet. Didn't need to ask who she meant by "they." Other Voyants. People like me. Not sure when that'd started to roll off so easily. Or why it still felt like I'd switched sides, when really there'd never been any sides, to begin with.

I picked up her card.

"I'll let you know."

"I'm looking forward to it."

The red dots on my chest winked out half a second before I lowered my Colt.

Stern's card burned a hole into my pocket all the way back to the Fringe, where I'd found a small place for Aris and me, far enough out of the way I didn't have to worry about getting a face full of lead whenever I stepped out of the door.

I ignored the pins and needles in my knee and took the long way back, across the East River and through the tangled back roads of the Outer Core, to be sure Stern hadn't put a tail on me. As far as job interviews went, this'd been one of the weirder ones. It'd half convinced me the only way to dodge a bullet, in the long run, was to pack up and clear out of Helos while I still could. Only the other half of me already saw the bullet coming and turning my back to it wasn't going to help.

That train of thought derailed when I got to the apartment and found the door unlocked.

"Aris?"

No answer. A spike of panic drove into my gut. I never heard the clatter of my cane hitting the ground behind me, because I'd already gotten both hands on my Colt and burst through the door.

And found Raeyn leaning over a very pale Aris.

"Oh. You."

Raeyn froze. For a second the only sound in the tiny living room was the fizzing of a handful of pills he'd dumped into a glass of water. One of Aris's teacups lay on the floor, tea seeping into the gray carpet in a greenish stain.

Aris held up a shaky hand, his voice muffled by a bloody towel he was holding to his nose. "I called him. You weren't here and..." He pinched the bridge of his nose and tilted his head back against the wall. "Damian, please."

I sighed and ran a hand through my hair. Aris hadn't had a seizure in two days now. Should've known it wouldn't last. I shouldn't have left him alone. Whatever'd happened when the Voyance burned out of him must've shorted out something in his brain. One moment he'd be fine, the next he'd fall, convulsing, and all I could do was lie him on his side and make sure he wouldn't hurt himself any worse than he already had.

That's why we'd moved in together in the first place. Aris couldn't live by himself and I... Well. Let's just say some habits are hard to kick and Aris was the last of the Shadows I could still look out for.

At least this time, he was pretty much with it, never mind he looked like shit, nose still dripping red and his knuckles bloody where he must've hit the corner of the table.

I put my Colt down and took off my sunglasses. Regretted it immediately, because even with the blinds down, the apartment seemed too bright with Raeyn in it. I felt another migraine coming on, clawing at the edge of my vision. Fucking Voyance headaches.

"I should leave." Raeyn wouldn't look at me. He pushed the glass toward Aris. "The pills should help with the seizures. Here." He put a blister pack on the table. "Don't take more than two at a time. Call me if..." He trailed off when he caught me looking. "I should go."

"No," Aris said. "Stay. You two need to talk."

He knocked back the rest of the water and pulled himself up from the couch, swaying only a little as he shuffled to his room, one white-knuckled fist clenched around the blood-spattered towel. "Try not to kill each other. I'm sure the neighbors wouldn't appreciate the noise." He gave me a pointed look and pulled the door shut behind him.

Which left Raeyn and me standing there, two people stranded on an island with too much and at the same time too little space between us. Something moved under the couch, and Dust peeked out, stalked over to Raeyn and rubbed against the back of his leg. Raeyn cracked a smile, leaned down and scratched her head. For a while, happy purring filled the quiet.

"You and Aris are living together." Raeyn kept his voice perfectly neutral.

"We're not..." I couldn't make eye contact. "This isn't..."

"Of course." Raeyn nodded, the motion clipped and stiff.

I turned away and picked up Aris's cup. When I straightened, Raeyn's hand was on my shoulder, his fingers a whisper against the back of my neck before he pulled away.

"You're right," he said into the empty space between us. "This was a terrible idea. I should leave." He took a step back.

I turned the cup over in my hands, ran a finger over a chipped corner.

"I missed you," I said quietly. "Now how fucking stupid is that, huh?"

I set the cup on the table because it was either that or throw it against the wall and watch it shatter into a thousand pieces. "Go ahead. Laugh. I deserve it."

Raeyn didn't laugh. "I didn't lie to you."

I glanced at him, expecting the lie to flash in his eyes. Instead, he just looked thin and tired. Like he'd stopped eating. Stopped sleeping.

Raeyn licked his lips. "Father was right, you know. I lie. I use people. It's what I do."

He made an impatient gesture at that, as if his fingers itched for a lighter and a cigarette. "I'm not going to pretend I'm going to change. We both know better. But I want you to know what happened between you and me was real. And I'm sorry I fucked it up."

Liar. I wanted to shout at him. Hit him. Kiss him more than anything.

I sat down on the rickety armchair in the corner, elbows on my knees. "You know what's sad? I want to believe you," I said, more to the muddled gray carpet than to him. "But I'm fucking tired of everyone playing their own fucked up little game with me. Valyr, Nymeron, Aris. You. I'm done, Raeyn."

He watched me with the weirdest expression.

"Okay," Raeyn said softly. "No more games. Though I should warn you. You're not going to like this."

"Try me."

The corners of his mouth twitched, a muscle in his throat fluttered as he swallowed.

"I'm in love with you."

The silence was heavy enough to choke me. I got out of the armchair. Closed in on him.

"Get out."

"See, that's what I meant." A nervous laugh teetered on the edge of Raeyn's voice. "You always do this, throwing me off in the most crucial situations." He cleared his throat. "Um, okay. Let's pretend my sudden bout of blunt honesty temporarily short-circuited something between your ears and your brain. Let me repeat, slowly this time. I love you."

"Shut up," I ground out between clenched teeth and shoved him toward the door.

I wanted him gone. Didn't want to see the shock on his face, like he didn't get it. Like he didn't realize how I needed him to stop talking *now*.

"I know how it sounds. Trust me, I'm still getting over it myself. I mean, you're stubborn and mouthy, and let's not forget homicidal and ridiculously volatile." Against my grip, I felt his pulse jump, his breath catch. "Hells, half the time you hate me and you're full of ideas that will absolutely get us killed someday, but I can't help it, I—"

"I said *shut up*." The words tried to strangle me. "Don't tell me what you think I fucking want to hear. Out. Now." I reached past him and yanked the door open.

"Damian, please." He tried to touch me, but I pushed his hands away.

"We're done, Raeyn."

Something went out of him then and he let go. "I see." He left without another word.

I closed the door against the broken hunch of his shoulders as he walked away.

I had no idea how long I sat on the floor with my back against the door and my knees drawn to my chest, staring at the carpet before Aris pushed a green mug into my hands. Beyond the coffee, I smelled the bite of whiskey.

"Figured you could use it," Aris said. "I see the carpets got away clean."

I kept silent and drank my coffee. The whiskey chased a warm tingle down my throat.

"You know, back when, I probably could have told you if he was telling the truth," Aris tapped the side of his forehead. "But I think you already know."

He'd overheard it all. Guess the shouting'd been hard to miss. I should've been embarrassed. Maybe angry. But all I felt was numb.

"Why're you telling me this?"

A small smile curved Aris's lips. "That's the question, isn't it?"

He sat next to me with his legs crossed and his back against the wall, and I could almost imagine we were back at the *Shadow*, outside Iltis's study, waiting for her to send us out on another run.

"I'm leaving." The words seemed to echo against the cracked plaster walls. "There's a Temple up north," Aris went on, like he was worried I'd interrupt him. "Aemelia told me, before—" He closed his eyes, pinched his lips into a thin line. "I didn't know about the airstrike. Father—Nymeron must've gotten the Temple's location from one of his spies. Maybe he's known all along and just waited—If I'd known, I would have moved sooner. Warned you."

Aris shook his head, stared off into space. It took him a minute to find his voice again.

"The pills Raeyn gave me should help keep the seizures down, so I should make it."

He paused. Gave me a sidelong glance, waiting for me to argue. Maybe I should've.

But all I could say was, "Okay."

Aris blinked. "Okay." He let out a long breath, the tense set of his shoulders relaxing.

"Did you tell Laras?" I wanted to take back the question as soon as it was out.

"We talked," Aris said. "She's going to come with me. We'll have the baby as far away from the capitol as we can."

"Ah." The words died in my throat. I didn't have a problem pointing a gun to the godsdamned president's head but talking about Aris having a kid with Laras of all people was enough to make anyone's head explode.

"Don't look at me like that. I'm not running off to play house. But I'm giving this a chance. I'm not skipping out on her. On either of them."

"Right. Um. Good luck."

"Thanks. I'll need it." Aris grinned. It lit up the hollows in his face, and for the first time in a long while he reminded me of the kid I'd first met. Who'd taken my hand when I'd first come to the *Shadow* and asked me if I knew how to pilot a space ship because he knew this girl who swore someday she'd make it fly again.

Past the knot in my stomach, I felt myself returning his grin. "You'll do okay."

"Thanks," Aris said again. "For everything."

He broke off, all the unsaid things hanging between us like a bomb about to drop. There was too much and too little to say. We'd have to bury it along with everyone else we'd lost.

It was the only way to move on.

Aris got to his feet. "About Raeyn," he said carefully. "Don't fuck things up just because you're too scared to try." He looked down at me, his smile tinged with a mix of hope and regret. "You deserve something good, you know."

29

Something Good

FIGURED THEY'D TAKE my gun before letting me anywhere near Stern's office, but the security guard by the metal detectors just nodded and waved me through.

"The president is expecting you, Mr. Nettoyer." She tossed me a plastic clip-on badge with a red V on it. "Elevator's on the left. Thirty-fourth floor. Can't miss it."

I muttered a quick thanks and stuffed the badge into my pocket. It took all I had not to keep looking over my shoulder waiting for uniforms to come running and arrest me. No one even gave me a second glance as I crossed the brightly lit lobby of what used to be the Finger of Light, but now had been remodeled into the headquarters of Federal Security. The new building smell of plywood and floor cleaner followed me up the elevator. It reminded me of the disinfectant they'd used down in the cells to cover up the stink of sweat and piss.

By the time the elevator dinged open on the thirty-fourth floor, the novelty of walking around a government building without handcuffs had worn off. It popped like a soap bubble when I walked into Stern's office and found Raeyn sitting in front of Stern's massive desk, two stone-faced guys in gray uniforms posted at his sides.

Well, talk about killing two flies with one fucking stone.

"Mr. Nettoyer." Stern stood facing the window wall that covered the south side of her office. "You're joining us right in time."

No shit.

Raeyn opened his mouth but didn't say anything. I shot him a look that said to let me do the talking for once so I could try and save his sorry ass. He didn't look hurt. At least not where I could see.

"We were just discussing how to deal with the obvious remainders of the old Empire," Stern said. She didn't move from her perch by the window. Her office overlooked Lightsquare, the East River a glittering ribbon under an overcast sky. The former palace sprawled along the riverside, an island of glass and steel. Most of it was boarded up now, the glass cupola cracked and black with soot, white walls dark with jagged graffiti. "It's probably best to get rid of it. Tear it down. Erase all the symbolism. People will forget eventually."

Something in the way she said it made my throat go tight, my heart kick against my ribs, because I didn't think she was talking about the palace at all. Not with the most fucking obvious remainder of the old Empire sitting right in front of her desk.

"You don't need to kill it!" I said quickly.

Raeyn raised an eyebrow.

"I mean, you want to send the right signal, right? Make nice and integrate and all that. Turn it into a museum. Or a hospital. Something you can use."

And there I went, parroting exactly what Stern'd been on about the day before, never mind how fucked up it was. I'd worry about being a hypocrite after I got Raeyn out of here.

Stern nodded. "I like the way you think, Mr. Nettoyer. Very efficient." She turned from the window. "You've thought about my offer?"

"Yeah," I said. "I'll take it. But he gets to leave with me." I nodded at Raeyn.

Stern frowned. "That, I'm afraid, is up to Mr. Nymeron. But yes, we are done here." She turned to Raeyn. "Unless you have any further questions?"

Raeyn got up, half smile in place. "Not for now. It's been very enlightening."

"Indeed." Stern shook his hand.

To me, she said, "Welcome to the Firm, Mr. Nettoyer. I'll see you tomorrow at nine. Someone will be down to show you around your office and the briefing room."

"I'll be there."

"Splendid."

Fortunately, she didn't push the handshake, because the hand that wasn't on my cane was clenched around Raeyn's shoulder. He didn't complain when I steered him away from Stern's uniforms and out the door.

It took me all the way down the elevator, through the foyer, and out the building, past the security guards to get my breathing back to normal again.

"Damian?" Raeyn asked after I'd finally let go of him. "Are you okay?"

I stared at him, watching me with pale eyes, his hand twitching as if he wanted to touch me, but couldn't quite bring himself to. He still looked too thin, worn out and rumpled around the edges, like he'd spent weeks on the run. His hair'd grown out, curling around his ears, at the nape of his neck. He wasn't wearing his hat. It made him younger, though still sharp enough to cut myself on. And still I ached to touch him, no matter how much I should know better.

"I'm an idiot," I said, and once I'd started, the words kept spilling out. "And a hypocrite. I mean, you lie, I kill people for a living. Doesn't look like I've got any room to criticize. I'm sorry. I should've told you. I just, I want—"

I swallowed, tried to get my voice back under control, but it was like falling: once you'd taken the plunge, there was no going back. "I want you. Just you. I mean, if you still want me..." The words trailed off.

Neither of us moved. Those inches between us could've been light-years.

Raeyn was the first to unfreeze. "Come here." His voice was rough, as were his fingers catching handfuls of my shirt, dragging me closer. It was all the encouragement I needed. I leaned in hard, pinned Raeyn against the glass and kissed him, reveling in the soft little sound he made in the back of his throat, his lips hot on mine, neither of us letting go until we were both panting, breathless and bruised.

"Better?" Raeyn asked, his head warm on my shoulder. It'd started to rain, the water like icy fingers reaching down the back of my collar. It didn't matter. I could've stayed there with him forever. In the glass, I could see the reflections of people hunched under bright umbrellas scurrying past, most of them in too much of a hurry to get out of the wet to stop and stare.

"I thought she was going to kill you," I said against Raeyn's damp hair.

"Who? Stern?" He lowered his head against my chest and I felt his shoulders shake. "Oh, darling."

I almost let go of him then. "Are you seriously laughing at me? After—"

Raeyn shook his head. Cleared his throat before he looked me in the eye, but even then the grin kept tugging at the corners of his mouth. "She offered me a job. And conveniently verified I truly didn't know anything about my mother's whereabouts." Raeyn made a face. Valyr'd been in the wind, and consequently in the headlines as the subject of one wild speculation after another. No one believed she was gone for good. Clearly, the new president was no exception.

"Stern wants to keep me close, of course. There's going to be an inquiry about what happened with the Empire." Raeyn's face slipped, and I saw the exhaustion cracking his smile. "Stern wants me around for that, of course. But in the meantime, she wants me to continue my Voyance research. Strictly volunteers this time. That's why we were talking about the palace. We thought it might be a good location. If a bit...tainted." He rubbed his eyelids. "Gods. No wonder you looked like she was ready to drag you out back and shoot you."

"The guards," I said, suddenly realizing how stupid it sounded. "I thought—"

"Ah. That. Apparently, it's protocol now. I guess someone tried to open fire on her at a cafe yesterday." He gave me a sidelong look. "You wouldn't know anything about that, would you?"

I didn't say anything.

Raeyn sighed. "Darling, you are a piece of work." He brushed a wet strand of hair out of my face, his palm warm against the roughness of my cheek before he kissed me again.

"Come on. Let's get you out of the rain. You look like you could use some pancakes."

A laugh bubbled up in the back of my throat. "Gods, could I ever."

I let him take me by the arm and together we walked through the downpour.

Aris'd been right. Maybe it was time for something new, something good.

Maybe I could stop running for a while.

Acknowledgements

This book is dedicated to found families for many reasons. I could never have done this without the help of so many people who have become family to me over the years.

Thank you to my publisher Rae, my editor Sam, and the rest of the wonderful team at NineStar Press, for taking a chance on this book full of queerness with a chance of explosions, and thank you to Natasha Snow, for creating the perfect cover, bringing Helos to life.

Thank you to David R. Slayton, one of the very best humans I know and who kept pushing me to be kind, be persistent, and above all, to keep writing. Also for founding the Speculators, our amazing online writing group who may be plotting to take over the world. Helen Corcoran, Liz Freed, David Meyer, Anitra Van Prooyen, Kat Cho, Axie Oh, Rena Barron, Erin Kennemer, Nikki VanRy, and Amanda Blixt, thank you all for commiserating and squeeing along the way.

To Eleanor Boyall, Helen Corcoran, Alice Loweecey, Barbara Ann Wright, and everyone else who suffered through the messy, early drafts of this. Special thanks to Judy Elsley and Sîan Griffiths for letting me swear up a shitstorm in their college writing classes.

A shout-out to my critique partners, the Dark and Stormy Nights: K.F. Silver, who may finally have taught me a thing or two about blocking, J.T. Moore, who made sure I described Damian's hair right, Terra Luft, who cusses at least as much as I do, and Jenni Wood who fiercely defended me against people insisting on scribbling out all the fucks in this manuscript before reading it.

To the Infinite Monkeys and the Salt City Genre Writers who showed me that a queer author writing hella sweary queer sci-fi indeed has a home in the Utah writing community.

More than a thank you to Tori, who is my sanity check, brings me coffee when I need it most, puts up with my shit, and reminds me to sleep and eat. Love you and I'll try not to adopt any more cats. Probably.

And finally, thank you to everyone who is reading this book. I couldn't have done this without the support of each and every one of you. Thank you for being along for this wild ride. I hope you're ready for more

About the Author

Alex Harrow is a genderqueer, pansexual, and demisexual author of queer science fiction and fantasy. Alex's pronouns are they/them. When not writing queerness with a chance of explosions, Alex is a high school English teacher, waging epic battles against comma splices, misused apostrophes, and anyone under the delusion the singular they is grammatically incorrect.

A German immigrant, Alex has always been drawn to language and stories. They began to write when they realized the best guarantee to see more books with queer characters was to create them. Alex cares deeply about social justice and wants to see diverse characters, including LGBTQ+ protagonists, in more than the stereotypical coming out story.

Alex currently lives in Utah with their equally geeky wife, outnumbered by three adorable feline overlords, and what could not possibly be too many books.

Facebook: www.facebook.com/alexharrowsff

Twitter: @AlexHarrowSFF

Website: www.alexharrow.com

Also Available from NineStar Press

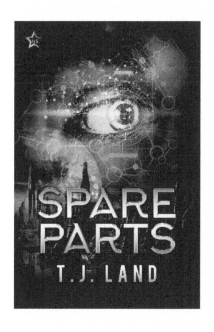 

Connect with NineStar Press

Website: NineStarPress.com

Facebook: NineStarPress

Facebook Reader Group: NineStarNiche

Twitter: @ninestarpress

Tumblr: NineStarPress

Made in the USA
Las Vegas, NV
08 December 2020

12407443R00173